Those Sci-Fi Guys

The Parody From Space

R. Jay Carissimo

tredition

Copyright © 2017 R. Jay Carissimo

Publisher: tredition, Hamburg, Germany

ISBN
Paperback: 978-3-7323-9097-7
eBook: 978-3-7323-9099-1

Printed on demand in many countries

THOSE SCI-FI GUYS

The Parody from Space

By

R. Jay Carissimo

To my Uncle Mickey & my Uncle Raymond; they always told such funny stories.

CHAPTER 1
THOSE SCI-FI GUYS VERSUS THE TARANTULION
COSMIC-CALENDAR.2399.04.25.4/30

The tarantulion was not a hideous monster with oily, black hair, spindly legs and a huge head swathed in black mane, bearing fierce fangs; it was simply one of the many new life forms one routinely encounters when in the service of Cosmos-Corps. At least that is what Captain Gene Lucas Seasqrd tried telling Commander Sam Parseck while Commander Parseck hung helplessly in the tarantulion's web but for some reason the commander did not see it that way.

"Oh, save me. Won't you help me," Sam Parseck cried out as the gaping jaws of the gigantic tarantulion drew closer towards him. "Seasqrd! HELP!"

"I'm not sanguine about doing harm to an alien life form until its hostility has been confirmed, Sam," Seasqrd said.

"When it eats me, will its hostility be confirmed?" Parseck asked.

"I see your point." Seasqrd nodded. "Fear not. You can rely upon my genetically enhanced strength."

Seasqrd placed his hands about a small boulder. He lifted the rock up over his head and tossed it at the tarantulion. The perfectly aimed shot not only stunned the tarantulion, but tore through the web that had trapped Commander Parseck. The rock fell to the ground and the tarantulion fell on top of it. Sam dropped down from the silky thread he clung to, landing on the belly of the monster and bounced to the ground next to Captain Seasqrd.

"You took some time before doing something!" Parseck said as Seasqrd helped him to his feet.

"You're welcome," Seasqrd replied.

Commander Parseck withdrew his conclusionator, holding the small device in the palm of his left hand while he

7

tapped buttons on its diminutive keyboard with his right. The small v-shaped antenna that sprouted from the top spun about then popped out and fell to the ground. Seasqrd watched with askance and asked, "What conclusions has your conclusionator reached?"

"Nothing!" Parseck said. "It's not working."

"What are you doing?" Seasqrd tugged at Parseck's arm as the commander withdrew his plasma-pistol.

"I've reached no conclusions as to whether it's alive or dead and I'm not giving that thing another chance at us," Parseck said, while taking aim, but the plasma-pistol remained inoperative. He kept squeezing the trigger. "Our gadgets seem useless on this planet."

Captain Seasqrd was about to rebuke the commander when the tarantulion awoke. After shaking its furry head, it looked up, eyeing the two Earthmen with an angry and ravenous look. Seasqrd did not need a working conclusionator to conclude the creature viewed them as prey.

"What do we do?" Parseck said. "Our machines won't help us!"

"We are not helpless without machines. There is no problem the heart, bone, sinew and soul of a human cannot solve," Seasqrd said. Then he pointed at the computer portal in the middle of his forehead. "Leave it to me."

Seasqrd left Commander Parseck staring in wonder as he leapt into action, tearing down what was left of the web. "Sam, grab the other end!" he yelled.

As the tarantulion attempted to charge, it was seized by its own webbing, which Parseck and Seasqrd wrapped about its numerous legs as they circled around and around. Seasqrd took the loose ends and tied them about the rock he had just thrown.

"Seasqrd!" Parseck shouted. "Look out!"

The tarantulion snapped its jaws at nothing but air after Captain Seasqrd dove for safety. Sam Parseck began pelting the fierce beast's snout with rocks and stones.

"Good work, Commander Parseck!" Seasqrd knew he had just enough time to run forward and shove the boulder down the side of the hill. Just as the tarantulion was about to close in on Parseck, it was dragged away by the rolling stone. Captain Seasqrd and Commander Parseck crept to the side of the hill, looking downwards and spotted a slow moving lump. The tarantulion slowly pulled itself from the webbing that bound it to the boulder and limped away.

"He's had enough," Seasqrd said. "That was good team work."

"It would've been a whole lot easier if we could've used this." Sam Parseck held his plasma-pistol and tapped the side of it repeatedly. "What's wrong with this weapon?"

"Sam, put that thing away," Seasqrd said. "We've come to this planet on a peaceful mission to advise the Animazons if and when the Zlythetaur Empire invades."

"Well, I would say the peaceful end of this mission ended when the Saturn Seven was shot down," Parseck said.

"Our spacecraft simply crash landed," Seasqrd said.

"That's impossible." Parseck raised his hand in objection. "I checked the Saturn Seven from posiprow to silistern before we launched. Something inhibited that ship as we flew to the Animazon city."

Seasqrd had never worked with Parseck before but he knew his type. "You just can't stand it when one of your toys breaks can you?"

"Well, without conclusionators it could take quite some time to look for the Animazons and without our weapons we might fall prey to more creatures that dwell on Zaftig." Commander Parseck said. "And speaking of plasma-pistols why didn't you go for yours when you saw that creature was about to swallow me. What are you squeamish?"

"It wouldn't have worked," Seasqrd said.

"But you didn't know that," Parseck said. "You should have fired on it."

"No!" Seasqrd shouted. "We're in Cosmos-Corps. We only search out new life. We don't destroy it."

"Strange for a man to say that," said a mysterious voice behind them.

Seasqrd whirled around trying to use his super-sensitive hearing to locate who just spoke. Then he felt a tap on his shoulder.

"We don't have to look for the Animazons anymore," Parseck said while motioning with his thumb.

Stepping cautiously from the forest were three Animazon warriors. The women were very tall, with wide shoulders and narrow waists. Their thick-heeled boots made them appear even taller and more slender. They were clad in black uniforms that covered very little, but even more eye catching than their shapely figures were the tails that sprouted from the bottom of their backs and dangled about touching their calves. They encircled the two Earthmen who offered no resistance, but merely eyed the Animazons from the tips of their leather boots all the way up to the fine, white hair that spread across their shoulders like silky mane.

Though their appearance was both imposing and provocative, Seasqrd found the aspears they pointed to be particularly lethal. The long rods of the weapons were wrapped in reptilian scales. At the tip grew a crescent shape hook. While the lower end of the hook formed a serpent's tail that drew into a sharp point, the upper end resembled a viper's head. Seasqrd and Parseck stood back to back as the three female warriors surrounded them.

"We mean you no harm," Seasqrd said.

"You mean you can do us no harm," said one of the Animazons, "we on the other hand."

She raised her aspear. Sam Parseck said, "Now, look sister—"

"I am Captain Gene Lucas Seasqrd and this is Commander Sam Parseck. We come to the planet, Zaftig, on a diplomatic mission from Earth on behalf of Cosmos-Corps. We wish to assist and advise just in case you happened to be invaded by the Zlythetaurs."

"We do not need the advice or the assistance of men," said the Animazon. Suddenly, the women froze. All three stood silent as if they were locked in deep thought.

Seasqrd nudged Sam Parseck and said, "Look at their chests."

"I know they are —"

"No," Seasqrd said as he pointed his finger. "Look at the pendants that hang from their necks over their chests."

The pendants the Animazons wore looked like small, crystal clumps of leaves. They were silver but soon flashed orange then changed to blue. When the pendants turned silver again the Animazon women unfroze. One of them pointed her aspear at Seasqrd and said, "The clemency that this one showed the tarantulion has intrigued our queen."

Another Animazon pointed her aspear off towards the distance and said, "Come Earthmen! We're taking you to our leader."

Seasqrd nodded oblingly and marched along with Parseck at his side through the wooded terrain. The forest landscape grew thinner and thinner until it disappeared into a rocky wasteland of stony soil. The sun beat down relentlessly on the two Earthmen. Captain Seasqrd took a small handkerchief from his back pocket, one that bore the symbol of Cosmos-Corps, and draped it over his bald head. After he made sure the portal that went across his forehead was shielded from the sun's rays, he began sucking in deep breaths, filling his lungs with air. Seasqrd began reflecting on how this would sound in his Cosmos-Corps Reflection Entry.

Of course like all members of Cosmos-Corps he hated doing reflection entries; they were tedious and time consuming but Cosmos-Corps deemed them necessary. It was just a way for those with very little experience to be able to evaluate those with vast experience; then they could act as if they actually knew more and finally the inexperienced could tell the experienced what to do. Seasqrd recalled reading somewhere once that it all began with the mistreatment of teachers in the early twenty-first century.

Seasqrd thought of what he might say. *Cosmos-Corps Reflection Entry: Commander Parseck and myself have been captured by Animazon warriors; no wait let's try we were being held by Animazon warriors; no that gives the wrong idea. We were led by Animazon warriors across a desert terrain. My genetically enhanced physique has had little trouble coping with the situation but Commander Parseck worries me. Beads of perspiration are covering his round cheeks and flat nose; his once ebony skin seems a bit pale and he's walking with a limp. No, I can't use that it makes the poor little guy seem as if he's withering.*

Seasqrd turned back to check on his compatriot; Parseck stumbled over some stones. He was obviously finding it difficult to keep pace with the long-legged Animazons. Seasqrd put his hand under Parseck's arm, helping him regain his balance.

"I can't keep up this brutal pace," Parseck moaned.

Seasqrd looked at the sweat that drizzled down from Sam's curly hair; his dark eyes seemed glassy. Then he said, "But we've only been at it for five microns."

"I know but I am used to machines doing all the hard stuff," Parseck said as he clutched his hands against his narrow torso.

"Come on, Sam," Seasqrd said as he tried assisting his undersized shipmate along. "Try breathing in through your nose and out through your mouth. You may not have a genetically enhanced pulmonary system like I do, but it should help."

"I know; I'm just a man, not a Geneti-Man you don't have to remind me." Commander Parseck pulled away. "And by the way, plasma-pistols have a stun setting!"

"Remember, Commander, it was this Geneti-Man, not a plasma-pistol, that saved you from the tarantulion," Seasqrd said.

Sam Parseck stopped in his footsteps. He looked up at Gene Lucas Seasqrd; his chin was pointed at Seasqrd's brawny chest. Parseck asked, "Do you want me to kiss that portal in your forehead, Seasqrd?"

"No, I don't and I'd wish you'd pronounce my name right. It's not 'Saysqwad.' It's 'Sea squared'; it's like Mediterranean times Mediterranean," Seasqrd said.

"Sorry, sir; I didn't mean to offend your genetically-enhanced feelings." Parseck formed a wide, toothy grin across his fatigued face.

Seasqrd looked down at him and said, "You know I am going to put all this in my reflection entry after all."

Commander Parseck was about to answer when one of the Animazons shoved him. She said, "Move along, man."

They began marching along. In between panting Sam said, "You Geneti-Men are awfully proud of all those genetically enhanced muscles, reflexes and abilities they programmed into your brains."

"Well, I wouldn't put it like that," Seasqrd said. He did not bother to look around at Commander Parseck; he just kept walking behind the Animazon in front of them and said, "I'm proud of the powers the human body has."

Seasqrd hoped that would be the final word in this conversation but then he heard Sam say, "Well that's how I feel about my machines. I'm proud of the power our technology gives us."

Seasqrd paused, slowing his step then he turned and raised his finger at Sam and said, "Don't be too proud of your technology, Commander, the power of your plasma-pistols, conclusionators and even your mighty cosmicrafts pale in comparison to the power of the heart, bone, sinew and soul of the human body."

"You don't say," Parseck replied as if he'd just been insulted.

"I do say and I'll tell you something that we Geneti-Men say amongst ourselves regarding genetically enhanced reflexes, stamina and abilities," Seasqrd stood waiting.

Parseck became impatient and said, "What do you say?"

"We got the power." Seasqrd poked his thumb at his own chest then waited to see if Sam would have any reply. The commander was just about to answer when he got a less than gentle nudge from one of the Animazons behind them.

"You talk too much, man!" she said.

Sam Parseck stumbled forward then turned and stood defiantly as if he wasn't just awaiting confrontation with the Animazons but he welcomed it. Seasqrd had to admire the little man's fortitude but he was no match for these women and they very quickly demonstrated that. The Animazon approached; she stood looking down at Sam and while her tail was wagging furiously she pointed her aspear at a stone. The viper's head at the tip of the spear opened its jaws and a venomous spray was let loose. Captain Seasqrd and Commander Parseck watched the stone disintegrate under the acidic discharge of the aspear.

"Pretty potent weapon you have," Seasqrd said.

"Too bad our plasma-pistols aren't working," Sam Parseck said. "You'd see some real potency."

"Don't start this again, Sam," Seasqrd said with his hand against his forehead.

Sam was about to continue when the Animazon, leading the path turned and spoke. She said, "Stop complaining about your machines, man. Your mechanical devices will not work under our chlorofield."

"Chlorofield?" Seasqrd said.

"This will be difficult for a man to comprehend, but all living things give off energy. The females of this world have learned to harness those energies and focus them so as to make

14

them work for us. The chlorofield is a force field surrounding our city. It immobilizes any mechanized technology."

"That's what happened to my Saturn Seven!" Parseck snapped his fingers.

Captain Seasqrd ignored Sam Parseck's redemption and asked, "But how are you able to focus these bio-energies?"

The Animazon slowed her pace, turned and held up her flower pendant. "We call it tulipathy," she said.

"That is how you were able to communicate with your queen," Seasqrd said.

"Yes," the Animazon nodded. "It also allows us to communicate with each other, the bio-genetic creations we've bred and all living things on our world."

The Animazons led the two Earthmen through a small grove of trees.

"The zoological cross-creations of Animazon women are famous back on Earth," Seasqrd said.

"Yeah, that tarantulion you made was especially fascinating to us," Commander Parseck said, nodding his head in mock agreement.

"The tarantulion serves a great purpose," the Animazon replied. "It gets rid of pests."

"Sam, you're making them vexed," Seasqrd said then he stopped short. "What in the heliosphere is that?"

In a clearing at the bottom of the hill was a magnificent yet weird creature. The beast was tall with great bulk. Its gray skin was leathery and coarse, but its wings were a wide panorama of bright, silky colors. Captain Seasqrd and Commander Parseck stood dumbfounded watching the creature grasp clumps of grass with its trunk and shove them in its mouth.

"What's wrong Earthman?" asked the Animazon. "You've never seen a butterphant before?"

"You women are truly geniuses at bio-technology," Seasqrd said. "You must tell me how—"

15

Suddenly, the pendants began to flash. After the Animazons unfroze Seasqrd asked, "What is wrong?"

"It's our queen," said the Animazon. "She grows angry."

"Have we committed a breach of protocol?" Seasqrd put his fingers to his chin.

"No," said the Animazon. "She wishes me to stop explaining everything otherwise she'll have nothing to talk about when you arrive."

"I see," Seasqrd said.

"Climb aboard, man!" The Animazon commanded. "Our butterphant is taking us to Photocitysis."

CHAPTER 2
THOSE SCI-FI GUYS AND THE CITY OF ANIMAZONS

To Captain Seasqrd's surprise, the butterphant flew with great grace for such a mammoth beast. From the height of gliding clouds he viewed the world of the Animazons; it was a land of rolling pastures, verdant forests and crystal streams. Sam Parseck patted Seasqrd's arm and pointed in the distance to the city of Photocitysis.

It was a magnificent metropolis that seemed to grow from the ground. Trees of enormous size had grown wooden girders from their gigantic trunks. What seemed to be concrete and tile to Seasqrd's first glance was actually some sort of coral growth that fastened itself to the girders forming small buildings and dwellings. Gigantic leaves, woven together with vines as thick as cables, formed roofs and a palisade wall made from thorny canes surrounded the whole city.

"It's incredible," said Seasqrd. "It's an entire society free of mechanization; so no devices or doohickeys; no gadgets or gizmos!"

"Don't be too enthralled by the Animazons," Parseck whispered.

"Relax," Seasqrd whispered back. "I'm merely admiring their natural attributes."

"Can't say that I blame you." Sam patted his arm again.

"I meant their bio-technology."

Atop the tallest tree was a revolving satellite dish that really was not a satellite dish but a huge flower. Its petals formed a circular plate and its center stamen protruded out like an antenna.

"That is your tulipathy," Seasqrd said, pointing upward.

"Yes," said one of the Animazons. "Unlike you we can communicate with our environment."

The butterphant flew ever higher, circling a conical tower that resembled a spiraling redwood. It came in for landing upon a leafy runway. Two of the Animazons pointed their aspears at the Earthmen and led them to a wooden stairwell connected to the tree tower while the third patted the butterphant's head and stroked his trunk; she then quickly joined the others. After touching her flower pendent a long, thick vine descended upon them and a huge leaf was unfurled before their feet. The Animazons stepped off the stairwell and onto the leaf and commanded the men to follow. Soon the vine was escalating them upward to a grand entranceway.

The Earthmen stepped off; the Animazon women motioned with scowling faces to march forward. Beyond the entranceway was a grand hall that led to tall, wooden doors that swung open revealing a circular courtroom; the walls of the courtroom seemed to be made of blocks of carved jewels. A long scarlet carpet lay at Seasqrd's and Parseck's feet and led the way to a dais that rose from the tiled floor. Though Seasqrd was impressed by the grandeur he could not help notice the menace of the strange looking guards before them.

Two large animals stood at opposite ends of the dais. They had the bodies of horses but at the top of their equine forms were the muscular torsos of gorillas. Long black horsehair dropped from their primate heads; their eyes never left the two Earthmen. They stood snorting and staring.

"Beware of the gorillataurs," said one of the Animazons. "They're trained to protect our queen."

Seasqrd looked at the throne made of bronze branches and emerald leaflets and saw it was empty. "Where is your queen?" he asked.

The Animazons did not reply; there was no need. Seasqrd gazed from the watchful gorillataurs to the back edge of the dais. There was a beautiful head of red hair rising over the edge and upon it was a tiara which seemed made of golden vines. As the woman's head rose higher, Seasqrd saw the most beautiful face he'd ever seen beneath the golden tiara and red hair; her eyes were a glimmering green and her rosy cheeks formed perfect crescents that ended in the most sensuous jaw line.

As the women stepped up further onto the dais, her cape of silver feathers was revealed and beneath the cape was a glossy white tunic that hugged the woman's figure tightly. She finally climbed to the top of the dais and the warriors and gorillataurs bowed before their queen. After a not so gentle poke from an aspear, Sam and Seasqrd bowed too. The queen let her tail untwine itself from about her bare thigh as she crossed the dais. She shed her feathered cape, displaying her porcelain like shoulders and draped her garb across her throne. She swung her long hair of red back over her shoulders and looked down at the Earthmen.

Sam Parseck whispered, "She certainly is the queen of Zaftig."

Seasqrd was happy the Animazon warriors did not hear Sam's words but he couldn't blame the commander for saying what he said. The queen was incredibly beautiful. Seasqrd finally pried his eyes off of her and said, "We have come from the planet Earth to—"

He stopped when the Animazon behind him batted his shoulder with her aspear and said, "You have not been given permission to speak."

The queen looked over them, standing like an aristocratic giant and finally said, "You are both men from Earth yet you do not appear to be alike."

"Yes, this is true," Seasqrd said. "We are not alike in appearance but that is the way of Earth. On our planet different races have learned to live together in friendship just as our entire species has learned to live in harmony with our environment. It is the mission of Cosmos-Corps... I guess you want to talk some more now."

Seasqrd bowed his head as the vexed queen replied, "You do not have to lecture the females of this world as how to live in environmental harmony. A thousand of your years ago when the men of your planet were charting sea routes to explore unknown continents the men of our world sailed through space discovering new worlds. They even reached your home world, returning with some of your more exotic species."

"Yes," Seasqrd said with a nod. "That explains the resemblance of some of your life-forms to—"

"Silence," said the queen.

Seasqrd shut his mouth. He looked at Parseck and heard him click his tongue against the back of his teeth with shame. Seasqrd shrugged.

"But it was the women who made the greatest discovery when we found that the machines, motors and engines that our men had made were poisoning this planet."

Seasqrd cleared his throat; softly at first, then a bit louder the second time, causing the queen to pause. Seasqrd pointed at his own chest and the queen nodded, finally granting permission for him to speak.

"Yes, we too on Earth once faced a similar climate crisis, but we found new technologies and we now have machines that do not pollute the planet," Seasqrd said.

"We?" the queen said. "What do you mean we found new technologies? You are men and men are evil, capable of nothing but environmental disasters. Our men neither had nor sought any solutions to our climate problems and so the female takeover began. The result is what you see before you; we have a world of organic, not mechanic, technology where we live in harmony with the plant and animal kingdoms."

"If you don't mind me saying so," Commander Parseck interjected, "it seems like you lovely ladies have a rather prejudiced society. Men and their machines aren't all bad. Why back on Earth some of my best friends are men and some are machines."

"Sam, I think it would be better if I handled this," Seasqrd said.

"But I have something to say," Parseck said.

"Please, it's my mission." Seasqrd hoped that would be the end of the discussion. It wasn't.

"But they wouldn't have sent me along if there was nothing for me to contribute," Parseck said. "I'm the one with the talent for technology. Let me speak on behalf of our machines, G-Man."

Seasqrd noticed the Animazons and their queen exchanging looks of disgust. Seasqrd patted his hand against the air, never looking at Sam, but whispering through the side of his mouth, saying, "I'm the captain; I'll do the talking."

Sam Parseck spoke in a firm, clear, voice and said, "I'm a captain as well."

Seasqrd stared at the queen; he smiled and nodded. He leaned to the side hoping he could end this argument with Sam before it began.

"You're a commander." Seasqrd turned about and looked down. "You're not a captain."

"I'm captain of the Saturn Seven." Parseck folded his arms against his blue uniform.

Seasqrd shrugged. He looked at the Animazon queen; she folded her arms and stood waiting impatiently. Seasqrd turned to Parseck again and said, "But we're not aboard your ship so you're a commander and I'm a captain." He then patted the insignia on the sleeves of his burgundy uniform. Sam tilted his head to one side and sneered.

"I have no ship to pilot," he said, "My devices won't work for me, I have no weapons to fire and now you won't let me speak my mind. So why was I brought on this mission?"

"To be candid," Seasqrd said. "I've been asking myself the same thing."

Parseck paused for a moment, staring up at Seasqrd, and then said, "As long as we are speaking candidly, sir, I've always thought you Geneti-Men to be more arrogance than action. It seems the bigger your genetically enhanced muscles get the bigger your egos get... sir."

"Well as long as we're off the record, Commander," Gene Lucas Seasqrd said. "You space-men of Cosmos-Corps do not exactly thrill me. Your lack of physical abilities is surpassed only by your dependence on things that flash and hum and never seem to work when we need them the most."

"It was my machine that got you to this planet!"

Seasqrd nodded his head rapidly and said, "Sure the Saturn Seven did a great job until it crashed."

"That wasn't my fault; it was them!" Parseck pointed at the women. "And don't insult my ship."

Seasqrd pointed down at Parseck's nose. "You are addressing a superior, Commander Parseck."

Sam fixed his eyes on Seasqrd's finger which was only a centicam away from his flaring nostril and replied, "And if you are my superior then that makes me an inferior, right G-Man?"

"And they wonder why we frown upon mankind," said the queen while walking down from the dais and stepping in between them.

Gene Lucas Seasqrd was already mad at Sam Parseck's insulting insubordination and mocking grin but when he realized that the little commander was jeopardizing his diplomatic mission to Zaftig Seasqrd became angry; he became very angry.

"I've never failed on a mission," he got caught in the gaze of the queen's beautiful eyes, "but you... I... he...."

"You better ease up on the way you look at her, sir; if you were a computer I'd say you're in need of a soft boot." Parseck's mocking grin was now an obnoxious scowl and that became too much for Seasqrd.

"I was thinking the same thing about you!" he lifted Sam Parseck up by his collar.

The queen stepped back and the Animazon warriors attempted to pull the Earthmen off of each other, but Seasqrd was mad and proved too strong for their restraint; he pulled the two tall females off their feet and swung them around to the floor. He heard the queen order her gorillataurs to seize him but he didn't care; he was too enraged to care, but Sam too was mad.

He yelled, "I'm not afraid of that chrome-dome!"

With that he jerked away from the Animazon who held his arms with all his might and when that failed he stomped on her boot. As she fell off balance, cursing at Sam, he wrenched free of her hold only to topple into the back of the queen's legs, knocking her over onto the steps of the dais. She lay across the steps with her skirt up over her waist and her tiara hanging over her eyebrows.

The Animazon warriors pinned Sam Parseck down with the points of their aspears, staring at him in disdain. The gorillataurs who held Seasqrd by his arms and wrists stood with their jaws agape. The queen lay still across the steps; one of her warriors offered her a hand but she refused the help. She fixed her tunic of white and straightened her tiara of vines so it rested straight on her head.

Then the queen rose to her feet and said, "Earthman you have assaulted the Queen of the Animazons. I sentence you to death."

Seasqrd suddenly realized what his display of anger had wrought and yelled. "No! It was my fault. I'm in command of this mission. Punish me!"

"It was he, not you, who assaulted our queen," said one of the Animazons.

"No, it was my outburst of temper that started this," Seasqrd said.

"You intrigue me, Earthman," said the queen. Standing eye to eye with Seasqrd, she placed her hands on his torso, tracing her fingers over the burgundy uniform that covered his bulging pectorals and well-formed arms. She made a circle around the golden sun that was centered in Seasqrd's chest, bearing the symbol of Cosmos-Corps then poked her finger into his rock-like abdomen. She said, "I will spare him if you perform a service for me."

Seasqrd looked about as he felt the tension mounting. The Animazon warriors stood in silent shock. Even the gorillataurs' eyes opened wide. Seasqrd looked back at the queen who smiled slyly. He then looked down at Sam; the pathetic little guy looked helpless.

"Don't do it, Gene Lucas," Sam Parseck said, while he stared down the point of an aspear. "It sounds like she has some ulterior motive."

The queen turned and reached down, grabbing Sam Parseck by his collar and hoisted him to his feet. She turned to Captain Seasqrd and said, "You have two choices. He suffers death by aspear or you perform the ritual of Anjhee-Nah."

Captain Seasqrd looked at Sam Parseck as he dangled in the queen's grip, then back at the grinning Animazons. He tilted his head to the side. "Could I have those choices again?" he asked.

The queen repeated the choices.

"Well, I know what the aspears can do. So I guess I'll take performing Anjhee-Nah." Seasqrd tilted his head to the opposite side. "What is it?"

"Our copulation ceremony," said the queen. "I must warn you though; few men have survived Anjhee-Nah with Animazon queens."

While the females wagged their tails in zeal, Seasqrd shrank back, forcing the gorillataurs to pull him forward to his feet again.

"Am I to understand you're going to force me to have sex with you?" Seasqrd asked.

The queen nodded. Sam Parseck freed himself from the queen's grip and stood in front of his compatriot, shouting, "No! It's not fair. I committed the crime. Let me suffer this Anjhee-Nah!"

"Sorry, puny Earthman, it's doubtful you'd survive a kiss on the cheek. It is this one who will perform Anjhee-Nah." She shoved Parseck aside, took Seasqrd by the wrist and pulled him along.

"Wait!" Seasqrd said. "Can't we talk first... get to know each other better."

She pulled Seasqrd around the dais and down a narrow hallway while he listened to Sam Parseck screaming. "You call this justice? Take me instead. I swear I'm quite the criminal!"

CHAPTER 3
THOSE SCI-FI GUYS AND THE ANIMAZON QUEEN

The royal bedchamber was ornate and beautiful, but Seasqrd was still nervous and apprehensive. At the center of the room a curtain made of white leafed vines rose on the queen's command, revealing a large, circular bed. She took Seasqrd in her arms and pulled him onto the fluffy cushions and pillows.

"Let us begin the Anjhee-Nah," she said as she tossed her golden crown across the room, kicked off her shoes and pulled his burgundy shirt from his body.

"Now hold it!" Seasqrd said. "Wait, I didn't mean that."

"Why are you so nervous?" she asked just before she began kissing his neck.

"Well wouldn't you be if you were about to risk your life in a copulation ceremony," Seasqrd said.

"Oh don't worry about what I said before." The queen wrapped her arms about Seasqrd's shoulders; she held him tight. "You'll have no problem surving the Anjhee-Nah. I just said that to add some excitement to our ritual."

"You did what?" Seasqrd took the queen's wrist and stood up on the bed. She offered no answer; she seemed too shocked to speak. Seasqrd couldn't decide whether she was pleased by his courage or outraged that someone actually dared stand up to her. He didn't care either way. Seasqrd stepped off the bed, trying to keep his distance from the Animazon queen. Her long, red mane of hair seemed to glisten in the soft light. Her muscles tensed and her tail shook while her glowing green eyes fixed on Seasqrd.

"You're most extraordinary. You may prove to be the sire of an incredible, warrior dynasty," she said with a smile. "I've got to have you."

She rushed forward, wrapping her arms about Seasqrd's waist and, suddenly, he was up in the air looking down at her cleavage. He tried to get free, but the queen maintained a tight grip, keeping her body pressed tight against his as she turned around and gently dropped them him back on the bed.

As she sat next to him and ran her fingers all about his chest and shoulders, Seasqrd said, "Now see here, your majesty. You can't treat a member of Cosmos-Corps this way. I'm here on a mission to save the planet, Zaftig, from the Zlythetaurs and that's all."

Seasqrd rose to his feet, standing at the edge of the bed. The Animazon Queen remained on the bed; she lifted her foot and her white tunic slid across her leg revealing here knee and thigh. She moved her foot so that it gently slid from his knee up around his waist then back down to his knee. Seasqrd wanted to move away but he didn't. The queen asked, "Is that all you have on your mind at this moment."

After the queen finished her question she moved back just slightly; she lay across the bed running her hand over her knee and around her thigh then back down around the calf of her leg as she awaited an answer.

Seasqrd folded his arms, stuck out his chest and replied, "No of course not I want your planet to join the Earth Alliance. I want you and your Animazons to share their bio-technology with us and I want us to share our environmentally safe mechanics with you. I want you... holy nova do I want you!"

Seasqrd fell across the bed; he lay next to the queen and their arms and legs were intertwined. Seasqrd sat up, shaking his head. He said, "No, no; I don't want to do this."

Seasqrd sat at the edge of the bed with his chin resting in the palms of his hand. The queen slid off the bed; she stood before Seasqrd and asked, "You find me not attractive?"

Seasqrd lifted his head; he slowly looked her up and down and muttered, "Well... the long legs and shapely figure plus the beautiful eyes are certainly stimulating but... uh...

28

well...let's just say you're not the kind of girl one brings home to mother Earth."

The queen twisted her hips and drew the palm of her hand right across Seasqrd's face. He rolled back across the bed and landed on the floor on the opposite side of the queen. While rubbing his sore cheek, Seasqrd said, "Don't take this the wrong way but you're just a little aggressive."

The queen circled around the bed; she stood before him and pointed at the royal bed and said, "How dare you insult me! Get into that bed and Anjhee-Nah me!"

"I'm sorry that I hurt your feelings." Seasqrd never got a chance to finish his apology. The queen grabbed his arm and flipped him onto the bed. She stood over him with her heel pointed into his chest.

"I will not spend the rest of my life serving under you!" Seasqrd batted his hand across her leg. The queen stepped back, off balance, and then fell across to the other side of the bed. Seasqrd rolled over to the opposite side of the bed and began placing pillows between him and the queen. He sat on the other side of his fortification and pointed a finger at her. He said, "I'm a Geneti-Man of Cosmos-Corps. I'm to be treated with respect."

"A Geneti-Man is still a man," the queen said, "and men on this planet do not gain respect until they learn to do as they're told."

Seasqrd piled the pillows higher. He said, "You can't order me around."

The queen stood on the other side of the bed looking at him with frustration then she straightened the wrinkles in her tunic and said, "Alright then I won't tell I will ask; I will ask if you'd like to share a drink with me. We can toast an alliance between your planet and mine."

"You want to toast what?" Seasqrd said. "Oh, that's a wonderful idea."

He was somewhat surprised but he did not want to let the queen know that. He just assumed he had won her respect with his amazing attributes and by standing up to her. He was probably the first person ever to do that he thought. He watched her walk to other side of the room. She didn't really walk; she glided. She pulled a branch that grew from the wall. A door behind her opened and a being limped in, carrying a tray. The queen snapped her fingers and the diminutive being crept over to Seasqrd who took a glass off the tray. As the ratty haired being made his way back around the bed, the queen reached for the other glass upon the tray and pointed at the door.

"Away with you," she said.

With his tail between his legs the pathetic being slipped away and the door closed behind him.

"What do you call that bio-genetic creation?" Seasqrd asked.

"What creation," said the queen. "He's a man."

"What?"

"As we Animazon women took control we evolved into the physically elite warriors you find us as today, our men were reduced socially and genetically."

"You mean they are slaves!"

"I wouldn't call my little brother a slave."

"Your brother?" Seasqrd's eyes opened into a wide stare.

"Why don't you relax?" the queen circled around the bed. She reached forward to guide Seasqrd's glass to his lips and said, "Have a drink and then we can get down to the Anjhee-Nah."

"No, your majesty; I thought I was getting through to you but we must discuss this further."

"After our drink," she said.

As the glass made its way towards his mouth, its vapors floated beneath Seasqrd's nostrils and his enhanced sense of smell detected a trap. He slammed the glass against the wall. The queen stepped back in shock.

"You are a manipulative, power-mad bi—"

"No man has ever dared speak to me like that!" She flung her glass against the wall.

"I told you before; I'm not a just a man," said Seasqrd, "I'm a G-Man of the Earth's Cosmos-Corps. I will not be petted, fondled, stroked, like I was some prisoner of your love. I'm a free G-Man."

"Does this mean no Anjhee-Nah?"

"Anjhee-Nah with you?" Seasqrd scoffed. "Talk about a gross encounter."

"Do you prefer death?"

"I'd rather die then have Anjhee-Nah with you!"

"You mean you —"

Lunging forward the queen drove Seasqrd back on the bed, pinning him down. Seasqrd struggled against her, but the queen would not relent.

"Remember, if you don't give me Anjhee-Nah, your friend dies."

Seasqrd felt her moist lips against his neck and her hot breath blew against his ear.

"No," he muttered. "You are a dictator… you are a tyrant… you… you should keep doing that."

She kissed him again and again and Seasqrd wrapped his arms about her waist and said, "Oh, alright but it's only to spare Sam."

Then the ground moved.

"Oh, Earthman," the queen muttered.

"Wait, I haven't done anything," Seasqrd said. "Something crashed on your planet."

The ground shook again as an explosion was heard. Another explosion followed, knocking the queen and Seasqrd off the bed.

"Come with me," said the queen.

Seasqrd followed the queen out onto a balcony; she stood before a small tree rooted in a large urn. The tree had a narrow trunk that ran branchless until at the top it split into a cluster of twiggy branches, which formed a sphere. Seasqrd prepared himself for what the plant might do, knowing the fascinating bio-technologic breakthroughs these women had achieved, but in spite of that what he saw astounded him. As the queen placed one hand upon her pendant, she waved her other hand over the orb of branches atop the small tree. The thin branches suddenly sprouted leaves and the leaves grew and opened and spread until the orb of branches became a solid ball. The interwoven leaves changed from green to blue then became clear.

"It's starting to resemble what was once called on Earth a light bulb," Seasqrd said. "What do you call this plant?"

"It's a telemetree." The queen opened her eyes, freed her hand from her pendant and pointed at the glassy bulb atop the narrow tree trunk. "We use them to keep a watchful eye on our environment."

Within the telemetree appeared an image. Off in the distance hills beyond the walls of Photocitysis they saw what appeared to be two gigantic pods buried deep in the green fields. Another pod flew across the sky, descending down upon the ground like a meteorite and impacted into the surface, driving mounds of ground into heaps.

"Z Asterwaroids! This is the Zlythetaur invasion. You must call your warriors. We must act now," Seasqrd said.

"Any actions by the Zlythetaurs would be a futile gesture." She wrapped her arms about Seasqrd's arm and kissed his cheek. Her tail wiggled. "Now, I have some other actions for you and me."

"But you cannot let the Z war machines gain a foothold," Seasqrd said.

"No machine can penetrate our chlorofield," the queen said, shaking her head.

"Perhaps the Z have figured out a way around that. They're quite resourceful."

"Alright, alright; sometimes men must be indulged like temperamental children," said the queen.

She touched her silver leaf pendant and closed her eyes while muttering orders under her breath then she put on her shoes and grabbed her crown. Seasqrd nodded and put on his shirt. They exited the royal bed chamber and walked back out into the throne room. They were surrounded by Animazon warriors and gorillataurs who awaited further orders from the queen. Sam Parseck was seated at the bottom of the dais tied up in vines. Seasqrd lifted him to his feet and tore the vines apart.

Sam stood shaking his hands and said, "Thanks."

"You're coming with me," Seasqrd said.

"I thought you had to go somewhere with her," Parseck said.

"We were but now we all have to go together." Seasqrd patted Sam's back. "Ooh sorry."

As Sam reached up for Seasqrd to help him up off the floor he said "All of us together?"

"Yes, together!" Seasqrd said. "And sorry sometimes I don't know my own strength."

Within moments, Seasqrd found himself riding on a gorillataur against the wind with the Animazon queen at his side; unfortunately there would be no Anjhee-Nah at least for awhile. They all rode at a full gallop until the gorillataurs ascended a high hilltop outside of Photocitysis. Seasqrd turned to see if the others were still right behind. Sam Parseck had been clinging to one of the Animazon's tails as she and he came up to the hilltop and now he used her tail to lower himself down from the gorillataur.

"Thanks!" Parseck said. The Animazon warrior nodded with a brief a scowl. Two more warriors rode up on gorillataurs, carrying aspears. Parseck backed off in haste, making his way down from the hilltop where he began examining the Z Asterwaroids.

The Asterwaroids lay dormant in smoldering craters. The only activity was the pulsating hum that emanated from their shriveled shells.

"He complained the whole journey," said the queen. "Why did we have to bring him?"

"These are the Asterwaroids of the Z. They use them to transport their invasion forces and Sam is more of a tech-expert than I. He should be able to deduce what we're up against," Seasqrd said. He put the palms of his hands at the corners of his mouth and yelled, "Sam! Anything inside?"

Sam held up a finger. "Give me some time, G-Man."

"Hurry Earther," added the queen.

"Sorry, your mighty majesty, I know you want to get back to your diplomatic accords, but it's hard to reach conclusions without a conclusionator," Parseck said.

"Try acting on a hunch," Seasqrd said.

He watched Parseck touch the Asterwaroid, but then draw his hand back quick. After realizing he suffered no burns or other ill effects he placed his hand on the Asterwaroid's shell, rubbing it against the crevices and crags.

"There's definitely something inside, but my guess is it is non-mechanical," he shouted back to Seasqrd.

"Of course, they can't be machines," the queen said impatiently. "I did not need him to explain there can be no machines within the chlorofield."

"But the Z would not land Asterwaroids as a sign of peace. I have a hunch that the Z have come up with some sort of organic war machine especially designed to penetrate your chlorofield," Seasqrd replied.

"I concur," Parseck said while ascending the hilltop. "It would be consistent with their past methods of conquest like when they used their Furnacesaurus against the Glacions of the planet, Brurh."

"Yes, I was there on Hydros when they landed a fleet of Petroleviathans," Seasqrd said to Sam then he turned to the queen and added, "I had a devil of a time defeating them."

"I just wish my conclusionator was working. I could tell you exactly what's inside," Parseck said.

Just then, the low hum of the Asterwaroids became louder. It became a throbbing shrill. Sam stepped back with his hands over his ears and said, "But I think we're about to find out."

The Asterwaroids began to crack. Their massive shells slowly splintered. Fissures split their rough-hewn casings until finally they exploded into thousands of shards. The Animazons and the Earthmen turned away, shielding their eyes from fragments while the gorillataurs reared up.

"Sam!" Seasqrd yelled. "Get out of here!"

Sam Parseck yelled back, "I think we should all get out of here!"

"No Sam, you must go!" Seasqrd said as he pointed to an Animazon then pointed at Sam. "I'll stay; I got the power."

As Seasqrd pointed his thumb at his chest Sam yelled, "But wait what about me? I can help; I have power."

Commander Sam Parseck would have continued shouting and arguing but an Animazon on a gorillataur swept him up in her arms grabbing him by the burgundy collar of his blue uniform and draped him across her lap before galloping off to safety. Seasqrd watched the brave, little commander as he went bouncing down the other side of the hill and saluted him. What Sam did in return was not a hand gesture that could be interpreted as a salute and certainly was not going to be mentioned in the reflection entry. Seasqrd ignored Sam's behavior and turned towards the Z invasion force. Spilling across what was left of the Asterwaroid was a pool of tar that spread like an oily flood over the green grass. The tar acted as if it were alive, seeking out plants and animals splashing and drowning them in sludge.

"Your majesty!" One of the Animazons pointed to the other pod. The other Asterwaroid had broken open and out of the rubble fumed bubbling acid. The corporeal acid sizzled towards the pool of oil, leaving scorched, barren ground behind.

"I must stop this!" yelled the queen.

"No, your majesty," said an Animazon.

"Leave this to me," said Seasqrd as he charged forward on his gorillataur chasing the queen.

The queen had dismounted, holding her aspear and spraying acid upon the acid. Seasqrd circled about, jumped off his mount and shouted, "You're making it stronger!"

"You could be right, Earthman," said the queen when she found herself being surrounded by the tar pool and the acid.

Seasqrd jumped high in the air, landed in the middle of mound that had become encircled by acid and tar. He picked the queen up in his arms and leapt upward once again. He and the queen landed beyond the pools of oil and acid, which were now beginning to merge.

The queen touched her pendent and suddenly two gorillataurs appeared ready to gallop up the hilltop. From there Seasqrd and the queen watched the last Asterwaroid crack apart. Trotting up behind them was another gorillataur with an Animazon warrior on his back and Sam Parseck cradled in his arms.

"The tiny Earthling wishes to speak to the large Earthling, my queen," she said with a salute.

"What is it, Sam?" Seasqrd asked as he dismounted his simian steed.

"I have a theory and it's an amazing one, G-Man; on a planet ruled by bio-natural forces the Z drop living toxic pollutants." Sam spread his arms out wide and raised his palms upwards as if he expected applause. When he didn't get any he quickly continued, "They're non-mechanical but deadly and destructive."

Seasqrd snapped his fingers. "That's why the chlorofield has no effect on it."

Parseck remained in the gorillataur's arms and pointed at the tar and acid. "Look!" he cried out. "See how the acid and tar have converged into a molten bubbling mass. Now if I'm not mistaken the streams of mercury pouring from the last Asterwaroid will form flagellum."

Seasqrd put his arm around the queen's waist as they watched what was to happen below. The strands of silver chemicals that squiggled from the broken pod flowed across the valley like menacing serpents until they attached themselves to the pool of tar and acid.

"See, artificial pseudopodia," Parseck said. "I was right."

"Very good, Sam, and you did it without a conclusionator." Seasqrd turned to the commander and pointed to his head and then to his own. "See, the best machine is up here."

"Thank you, sir!" Sam locked his hands behind his head as he remained cradled in the gorillataur's arms.

Then Seasqrd asked, "Any theory on how to stop that glob before it oozes its way right to the walls of Photocitysis?"

"Hey," Sam Parseck touched his finger to his head then waved it at Seasqrd, "a glob; that's a great name for it."

"Come to think of it is." Seasqrd watched the glob continue in its path of destruction then he smiled at Sam.

The queen whipped around suddenly and dug her fingers into their chests clutching the two Earthmen by their uniforms. "Would you two shut up and do something! My city is in danger!"

Seasqrd batted her hand away and mounted his steed. "Prepare your defenses your majesty."

"I've already summoned my army," the queen said as she hopped on top of her gorillataur and drew her hand down from her pendent. Suddenly, the gorillataurs broke into a gallop and Captain Seasqrd and Commander Parseck bounced along, following the Animazons on a path to Photocitysis. The gates of the city opened allowing the gorillataurs to trot up a long rampart towards a wide parapet that looked over the city fortifications. Seasqrd and Parseck leaned over the wall to watch marching plant men. Their heads and hands were beautiful buds but their torsos were unfurled leaves and their arms and legs were stems covered in thorns.

"Our rosebots will annihilate that glob," said the queen while waving her hand over a telemetree.

Sam Parseck stood staring at the tree then glanced down at the urn and poked his finger at the roots. He looked at Seasqrd in amazement. Seasqrd pointed at the image in the tree branches and replied, "They call it a telemetree. They use it to keep abreast of things... Sam, don't say it!"

Within the telemetree's picture, the rosebot column trudged over a ridge to face the glob that attacked their world. Wheeling behind the rosebots was a towering plant that appeared to be a motorized cactus. Its rigid, green wheels slowly propelled it forward, its sword like needles were catapulted forward bombarding the glob.

"Our cactoid will shred that glob into a million droplets," said the queen.

Seasqrd and Parseck exchanged glances of doubt as they watched the queen's forces move to intercept the immense glob. Parseck asked, "Where do they get these names?"

Seasqrd raised his hands upward as he lowered the corners of his mouth. Parseck pointed into the clouds and asked, "And what do you call those things, your exalted sexiness?"

"Tomatons," said the queen.

Flying over them were helicopters made of vines, carrying circular, red bombs. They whirled off over the horizon.

The tomatons appeared on the telemetree as they hovered over the combat zone. The tomato bombs exploded, splattering pasty splotches of crimson slime across the glob, but it continued to ooze forward. The rosebots fired thorns from their arms that simply melted into the bubbling body of the glob; its mercury tentacles then reached forward seizing the rosebots and flipped them backwards into its own acidic mass. As the rosebots dissolved into acrid puffs of smoke, the cactoid rolled forward ramming into the glob. Seasqrd saw a moment of hope on the queen's face while she stared at the telemetree and watched the glob roll back, but just as quickly did the glob ebb backwards it surged forward, engulfing the cactoid and burning it into ashes. The glob returned to its advance on Photocitysis.

"Your majesty, that glob is specifically designed to devour the natural technology of your world," Seasqrd said.

"I don't understand," said the queen.

"He's trying to say you are wasting your time," Parseck said.

"You want to be fed to that glob next?" the queen turned about ferociously.

"I'll bet I'd be more effective than the arsenal of salad you sent!"

Seasqrd placed himself between the queen and Commander Parseck and said, "Your majesty, this is what we've been trying to warn you about. The Zlythetaurs are masters of CGI warfare."

"I still don't understand," said the queen.

"Shame her brains aren't as big as her—"

"Sam!"

"What did you call it? Masters at... what did you say?" asked the confused queen.

"The Z are masters of what we call CGIsms or Cyber-Genetic- Inventions. You see, on Earth we have developed technology that works with nature, while here on Zaftig, you have made nature into your technology. But the Z have merged genomics, weaponry, biology and toxicology into one evil technology. I've seen their vile cybernetic organisms crush the defenses of their enemies and this glob must be their latest breakthrough. They use these mutant machines to destroy the environments of other worlds. Once the planet is uninhabitable they drain it of its resources," Seasqrd said. "But we of Earth have stopped them before."

"What he's trying to say is the Z believe that since they've wrecked their environment ages ago why should anyone else enjoy a prospering one," Parseck said.

"You mean the Z do what we've accused you Earthmen of?" the queen tilted her head to the side.

"Now you got it!" Parseck said then he slapped his hand across his forehead.

Seasqrd placed his hands about the queen's shoulders. "Fear not though, my queen. Gene Lucas Seasqrd is here. I know what to do." He turned to Sam Parseck and asked, "Sam, you know science and tech-stuff. How do we stop this invasion?"

"I see no way to stop it," Sam Parseck said shaking his head. "But wait, there could be a way to slow it down... freeze it in its tracks!"

"What do you mean?" asked Seasqrd.

"You know freeze it; come on Seasqrd, it's as plain as the nose on Tyco Brahe's face," Parseck said.

Seasqrd stood silent trying to figure out what Sam's strategy was and why he was so excited about it. He would look up Tyco Brahe and his nose later. Seasqrd looked down at Sam through squinted eyes. Sam closed his eyes; he sighed as he lowered his chin and when he lifted it back up he said, "We can use Lox!"

"We feed it salmon?" Seasqrd asked.

"No, liquid oxygen. We fly the Saturn Seven over the glob and jettison its lox tanks."

"But the Saturn Seven can't make it through the chlorofield," Seasqrd said. He turned to the Animazon leader and asked, "My queen, can you temporarily lift the chlorofield?"

"No," said the queen. "It's a living force. It would be like stopping gravity."

"Isn't she smart," Parseck said. Then he snapped his fingers and said to Seasqrd, "I think we better get STPD."

"In your case, you mean more stupid," the queen said.

"Watch your mouth, your high and buxomness. I meant the Satellite Tracking & Piloting Device aboard the Saturn Seven."

"Yes!" Seasqrd said. "I see your idea. STPD could guide us just far enough in so as to thwart the glob." He turned to the queen and added, "This could be your only chance."

"It's risky; it's very risky," said the queen.

"I have a hunch Sam's plan will work," Seasqrd said.

"No the risk is in trusting men not to screw it up," said the queen.

"What's wrong your royal pulchritude? You just can't deal with the fact that this lowly, Earthman has the key to saving your planet," Commander Parseck said while holding up the key to the Saturn Seven.

"Condorox!" said the queen as she clapped her hands.

"What did she say?" asked Parseck as he hid behind Seasqrd.

A shadow crossed over the two Earthmen. Looking up in the sky they saw a magnificent bird. Its wing span seemed to go on forever. The base of its long craning neck was ringed in black fur and at the end of its neck was the head of a bull. The condorox flew down closer, landing upon a long, thick branch.

"What's that attached to its back?" asked Parseck.

"My chariot," said the queen. "Come Earthers."

Parseck turned to Seasqrd and said, "Wait, she's coming with us; we don't need her. I'll pilot the Saturn Seven and —"

Sam stopped abruptly when he noticed the business end of an aspear being pointed at his face. The queen held the weapon and said, "But the condorox will only obey me and the glob is almost upon my city. Now I do not propose to argue with you while Photocitysis is in danger."

Seasqrd placed his hand across the aspear, forcing the queen to lower it. "We have to work together on this — Animazon and Earthmen — Space-man and G-Man; right?"

"For your sake I will spare him," the queen said.

41

"She spares me? Who is saving who again?" Commander Parseck asked.

Seasqrd couldn't believe it but he actually felt sorry for Sam. He had lost his ship; he was a mechanical genius on a planet with no mechanics and he had been bullied by Animazons throughout the entire mission. Seasqrd very gently patted Sam's back; he wondered how he might feel if he had crash landed on a planet where no one was in awe of his genetically-enhanced attributes. Then he wondered if Sam had been right when he said all Geneti-Men were arrogant. But Seasqrd didn't have to wonder what Sam was thinking as they watched the combat below.

*   *   *

Sam Parseck appreciated the pat on the back from Seasqrd. As the condorox stretched its wings, the chariot was drawn through the clouds and Sam Parseck watched the battle of Photocitysis. Down below the glob was bubbling its way upwards over fields and hills consuming all that was green and natural, leaving a path of devastation and drawing closer to the gates of the city. What was left of the rosebots and tomatons tried in vain to halt the glob's assault while fleeing Animazon warriors rode their gorillataurs back into the city. Sam wasn't the type to rub it in, especially when the one he'd like to rub it into carried an aspear, but he did not mind seeing the queen's organic army destroyed.

In a deep, dark way he kind of wanted to see the Animazon queen and her warrior women get theirs, but he knew that was not the way of Cosmos-Corps and he knew what Seasqrd would say and he knew the G-Man would be right; he also knew if the Z won Seasqrd would never let him hear the end of how he failed due to over-reliance on machinery. Sam had to admit it; he looked up to Captain Seasqrd, not just because the guy stood head and shoulders above him, there were other things. Seasqrd was the hero type; he had these great big muscles; he had a firm jaw and these very serious brown eyes that always looked like he could get the job done but more importantly he cared about others and really truly believed in the principles of Cosmos-Corps. Before Sam had accused Seasqrd of being arrogant but the truth was the captain was just confident; he was confident of his skills and all that malarkey about heart, bone, sinew and soul. And he knew how to lead; he even had the Animazon queen following his instructions. Sam smiled as he thought about the queen and the captain when suddenly Seasqrd spoke.

"There is the Saturn Seven below!"

Seasqrd pointed to the spaceship wedged within the crevices of the canyon. Commander Parseck turned and said, "Yes, fortunately, I managed to land it beyond your chlorofield."

The queen nodded in mock approval of Sam's piloting skills while she touched her pendant. The condorox seemed to nod in comprehension of its queen's orders and slowed to a halt as it landed next to the Saturn Seven. Withdrawing the keys from his uniform, Sam pressed a button on the key chain but grew frustrated aiming the button pusher at the hatch then he held it directly over the hatch.

"What is wrong with this thing?" Parseck said as his button pusher beeped and beeped. "Why won't it open the hatch? Unlock!"

"Men and their machines," the queen said. She turned to Seasqrd. "We have no time for this."

"Sam, she's right. I'll open the hatch," Seasqrd said.

Seasqrd grabbed onto the handle of the hatch and tugged at it. He seemed to be pulling with all his super-human strength, but the hatch did not budge. Soon the queen reached up and placed her hands about his and together they pulled slowly tearing the hatch from its bolts.

Sam grew impatient and slammed his fist into his palm banging the button pusher forcing it to give out one loud beep.

"This doo-hickey has got to work!" Parseck said. Then suddenly the hatch unlocked. Both Seasqrd and the queen fell back, while the hatch tore off its hinges and flew backwards.

"Oh no," Commander Sam Parseck said.

"Sam!" Seasqrd yelled. He lifted the heavy hatch door off him and asked, "Are you hurt bad?"

Sam Parseck did not bother to answer; he focused on trying to breathe again.

"Let's help him up," Seasqrd said, gesturing to the queen.

"No!" Parseck gasped.

"Sorry, Sam," Seasqrd said, backing away. "I keep forgetting how fragile your ordinary physique is."

Sam looked up at Seasqrd with angry eyes as he felt tears roll down his cheek. Seasqrd looked down and said, "That came out the wrong way, Sam, but what do we do?"

"Only one thing to do, G-Man, you must pilot my ship," Parseck groaned.

"Me, pilot the Saturn Seven?" Seasqrd placed his hand over his own bulky chest. "I'm biologically programmed for strength, endurance and agility. I'm not one with machines like you."

"Just do things the STPD way," Parseck said.

"No one could be as good at that as you are, little Earthling," said the queen.

"Thank you, oh sexalted one," Parseck said. "Wait, the mighty, mouthy majesty has given me an idea."

He slowly reached into his pocket and gently withdrew a small communication device. He held it up before the queen, hoping its odd shape would confuse her and the Zaftig monarch did not disappoint.

"What good is a giant animal fang going to do?" the queen asked.

"It's not a fang. It's my sabretooth."

Sam Parseck slowly clipped the device in his ear so that its wide tip was juxtaposed to his earlobe while the narrow tip dangled near his mouth. After letting out one more groan of pain he said, "With my sabretooth I'll be able to stay in contact with the Saturn Seven and help guide you. We will be one with the ship."

"Excellent deal, Sam." Seasqrd nodded.

"Aye, sir," Parseck said. He winked and then added, "I also get 500 microns each solar month and weekends are free."

Gene Lucas Seasqrd knelt down; Sam reached up and they locked arms then Seasqrd clasped his hand over his friend's shoulder. Parseck let out a slight moan; he tried to cover it up quickly before his compatriot realized the pain he had just inadvertently inflicted. Seasqrd raised his hand up then very gently placed it back on Parseck's shoulder, patting it carefully.

"Sorry my friend," Seasqrd said. "Like I said, sometimes I don't know my own strength."

Sam Parseck nodded and handed the keys to the Saturn Seven to Seasqrd.

"Do you two need to be alone?" asked the queen.

"You!" Seasqrd rose to his feet, pointed at the queen and said, "You take care of my friend while I pilot his ship."

Sam was impressed.

"You can't talk to me like that. I'm the ruler of Zaftig!" shouted the queen.

"You just do as I say!" Seasqrd jumped up onto the wing of the Saturn Seven and climbed down into the open hatch. A moment later a medicocoon was tossed out and landed in the queen's hands.

"Who does he think he is ordering me around?" asked the queen.

"He's Gene Lucas Seasqrd... the best of the G-Men." Sam Parseck said with a smile. He looked at the queen and asked, "What's wrong your voluptuousness? Kind of gets your heart pumping when he takes command, doesn't it?"

The queen turned, lowering her sights on Commander Parseck, as he lay helpless on the ground. Parseck, not caring for the sinister look in the queen's big, green eyes, began to squirm away as best he could. The queen plopped the medicocoon down next to Parseck. She unrolled the bundle of shiny plastic and asked, "What kind of machinery is this, man? It looks like gigantic slipper?"

"Only a slipper that big would fit your feet," Sam said with a sneer.

"For someone so little and frail you've got a big mouth," the queen said as she lifted her foot up, preparing to stomp on Sam's face.

"Watch your temper; Seasqrd wouldn't like it if you hurt me," Parseck said. The queen stood back. Sam said, "Now place me in the medicocoon."

"The what?"

"The medicocoon; when the patient is placed inside it fills with analgesic salves and pain-relieving ointments. Now slip me into it as gently as possible."

"Certainly," the queen said slyly.

Sam was a little concerned by her tone of voice but Seasqrd had just popped his head out of the forward hatch atop the Saturn Seven; Sam knew he was plugging the STPD lines into the guidance system but he also knew the Animazon queen would be pleasant while he was watching.

"Have no fear Earthman, on this planet we have a natural capacity for natural medicine," said the queen loudly making sure Seasqrd heard every word. Then she acted like she was counting on her fingers. "We have plants and herbs that can be made into any remedy; we have buds and berries that will create any cure; we even have shoots and roots that produce panacea-like potions."

"Yes," Seasqrd said as if he was very impressed by her numeric substantiation. "The medicinal knowledge of Zaftig is renowned throughout space."

"But don't forget our most important healing element," said the queen; both Seasqrd and Parseck waited patiently then the queen finally said, "The female of the species always possesses an inherent instinct for care giving."

"That is undeniably true, my queen." Seasqrd said and lowered himself back down into the Saturn Seven.

Once he was gone the queen's pleasant tone vanished. She said, "I'll take care of you, my fragile little friend."

"Ow!" Parseck said as he was grabbed and shoved into the medicocoon. "Thank the stars I am in such capable care!"

After his final grunt of agony was over Parseck's injured body began submerging in orange medical gels; it felt a little cold and damp but soothing. He looked at the aspear of the Animazon queen pointing at him and swore it was smiling at him. The queen asked, "You should be fine now; I will leave you here to heal and see if Seasqrd needs any assistance."

"But wait," Parseck said. "What if I need some assistance; I'm trapped in here."

"You'll be better if left alone," the queen said, "and besides I'd rather be with him."

Sam watched the queen walk away and said, "So much for the natural capacity of a woman."

* * *

Down in the auxiliary bridge of the Saturn Seven, Seasqrd was trying to figure out how he'd enter this in his reflection entry.

Mission Entry: With my genetically enhanced … Sam is right I am a bit arrogant.

Right now he wished he had some of Sam's engineering skills. But even if he did he couldn't concentrate; he kept thinking about the queen. Then he told himself to think about the mission and his reflection entry.

Cosmos-Corps Mission Entry: the Animazon Queen had risked her neck and now it's up to me, Gene Lucas Seasqrd, to save her skin. That sexy neck and that smooth, soft, sensuous skin.

Seasqrd shook his head.

Cosmos-Corps Mission Entry: Let's try this again; unfortunately the Saturn Seven had been wrecked on its final leg of our journey. Oh what legs! Why bother?

Seasqrd shook his head again then his super-acute hearing heard someone jump onto the wing of the space vessel, then he saw exquisitely shaped calves and thighs climbing down the ladder and he began working even harder to prepare the ship for flight.

He heard her say, "Your friend is healing in some enormous slipper; I can't recall what he called it."

"I know what it is," Seasqrd said while trying to focus on the mechanical mess in front of him instead of the very attractive woman behind him.

"Why are you ignoring me?"

Seasqrd remained focused on his work. The queen stepped in front of him.

"How does the task progress?" she asked looking from the burnt out computer components back towards Seasqrd and then at the various spare parts strewn about the floor plates. "Will this machine be ready to fly?" she asked.

"I'm not the engineer Sam is," Seasqrd said. "But I think all we need is for these relativity relays to power up."

The queen knelt down, helping Seasqrd and their hands touched against one another. The queen wrapped her fingers about his and said, "I must thank you. You are doing this in spite of the way we Animazons have treated you. Why?"

"It is the nature of Earth people to help those in need, and we know too well the evil of the Zlythetaurs," he said clasping her hand.

The queen placed her other hand about Seasqrd's shoulder. Her tail wagged so widely it brushed against his bicep as he wrapped his arm about her waist. She leaned forward and kissed him. Suddenly, the queen pulled back and said, "Your relays are getting hot."

"What?" Seasqrd said. Then he glanced around at the control panel and said, "Oh, yes, they're ready. The ship is ready."

"Before, you go I want you to have this." The queen reached about to the back of her neck, twisting her hands about as they dwelt underneath her luxurious red hair. When she pulled her hands back around she had her pendent in her hand and she placed it in Seasqrd hands.

"I can't take this," he said, looking at the silvery leaflet. "This is your connection to your environment."

"No, I want you to have it, it is very precious, it has great power and it could save your life someday just as you saved mine," said the queen.

He replied, "But it is too valuable."

"Worry not." The queen waved her hand. "I have a dozen more just like it."

Seasqrd placed the pendent about his neck. The queen leaned forward to kiss him again.

"Your antenna is going up," said the queen.

"What?" Seasqrd replied. "Oh, that."

"Hey, inside there!" Sam Parseck's voice shouted over the tele-antennae that rose from the center of the control panel. "Why are you two wasting time?"

"So, Sam," Seasqrd said as he leaned over the tele-antennae. "I see your set with your sabretooth."

"Never mind that; you got the ship ready to go?"

"Affirmative," Seasqrd said. The queen stood behind him, rubbing his shoulders and resting her head upon the back of his neck. "I'm ready for lift off," he said.

"So what are we waiting for?" asked Parseck.

The queen turned Seasqrd around, pressed her moist lips against his and wrapped her arms about his waist. The queen finally ended her long, moist kiss. Seasqrd looked into her gleaming eyes and said, "It's time for me to launch."

She kissed him again, quickly and said, "Not now, first, get this ship in the air."

CHAPTER 4
THOSE SCI-FI GUYS VERSUS THE GLOB

Sam Parseck lay encased in his medicocoon, trying to think of how this would go into his Mission Entry.

After the hatch landed on me... no that doesn't sound good. A lesser man would've been completely crushed; I was only... no! How about I was knocked to the ground? So there I was in a medicocoon after sacrificing myself. Yes, that sounds good. After I was incapacitated I left Seasqrd in command of my ship. At first Gene Lucas was apprehensive but after my words of encouragement he was filled with confidence.

Seasqrd's voice broke up Sam's thoughts. Sam listened as Seasqrd said, "Now I think we've got it. I've rebooted the navigational components and I'm about to recharge the photonic cells."

"No you idiot," Sam said. "You have to recharge the photonic cells first!"

"How dare you speak to him that way?"

Sam shifted his eyes up and saw the Animazon Queen's upside down face standing over him. Unfortunately the viper on her aspear was looking right at him.

"I mean it would be more conducive if you were to do it the opposite way around in reverse, my friend," Commander Parseck winked and smiled at the queen.

Seasqrd's voice came through the sabretooth once again. "I am Sam. And I think we're ready."

Sam Parseck lay still watching the Saturn Seven hovering above. He felt so strange like he was at odds with the ship he had piloted for so long, but at least with the sabretooth, he could keep in constant contact with this new pilot in case he started to mess up. The Saturn Seven rose up into the sky; from out of her stern shot a small missile.

"There goes STPD," Commander Parseck said.

"Do not speak of him that way," said the queen. "He's the only man who has ever touched —"

"No, I mean the satellite. That is the satellite in the Satellite Tracking & Piloting Device. See it?" said Parseck.

The queen looked upward and spotted the small spinning orb with the long satellite dish on top. "I see it!" she said and looked down at Sam Parseck. "Are you sure you and your devices will help Gene Lucas Seasqrd succeed?"

"Don't worry, queenie, my whole life has been about machines?"

"Your death will be about them too."

"Say again." Parseck shifted uneasily in his gel.

"If any harm comes to Seasqrd due to the machinations of your machinery, you will pay with your life," she said aiming the head of her aspear at Sam's face.

"I see your point," Parseck said as he gulped down.

"Seasqrd to Parseck... Seasqrd to Parseck," said a voice emanating from the sabretooth. "Sam are you there?"

Sam Parseck was still quivering under the icy stare of the Animazon queen when he finally responded, "I'm here, Captain Seasqrd."

"Sam, we have a problem."

"I really wish you hadn't said that." Sam's eyes crossed as they bore down at the point of the aspear that pressed against his nose then he heard the mechanized voice of STPD in the background.

"*You will need to increase altitude,*" STPD instructed.

"We're losing altitude," Seasqrd said.

"No problem. Divert auxiliary power to the gravi-pads," Parseck said.

"*You will need to turn four degrees to starboard,*" said STPD.

"Sam! The converters just crashed! Now the navigatrometer has shorted out. I don't think I'm going to make it," Seasqrd said.

"Yes you will… yes you will!" Parseck said while looking at the queen's glaring green eyes. He pressed the sabretooth close to his mouth and said, "This can be fixed. Grab the bag of smartools under your seat."

"I don't know how to fix these things," Seasqrd said.

"Just listen, G-Man, the tools are smartools. They'll tell you what to do," Parseck said.

Commander Parseck sank deeper into his medicocoon. The queen was obviously surmising from Sam's side of the conversation, and the sweat on his brow, that something was amiss. She tightened her grip on her weapon.

"Have you got the multiwrench?" Parseck asked while faking a smile.

"Roger," Seasqrd said. "I tore open the command console and have engaged the multiwrench. You sure this tool knows what it is doing?"

Parseck replied, "Yes, it does."

"It just told me right tightens and left loosens," Seasqrd said.

"Listen to it, Seasqrd!" Parseck said as he stared at the serpentine eyes of the queen's weapon.

"We will now begin our descent," STPD said.

"I fixed the converters but, we're losing orientation!" Seasqrd said.

"Just use the plasmapliers to increase the power flow to the stabilizers," Parseck said.

Seasqrd said, "The plasmapliers just told me they're insulted that the multiwrench was used first and now they won't talk."

There was some static and Seasqrd broke off. "Gene Lucas, come in!" Parseck yelled.

"Now the multiwrench just yelled at the plasmapliers; it said the pliers were being too snippy," Seasqrd said.

"I forgot to mention, Seasqrd," Parseck said, "smartools do not get along."

"Sam, we have a problem," Seasqrd said.

"I wish you'd stop saying that," Parseck gasped. He looked at the queen; she was not pleased.

"I'm heading directly into the glob!" Seasqrd said.

"Eject!" Parseck said.

"I am," Seasqrd said. "I am going down below to eject the lox tanks manually!"

"Seasqrd! I meant you should eject!" Parseck said. He waited for an answer then yelled, "GENE LUCAS!"

Then came a voice over the sabretooth; it was STPD. The voice said, "*You have reached your destination. Hope you had a great flight.*"

Sam Parseck lay in his cocoon of medical salve, listening to an explosion in the distance then static over the sabretooth. He slowly looked up at the queen, and saw a smoke plume over her shoulders.

"What has happened to Seasqrd?" she asked.

"I'm sure he got out of there before it impacted," Parseck said. "How about you? You think he's okay?"

The queen did not answer. She held up her aspear then drove it into the soil next to Sam's head. She reached down, grabbing the medicocoon by the handle that protruded over Parseck's pelvis. Lifting the medicocoon up in the air she carried Commander Parseck back to the condorox.

"Come with me, tiny Earthman!" she said, and soon they were in flight back to Photocitysis.

* * *

Commander Sam Parseck watched every move of the Animazons with caution. They all stood at attention while staring at their queen; the queen kissed her fingers and touched the block of ice that encased Gene Lucas Seasqrd. His strapping arms extended outward from his burly chest as if he was about to embrace the Animazon queen yet his eyes were lifeless. The queen seemed genuinely sad as did Sam, and he hoped her sorrow had caused her to forget her promise regarding Seasqrd's demise.

The glob, once a menacing pool of toxic sludge and chemicals, now lay before the gates of Photocitysis like an ebony glacier. Its silvery tentacles had snapped off and shattered like fallen icicles and white fissures had split the bubbling pockets of acid across its surface. Next to the glob was the smoldering fuselage of the Saturn Seven.

"What a shame such a magnificent life had to be sacrificed," said the queen.

"It's not that bad, I might be able to salvage her," Commander Parseck said then he bit his tongue.

"I meant Gene Lucas!" She turned with her tail remaining limp between her legs; she snapped her fingers. At once the Animazon warriors took their weapons and surrounded Sam Parseck as he squirmed and sank down in his medicocoon.

"I told you I would hold you responsible if anything were to happen to him," the queen said. She stepped forward, ripped open the medicocoon, spilling salve across the ground, and pulled Parseck to his feet as she said, "Anything to say about your fallen fellow Cosmos-Corpsmen."

Sam Parseck stood wiping bits of salve and gel from his Cosmos-Corps uniform and looked at the aspears that were pointed at him. He swallowed hard, trying to think of a reply. He stood as tall as he could and cleared his throat.

"Captain Gene Lucas Seasqrd was one of the greatest officers I ever knew. He was the finest student at the academy and the prototype for all Cosmos–Corpsmen... and... uh... of all the beings I've known, he was the most super-human."

"Strong words from such a scrawny human. Go on Earthman," said the queen.

Sam was happy; the queen seemed touched by his words and that made her seem less hostile. He cleared his throat once again while trying to think of more to say but what else was there to say? He cleared his throat one last time then he said,

"Gene Lucas gave his life for the spirit of Cosmos-Corps and the spirit of man cannot be stopped."

Sam Parseck tilted his head until his chin touched his chest. When he looked up the queen and her Animazons seemed moved by his brief yet poignant eulogy of Gene Lucas Seasqrd. The queen approached him; tears filled her eyes. She placed her hand on Sam's shoulder and leaned down, but she needed to pause before she spoke.

"What do you mean by spirit of man?"

"Wait, you can't be mad at me for that." Parseck raised his hands up. "Throughout history we've used terms like mankind."

"History?" said the queen. "Not Herstory."

"Oh, I give up, go ahead and kill me," Parseck said.

The queen stood back allowing her warrior women to close in on Sam Parseck. Sam shrank back, dropping to his knees.

"How little you have learned about Earthmen," said a voice.

Sam thought he knew who it was but that would be impossible but then again for a Geneti-Man nothing is impossible. Sam clasped his hands together in hope; he said, "Gene Lucas, you're alive?"

The queen and her Animazons turned around. Sam Parseck peered around the venomous weapons and shapely legs to see Captain Gene Lucas Seasqrd standing up to his ankles in melted slush. About his neck hung a pendent that seemed to be burning brighter than the binary suns of Zaftig.

"Yes, Sam, I am quite alive." Seasqrd flexed.

"The power of tulipathy has given him life!" the queen said as she put her hands over her chest. She beamed at the Seasqrd and said, "I am glad to see you unharmed, my hero."

"I am glad to see you and all of you," Seasqrd said. He stepped out of the melted ice and said, "But I am disappointed. I am out of it for only a brief time and already you revert back to your old ways and are ready to pounce on this pathetic man."

"But Seasqrd... he... I...." the queen lowered her head, offering no further excuses while Seasqrd cast a stern look at her and the other Animazons. Having to listen to one of Seasqrd's speeches would be just the punishment these Animazons deserve Sam thought.

Gene Lucas waved his hand at Sam, motioning for him to come to his side and Sam warily walked around the Animazon women and joined his compatriot. Seasqrd placed his dripping hand on Parseck's soggy shoulder and said, "I know you think of him as simply a man... an obnoxious, little man who shows more feeling for tools and machinery than he does for living things and I cannot say that I blame you. But it was his idea that saved you all and I have come to know him as a friend."

Parseck looked up at Seasqrd and smiled.

"Ask not for the logic of this statement for there is none," Seasqrd said. "He and I are as different as an electron and a proton, but perhaps in the bond that joins such things together you can see the ways of our Earth. We have learned to combine the tools and the machines of our technology with the natural forces of our environment. The mission of Cosmos-Corps is to protect the ecologies of Earth and all our allied worlds. We can cite numerous examples of newly encountered civilizations that have prospered from our technologic aid but have maintained environmental stability. Now we do not pretend that the Earth has achieved perfection, but we do have a system and it works, or at least it works a hell of a lot better than anything I've seen on any other planet, especially this one."

"That is for sure." Sam Parseck nodded in agreement. The queen and her warrior women lowered their heads as Captain Seasqrd continued his reproach.

"Forgive my bluntness, but the choice is yours. Join with Earth against the Z or stand alone and face environmental destruction."

The queen stepped forward and said, "I understand your words, Seasqrd. Perhaps we Animazons can learn from you Earthmen. I wish Zaftig and Earth to be allies. I want you and me to be together always. Let me join you in your struggle to right the wrongs of the Z."

"My queen, there are so many wrongs that you must right on your own world first." Seasqrd smiled.

"So you will be leaving me," the queen said.

"I'm afraid so, my queen, but I still stand prepared to serve my punishment," Seasqrd bowed to the queen.

"I do not understand, Gene Lucas," the queen said with her tail drooping and her head tilting.

She didn't know what Seasqrd meant but Sam did; he winked at Gene Lucas. "I think he wants to complete this diplomatic mission with a final consummation between your world and ours."

The queen was more perplexed than ever. She asked, "What does he mean, Gene Lucas?"

Seasqrd smiled at Sam then went before the queen and said, "I believe we have some Anjhee-Nah to finish."

"Oh, yes!" the queen said gleefully.

"Just remember one thing, queenie. He has never failed on a mission," Sam Parseck said as he clasped his hand over his friend's massive shoulder, "and he has the power."

*   *   *

Seasqrd plopped down on the queen's bed. She nestled up against him, tracing circles around his wide chest with her fingernails and kissing his balding head. Her tail whipped about when he began caressing her long red hair.

"I've always believed there's nothing the heart, bone, sinew and soul of a human couldn't overcome but are you sure I'll survive this?" he asked with a smile.

"I'm sure. You are unlike any man we have here on this world," the queen said but her words trailed off as if she were lost in thought. Seasqrd saw she was looking at his forehead;

actually she was studying the port in his forehead. She said, "I've been meaning to ask you something."

"Why this is my power port; all of us Geneti-Men have one." Seasqrd poked his forehead. "They used it to load me up with all kinds of genetic programming."

The queen was still studying his forehead as she asked, "Like what?"

"Oh, for instance, I have ape DNA for enhanced strength and falcon DNA for enhanced eyesight; there's some stallion DNA for stamina too I believe." Seasqrd held his fingers against his mouth as he became pensive. "I think there was some rabbit DNA for enhanced hearing; not to mention cat DNA for quickness and agility. I'm a master of over twenty martial art forms."

"What's with the tiny little lights on the side?" she asked.

"They light when the brain and the genetic programming get really active," he replied.

"I see." She moved closer and Seasqrd could see and feel the little lights flashing over his brow. She teasingly asked, "What other powers do you have?"

Seasqrd said, "*Kiss me!*"

She did then she pulled her lips away in awe and asked, "How'd you make me do that?"

"With my power voice," Seasqrd said, "We Geneti-Men are so confident and forceful that we can make, well let's just say, very powerful suggestions."

"I see," the queen began fanning herself with her hand, "you really know how to take a woman's breath away."

"Actually I couldn't have made someone as strong willed as you kiss me like that unless you already wanted to but you'd be amazed what I could make a weak willed person do or believe."

The queen tilted her head back like she was ready for another powerful kiss. "Tell me more about the stallion stamina in you."

Seasqrd leaned forward. "And don't forget the rabbit."

They kissed then Seasqrd said, "But you will free the men of this world from their second-class citizenry?"

"Oh, of course," said the queen as she snuggled closer.

"And you will give them equality," he said.

The queen kissed him and said, "Yes... yes, of course."

They kissed more and the queen began nibbling on his neck and around his ear; Seasqrd pounded the side of the bed with his hands.

"Now you're not just saying this?" Seasqrd asked. He looked into her big green eyes and said, "You are going to put a stop to keeping your men as mere slaves?"

"I have begun to see your wisdom, Gene Lucas," the queen said in between sighs.

"That pleases me for it is the way of Cosmos-Corps to spread knowledge and justice throughout the galaxy," Seasqrd said. The queen rolled on her side and tapped her fingers in his belly. Seasqrd ignored her impatient fingers and continued, "Back on Earth we have faced many cataclysms but we have always found the humanity not to let self-destruction—"

"Gene Lucas," whispered the queen while her fingers were over his lips. "I have two words for you: Anjhee-Nah."

Seasqrd realized he had been talking too much and embraced the Animazon queen. He pulled her into his strapping arms.

"Why are you smiling?" she asked.

"Your tail is tickling me," he said.

"Oh, Gene Lucas this is going to be fantastic Anjhee-Nah!"

Just then, a pulse running through the wooden wall opposite the bed took Seasqrd's attention away. He watched the pulse travel along the grain of the wood, through the ceiling and down the wall adjacent to the bed causing a branch to sprout up and a broad leaf to unfurl from the tip of the branch. The queen looked at the leaf as it changed from a shiny green to a deep blue. She placed her hand over her head and sighed, "A communication."

Seasqrd stared in amazement as the blue leaf rolled itself into what looked like an old fashioned conical speaker and from it came a woman's voice.

"Your majesty, a thousand pardons for disturbing your Anjhee-Nah."

"What is it?" The queen sat at the edge of her bed.

"We have something entering our chlorofield —"

"It can wait," said the queen.

"But the other Earthman says it's from their Cosmos-Corps and —"

"I'm busy," said the queen.

"But my queen, the object is heading —"

"Leave..." the queen said, slamming her fist against the speaker, "us..." she slammed her fist again, crushing the leaf, "alone!"

The leaf broke off the branch and the queen rolled over back the next to Seasqrd.

"Where were we?" she asked.

"Your majesty," said Seasqrd. "Temper; temper."

"I'm sorry, but I want nothing to ruin this moment," said the queen.

"Nothing will," said Seasqrd.

Suddenly, the roof caved in. Shards of wood exploded across the queen's chamber. A rocket speared into the floor, its tail still burning and producing plumes of smoke. The rocket went still and across its tubular frame a monitor screen lit up. The queen and Seasqrd shared looks of bewilderment. Seasqrd sighed and said, "Well, unless I get an urgent txt messile from Earth."

The chamber doors opened. Into the royal bedroom came charging Animazons followed by Sam Parseck.

"How dare you disturb Anjhee-Nah?" the queen said.

"We beg forgiveness," said one of the guards.

"I don't," Parseck said as he approached the txt messile. "I'm anxious to see what is so important."

"No need to read it to me," Seasqrd said, holding his hand up, causing Sam to close his mouth. "My genetically enhanced vision can see the message of the messile fine from here."

The message read: **Seasqrd RUT? U need 2 CRB 2 C-C Intell ASAP. S2S we had an intruder invade the Rozwelles lab. AFAIK _it_ is still safe but I'm SMHID over the security breach. ATM we're only on minimal alert but TPTB want U 2 rtrn 2 Earth. IAE I need U & TSTB. ACK, Quasar.**

"O-M-G," Commander Parseck said. "Sounds like someone wanted you away from Earth, Gene Lucas."

"Where are you going?" asked the queen while watching Seasqrd wrap a sheet about him and get up from the bed. Seasqrd did not answer, but simply grabbed his uniform and went behind the vines that hung across the back of the bed.

"Sam, send a reply txt messile," Seasqrd said from behind the curtain of golden vines. "Tell Quasar: B-B-S A-E-A-P."

He then heard the queen ask, "What is going on, Gene Lucas?" Her figure formed a shapely silhouette across the curtain as she asked, "What is B-B-S, A-T-M and S-2-S?"

"Txt speak, your legginess," Seasqrd heard Parseck reply as he put on his pants and shirt. Sam's narrow stature formed a smaller silhouette next to the queen's as he said, "Our ancestors were too lazy to type complete sentences with properly spelled words so they utilized an argot language to send messages. In the years that followed, schoolchildren began to think of this as proper spelling and grammar so txt speak was eventually adopted as an official language. I'm fluent in it."

"So as your computers became smarter your species became dumber," the queen said.

Seasqrd opened the vines after he pulled on his boots; he shook his head at the queen's comment but the queen was preoccupied with harming Sam.

"B-I-O-Y-A," Parseck said as he sneered at the queen.

"I'm sure I don't need a translation for that you obnoxious Earthman," the queen said with her fist raised back, but before she could land it on Parseck's cowering head, Seasqrd had taken her by the wrist.

"Your majesty, you're disappointing me again," Seasqrd said.

The queen looked at Seasqrd dressed in his uniform; her eyes opened wide and her jaw dropped. He did not bother explaining. He stood before Sam Parseck and asked, "What needs to be done to the Saturn Seven?"

"Well, the Animazons helped me reload the lox tanks. The retassitators were damaged, but I jerry rigged them. The flux fuses were shorted out in your crash; they can be replaced easily and speaking of a crash." Parseck ducked away from the queen.

Seasqrd turned just in time to watch the queen smash some very large pieces of furniture while throwing a royal fit that caused the other Animazons to flee. Seasqrd rushed to stop her. He grabbed an ornate wooden chair, saving it from being shattered into splinters.

"Your majesty, you must stop this," he said.

"Seasqrd, I'd like to tell you something," Sam Parseck said.

"Not now," Seasqrd held up his hand.

The Animazon queen tore the vines that hung from the ceiling down and fell upon her bed, pounding the pillows, screaming into the sheets, her tail swishing violently the whole time.

"But Seasqrd," Sam Parseck said.

"Sam, please, I'll handle this," Seasqrd said.

Seasqrd sat on the edge of the bed. He gently caressed the queen's soft red hair after batting her swinging tail away from his face.

"You see, my queen, I am a G-Man of the Cosmos-Corps. I am a creature of honor and duty as you are. My first duty is to Earth. When my home planet needs me I must answer the call."

The queen hammered the bed with her fists, swinging her feet as her temper tantrum continued. In between the queen's screams, which were muted by her head being buried in the pillows, Parseck tried once again to interrupt.

"Seasqrd, I must tell you something," he said.

"What is so blasted important?" Seasqrd said, as he turned his head. He looked at Sam and asked, "Why aren't you getting the Saturn Seven ready?"

"That's just it, I can fix all the little things in no time, but the loxinator will take at least eighteen macrons to fill the liquid oxygen tanks," Parseck said.

"A-Y-S?"

"I'm quite serious, I have to have eighteen macrons," Parseck said.

"I see." Seasqrd nodded knowingly. He turned to the queen. Her face was still buried in the pillows. Her tantrum had not subsided.

"There, there, my queen," Seasqrd said, stroking her back. He took in a deep breath and said, "As an interstellar hero my first duty is to my home world and the preservation of my species, but in the meantime while Sam prepares the ship what's wrong with a little Anjhee-Nah?"

Sam Parseck took his cue and left the royal bedchamber in great haste and said, "T-T-Y-L."

CHAPTER 5
THOSE SCI-FI GUYS & THE RETURN OF DARKLONE

Sam Parseck listened to the battered hull of the Saturn Seven rattle its way through Earth's atmosphere as he brought his vessel in for a landing at Cosmos-Corps Command. Sam patted the wheel and said, "Easy big seven; we're home."

Cosmos-Corps Command stood like a forest of glass towers. Each one was a shining cylinder of engineering might and that made Sam happy to see. Seasqrd tapped his shoulder and said, "Down there."

Sam had been lost in thought and not seen the landing crew awaiting them down below. The Saturn Seven was a bit sluggish; Sam cut power and then power cut out altogether.

"Uh-oh," Sam said as the ship plopped down on the landing field. After the ship stopped vibrating Sam sucked in a deep breath and said, "Any landing you can walk away from."

Sam got no answer from Seasqrd and suddenly realized it was because the G-Man was already out of his seat and up the hatch. Sam rushed to follow; Seasqrd leapt to the landing pad and ordered the men to take him to Quasar. Immediately, Sam and Seasqrd were escorted to the HQ of C-C Intelligence, where Commodore John Quasar of the Geneti-Men met them.

He and Seasqrd saluted, bumping their hands against the power portals in their foreheads; like Gene Lucas, John Quasar was tall and very muscular but had a balding head. Sam tried not to laugh out loud but he wondered if very little hair on your head was the price you paid for having all that genetic engineering pumped into it.

"Good to see you again, Gene Lucas," Quasar finished shaking Seasqrd's hand, "by the way, did I mention my nephew was accepted to Cosmos-Corps Academy after you wrote that letter of recommendation?"

"I wrote a recommendation for your niece," Seasqrd said, placing his hands at his side.

"That is right," Quasar said then suddenly he withdrew a weapon and aimed it at Seasqrd's head.

Sam took his hand off his plasma-pistol when he realized Quasar held an eyedentifieray gun.

Quasar shot a beam at Seasqrd's surprised face allowing the red light to probe the Captain's cornea and retinas. Quasar glanced at the readout of the eyedentifieray and nodded.

"It is you, Seasqrd," Quasar said. "How did the mission go with the Animazon women?"

Seasqrd rubbed his eyes and began blinking rapidly. Then he said, "There were more dangers than anticipated, but as you may have expected, we were able to save the Animazons from certain destruction by the Z."

"That should improve our interstellar relations in that quadrant," Quasar said.

"Oh, Seasqrd really improved relations," Parseck said.

"Sam!" Seasqrd said.

"You don't have to tell me of his diplomatic skills, I accompanied him on an ambassadorial mission to Gamma Alpha Beta," Quasar said.

Seasqrd stopped blinking; he turned to Quasar and said, "You were supposed to accompany me to Gamma Alpha Beta but at the last minute your orders were changed. What the devil is going on here? Why was that txt messile sent?"

"Someone broke into the Rozwelles labs and the good doctor is disgusted... as is usual," Quasar said.

"So why the eyedentifieray?" Seasqrd asked.

"Sorry, Gene Lucas," Quasar said. "I had to be sure it's really you. Come with me."

Seasqrd and Parseck followed Quasar into his office. The commodore offered them seats as he took a moment to feed the fish swimming about the large circular tank housed in the wall. "Please sit and be comfortable," he said.

Sam Parseck looked over the rest of the office. The room was decorated with paintings of ancient sailing vessels and replicas of the old Apollo moon rockets and NASA space shuttles. Seasqrd wanted to sit but found the chairs were occupied by half completed models of early space probes.

"Be careful Seasqrd or the Voyager might make another trip beyond Uranus," Parseck whispered.

"Sam!"

"How's that?" Quasar turned with a look of puzzlement.

"I was saying I find all this hard to believe. Before I embarked for Zaftig, I left orders for three G-Men and a contingent of Cosmos-Corps secureaday guards to protect the Rozwelles labs. How could someone breech that defense," Seasqrd said.

"Well, our secureaday guards never really do much," Parseck said.

"That's true, but still three G-Men," Seasqrd said.

"Someone of extraordinary power must be behind it. The G-Men were not only defeated but were rendered helpless. We found them drooling and babbling; all their power gone," Quasar said while tapping the portal in his own forehead.

"Was it him?" Seasqrd said. His portal glimmered slightly.

"Who else?" Quasar asked. Then his forehead lit up.

Commander Parseck was a bit confused. "Who is him?" he asked.

"Sam, please," Seasqrd said.

"Now we must try to get one step ahead of him," Quasar said.

"That won't be easy," Seasqrd said.

"Are we referring to Darklone?" Parseck asked. He noticed at the mention of Darklone's name, Seasqrd's forehead flashed brighter and brighter. He looked as if he wanted to explain something, but then turned back to Quasar, stretched his shoulders back and stuck out his chin.

"No wonder you wanted me back immediately. You would need the finest of the Geneti-Men to match that renegade," Seasqrd said.

"No, not quite," Quasar said.

"What?"

Commander Parseck, looking at the wounded expression on Seasqrd's face, brought his hand to his mouth so that neither of the G-Men would see the smirk on his face.

"You are the best we have," Quasar said. "But as I told Cosmos-Corps Command, we need Gene Lucas Seasqrd here to help us match Darklone's wits not his strengths. Specifically, you serve two purposes in thwarting that renegade G-Man. First, you better than anyone knows how he thinks... for obvious reasons."

Seasqrd gave a grudging nod and said, "Yes, yes that is true. Go on."

"And by having you here it may prevent Darklone from using his usual ploy to gain the element of surprise on our fellow G-Men." Quasar pounded his fist into the palm of his hand.

"Is he using that trick again?" Seasqrd asked.

"What are you two talking about?" Parseck asked.

"How else could he have gained access to the Rozwelles Labs?" Quasar asked. "He broke into the labs but did not steal the—"

"No, thank heavens I had it moved, but if you can deduce where it is hidden, so can he. So where do you think it was moved to?" Quasar said.

Seasqrd paced back and forth; he tapped his fingers against his lip.

"The Plexagon," Seasqrd said.

Quasar pointed at Seasqrd and winked.

"No," Parseck said shaking his head. "Even Darklone would never dare strike there."

"Never underestimate him," Seasqrd said. "Very well, then I shall use all my genetically enhanced abilities to put a stop Darklone."

"I knew you would and I shall be there to help you. I still owe you from the time you saved my life during our assignment to Delta Zeta Tau," Quasar said.

"It was Epsilon Omega. Delta Zeta Tau was our old fraternity and would you stop testing me. It's me I tell you, not him!" Seasqrd bellowed.

Sam Parseck raised his hand, waving it at the two G-Men and said, "Count me in too."

"Good," Seasqrd said. He patted his hand across Parseck's back. "Then we are united as Cosmos-Corpsmen should be."

Seasqrd leaned over to help Commander Parseck back up on his feet. "Sorry about that. I did it again."

"I'm okay," Parseck wheezed. He sucked in a deep breath and said, "We had better fly to the Plexagon right away."

"I must log out of a few things up here. I'll meet you downstairs," Quasar said as he pointed at the door. "We can take my new set of pads."

"Thank you, John," Seasqrd said then he and Sam Parseck walked out of the office and entered a jetevator.

As they careened down to the nearest launch pad, Sam Parseck scratched his jaw and rubbed his chin. He said, "Seasqrd you and I have been through a lot on this mission. So I think I have a right to speak frankly. There's something you G-Men are hiding. What is the connection between you and Darklone?"

"Sorry, Sam, I'd rather not discuss it right now," Seasqrd said.

"Fine, it's no ice off the tail of my comet," Parseck said. The jetevator doors opened; Parseck followed Seasqrd to the launch pad. As they passed saluting spacemen, he continued, "It certainly seems that C-C Intell doesn't seem to trust you."

"Quasar just wanted to be sure I am the real Seasqrd," the Captain replied.

"That's just it," Parseck said, placing his hand on Seasqrd's muscular shoulder. "Why did he do that? And why didn't you check him? And why didn't they check me?"

Gene Lucas Seasqrd stopped and sighed before answering. "I know John Quasar and he's one of the finest Geneti-Men they ever made."

"So was Darklone."

Seasqrd pulled away, motioning for Parseck to follow. He finally whispered, "I assure you we need not worry about Quasar so let's just drop it."

Sam Parseck stepped in front of Seasqrd, shoved the lobby door open and stomped out onto the launch pad. He turned back to Seasqrd and said, "You G-Men really stick together, but mark my words, John Quasar is...." Sam turned back around to see Quasar in front of him, "the owner of one great revulsion car."

"Thanks, Commander Parseck." Quasar said. He looked at his new set of pads and asked, "What do you think of my new ReVolt?"

Sam stood in awe. The car stood like a wide-based pyramid of plastic and glass resting on a set of four rectangular metallic crates. There were three long mirrors resting on the hood and two accelejets on the back.

"Nice," Seasqrd said.

"Nice? It's the latest in revulsion propulsion," Parseck said.

"It really is revolting isn't it?" Quasar asked with pride.

"Gentlemen, time is of the essence," Seasqrd said.

"Two revulsion pads and how many solarnators?" Parseck asked while circling the ReVolt.

"Six," Quasar replied and pointed to the mirrors on the hood. "Fed by these three solar cells."

"What's the revulsion ratio?"

"I get 110km per volt locally and 725 on the hoverway."

"We should go," Seasqrd said.

Quasar nodded, pressed a button on the remote of his key chain and the glass dome atop the ReVolt slid open. "Here Sam," Quasar said, tossing the keys to Parseck. "Want to take her for a flight?"

"Love to!" Sam Parseck said as the keys dangled from his fingers. Quasar hopped in while Seasqrd tapped Sam's shoulder and gestured for him to climb into the cockpit and stop gawking at the ReVolt.

"He's a great guy," Parseck whispered to Seasqrd.

"Glad to hear you say that, Sam. Let's go!"

Within moments the ReVolt's revulsion pads lifted the car off the ground. Sam engaged the accelejets and the ReVolt began hovering across the launch pad and down the road.

"She floats like a cloud."

"Thanks, Sam," Quasar said.

The ReVolt drifted down a ramp and onto the hoverway. Sam could feel the revulsion pads lock onto the magnetic rails and the ReVolt suddenly took off. "At this rate, we'll be at the Plexagon in no time," he said.

"Sam it's getting overcast. Why don't you pull over to the next statitower and make sure the reserve cell is fully energized," Quasar said.

"No, I can tell the solar cells are doing fine. We can get enough sunlight between those clouds," Parseck said.

"Perhaps you should listen to John," Seasqrd said.

"Captain, I know my machines," Parseck said as he piloted the ReVolt past a statitower and flew down the hoverway. Then the gauges dimmed and energy levels dropped.

"Uh-oh," Sam Parseck said.

A macron later the gauges and energy levels were still dead and Sam was vexed. But if he couldn't get any power out of the ReVolt he was determined to get answers out of the Geneti-Men.

"Now can you tell me what the connection is between you and Darklone?" Sam Parseck asked.

"You're going to have to speak louder," Seasqrd said. "Even my genetically enhanced hearing isn't that good."

Sam leaned over to shout at Seasqrd and Quasar as they held the ReVolt over their heads and carried it along the side of the hoverway. "I asked what this connection between you and Darklone is."

"An open hoverway isn't the best place to discuss such matters," Seasqrd shouted back.

"You know I feel bad," Parseck said. He looked at the gauges and shouted, "Commander Quasar, you should have these solarnators checked. They must be out of alignment."

Parseck felt the ReVolt rock as Seasqrd and Quasar changed their grips on the revulsion pads.

"Do you see a statitower nearby, Sam? Even my genetically enhanced triceps are growing weary," Quasar said.

"It's right here!" Sam Parseck looked up at the edifice of steel girders and wires, piercing the sky.

The two G-Men dropped the ReVolt on the statitower's nearest charging bay. Parseck grabbed the energizer an opened the ReVolt's motorositor. He glanced up at the statitower's main aerial, watching wisps of green and blue shafts of electricity being drawn from the gray clouds and fed into the tower's central core.

"And you G-Men think you have power." He pointed upwards. "Millions of volts of static electricity at our disposal and no pollution. Shame your girlfriend from Zaftig can't see this."

"While you're admiring your phallic technology don't let the energy flow overflow." Seasqrd pointed at the ReVolt.

"Don't explain how these devices work to me." Parseck placed the energizer on the plate of the motorositor. Instantly, the stem of the energizer moved back as glowing threads of electricity began to flow from it to the motorositor. "The flow is fine. Now explain to me about you and Darklone."

"If I were to tell you you wouldn't understand," Seasqrd said.

"Why because I don't have a blinking computer port in my forehead," Parseck said.

"I'm afraid you'd find the whole thing disgusting," Seasqrd said.

"Try me," Parseck said, while guiding the energizer's flow steadily into the ReVolt.

Seasqrd cleared before saying, "Darklone is my brother."

"I don't understand," Parseck said.

"I knew it," Seasqrd said.

"I've read up on you, Gene Lucas," Parseck said. "You have no siblings."

"Uh, Sam," Quasar said.

"Yes and no. He is my clone," Seasqrd said.

"Eewh!" Parseck frowned. "That is disgusting."

"Sam!" Quasar said.

Sam Parseck ignored Commodore Quasar's interruption as he hung on the words of Captain Seasqrd.

"I knew you'd react that way," Seasqrd said, raising his hand and pointing at Sam. "But at least now you can see how it has been easy for him to sneak his way into Cosmos-Corps installations."

"Well then how... ow!"

A jolt of static electricity struck Sam's chest like a battering ram. A moment later he tried to raise his head off the concrete but was too dizzy. He tried focusing on the two blurred figures standing over him.

"Well, you warned him," one said.

"We better get him to a medi-comm," said the other.

"Do you think that's wise?"

"Fear not!" The blurry figure stood with his hands on his hips and said. "We'll get to the Plexagon before Darklone."

As the center of Earth's worldwide military complex the Plexagon Building was shrouded in superior security defenses. As he methodically slipped by the last security door Darklone knew the weakness was not in the superior technology of the Plexagon's defenses but in the inferior weaklings who enforced it.

He slammed his hand against the door in front of him squeezing his fingertips into the doorjamb. Slowly, he wedged his whole hand in and dragged the sliding door open. He was about to enter the Top Secret File Room when his genetically enhanced hearing heard footsteps nearby; Darklone turned.

"Captain Seasqrd," said the bulkily built guard. "Is all well?"

Darklone smiled. He had worried that he would encounter no prey during his incursion of the Plexagon and now standing before him was a Cosmos-Corps secureadv guard, who had fallen for his disguise perfectly.

"Splendid, I've simply come by to examine the W.H.Y. files. Would you please let me in," Darklone said. He then casually brushed his Cosmos-Corps uniform with his fingertips as if he was more concerned with lint on his Geneti-Man costume than the force field before him.

"Yes, Captain Seasqrd," said the secureadv guard. He walked to the force field blocking the portal and pressed the button on the computer screen in the wall then said, "X is in the top, left square and lower right."

Darklone stared at the tic-tac-toe board that had materialized on the screen. "I have no time for children's games. Lower the force field."

"Captain, was it not you who suggested the tic-tac password protocol?" the secureadv guard asked.

"Oh, yes, of course I did. I was merely testing you." Darklone folded his arms trying to imitate the gestures of his double while he thought of a way around the password.

"Captain Seasqrd, I am affronted." The secuready guard stood back. "I have always taken my job quite seriously. Back at the academy I received top marks in martial skill, surveillance proficiency and bellicose speech."

"I see you are a fine example of a secuready guard." Darklone nodded. "Now lower the force field."

The secuready guard was about to place his compkey in the slot when he turned and said, "Very clever Captain Seasqrd. X is in the top left and lower right."

"I'll take O in the center to block," Darklone said.

"Captain Seasqrd, are you still testing me?"

"No." Darklone had lost patience. "You are a fine secuready guard, but the problem with being a Cosmos-Corps secuready guard is when there is danger you are always the first ones to fall victim to it."

"You're not Captain Seasqrd!" the secuready guard cried out. "You're the evil Darklone!"

"Yes," Darklone said fiendishly.

The red shirted sentry nervously raised his plasma-pistol and said, "Stop or I'll shoot!"

Darklone looked the fool up and down, smirked with disgust and replied, *"Pain."*

The young guard crossed his eyes and dropped to his knees while Darklone waved his hand and said, *"More pain."*

"I can't take it," murmured the guard while doubling over in tortured agony.

"Did you really think an ordinary man like you could stand up to the 'power voice' of an extraordinary man like me?" Darklone kicked the plasma-pistol from the squirming secuready guard's hand and took his compkey. Slowly, the blue light of the force field dimmed into nothingness while the top and bottom portions of the portal withdrew into the ceiling and floor. Darklone quickly found the locked file he was searching for and tore it open with his bare hands.

Inside the cabinet was an hour-glass-shaped computer drive suspended in a blue solution contained within a crystal test tube. He scooped up the test tube and tossed it into the pouch that hung from his belt. Then he heard an angry voice say, "Turn around!"

Darklone spun about. Standing behind him was another secureaged guard. Darklone raised his hands as the crimson-coated sentry raised his plasma-pistol upwards. He slowly spun his fingers before the secureaged guard's eyes and said, *"Sleep. You must go to sleep."*

The plasma-pistol of the guard fell to his side as his dreary eyes drooped then he collapsed into a placid mass.

Turning to run, Darklone heard the first groveling guard holler, "How come he got to go to sleep and I got pain? Come back here!"

Leaving the whining guard behind, Darklone spied down the corridor then ran to the far stairwell. Sensing he was being pursued, he hastened his egress. Jumping with the ability of a Capellan kangaroo, he leapt to the top of the stairwell in one bound and bashed opened the doorway to the hovercopter hangar.

Suddenly, a cohort of secureaged guards appeared and flanked him. A barrage of plasma beams was fired at Darklone. With the agility of an Antarrian antelope he dodged their assault drew his plasma-pistol and fired at the legs of the guards. The guards tried to escape Darklone's attack but with nimbleness that matched their aim they collided into one another.

Like a Rigelian rhino he charged through the guards, ramming his way towards the nearest hovercopter and with the strength of a Gammarian gorilla, Darklone ripped the door of vehementine steel off the hovercopter and climbed into the cockpit.

One blast from the hovercopter's blazer-bazooka opened the hangar doors and in moments Darklone was in the air over the Plexagon. Knowing they were tracking him, Darklone flew his coptor up over the clouds and down into a grove of trees where the portahole to his getaway shuttle had been left.

As he climbed out of the hovercopter, a chill raced down his back. He knew the feeling well and knew who was approaching. Glowing lights flickered in the night air. Stepping out of the brush was a tall bald-headed man. Across his forehead were two tiny lights; they seemed to pulse with radiant life, turning from red to orange. Darklone wondered what the fool would say. Commodore John Quasar stood before Darklone staring and pondering. Obviously the dolt could not determine the true identity of his foe.

"Are you Darklone or are you Gene Lucas?" he asked.

"Can't you tell, old friend?" Darklone asked hoping to keep his playful ruse going.

"X is in the top left—"

"Oh not that tic-tac-toe garbage again," Darklone roared.

"Hands up, Darklone!" John Quasar pointed his plasma pistol. "You are a disgrace to the Geneti-Men."

Darklone said, "I never wanted to be part of your team. I wanted to be the only one."

Darklone pointed his finger at Quasar and said, "*Pain!*"

Quasar stood firm and smiled. "Your power voice won't work on a fellow G-Man."

"So you think," Darklone said. "*Torturous pain!*"

Quasar stood strong.

"*Sleep... you must sleep.*"

Quasar stood strong and awake.

"*Cramps... migraine, sciatica!*"

"My power is too strong." Quasar pointed his plasma-pistol at the Plexagon and said, "You're coming back with me. Drop your weapon, hand over the W.H.Y. files you stole and what is that hanging from your belt?"

"Oh, this, it is a mere invention of my own design." Darklone dropped his plasma-pistol then grabbed the narrow cylinder at his side.

"Stop!" Quasar said, but it was too late; once in Darklone's hand the intelli-whip was activated. A long electrical cord snaked its way from the end of the cylindrical handle and lashed at Quasar's hand. As Quasar's pistol fell from his hand, Darklone said, "But is your power too powerful for this?"

The tip of the intelli-whip attached itself to the port on Quasar's forehead. Still in shock, Quasar dropped to his knees. He was trapped in Darklone's brain-drain.

"Your power to my power. My power has your power," Darklone said while he watched the glow from Quasar's bald skull dim.

Suddenly, a shadow descended down from the night sky. The intelli-whip was torn from Darklone's hand as he was sent crashing into the trunk of a tree. When he looked up Darklone saw the angry face of Gene Lucas Seasqrd beneath the bright light of an illumilantern. Seasqrd released the lantern's handle and it levitated over their heads shining bright down upon Seasqrd leaving Darklone in the shadows, which he thought was quite appropriate.

"Quasar, are you alright?" Seasqrd asked.

"Twinkle, twinkle little star," Quasar said, pointing at Seasqrd's forehead.

"You drained his brain; he has no power you fiend." Seasqrd's eyes squinted. "Is there no good in you at all?"

"How can you ask that, my brother?" Darklone said. "We are one of a kind. Why not join me? The best will get better while the losers will be beaten."

"That's insane!" Seasqrd said. "And don't refer to me as your brother; we're just clones."

"Regardless we share the same philosophy. Do we not?" Darklone nodded and smiled.

Seasqrd became distraught. He said, "I would never conceive of such a cruel philosophy."

Seasqrd spoke his words so rapidly Darklone was convinced he had hit his mark. He continued to taunt Seasqrd. "But if I think it then you must have too."

Darklone watched Seasqrd grab his plasma-pistol, set its force to kill and aim right between Darklone's unblinking eyes. The port across Seasqrd's forehead flashed rapidly yet Darklone remained cool.

"You know you cannot destroy me," he said. "You are too weak."

Seasqrd lowered his plasma-pistol and said, "You're right, but you cannot destroy me either. You came from me. You are part of me. You would be nothing without me."

Darklone stepped back. "No! I owe nothing to you. You're just trying to make me weak like you," he said.

"It's not weakness to feel sorry for the weaker." Seasqrd gestured with his free hand to John Quasar who had just removed his boots so he could count his toes.

Darklone took another step back. He grasped his stomach, clutching his fake uniform like he was in pain. He knelt down mumbling.

"What is it you said?" Seasqrd asked while walking forward.

"You are right," Darklone said. But he refused to raise his head and look his foe in the eye. He looked down at Seasqrd's boots as they stood over his intelli-whip and said, "You've weakened me. I've grown so weak. I'm too weak to fight. Now, don't you feel sorry for me?"

"Perhaps just a little; you and I may be enemies but we're still made from the same heart, bone, sinew and soul," Seasqrd said and as he took in a long breath so as to continue his pontificating he stepped forward to place his hand on Darklone's shoulder and he finally lifted his foot off the intelli-whip. Darklone lunged for his weapon.

"Tricked you Gene Lucas!" Darklone sprang to his feet and the tip of the intelli-whip flared upward cracking Seasqrd's wrist; as the plasma-pistol fell to the ground, Darklone said, "And would you please stop with that sinew and soul speech."

Seasqrd was about to dive for his weapon when Darklone hauled back with his whip and cracked it at Seasqrd's face. Seasqrd took a step away, almost tripping over Quasar's bare feet.

"This little piggy flew to Mars and this little piggy flew to...." Quasar whispered.

"You see my brother you could never destroy me because whether you wish to admit or not I'm doing all that you always wanted to do." Darklone took a footing between the plasma-pistol and Seasqrd. "If I came from you, then I have the same feelings you do towards the inferior. I'm acting on what you always felt, but your sense of ethics and duty and honor forbids you to be as I am."

"Damn you, Darklone," Seasqrd said.

Darklone gleefully anticipated how much power the brain-drain of Gene Lucas Seasqrd would add to his own; he raised his weapon. The intelli-whip was just about to latch itself onto Seasqrd's head and bore its way into his genetic programming when it was blasted from Darklone's hand. Darklone drew back in surprise while a small Cosmos-Corps officer with scorched hair stepped into the light of the floating illumilantern.

"An excellent shot, Sam," Seasqrd said.

Darklone looked at the scrawny Cosmos-Corps spaceman who aimed his plasma-pistol at him then looked back at Seasqrd. Darklone had quickly sized up the situation and developed a strategy.

"Farewell my old friend." He jumped backwards and landed on his portahole and just before dematerializing he heard Seasqrd screaming, "DARKLONE!"

* * *

80

Captain Seasqrd and Commander Parseck sat next to one another on the ground in silence. The lantern was still hovering above; John Quasar was stumbling about below, bumping into trees and tripping over shrubs. Seasqrd was not sure who was more depressed him or Sam.

"The bitter taste of defeat lingers in both our mouths." Seasqrd was about to pat Sam on the back then thought better of it; the man had suffered enough.

"Want to taste *deez* feet?" Quasar asked as he shoved his bare foot at Sam's mouth.

"Sam thanks for saving me. Seems like we've gotten into the habit of rescuing one another," Seasqrd said after watching Sam bat Quasar's foot away.

"But I let him get away," Parseck said, pointing at the portahole that lay before them. "You should've let me pursue."

"No, we don't know what was on the other side and with Darklone expect the unexpected," Seasqrd said.

Parseck sighed deeply and said, "I guess if I only had genetically enhanced reflexes he wouldn't have escaped."

"I'm a genetically enhanced fool," Seasqrd said. He turned his head so as to look his friend in the eyes and said, "You were right about me, Sam. I believed in my superiority; not just physical but my character as well. But you see if Darklone was made from me then I must have the same evil in me somewhere. He thinks he has the right to do these dastardly deeds to the weaker because he's stronger but I was too arrogant to believe anyone who was me could be that evil."

"No, you're wrong," Parseck said. "I was wrong about you; besides we all have a little bad in us but there obviously must be much more good in you than there is bad because look at all the good things you do. Just the fact that the mere thought of evil being in you bothers you so much proves how really good you are, Gene Lucas."

Seasqrd appreciated Sam using his first name for a change and his attempt to cheer him up but it was to no avail.

Seasqrd said, "Look at all the good I did this evening; I let Darklone deceive me and he got away."

"I failed there too and now the plans for a super-weapon are in his evil clutches," Parseck said as he placed his face into the open palms of his hands.

"And it's only a matter of time before that madman turns it loose on the Earth." Seasqrd placed his face into the open palms of his hands.

He heard Sam say, "But just because he has the plans doesn't mean he can build it. It may be years before a power source strong enough for the weapon is developed."

"I like your optimism, but it still remains a matter of when not if," Seasqrd said, as he finally lifted his head. "It will hit us someday."

"Well, I'm reminded of the platitude used in the late twentieth century when humanity was faced with ecological problems, global warming and a mounting climate crisis," Parseck said, raising his head back up.

"What platitude?" Seasqrd asked.

"Let the next generation worry about it."

CHAPTER 6
THOSE SCI-FI GUYS & THE NEXT BUNCH OF CHARACTERS
COSMIC-CALENDAR.2523.09.19.3/31

Peter Pulsaar hated going to the bank. Intergalactic Telling Machines was where high-tech and high finance merged; just another example of the problems of the human race being solved by its super-technology. It was all part of the perfect life machines had created for humanity and Peter Pulsaar hated anything that was perfect. He reminded himself he needed fast cash and the people he owed were not well known for their patience. So as much as he hated dealing with the ITM he had to do what he had to do.

Peter Pulsaar entered the ITM dome and approached the metallic cabinet that housed the Personal Accounting Liaison screen, took in a deep breath and put his finger in the pin coder. He felt the warmth of the laser needle against his finger tip as the silvery screen displayed the image of a double helix. A computer voice stated laconically, *"DNA recognition complete."*

Slowly, the cabinet opened and the next sound was the soft, shy voice of the Personal Accounting Liaison program. Peter Pulsaar rolled his eyes back while he put his finger to his mouth. The PAL program very rarely lived up to its name in his opinion.

"Hello, Peter. How may I be of service to you?"

"Hello, PAL." Peter looked into the red dot at the center of the speaker screen. "I'd like… that is… I need some money."

"Of course, Peter, how much would you like?"

"I need 30,000 credollars." Peter nibbled on his fingernail, anticipating PAL's response.

"That's a lot of money, Peter. What do you need it for?"

"Look, PAL, we've been through this before," Peter said, trying not to sound too angry.

"Peter, have you been gambling again?"

"What? I don't gamble and it's none of your business even if I did." Peter leaned against the screen as if the computer had a tough time hearing. "I'd like my money, please."

There was a moment of silence before Peter heard the usual reply.

"I'm sorry Peter, I just can't do that."

"But it's my money," Peter said.

"But you will never learn responsibility if I'm always here to aid financially."

"You're my PAL not my mother!" Peter said.

"Now, now, Peter, mind your temper," PAL said.

"PAL!" Peter measured off the monitor screen. "I need the money!"

"Sorry, Peter —"

Sparks popped through the air and Peter Pulsaar pulled his fist back. The red dot that showed the PAL program in use faded away. Peter stepped back into the decompression chamber; he put on his space helmet and zipped up his silver life support suit. After pressing the outer chamber lock, the hatch slowly rose and Pulsaar was pulled into the vacuum of space.

He quickly tugged at his tether line, pulling himself closer to the Aeon Owl. He opened the hatch and crawled into the cockpit of his spaceship; he turned for one quick glance at the ITM port. The glass dome was filling with smoke. The engines of the Aeon Owl roared to life and the ship spiraled through the troposphere down towards the Earth. Peter Pulsaar locked the Owl on automatic pilot as he tried to figure out another way to pay off his debt to the greenfellas.

* * *

Captain Sam Parseck reminded himself that old space commanders never die they just fade away into the stars or to be more specific the Cosmos-Corps retirement home on Alpha Arthritis II. But the place wasn't all that bad; it was a normal day as all the retired officers played golf, which of course, was the only thing to do on Alpha Arthritis II for the entire planet was one big golf course. The whole planetary surface had been landscaped and manicured into endless miles of tranquil fairways, placid greens and sandy, pristine bunkers. What he would not give to be back in action with good ole Gene Lucas.

Clubhouse communities had been established in between the links where retirees from Cosmos-Corps ate, drank and talked about their bygone encounters with alien races and outer space menaces and enjoyed their convalescence. Problem was what did one do when there was nothing to convalesce from. Sam thought about his first adventure with Gene Lucas Seasqrd back on Zaftig and all the many adventures that followed but Sam didn't have a genetically enhanced physique like his friend Seasqrd and had grown too old to be an outer space hero and so here he was.

Sam had been hovering through the back nine thousand on his gravi-cart when suddenly he had an urge. Nature had a tendency to call at the most inopportune moments but there had to be a pottybot on its way. He looked around and with great relief saw the faithful pottybot flying in. The pottybots on Alpha Arthritis II were kept busy but there had not been a major accident in years. Floating down on its chopper blades the pottybot landed in a cushion of grass. At its base was an enormous round septic tank surrounded by wheeled tracks. A cylinder shaped room made up the pottybot's center and affixed to the top of the cylinder was its helicopter blades and scanning devices, which had zeroed in on Captain Parseck. The tracks began to roll pulling the pottybot through the grassy field then slowed to a stop.

"Greetings, Captain Parseck, sorry about the delay." a speaker said as the door to the pottybot slid open and a ramp lowered down to the ground before Parseck's feet.

"Don't worry," Parseck ascended the ramp, ducking under the translucent dome and grabbed a recent issue of

<u>Popular Quantum Mechanics.</u> He then flipped the light and the pottybot's hatch slid closed.

Suddenly, Sam became nauseas and he knew it had nothing to do with the Jovian Jambalaya he had for lunch. He stood and pressed his face against the pottybot's translucent dome. Outside, an ominous shadow crossed over the fairways of Alpha Arthritis II.

Samuel Parseck could not believe his eyes as he watched the skies.

"Darklone finally did it," he whispered. "He really did it."

Then it attacked.

*   *   *

Peter Pulsaar cautiously stepped onto the rollowalk that flowed to the entrance of the Succulent Green Restaurant. He viewed a sign that read: WE LOVE SERVING PEOPLE.

Everyone in the Ultra Metro area knew of the Succulent Green, the restaurant where they put a little bit of themselves in every meal, but what few knew was the Succulent Green was just a front for the crime boss, "Lucky" Nucleano. Pulsaar entered the restaurant and was greeted by one of Nucleano's henchmen.

"Hi, how are you? I need to see your boss," Peter said.

Pulsaar could not stand the sight of these Martian gangsters or as they were known on the streets, greenfellas, and he knew they could not stand the sight of him. His slender build and sandy blonde hair that sort of flopped over his delicate face made him appear to be more like a potential victim of criminals rather than a reluctant partner.

The greenfella hooked one of his claw-like fingers. Peter accepted the gesture and followed him into the dining area. The room was dark; only the light of the illuminated table tops lit the room. There was a dozen or so of these tiny round tables and hanging over each one was a multi-mic that spread swinging music around. The dance floor was small and seemed crowded by only a few couples. Of course those couples had two heads each so Peter felt it looked more crowded than it really was.

Waiters darted about on multiple legs, serving entrees to various species seated about round illuminated tables. A small waitress carrying a bubbling broth of soup bumped into Peter. She offered a fast apology, walked away and winked at Peter with the eye in the back of her head. Peter smiled briefly at other passing waitresses but was taken aback when the grizzly bartender growled at him, demanding to know if he required a drink.

Peter looked at the bartender covered in thick black fur, wearing a brown leather jerkin, and quickly nodded no. The greenfella turned back towards Peter and yanked his arm. Peter followed obediently.

Sitting at an enormous rectangular table in the rear corner, with his back to the wall, was "Lucky" Nucleano. Sycophants and bodyguards surrounded him, reading to him from ledgers regarding his latest illegal ventures and spying for potential enemies. Slowly the inter-stellar gangster fixed one of his bulbous eyes on Peter Pulsaar and his four tentacles dropped their knives and forks.

"Pulsaar, my boy. I thought I'd have to send someone to bring you to me." Nucleano slammed his tentacle to the tabletop. All stopped and stared at Peter, who smiled nervously. Nucleano said, "Sit, Pulsaar. Enjoy the cuisine of my place. The veal armigian is very good or how about a bowl of feetsesuaz."

"No, thanks, I need some more time... if you do not mind?" Peter said.

"Pulsaar, Pulsaar, Pulsaar, we made a deal." Nucleano shook his head. "Now you come with no respect and worse you have no money."

"If you recall, I had my doubts about the deal. You greenfellas kind of forced it on me," Peter said. "But don't worry I can get the money."

Nucleano began with a ghoulish belly laugh before he said, "I wish I had a credollar every time I heard that."

"All I need is a little more time." Pete extended his hand casually in the air.

All the greenfellas began to chuckle fiercely. After Nucleano finished slapping his tentacles on his lap he said, "Bleep you; pay me."

"Watch your language, please," Peter said.

"Forget my bleeping language! If you can't take Martian curses then get me that bleeping money!" The wiry spikes that emerged from the top of Nucleano's head seemed to shimmer as he cursed at Peter. "You bleep-head!"

"I can get it!" Peter exclaimed. "I just don't have it right now."

Nucleano scratched his head his wiry skull and whispered, "Then I'll take your bleeping ship."

"I'd rather be dead than lose the Aeon Owl!"

"That's the idea," Nucleano said with a nod and his henchmen surrounded Peter.

"Don't get me mad," Peter said. Then he felt a claw-like grip about the back of his neck. He sighed and said, "Don't get me mad. You won't like it if I get mad."

*   *   *

Admiral Gene Lucas Seasqrd arrived on Alpha Arthritis II with despair in his heart and anger in his soul. The snow that was once deep now had turned to slush as the rain drizzled upon the grounds. Seasqrd looked through the fog and stared at the red pennant that had been placed in the cup of one of the few remaining greens. On the pennant's crimson field was a small sphere, being attacked by a z-shaped serpent. He watched his young yeoman grab the flag and toss it into a sand trap.

"Well, now we know who," the yeoman said. She looked at Admiral Seasqrd and asked, "But why?"

The admiral ignored the question as the commander of Alpha Arthritis II approached on a gravi-cart. He swooped in for a landing, saluted and said, "I was informed you wanted to begin a search for your old friend, Captain Parseck; if you'll just climb in."

Seasqrd helped his young yeoman into the back of the gravi-cart and then sprang into the front seat. The seats had grown hot under the burning sun and as the temperature rose so did Seasqrd's impatience.

"I'm surprised after the attack you didn't search for survivors sooner, Commander Mulligan," the admiral said.

Lt. Commander Mulligan shifted uneasily after the rebuke and replied, "Unfortunately, a shortage of manpower leaves us with quite a handicap."

"Of course. This erratic weather is certainly not going to help." Seasqrd said as the gravi-cart buckled under strong winds.

"That's a fair way of putting it." Mulligan nodded. "Sir, to save time I'm going to slice through this grove of trees and hook around this dog-leg."

Admiral Seasqrd remained silent. The wind grew into a gale, almost lifting the yeoman from the cart. Seasqrd turned, reaching back just in time; the yeoman clung to his arm.

"Keep this cart steady!" he said.

"I'm sorry Admiral, have I done something wrong? You seem teed off," Mulligan said.

"Is it necessary to work golfing terminology into every statement on this planet?" Seasqrd asked.

"That would be about par for the course," Mulligan said.

"Mulligan!" Seasqrd said. Then he took in a deep breath. "Just take us to the last known coordinates of Captain Parseck and keep quiet."

"Very well, I'll shut my trap." Commander Mulligan said.

Admiral Seasqrd placed his forehead against the palm of his hand as pellets of ice dropped on his back and shoulders. The yeoman leaned forward, dusted off the admiral's uniform and said, "Admiral Seasqrd, I know your worried about your old friend but—"

"There look!" Seasqrd shouted.

As the gravi-cart emerged over a knoll, the admiral pointed ahead. Off next to a distant bunker was a pottybot, and in the pottybot's dome was a waving hand.

"Sam!" Seasqrd yelled as he jumped from the flying gravi-cart and hit the ground running but slipped in the mud. He pulled himself up and began trudging onward. Just before he was about to open the pottybot the yeoman jumped on his back and shouted, "No! You'll kill us all!"

Admiral Seasqrd turned to the yeoman and asked, "Do you think there's radiation inside?"

"No, but think about the smell," whispered the yeoman.

"Yeoman, please... let me go! I cannot leave him to die in there!"

"It's too late, Gene Lucas," said a voice from within the pottybot. Slowly, Sam Parseck's head rose to the top of the transparent bubble atop the pottybot. Seasqrd climbed up and put his hands across the dome.

"Old friend," Seasqrd said.

"Looks like you'll be fighting this battle without me. I'm sorry," Parseck groaned.

"Try not to speak; I'll free you with my super-strength." Seasqrd said.

Parseck placed his hand on the glass so it was opposite Seasqrd's and said, "Nothing can save me, but you have been and always shall be the finest of Cosmos-Corps."

"Oh, be quiet Sam," Seasqrd said then the pottybot was torn apart and Sam Parseck lay in Seasqrd's arms. "Sam! You're gonna be alright!"

"Do not grieve, old friend; it was nice to be back in action again." Sam began to choke. Seasqrd wasn't sure whether it was due to injury or the egregious odor the Yeoman had warned about.

"Try not to speak Sam; save your strength." Seasqrd cradled Parseck in his arms. Then he pulled the tulipathy pendent from his neck. He held it before Sam and asked, "Do you remember this gift; it has incredible healing powers perhaps if you wear it."

Sam pushed the gift from the Animazon Queen away. "I don't need your magic charms. I need technical support; I need a cardiocator or a hemoputer or a cerebrograph or a pill or something."

"Some things never change." Seasqrd tried to laugh on the outside for his genetically enhanced heart was breaking on the inside.

Sam too laughed although it caused him great pain to do so. "We have always been opposites. You always admired the abilities of humans; I always admired the abilities of machines."

"Let me pick you up and we'll get you to some medical machinery," Seasqrd said.

Sam began waving his hands and in between gasps of breath he said, "No time for that, but I need to tell you what you're up against."

Seasqrd gently patted his friend's chest and said, "You can once we get you healed up, Sam."

"I may not last that long," Sam pushed the admiral's hand away, "and you've always relied on my technical advice."

"Yes," Seasqrd said, realizing he didn't want his last words with his best friend to be argumentative ones, "I've always relied on them."

"The ship that attacked us was a climate killer. My guess is it uses concentrated gravity waves to disrupt a planet's environment." Sam clutched Seasqrd's collar. "You must stop it from destroying all the environments Cosmos-Corps has preserved across the galaxy!"

"I will Sam!" he tried to pry Sam's fingers loose from his collar but he couldn't do so without hurting his comrade. "Just rest Sam."

Sam finally let go and closed his eyes. Seasqrd whispered through quivering lips, "Sam, my friend."

"Did I tell you my theory on their power supply?" Sam asked while he rose up.

Seasqrd shook his head and then looked at his startled yeoman who still had her hands clasped about her cheeks. Sam continued, "My guess is it could be a positon reactor of some sort."

"That's very good, Sam, but you really must rest." Seasqrd eased his friend back down. "Wait! Positon reactors are the most powerful energy source in the universe aren't they?"

"In theory; and I must give you my theory on how to destroy it but I can't go on." Sam draped the back of his hand over his forehead and let out one final breath.

Seasqrd looked at his dying friend and waited. Sam's eyes popped open as his finger pointed at Seasqrd's nose. "Negatons," he said.

"What?" Seasqrd said with Sam's index finger plugged into his nostril.

"Negatons cancel out positons; do you understand?"

"I think so," Seasqrd said.

"No you don't," Sam replied. "I can tell."

"Sam, don't you think this can wait?" Seasqrd pushed Parseck back on the ground.

"You were always all muscle and no brain."

"Sam, don't start."

"Our cosmicrafts are no match for that thing unless we had some super-tech of our own to even out the odds." Sam winked. "They can't fight what they can't see. Get it?"

"No," Seasqrd said.

"Oh maybe I should talk to her?" Sam pointed at the Yeoman.

"I think I know what he means, Admiral." The Yeoman nodded.

"Good," Sam said. "Now I can rest in peace."

Seasqrd looked down at his friend; their faces were covered in drizzling rain. Sam's limp hand lay in the mud. Seasqrd looked up at his Yeoman; he couldn't tell whether her face was covered in tears or rain drops. He pulled his tulipathy pendent from out of a puddle and said, "My poor friend, Sam, if only we had more time we could've have gotten him to Zaftig. There their knowledge of organic powers could have healed him I'm sure."

"Ooh, I remember that planet." Sam sat up again. "The women there were so... so... I think I can make it, Gene Lucas."

Seasqrd wiped the droplets from his smiling face. He looked up once again at the yeoman and said, "Don't just stand there; go get a medicocoon."

"Not another medicocoon." Sam plopped down in the mud again.

*   *   *

Admiral Seasqrd climbed out of the portahole and onto the deck of his shuttle ship. Turning around, he noticed his young aide having difficulty climbing out. He placed his hands about her waist. Once again he ignored the unspoken attraction between them, as all Cosmos-Corps heroes must do, and pulled her up out of the portahole.

"Thank you, Admiral," she said. She and Seasqrd looked out the viewing glass and watched a star-ambulance fly away. Seasqrd felt her head against his shoulder. "I'm sure your friend, Sam Parseck, will be just fine once the women of Zaftig have their way with him... I mean once they work their ways... I mean... you know what I mean."

"Yes, I do, Yeoman," Seasqrd said then he left a dent in the bulkhead after he punched it. "Sorry, I lose my temper and don't know my strength."

As he walked away he heard the yeoman say, "I'm sorry for all that you've been through."

"No time for regrets. We must get back to Earth!" Seasqrd said.

"But why would anyone want to attack a senior citizen colony?" the Yeoman asked, angrily. "It makes no sense. There has to be a reason!"

"It does make sense if you know the 'who.' Once you know who, then the reason why is immaterial. It was all a matter of when."

"You lost me; who's who?" the yeoman said.

The admiral looked about, making sure no one could hear. He took the yeoman aside and whispered, "Darklone."

"Darklone!" the yeoman said. She looked around and lowered her voice. "He was banished from Earth years ago."

"That was the official story," Seasqrd said with a nod, "but there were those of us who knew he would always be back."

"How can you be so sure?"

"He is me," Admiral Seasqrd said. He saw the look of puzzlement on the lovely face of his yeoman. In spite of his age, he had not lost the ability to appreciate an attractive woman. "As you know, Yeoman, I was once the commander of the Geneti-Men."

She pointed at her own forehead but kept her eyes on his. "Yes, a group of genetically enhanced super-warriors used on the utmost important missions by Cosmos-Corps."

Seasqrd poked at his power port in acknowledgement and said, "That was us and while I don't like to boast we were the best and I was the best of the best. And so it was saw fit to try the copyclator on me."

"The copyclator?" she asked.

"A device used for perfect cloning," Seasqrd said. "It was another invention of Rozwelles."

"I see," said the yeoman.

"The copyclator produced a perfect clone of me and the hope was that it could be the beginning of a new line of G-Men. But my perfect clone became twisted... he became warped—"

"He became Darklone," the yeoman said, pressing her fingers to her mouth.

"That is how I know how he thinks. Just as he knows how I think."

"I never knew that," the yeoman said.

Seasqrd whispered out of the side of his mouth, "It's not the sort of thing I like to brag about."

"Sir, are you sure you're alright?" The yeoman placed her hands around one of Seasqrd's biceps.

Ignoring the affectionate attentions of his pretty young aide, Admiral Seasqrd looked heavenwards and sighed, "This all too like the last time I encountered Darklone."

"Sir, if I may, before you begin the story I suggest we get our vessel before back to Earth."

"Affirmative," Seasqrd replied then he issued orders to his pilot and navigator.

As they prepared for a star voyage back to Earth, Seasqrd recounted the story of how he and Sam Parseck were too late to thwart Darklone before the renegade G-Man stole the W.H.Y. files, drained the brain of John Quasar, and then hunted down all the remaining G-Men.

"How terrible that must have been for you, having an evil double who was wreaking havoc on Cosmos-Corps, performing all kinds of sinister deeds and threatening the existence of your planet." The Yeoman clasped her hands about Seasqrd's.

"But you know what the worst part was?" he asked.

She said, "What?"

"I kept getting blamed for the all bad stuff he did," Seasqrd said with his hands at his waist.

"You'll have to forgive me Admiral, as I am a lowly yeoman my clearance is not as high as yours. I know nothing of the W.H.Y. files except that they must be between the W.H.E.N. and W.H.E.R.E. files."

"It's not like that," Admiral Seasqrd shook his finger in the air, "they got their name because you have to ask why you would ever want to build such a thing."

"I still do not understand, sir, what was in the files that the Darklone stole," the yeoman said.

"You've heard of Dr. Orson Rozwelles?"

"Earth's greatest scientist and the man who created the Geneti-Men," she replied.

"That's him," Seasqrd said. "The poor genius inadvertently came up with an ultimate weapon. It was the gravity-magnetron. A machine capable of projecting concentrated bosons in a narrow ray. The ray caused a chain reaction of eruptions in plate tectonics, explosions of seismic activity, severe climate shifts and general atmospheric upheaval. Of course his hope had been that the gravity-magnetron could be used to change hostile environments of uninhabitable planets to comfortable and cozy ecosystems suitable for human colonization. But Cosmos-Corps turned down Rozwelles' plan, fearing that, in the wrong hands, the gravity-magnetron could be used to destroy the friendly climates of inhabitable worlds. And fall into the wrong hands it did and now Darklone has a weapon that could destroy the environmental balance we've struggled so hard to preserve these last four centuries."

"But I still don't know why he would pick Alpha Arthritis II as his target. Why not head right for Earth?"

"He's managed to destroy almost all that's left of the G-Men over the years. This was one more attack by him on those who stood opposed to him over the years."

"And Captain Sam Parseck?" the yeoman said.

Seasqrd sighed; his lip quivered.

"Sam Parseck was my best friend. So this was his way of eliminating someone close to me one more time," Seasqrd said. He placed his hands at his hips and whispered, "And he shows us who is working with him."

The yeoman took in a deep breath and said, "The flag back in the cup on Alpha Arthritis II. It was the flag of the planet, Zygote."

"The Zlythetaurs have built a gravity-magnetron for Darklone and he'll turn his climate killer on Earth."

"And now you are the only G-Man left standing between Darklone and his revenge upon our world," the yeoman said with her eyes opening wide.

Seasqrd said, "No, there is still one more left."

CHAPTER 7
THOSE SCI-FI GUYS VERSUS THE GREENFELLAS

Peter Pulsaar stalked out of what was left of the Succulent Green Restaurant and darted behind an enormous garbage disintegrator. He always regretted losing his temper. He also knew the people who had to pay for the damages usually felt badly about it too, but in this case the greenfellas got what they deserved. Peter did not care about them, but he did worry about the innocent customers who were storming out of the wreckage. Two greenfellas finally limped out and stumbled down the stairs, shoving frightened patrons out of the way. "Lucky" Nucleano shoved his huge head out of a shattered window and screamed, "Do you see that son of a bleep?"

The greenfellas scanned about. Peter Pulsaar crept down behind the garbage trying to avoid the vision of their bug-eyes. He prepared for round two with the greenfellas when he heard the sounds of sirens. The policeyborgs landed; Peter peered around to watch as well as listen.

The greenfellas had suddenly lost their menace and took on the mien of innocent bystanders. As the policeyborgs floated down, the jet stream from the bottom of their metal boots kicked up mounds of dust. The first policeyborg was quite muscular. His broad shoulders bulged out from under the metal armor that wrapped itself around his torso. The black visor that shrouded the policeyborg's eyes turned and tilted up at Nucleano. As if he knew what was going to be asked the boss of the greenfellas said, "Seems we had someone who refused to pay his bill."

The policeyborg remained silent. His head moved slowly as if it were on a rusty gear; his gaze drifted towards the garbage disintegrator. Peter leaned back and listened.

"Sgt. Keanoo," said one of the policeyborgs.

"Yes, Officer Berata," said the sergeant.

"Nikti has ascertained evidence," said the other.

Peter peeked around and saw one of the policeyborgs waving her mechanical arm around the handle to the restaurant door.

"DNA scan on fingerprints completed," said Nikti.

"Oh great," Peter said.

He drew back and heard the policeyborg called Berata say, "Match identical to the perpetrator who destroyed the PAL."

Peter slid down along the oily ground to see what the next move of the police would be. The leader, called Sergeant Keanoo, pointed skywards and commanded, "We have a runner. Continue search!"

Instantly, the three policeyborgs blasted off, propelled by the rockets from their boots into the clouds above. The Martian mobsters gathered around where the policeyborgs had launched. Peter heard one of the greenfellas shout, "Boss, whadda we do?"

Lucky Nucleano's voice came booming from the restaurant.

"The policeyborgs will never find this bleeping pest. We'll get the Kredator!"

"Oh no," Peter said. He quickly looked around as he thought of ways to escape, but with the greenfellas stalking the streets and the policeyborgs surfing the skies it seemed there was only one way out. Peter lifted the grate to the sewer and said to himself, "If Admiral Seasqrd could see me now."

He embarked on a trail beneath the Metro Area through the labyrinth of sewer lines until he reached Domeboken. Peter knew it to be the perfect place to hide out for besides becoming a haven to those who could not do without their tobacco and resented the laws that prevented them from sharing their poisonous habit with others, Domeboken had also had become a refuge for interplanetary rogues. Peter was ashamed of it but the truth was one of these rogues had just come squirming up through a sewer grate.

Peter Pulsaar wiped the slime off his pants. He looked about; trying to see if danger was nearby, but he could hardly see his hand in front of his face. The smoke of Domeboken was especially thick this night. So bad that Peter could not even see the dome of white glass that stretched over the city's sky and kept all the cigarette smoke that was exhaled from the community's inhabitants from stretching across the Metro Area. Rapidly walking through a maze of back streets, empty lots and alleyways Peter could not shake the feeling he was being followed. He quickened his pace, weaving his way around boxes, garbage cans and oil-slicked puddles. He took in deep breaths through his nose and though he only caught the scent of garbage and smoldering butts he could not shake the feeling that something was lurking about, ready to attack at any moment. His genetically enhanced eyeballs had quickly adapted to the dark and he began looking around each corner while frequently turning around to see if anything stalked him from behind. He saw nothing, but could not believe he was alone.

"Got a light?"

"Me?" Peter said with his back to the wall and his hand over his chest.

"Yeah, you." The man held up an unlit cigarette.

Peter looked at the man and the woman next to him. They had appeared out of the shadowy smoke, looking like shadows themselves. Their faces were pale and sullen; their voices were raspy and wheezy.

"He asked for a light. Me too," said the woman as she held up a cigarette.

"I don't have one," Peter said.

"What?"

"He has no light!"

"You must be from the outside. You are a non-smoker!" said the man while pointing an accusing yellow-tipped finger at Peter.

"Sorry," Peter said. "Please don't tell anyone."

"Listen to how he speaks," the woman said. "The words come from his clean lungs with no trouble."

"No wheezing or hacking! He's not of our polluted body!" they man screamed. Then he hunched over in a fit of coughing. The woman held her fellow smoker and cursed at Peter as he ran off into the darkness.

He crept down next to the broken window of a deserted building and looked around to see if anyone followed, but when he looked upward what he saw on the rooftop amazed him. Crawling along was a living silhouette as if someone or something had painted itself to match the darkened sky and the filthy facade of the building.

"The Kredator," Peter whispered.

Pulsaar wasted no time and ran down a dark alley. While turning back to see if the Kredator followed he tripped and went sprawling into a stack of refuse bags. The horrible odor of the wet cigarettes in the garbage filled his nostrils, but Peter found the stench relieving since it blocked out the cigarette smoke. Then an even worse odor fouled the air; it was the smell of a hideous creature that acted as a loan collector.

Pulsaar felt the Kredator's claws about his throat as it hoisted him over the garbage bags and slammed him against the wall. The Kredator's chiseled body was dressed in a black net and from the top of its head sprang bands of hair-like skin. Its hands were like large paws with tapering fingers that extended into long, razor sharp nails. His eyes were pools of blood wrapped by yellow circles and his massive jaw dropped slightly as he breathed, displaying rows of fangs.

"You're making a mistake—"

The Kredator tossed him across the alley. Peter ricocheted off the brick wall and onto some garbage cans. He got up and said, "I wish you wouldn't do this."

The Kredator grabbed Peter by the arm and laughed diabolically.

"You're making me mad; you won't like it—"

Peter wrapped his fingers about the Kredator's scaly wrist and twisted. The creature was face down in the gutter. His strands of hair floated alongside a pile of discarded cigar butts.

"I wanted to warn you!" Peter said. "Don't make me—"

The Kredator swept Peter's legs and knocked him into ash canister. Mounds of sand, ashes and embers spread across Peter's face and chest. The Kredator was about to pounce when Peter picked up the large cylindrical ash canister and rammed it at the Kredator's head. Another roar ripped down the street as the Kredator's fury mounted.

"Don't make me mad," Peter said.

The two adversaries squared off against one another.

* * *

The cosmicraft Zenith Three was the pride of Cosmos-Corps and so naturally Captain Raymond J. Atamz felt he too was the pride of Cosmos-Corps. As his shuttle cruised from the ship's hangar through the Earth's upper atmosphere, he looked out the back portal at the Zenith.

Crowned by a dorsal fin that jutted over her stern she looked like a majestic fish with her two engines winging out the side of her hull; she even had the prettiest satellite cones atop her amidships.

"She is a beauty," Atamz whispered to himself. To him the Zenith was the perfect combination; she was as lovely as any woman with all the mechanization that the Earth's super-technology had to offer.

"Pardon me, sir, we're hovering over Cosmos-Corps Command. Are you ready to go through the portahole?" the pilot yelled.

"Affirmative."

Ray Atamz strode over to the glass disc that was centered in the deck plate. The silvery sphere was bordered by protruding antennae, which Ray liked very much. It made it look like the old-fashioned ship-wheels of ancient Earth history.

The pilot said, "Sir, if I may, you may want to re-boot—"

"Just proceed," Atamz said, impatiently.

"Yes, sir," the pilot replied just as he pulled the portahole lever. After the brilliant flash of light Atamz closed his eyes and jumped forward. Instantly, his body was sucked into the portahole.

When Atamz opened his eyes they were looking at a pair of feet.

"Hello, Ray." Admiral Seasqrd offered his hand. "It seems like you got stuck in the portahole again."

Suddenly Ray realized he was on the admiral's floor with no body.

"You bungler!" said Atamz as he squirmed within Admiral Seasqrd's portahole. "I should re-boot the seat of your pants?" Ray saw Seasqrd's perturbed face.

"No, sir; I didn't mean you. I meant that incompetent shuttle pilot," Atamz said, turning his head back and forth into the portahole forcing it to rock and yawl across the floor.

Just then the insipid voice of the shuttle pilot came through the space-time continuum. "Perhaps if I shut down the Meta-physical Teleportation Apparatus?"

"Don't shut down the MTA just select reconfigure on the dematerialization grid," Atamz shouted down into the portahole then looked up at the admiral with pursed lips. "This kid doesn't know his app from his elbow."

"Well, perhaps if I may assist." Admiral Seasqrd reached down under and around Ray's shoulders trying to get a firm grip.

"Admiral, you're pulling my epaulettes."

"I beg your pardon," said the admiral.

"My epaulettes," Atamz said. "I'm very proud of them and don't want them yanked off."

"Oh, your shoulder insignia," Seasqrd said. "Well, no man wants his epaulettes grabbed. Unfortunately, I have nowhere else to hold but up here."

Seasqrd grasped Captain Atamz's ears and said, "Sorry Ray, but remember last time it took four attempts as I recall and we are pressed for time."

Seasqrd let out a brief grunt while he lifted Atamz out of the portahole. Atamz let out a brief whimper as he rubbed his ears and said, "Three times, sir. The fourth was just for my pants. Remember?"

Seasqrd looked down at Atamz's boots and said, "Yes, I had forgotten. Ray, I need to talk to you. I fear a great menace approaches our world."

"What else is new?" Atamz replied.

"Ray, please." Seasqrd held up his hand. "Latest intelligence from Alpha Arthritis II tells me Darklone and the Zlythetaurs have joined forces. I feel something dreadful is about to descend upon us. I have an unshakable fear that something ominous lies on the horizon, an uncanny sense that some horror awaits us."

Suddenly, a monstrous, mechanical beast appeared in the middle of the room. Ray Atamz jumped up and into Seasqrd's arms.

"It's just a holograph," Admiral Seasqrd said.

"Of course," Captain Atamz said. "I was just shocked by the poor quality of the virtual image. Perhaps I could adjust the lens."

"No, no! No need for that," Admiral Seasqrd said pointing at the holographic image. "This is the Havoccraft; the latest super-weapon of the Z. It is three times the size of our cosmicrafts and ten times the fire power."

"How can the Z drive such a ship? What's their energy source? What could fuel such a mammoth, malevolent warship? And why don't we have one?" asked Atamz.

"You were always great with machines," Seasqrd said. "You tell me."

Captain Atamz scratched his head and said, "It could use a nuclear reactor the size of Olympus Mons or... positon power?"

"You've done it again, Ray." Seasqrd said. "Cosmos-Corps engineers made the same conclusion and speculate it feeds off space rubble to fuel its anti-magnetic accumulator."

"Incredible!" Atamz bent over and looked at the awesome spaceship, pointing his finger at the jaws that were mounted at its bow. "This is just a guess, but I would say the asteroids get sucked within this gaping maw that acts as the Havoccraft's fuel aperture. The teeth break the asteroids into rubble which then passes through an array of hammer rays that pound the rock into pulverized particles, which drift through an attachyon field that would demolecularize the debris into fuel to feed the anti-magnetic accumulator which forms the positon core that must be housed in a high-energy containment field. "

"Quite a guess; actually it's a fine analysis, worthy of my old pal, Sam Parseck," Admiral Seasqrd said.

"You got to hand it to the Z." Atamz clasped his hands together. "What a piece of super-tech!"

"And soon this piece of high-tech will be right at your Uranus."

"Ooh," Captain Atamz straightened up.

"Sorry about the bad joke," Seasqrd said. "Whenever I think of Uranus, I think of Sam or maybe that should be the other way around."

"Sir?"

Seasqrd shook his hand through the air and said, "Nothing; I was just thinking out loud."

"I understand Sam Parseck is recuperating on the planet Zaftig. I'm not sure how comfortable the former head of Cosmos-Corps Research and Engineering will be on a planet that allows no machinery," Atamz said.

"You've never met an Animazonian," Seasqrd mumbled.

"Sir?"

"I'm sure he'll be fine and I'm sure that after its attack on Alpha Arthritis II the Havoccraft will head straight for Earth. I intend to lead an intercept mission!" the Admiral said.

"So you'll need your finest cosmicraft Commander," Atamz said.

Seasqrd put his hands up and said, "No, Ray, I need you. I need someone to advise me on technology, machinery and assorted apparatuses just as Sam Parseck used to and I need your ship. The Venus Eight is in for propulsor realignment and the Mercury Two is having her hyperocitator fluid flushed."

"What about the Nova Five?" Atamz asked.

"Revulsion pads need to be changed."

"The Zephyr Six?"

"She's in for an overhaul of her plasmatic conduits," Seasqrd said. "The Zenith Three is the only available cosmicraft."

"One cosmicraft against that," Atamz said.

"Good point; Sam advised me on that. We have to fight fire with fire and super-tech with super-tech and thanks to Sam's contacts in Research and Engineering I have quite a surprise for Darklone and the Z; you might say they'll never see it coming," Seasqrd said.

Seasqrd circled around and pressed a button on his desk. A computer screen on the desktop lit up and pages of schematics were projected slowly before their eyes. Atamz studied the screen intently wiggling his eyebrows.

"Of course, it's still experimental, but it should work," Seasqrd said.

"Incredible." Atamz placed his hands about his cheeks. "I'll get my people on it right away. Or should we have your people. How about both our people? I just want this apparatus aboard my ship."

"Ray, I appreciate your love for machines but we need more. There are still some of us who believe the greatest power source known is the heart, bone —"

"Yes, sinew and soul of a human, sir, but whereas humans are limited, technology is not." Captain Ray Atamz drew in a deep breath and said, "They used to say that if humans were meant to fly they'd have wings but—"

"No one is as good with technology as you, Ray, but take it from a human who has lived through countless encounters with the Z and their CGIsms, it wasn't the technology of earth that saved the day it was the people of Earth," Seasqrd said.

Ray exhaled in disappointment. Not only had the admiral cut off his humanity's need for greater technology speech, but also he was charting a course that made Ray ill in his stomach.

"And I have a hunch that we're going to need the best people available," the admiral said.

Ray Atamz stepped back for a moment then asked, "You're making me nervous, sir."

"We need an ace up our sleeve, or should I say an ace-pilot," Seasqrd said.

"Oh, no, not Peter Pulsaar," Atamz rolled his eyes back.

"He could be our only hope."

"If I may, sir, if he's our only hope then we're hopeless."

"I need him. We need him. I'm not getting any younger." Seasqrd took a seat and poured himself a glass of water.

"He failed us!"

"Or did we fail him?" Seasqrd asked. Atamz tilted his head and shrugged his shoulders. Seasqrd got up, walked over, slapped his former student on the back and said, "I want you to find Peter Pulsaar in time for the Zenith's departure."

Atamz got up off his knees and said, "After dropping out of Cosmos-Corps Academy, there were those who tried keeping in contact with Pulsaar on MySpacebook. From what I know, Peter fell in with some pretty seedy characters. Finding him could prove to be a problem."

Seasqrd helped Atamz to his feet and said, "A problem worth solving and sorry... Sam hated it when I did that."

Ray Atamz waited for his ribs to finally stop vibrating then said, "As I was saying who knows what your favorite pupil got himself into."

Seasqrd rubbed his chin and said, "I am cognizant of what became of Peter Pulsaar but we need him and once we find him we must make sure the same error isn't made twice. That's why I took the liberty of recruiting special help for you on this mission."

While leaning over his desk, Seasqrd pressed another button and a buzzing sound came from the hall outside. Immediately, the door slid open and Ray's heart plunged into a gravity well. Dr. Jane MaCardiak was five foot two with eyes of blue, matching her medical uniform perfectly and her hair was still a brilliant red. The kind of color a giant star turns just as it is about to collapse into becoming a black hole Ray thought. Jane had not changed; she was still just as beautiful as ever.

"It's good to see you again, Ray" she said as she entered.

"I'm sure it is." Atamz through back his shoulders and sucked in his stomach, assuming a very authoritative posture. "I mean good to see you."

"Now we're all aware of how things used to be, but I'm asking the two of you to put all that aside for the greater good of the whole," Seasqrd said.

"I'm sure that will be no problem, Admiral," Dr. Jane MaCardiak said. She turned to Ray and asked, "Do you agree, Captain Atamz?"

"Certainly, Dr. MaCardiak." Atamz nodded his head abruptly. "Why should there be any problems? We're both mature officers. No reason why we can't get along is there? You do your duty and I shall do mine."

Seasqrd looked at the captain then back at the doctor and nodded approvingly before he said, "Very well, then Jane will be serving as Chief Medical Officer."

"Great! I'm Captain and she will be chief medical officer." Ray faced Jane. "You have hosp-hold and I'll take the bridge."

Jane nodded at Ray and said, "Fine."

"No reason to go over all the good times we had before Peter Pulsaar came into your life. Like when we were voted cutest couple at Cosmos-Corps Academy."

"Ray!" MaCardiak said then turned away from Atamz gritting her teeth for a moment. "You were saying, Admiral Seasqrd."

"Yes, let the admiral finish his debriefing." Atamz waved his hand. "I'll just check the schematics again to see if they're compatible with the Zenith."

"Shame you never paid so much attention to our compatibility."

"What did she say?" Atamz asked.

"Check the schematics, Ray." The admiral said. He paused, took a breath then said, "Jane, I want you to know that I know how difficult all this will be for you."

"I know, you know, Admiral."

Ray rolled his eyes back.

"And remember no matter how strong your feelings are for Peter Pulsaar you must remained detached."

"She's good at that," Ray Atamz murmured.

"What did he say?" Jane MaCardiak asked.

Captain Atamz kept his eyes focused on the schematics but heard Jane groan then she said, "I'll do my very best, Admiral Seasqrd. You know that."

"Yes, I know, but again I want you to know that it won't be easy for me either. For as you know, if anything should happen to Peter Pulsaar then the G-Men die with me."

Ray looked up and watched Jane place a loving hand on the sad, old admiral's shoulder and say, "I know."

Ray Atamz turned about, began walking around the desk towards the admiral and doctor.

"Now we all know what we need to know," he said. Then his feet sunk beneath him. Finding himself up to his neck in floor once again, he said. "But there's one more thing I need to know. I'd like to know if you can get me out of here then we shut off that darn portahole."

CHAPTER 8
THOSE SCI-FI GUYS VERSUS THE KREDATOR

Peter Pulsaar had left the Kredator buried beneath a pile of cigarette cartons that lined the curb, hoping the horrible debt collector would be sucked up by one of the vaccumators that swept Domeboken's streets nightly, but something told him that the Kredator would be back. Pulsaar quietly crept into the hangar he had been calling home the last few weeks and flicked a switch; he gazed at the Aeon Owl.

"We're going on a long trip, honey, but first you need re-energizing."

Peter grabbed a long cable and went to plug it into the generator when he was hit by a sudden shock. The power surge tossed him across the hangar floor. Over the ringing in his ears he heard someone say, "Our runner has stopped running."

Slowly he rose and found himself standing before three policeyborgs; he recognized them as the same officers outside the Succulent Green.

"You are under arrest," Sergeant Keanoo said. His mechanical fist shot across the room like it was on a long spring and it impacted Peter's arm, sending him across the floor again.

"Wait, you can't just arrest me. Don't I have some rights?" Peter pleaded as he got back to his feet.

Sgt. Keanoo's head slowly pivoted. He said, "You are suspected in the destruction of property, inciting a riot and assaulting peace-loving citizens."

Peter blocked Sgt. Keanoo's metallic fist before it struck him again.

"The greenfellas?" Peter said. "They are peace-loving citizens? I don't mean to argue, but I think you are making a mistake."

"Policeyborgs do not make mistakes," Keanoo said. "We are monitored to apprehend you."

"I know the evidence points to me, but if you would just let me explain." Peter got back on his feet.

"We are not authorized, programmed or interested in your explanations, but if you feel you are being falsely accused then you may select from our touch-tone litigation system."

Slowly, Keanoo's chest slid open revealing a nine-button menu board. His once authoritative police voice became a soothing feminine tone.

"To plead guilty, say or press one. To plead innocent, say or press two. For a bail bondsmen say or press three. To hear these options again, say or press four."

"I just want to talk to a human being so I can—"

"Sorry, but your response is not an option," Keanoo's voice became menacing and male again, "and has been interpreted as an obstruction of justice."

Officer Berata immediately approached and handcuffed Peter Pulsaar. The cold metal of the handcuffs made Peter's blood boil and his temper grew hot. Berata suddenly landed against the wall. Peter snapped the cuffs then picked up an enormous toolbox. He tossed it at Nikti, but her mechanical legs propelled her upward. The toolbox hit the generators, causing an explosion.

Pete stood away from the fire and kept his distance from Nikti. She slowly reached towards her waist. Her mechanical arms drew two stasis ray guns from within her legs and fired. Peter dodged the beams, grabbed a chryston crowbar and was about to attack, but suddenly he found himself in a headlock.

Officer Berata's fingers dug into Peter's arm as he tightened his grip. Nikti was about to squirt Pete with paralysis pepper spray when he flipped Berata over onto her.

Sergeant Keanoo floated in mid air above Peter and said, "Resisting arrest is futile!"

He enveloped Peter in a stasis ray and Pulsaar found himself immobilized within a giant energy bubble.

"You're making a big mistake," Peter said.

"The perpetrator will remain silent," Keanoo said as his boots lowered him to the hangar floor. The three policeyborgs walked around, positioning Pulsaar and the energy bubble that caged him before the hangar door; they were about to slide the door open when it collapsed upon them.

"It's back," Peter said. Standing on the battered door, crushing the three policeyborgs below, was the Kredator. It spread its arms out wide as it growled and screeched; it massive chest flexed and drool drizzled from its fangs. Still frozen within the stasis bubble, Peter watched helplessly as the Kredator approached him; it drew nearer and nearer.

* * *

"You're one ugly mother fu—" Peter said.

"It's good to see you too, you ungrateful creep," a man in a Cosmos-Corps uniform said.

Peter's head became clear. He realized he was not trapped in an energy bubble anymore, then after his vision became focused he said, "Ray Jay Atamz!"

"This is what you say after we saved you." Atamz shook his head.

"Ray, I thought you were the Kredator," Peter said; he looked around and realized he was aboard the Aeon Owl. "Wait the last thing I remember I was back in the hangar... hey who's piloting my ship?"

"I thought you were a Cosmos-Corpsman and here we find you under arrest after being threatened by interstellar hoodlums," Atamz said.

"Please, Ray. Don't pick up where you left off with the reprimands, rebukes and second-guessing." Peter rubbed his eyes and looked around. "Just tell me how you, me and her got aboard the Aeon Owl and what's she doing at the helm of my ship?"

Peter pointed to the woman who was sitting in the pilot's seat. She obviously heard Peter referring to her; she stood and turned. Peter wasn't sure if his vision was quite clear; he thought he was looking at an angel.

"This is my executive officer, Commander Dya Nammock," Captain Atamz said. Peter did not know what to say. He just stood and looked at Commander Nammock with his jaw dropped. If he had known there were commanders this pretty he might have stayed in Cosmos-Corps. Her dark blue uniform had a firm grip on her form and she had the most alluring eyes. Then Peter noticed that behind her jet-black hair were these amazing ears with earlobes that twisted upwards into the shape of antennae. Realizing he had been quiet too long Peter said, "Pardon me, I'm still recuperating. It's nice to meet you, Commander Nammock. You're from the planet, Youkan, I see."

Commander Nammock said nothing. She walked up to Peter and shoved a blue and burgundy Cosmos-Corps uniform at him.

"I hear people from your planet are known for their brutal honesty," Peter said.

"You smell like garbage," Dya Nammock said. "After you wash up you should put on your uniform, Lieutenant."

"Lieutenant?"

She did not answer. She turned to Captain Atamz and said, "Sir, the auto-pilot will guide us to the Zenith in microns."

Atamz nodded. Commander Nammock strode back to the pilot's seat.

As Peter unfolded the uniform he asked, "Why did she call me lieutenant?"

"Did I forget to tell you? It's all part of a deal we just made with the policeyborgs. They won't arrest you provided you do service by flying one mission aboard the ECC Zenith," Atamz said.

"That can't be!"

"It has been be... I mean been done," Atamz said. "So you have a simple choice. Serve aboard the Zenith or serve time with the policeyborgs for being a pawn for intergalactic villains."

"That's some choice, Captain." Peter looked at his uniform.

While the Aeon Owl rocketed upwards into Earth's orbit. Peter changed into his uniform. He then joined Captain Atamz and Commander Nammock at the helm. He didn't like anyone but himself sitting in the pilot's seat but in Dya's case he'd make an exception. Giant sliding doors drew closed behind the Aeon Owl as the swift spaceship floated to a gentle landing within the ECC Zenith's flight hangar. The side-hatch flipped open and a gangplank slid down to the deck plate.

"You had no right to do this!" Peter Pulsaar said as he walked down the plank side by side with Ray Atamz. "Those policeyborgs had no right—"

"This is not my idea. I am under orders from my superior, and as for the policeyborgs they were quite grateful to us for incarcerating that creature called the Kredator," Atamz said.

"Wait... you incarcerated the Kredator?"

"No," Atamz said. "Her."

Peter turned about and stared at Dya Nammock as she walked down the gangplank. She stood eye to eye with him and asked, "Why do you find this so hard to believe?"

"I didn't say anything," Peter said.

"You are obviously unfamiliar with the telepathy of my people," Dya Nammock said. "Nor are you familiar with the Youkan punch."

Nervously trying to make his mind a blank before the sexy commander probed some of his other thoughts, Peter said nothing but just shook his head. Ray Atamz interceded and said, "Why not give him an example?"

"As you wish, sir," Dya Nammock said. She stood in front of Peter squaring her feet and said, "My people have dedicated themselves to positive thinking which has enabled us with great powers."

She curled her hand into a fist and hauled it back. "By focusing all my positive thoughts into one point I am capable of delivering quite a blow."

Peter was hurled across the room, bouncing off a bulkhead. His shoulder throbbed and his ego was bruised as he plopped across the floor. As he lay across the deck plate, the captain had a good laugh. The door next to Peter swooshed open and, suddenly, he found himself being kissed on the cheek by Jane MaCardiak. Captain Atamz stopped laughing. Peter drew back and smiled half-heartily under the doctor's tender care.

"Peter! What happened?" Dr. MaCardiak said.

""He just got a demonstration of the 'Youkan Punch' courtesy of Dya."

Jane's eyes followed the direction of Ray's finger and stared at Dya coldly. She said, "You did this to him?"

Dya remained silent; she just raised an eyebrow. Ray Atamz moved so he was between the two women and said, "Jane, he's fine."

"I'm the doctor; I'll be the judge of that!" she replied.

"He'll be fine," Atamz said as he stood over them. Jane caressed Peter's hair and held his hand. Suddenly, Peter found himself back at the academy days when he was stuck between Jane MaCardiak and Raymond J. Atamz's like a neutron in between an electron and proton. The doctor helped him to his feet.

"I'm fine, Dr. MaCardiak, I'm just fine," Peter said.

"Doctor?" MaCardiak said. "You've forgotten my name?"

"No," Peter said. "Jane, I'll be fine."

"Come with me down to hosp-hold so I can check how fine you are."

Dr. MaCardiak led Peter by the hand until Captain Atamz stepped in front of them and said, "Alright, let us remember we're officers in Cosmos-Corps."

Dr. MaCardiak shoved Captain Atamz away, took Peter's hand again and replied, "I'd never forget such a thing. Have you forgotten it is my duty to examine new members of the crew, sir?"

"Yes," Atamz said. He pulled Jane away from Peter. "That is true but it's more important for Peter to complete a psychiatric evaluation first."

"Would you two stop it?" Peter slapped his hands against his thighs then let his chin droop.

Jane tilted her head in sympathy but Captain Atamz gave him a look of disgust. He then said, "Commander Nammock, will you take charge of the psych-eval?"

Peter lifted his chin and smiled; he turned around to the beautiful alien with the tremendous over-hand right and asked, "How many jobs do you have aboard the cosmicraft?"

"Proactive behavior and positive thinking allow my people to assume many tasks," Dya said. She turned to face the captain and doctor and said, "Were I to invoke a few positive suggestions I would say that Dr. MaCardiak should return to hosp-hold and prepare for Lt. Pulsaar's examination after my initial counseling session. Afterwards, the captain should take him on a guided tour of the Zenith. It will give you the chance to explain the mission to him as well as afford you the opportunity to break in on the doctor's examination early and keep her away from him."

"Thank you, Commander Nammock." Captain Atamz tilted his head down.

"Honest to a fault, isn't she?" Dr. MaCardiak added.

"If I may say so, you humans could learn to appreciate an honest opinion more. On my planet we consider explicit honesty as the true path to self-improvement," Dya said.

"Be that as it may, I place great value on a good bed-side manner." Dr. MaCardiak said. She wrapped her arm about Peter's. "You should let people know how you've thought about them every day. That's another way towards self-improvement."

"I got enough self-improvement plans under my first tour of duty with Cosmos-Corps." Peter pulled away from Jane. "I'm never going to amount to anything in this uniform. It was a waste of time Ray. You should've known that."

"It wasn't my idea," Atamz said.

Peter heard a familiar voice say, "It was mine."

Peter spun around; Admiral Seasqrd had just entered through the sliding doors to the hangar deck.

"I see we're all getting acquainted again. That's good!" he said.

The admiral extended a handshake to Peter Pulsaar. Peter kept his hands at his side; he did not wish to be rude but he just plain resented Cosmos-Corps.

Peter tugged at the insignia on his uniform and said, "I should've known you'd be aboard, Admiral, you're the only man in Cosmos-Corps who Captain Atamz would call his superior. So I guess this is all your idea."

Admiral Seasqrd withdrew his hand, smiled and said," Come with me, Peter."

The admiral put his arm about Pulsaar's shoulder and whispered, "We'll have a nice admiral to lieutenant talk. Ray, is your ship ready to depart?"

Captain Atamz turned to Commander Nammock and asked, "Has our time-bend trajectory been computed?" When she nodded affirmatively Ray said, "Then start the chronomotors and engage chronosphere." He turned to the admiral and said, "The Zenith is ready."

"I never thoroughly understood time-bend travel no matter how many times Sam explained it," Admiral Seasqrd said. "But just as long as we reach our destination in time."

Ray Atamz replied, "That is the best way to put it, sir, since that's what we will be doing within the chronosphere."

"That's the part that always confused me where the chronosphere travels but we don't." Seasqrd scratched his bald head.

Peter was getting a little tired of the cosmologic conversation but when Dya spoke up he suddenly got interested. She said to the admiral, "If I may, sir, think of the space-time continuum as a blanket and the chronosphere is a ball on that blanket. If you bend the blanket in the right way you can get the ball to roll where you want it."

"Yes, Sam used to employ the same metaphor," Seasqrd said. "He always got miffed when I asked, 'What if we roll off the blanket?' "

Peter laughed because he was about to ask the same thing as a joke; he was glad he didn't because Dya did not react to the humor at all. She said, "That wouldn't happen; our trajectory has been locked into our navigatrometer."

Dr. MaCardiak seemed like she was perturbed by Dya's statement and said, "I think the admiral simply wants to make sure your ship will get us there as fast as possible."

Now Ray Atamz seemed perturbed by Jane's statement and said, "Well, the Zenith can't travel fast due to time dilation, Jane."

"Say that again," Jane MaCardiak said in confusion and Peter wondered how long it would be before the shouting started.

"If we travelled too long at our top speed our time would be too slow," Atamz said.

"That makes sense," Dr. MaCardiak said with her hands at her hips.

Now Dya seemed perturbed and ready to retaliate; she said to Jane MaCardiak, "Doctor, what the captain simply means is that we'd age slowly at such great speed while time on

Earth would continue normally. We would age a few days but on Earth a century would have passed."

"I see... right... but we will get there," MaCardiak replied.

"More accurately," Atamz said, "there will get to us and that is the nature of time-bend travel, sir."

Ray Atamz waved his hands before Admiral Seasqrd who said, "Well then, we're definitely getting somewhere." He placed an arm about Peter. "So let us all get going; Doctor, you get to hosp-hold and you two do what you have to with time and space and velocity; okay?"

The admiral gave a salute to his senior officers and pulled Peter through the hangar doors. Moments later Peter Pulsaar and Admiral Seasqrd had turned the corner of a long passageway that led to Pulsaar's new cabin. As they approached the door and he saw his name on a plate that was bolted to the door, Peter turned and asked, "Why me?"

"When I am gone, you will be the last of the G-Men," the admiral replied. "You must accept that fate and join us in this fight against Darklone and the Zlythetaurs."

"What if I don't want to accept that fate?" Peter opened the cabin door.

"You must do what you feel is wise of course... wimp." Seasqrd stepped inside.

"What did you just say?" Peter stood in the doorway with the sliding doors jamming against his waist. "You called me what?"

"Peter, I didn't say a word." the admiral stuck his hand against the door.

"You think I'm a coward, just because I don't want to be like you." Peter stumbled backwards into his cabin. "Maybe I don't want to be a G-Man. Maybe I hate having genetically altered reflexes and superior strength. Maybe I hate having everyone expecting me to be perfect because of my amazing abilities."

"You sound as if that's quite a big problem"

"It is," Peter said.

"There's no problem too big for the heart, bone, sinew and soul of a human cannot solve."

Peter had wondered how long it would be before the admiral used that line. Peter plopped on his bed and said, "Maybe if I had known my real parents I wouldn't be like this."

"You're father was one of the first G-Men and a fine Cosmos-Corpsman. He would be proud of your abilities, as you should be," Seasqrd said. "And just be grateful you don't have to walk around with this stupid power port in your head."

Peter smiled. He looked upwards and said, "I wish I had known him."

"In time, you will have the answers to many of your questions," Seasqrd said.

"I'd like to at least know his name," Peter said, putting his hands up in the air. "Can't you share that answer, now?"

"Patience Peter," Seasqrd said, patting Peter's head gently. "First learn to use your power then learn of your past and then you will know your future."

"Maybe just his first name," Peter said.

"Let me guide you in the ways of using your power." Seasqrd pointed to his own forehead then pointed at Peter's. "This time it'll be different."

"No, it won't." Peter gently knocked the admiral's hand away. "When you have amazing gifts, people expect you to be amazing at everything. There was always too much pressure on me in Cosmos-Corps. It was like being at the center of the Earth. Sometimes I feel like flying the Aeon Owl into the Unknown Zone and then I could be by myself forever."

"Sounds like a very lonely existence," the admiral said.

"I've been alone my whole life." Peter put his face in his open hands.

"No." Seasqrd clasped his hand about Peter's shoulders. "I will always be there for you."

"Admiral Seasqrd! Admiral Seasqrd!" A message was piped in on the audio-alerter. "A txt messile from Cosmos-Corps Command has been intercepted."

"Oh, I have to leave now," the admiral said, as he looked down from the audio-alerter in the ceiling. "You can find Commander Nammock's office... it's just down the corridor." He hurried through the sliding doors and said, "We'll talk later, kiddo."

The cabin doors swooshed closed. Peter Pulsaar sat all alone.

CHAPTER 9
THOSE SCI-FI GUYS AND THE FANTASTIC VOYAGE OF THE ZENITH

Peter Pulsaar tried not to think about Commander Dya Nammock the way he had before. Even more attractive than her eyes, her shape and her cute antennae was her confidence; Peter found it compelling maybe because he lacked it. The doors to the counselor's chambers swooshed open and Peter Pulsaar walked in. He heard a voice, which he recognized as Dya's.

"Please sit and make yourself comfortable. I'll be out in a moment," she said.

"Take your time, I'll just sit and relax," Pulsaar said.

Relaxation was the furthest thing from his mind as he paced the floor, trying to keep his thoughts under control. He reached for a glass of water that had been left on the table and tried to think of other things.

When he turned, there stood Dya wearing an informal uniform of light blue with a burgundy belt wrapped about her narrow waist just above a very short dark blue skirt. She adjusted the C-C insignia on her belt, sat and crossed her legs. Peter gulped down the cold water and sat himself down.

"I'll probably embarrass you with my improper thoughts." Peter looked down at the floor and put his hand over his eyebrows so as to avoid accidently looking up and staring at her legs. "But you do look real pretty in that outfit."

"Very good, honesty is an excellent way to begin our session." Dya took out her compad; she keyed in a few notes. "Besides, my people did away with embarrassment ages ago."

"So, I did something right in spite of myself." Pulsaar asked as he looked up with a smile. "Where do we begin?"

"Why don't you tell me about your childhood?" she asked.

"Not very many memories, it seemed like I grew up pretty fast. You know you turn around and there you are at Cosmos-Corps Academy." Peter sighed; he was beginning to feel relaxed.

"Your species has always relied on technology to solve problems and make life easier, yet I sense in you a distrust of mechanization."

Dya's bluntness made Peter feel tense once again. "Perfect machines making life perfect; nothing was meant to be perfect," he said.

Dya began scratching her knee and rubbing it as she said, "So you believe humans should solve the problems faced by the human condition."

Peter tried very hard not to watch what she was doing as he replied, "Admiral Seasqrd always preached about the heart, bone, sinew and soul of a human being the best technology."

"On my planet we rely on the power of positive thinking," Dya said.

"My problem is my thinking is not very positive," Peter said.

Dya looked down at Peter's foot, which he kept tapping against the leg of the table. She looked up and said, "I'd like to ask if you're always this nervous around women you are attracted to."

"What makes you think I'm nervous?" Peter asked just before he knocked over a glass.

"Please try to relax," Dya said. "Tell me about your love life."

"I don't have much of one. I've never been too successful with women," Peter said. He raised his hand up and continued with an afterthought, "I am signed onto LoveisEternal.cosmic. Ever hear of it?"

"With over two billion participants it is the largest dating service on the cosmic infonet. I should imagine it derives its title from the human belief that true love lasts an eternity," Dya said.

"I think they're called that because it may take you that long to find someone."

Dya wrote some more. Peter twisted his neck, trying to spy on what was being written about him. When Dya looked up he sat back. She said, "Interesting, though you dislike technology you turn to it in search of romance."

Peter pointed at the Zenith's bulkheads and said, "It just goes to show even all this super-technology can't help a pathetic loser like me."

"Why don't you tell me why you feel the need to engage in self-disparagement?"

"I'd rather not."

"I think you do."

"Yes, you're right." Peter poured himself another glass of water and took a long sip. "But it's very complicated. I don't know if you'd understand."

"I submit that you are purposely not living up to your potential for fear that you may disappoint the ones who believe in you. In other words, if you never try to be a success, you never need to worry about failure."

"Boy, you understand a lot more than I thought." Peter sat with his eyes opened wide. "But I don't know if you could understand the real reason why."

"You know I would."

"Yes, you're right again." Peter finished the water. "It's not easy arguing with a telepath."

"I'm only truly telepathic with someone I'm truly, deeply connected with."

"Oh."

"Amongst my crewmates, my powers only allow me to know what they want me to know although I am getting strong signals from you." Dya put down her compad. "However, in order for us to get at the heart of your problem, we must delve deep."

Peter's brow rose.

"There's something you're hiding far down within." Dya approached Peter with her hands up. "We must open the dark recesses of your psyche."

Peter backed away. "What do you have in mind?" he asked.

"No, it's what you have in your mind." Dya picked up what looked like an old-fashioned magnifying lens except that the center of it was made of wire netting instead of glass. She backed Peter Pulsaar into his chair and whispered, "I must probe your mind."

"Get that thing away from me." Peter tried to stand, but Dya placed her hand on his shoulder forcing him back down. She whispered, "Have no fear. This is simply a mind-mesh."

She attached the wires that dangled from the handle of the mind-mesh to her antennae. She then lowered the mind-mesh over Peter's head.

"Be gentle," Peter said.

Dya was about to begin her mind probe when Pulsaar shot up off the couch like a missile and shouted, "That was fantastic!"

"Amazing," Dya said, "I've never encountered such a response to the mind-mesh."

"I feel so...."

"Self-confident," Dya said.

"That's the word," Peter said, placing his arms about Dya's waist.

"It has happened before. The abundant positive thoughts of my brain spill over and fill the void created by low self-esteem in another's brain, though I've never witnessed such a pronounced case."

"Maybe we have a stronger connection then you thought." He held her tighter.

"Please, Pulsaar."

"Let's do it again," Peter held the commander even tighter then turned about suddenly when he heard the doors swoosh open.

"Did I come at a bad time?" asked Admiral Seasqrd as he stood in the doorway.

"Admiral," Dya said as she stepped away from Peter. "I was just counseling Pulsaar and applying—"

"Interesting technique," Seasqrd said with a wry smile. "But I'd like to see Lt. Pulsaar. I felt bad about the way our chat ended."

"Begging the admiral's pardon, I have an appointment with the ship's doctor." Peter said with his head back and his shoulders wide. "Then I tour the Zenith with the captain. Afterwards, I look forward to discussing your proposed plans and the role I will play."

Admiral Seasqrd looked Peter up and down with admiration and said, "Later then. I like your confidence, Pulsaar."

"Thank you, sir." Peter saluted. "I've got the power.

Seasqrd returned the salute. "You certainly do."

*   *   *

Down in hosp-hold, Peter impatiently sat on a gravi-gurney. He was anxious to use his new found confidence; he was ready to take on the challenges of Cosmos-Corps and prove he was worthy of Admiral Seasqrd's praise and expectations, yet he was stuck under Jane MaCardiak's loving care. As he floated, he habitually looked up at the round disc that hung over his head monitoring his bodily functions. He kept glancing back at the glass squares mounted on the wall. Each light was a detector that indicated everything that could be wrong with the body from pain levels to athlete's foot. Meanwhile, Jane MaCardiak healed the bruise he received from the Kredator with a wave of her electroanestisizer and a shot of healamins from injecterdermic.

"Your super metabolism is doing fine but what's wrong with a little T.L.C.?" she rubbed Peter's arm.

It was not that Peter Pulsaar did not like the attention; after all Jane did have the prettiest hair that seemed to fall into the cutest curls as it draped over her back and she had the smoothest, creamiest skin, but he always felt uncomfortable the way she lavished it on, especially when Ray Atamz was around. The doctor pressed her body against him, while she ran her anatoscanner over his torso. Peter was starting to feel embarrassed as the doctor caressed his back and put her fingers through his hair. Suddenly, Peter could hear the heart rate indicator on the biochecker beat at a rapid rate. Without looking he was sure the temperature indicator was rising also.

"Is there anything else I can do for you?" she asked.

"No, you've done enough." Pete slid off the gravi-gurney.

"They should've let you come to me first, but there now, you're in perfect shape. Of course anyone could see that. Especially a young woman," MaCardiak said.

"Jane, I wish you wouldn't say things like that."

"About being perfect," the doctor said. "Don't let Ray and that automated first officer of his push you too hard."

"No," Peter said. He slipped his uniform back on over his naked torso. "It's just that I've always felt like I got in between you and Ray."

"There are many things between the captain and I," MaCardiak said. "You are not one of them."

Peter sighed; Jane reached her arms around Peter's waist, placing her head upon his chest and said, "I have missed you so much. Aren't you going to say you missed me?"

"Of course I missed you," Peter said as he stepped back. "You're a wonderful woman. Beautiful, smart but —"

"If I could just make you understand my true feelings." She took his hand and placed it against her chest. "Then everything would be explained."

"Some things are best unexplained." Peter pulled his hand away.

"Don't tell me you're becoming like Ray Atamz." MaCardiak's eyes squinted.

"You may find this hard to believe, but even though he was so tough on me back at the academy I think of Ray as a friend. He's a good man, Jane."

"Oh sure, he's a man who can put together a cosmicraft blind folded, but he cannot fathom the basic operations of the human heart," the doctor said as she stepped forward.

Peter continued to back away from the doctor and she continued to pursue; they circled about hosp-hold until Jane stood beneath the disc of her biochecker. She said, "Some men it seems have to be programmed for love."

The brain activity light fluctuated and the needle for blood pressure began to bounce.

"Shame there is no way to re-calibrate their hearts."

Peter looked at the lights on the biochecker's stress monitors as they began flashing yellow then changed to red.

"And when you try to talk things out the way humans should do, they claim they want a woman to be maintenance free!"

The indicators seemed ready to burst.

Just then, Ray Atamz entered through the sliding doors of hosp-hold. "What seems to be the matter with your equipment?" he asked.

"Always more worried about machines than people," MaCardiak said and slapped the captain across the face before storming out of hosp-hold.

Peter stood back in shock, while Ray Jay Atamz just rubbed his cheek and asked, "Ready for our tour?"

Peter nodded and followed Ray. Together they toured the Zenith from her graviton gyros to her silicon sump pumps and finally wound up on a deserted deck not too different from the many others save for a strange plaque mounted before two very large doors which read Imagarena-A. Ray Atamz, still acting as the tour guide, said, "And for recreational purposes the crew may relax here where virtual simulations make imagination come to life."

"I've seen these before," Peter said quite anxious to pop the captain's egotistical bubble and bring the tour to an end. He gave a knowing nod and said, "You can sit and watch shows as if you were really there in three dimensions—"

"It gets better aboard the Zenith!" Atamz interrupted. "Our virtual imagery is composed of corporeal energy held in a cohesive state, thus allowing the participants to interact physically."

Peter Pulsaar paused and looked at the plaque, then looked back at Captain Atamz and said hesitantly, "So then it's possible on these decks to... I mean you could create a simulation where you could... couldn't you?"

"Leave it to you to come up with that purpose for such a wonderful piece of technology." The captain patted the plaque affectionately.

Peter tilted his head from one shoulder to another as he said, "I didn't mean anything by it. I just mean a techno-genius like you never dreamt up a program or two where—"

"Please."

"Maybe a nice romantic program, just for two, where you could invite your chief medical officer." Peter held up his two index fingers and bounced them against each other.

"Pulsaar!"

"What?" Peter smiled. "I just thought you and her might be able to settle some differences."

"Unfortunately, there will always be one man in her heart." The captain grew stern. "And that leaves room for no others."

"Peter's chin drooped down over his chest as he muttered, "I never gave her any encouragement."

"Why would you have to? She has always seen you as the paragon of perfection," Ray tilted his head, "despite your less than perfect record."

"So you're blaming me for your failed romance with Jane?"

Ray answered, "I'm not blaming you, Peter I just think it's your entire fault."

Peter's posture slouched and his smile became a frown. Just before he was about to say something, Ray looked up and watched the hatch in the ceiling open.

"Watch it." He pushed Peter aside. A series of metal rungs dropped from the open hatchway. The captain said, "Someone is coming down the escaladder."

Climbing down was Admiral Seasqrd. He smiled at Peter and asked, "So how's my little G-Man? Ready to begin your training?"

Ray Atamz folded his arms as he looked at Peter with disgust. Peter put his head down. He felt so guilty about Ray and Jane; there were also a lot of other things he felt should have been different.

The admiral continued, "You got the power; I got the power; we got the power!"

"I got nothing," Peter said as he sulked away down the corridor, sank to the floor opposite his commanding officers, folded his legs and placed his face between his hands.

"What's he doing?" asked Admiral Seasqrd as he stared in disbelief.

"I believe he's pouting," Ray Atamz said very as-a-matter-of-factly.

Peter awaited another speech about heart, bone, sinew and soul, but the admiral simply asked, "Why?"

Peter listened intently, waiting for Ray's explanation which he was sure would contain plenty of criticizing and complaints, but the captain simply said, "I warned you he's prone to breakdowns."

Peter found himself growing very mad at his captain when, suddenly, he felt a boot against his knee. The Admiral's yeoman had just turned the corner of the intersection and tumbled over Peter, landing at the other side of the passageway. Admiral Seasqrd hurried to her side and picked her up.

She said, "Sir, we have intercepted txt messile with a priority alpha attachment."

Ray Atamz took the admiral's arm and said, "Sounds as if it might be important."

Peter remained on the floor watching the admiral stare at Captain Atamz for a moment before he said, "It certainly could. Have it sent down to my cabin, Ray?"

Seasqrd looked down at Peter as if he was going to say something. Peter buried his face in his hands again and heard the admiral say, "And Captain, please assemble your officers in the ready room. I have a hunch the Zenith is going to be needed sooner than we expected!"

Peter shook his head in self-despair.

*   *   *

Inside the ready room, Ray Atamz lay sprawled across the floor with Admiral Seasqrd standing over him. The admiral had begun his briefing and required a three-dimensional map of chartered space. Ray Atamz had insisted he could increase the quality of the resolution and fumbled beneath holographic map projector.

"I believe that does it," Captain Atamz said. He stood, brushed off the pants of his blue uniform then looked at a small, bright sphere spinning over the table's center.

"They say the universe is shrinking but this is ridiculous," Seasqrd said.

"You've just shrunk known space to the size of a golf ball," Jane MaCardiak said.

"I can't understand it," Atamz replied. He dove under the table again and fine-tuned some knobs and dials. He asked, "How's that?"

He rose to his feet only to find the holograph now encompassed the room. He was going to say something to the admiral, but found it difficult to talk to him while his face was covered by the Crab Nebulae. He dove under the table once again.

"Captain, please just return things to as they were. Thank you," the admiral said.

The sliding doors to the ready room swooshed open. Peter Pulsaar entered, hanging his head down and muttering brief excuses as to why he was late.

"No apologies necessary," Seasqrd said.

Ray Atamz tried not to show his disdain for the admiral's all too forgiving nature towards young Pulsaar. He watched Admiral Seasqrd touch a small planetoid hovering about within the holographic imagery and, suddenly, the planetoid expanded to full-scale size.

"Now this three dimensional virtual dispatch was sent by Captain Isaac Tope just as the Havoccraft attacked Deep Space 1999. This outpost as you know was settled on a perfectly hospitable world. Now see for yourself." Seasqrd pointed towards the menacing Havoccraft that floated over the space station. From beneath the holograph of the Havoccraft appeared two rods. As they spread apart, a blue wave of lightning shot from the tip of one rod to the other. The rods began spinning and finally the wave of lightning turned red and shot like a tornado wreaking havoc across the surface of Deep Space 1999.

"Hurricane winds followed by blizzards, then volcanic eruption and after that a searing heat wave. And all in a less than a day," Seasqrd said. "Commander Nammock, what is your analysis of that force ray?"

"I would submit that it is composed of bosons," she answered.

"Precisely, a graviton beam of pure anti-bosons... absolutely pure."

"Boy, what technology," Atamz said while staring mindlessly at the three dimensional imagery.

Seasqrd continued by saying, "Recent intelligence puts the Havoccraft's position here." Seasqrd pressed a button and an asteroid field was highlighted. "To the best of our knowledge the Havoccraft's positon core needs to be fueled by munching on giant asteroids. My hunch is that Darklone will refuel the Havoccraft to its utmost capacity then head straight to Earth."

"Then it's up to the Zenith to combat the Havoccraft while still in a weakened condition," Atamz said. Then he looked up at the ceiling. "Captain to Zenith computer. Correlate an attack plan—"

"No need for all that computation. I have come up with a plan." Seasqrd pointed to his head and pressed another button and a blue squiggly line lit up through the holograph. "I propose we take an intercept course to the Havoccraft. Our fighters, led by Lt. Pulsaar, will fly recon until the exact position of the Havoccraft is found. With the Zenith's new top secret device we should be able to sneak up on Darklone before he knows what has hit him."

"Admiral, there might be a problem," Atamz said.

"And we all know what it is." Peter Pulsaar stepped forward. "I am to lead the fighters."

"I was referring to how dangerously close this course takes us to the Unknown Zone," Atamz said, highlighting the area of static gases and ionic maelstroms.

"It's a risk we must take," Seasqrd stated.

"Yes," Atamz said with his fist in his hand. "Risk is the business of Cosmos-Corps. Risk is what brings us into deep space. That's why we're aboard the Zenith."

"Peter, you're the best pilot I've ever seen." Seasqrd pointed his finger at the lieutenant.

"Of course he is," Dr. MaCardiak added.

Ray Atamz sadly realized no one was interested in hearing the rest of his speech on risk taking and changed the subject.

"We might need a more experienced fighter pilot," he said. "It might be better if we had Commander Nammock lead the fighters."

Ray noticed Peter looking at Dya Nammock incredulously. She responded with a confident smile and said, "I am also the squadron leader."

Peter dropped his lower jaw, looked at Ray and said. "My ship is faster than anything the corps has and you know it, Ray."

"I know, I helped you build it, remember?" Atamz nodded.

"Wait! Don't tell me you're going to fly against the Z in that rusty old space crate you two built back at the academy," MaCardiak said. She ran to Seasqrd's side and said, "Admiral, don't let him—"

"Wait a micron!" Dya Nammock stepped forward in front of Dr. MaCardiak and said, "This could be the opportunity for Lieutenant Pulsaar to prove himself."

"You can't push him." Dr. MaCardiak raised her fist. "If he's ready he'll do it!"

"Doctor, Lt. Pulsaar lacks the ability to think positively since he lacks confidence due to his past record of underachievement," Dya said.

"And you think that putting him in situations he can't deal with is going to help his confidence?" the doctor screamed. "What kind of callous, inhuman cold-heart would conceive of such a thing?"

"How would you like to be on the receiving end of the Youkan punch?" Dya asked.

"I promise to fix the broke nose you're about to get?" MaCardiak said.

As the two women charged towards one another, Ray Atamz and Admiral Seasqrd dove forward trying to get in between them.

"Peter Pulsaar will lead the fighters!" Admiral Seasqrd held Jane MaCardiak back and swung her around. "And Commander Nammock will co-pilot the Aeon Owl."

"Sounds good, sir!" Ray Atamz yelled while pulling Dya Nammock back, and then he looked down at Peter. The little, spoiled baby was pouting again.

He looked up at Ray with his sad eyes and said, "This is my entire fault."

Ray thought — *our hero*

CHAPTER 10
THOSE SCI-FI GUYS VERSUS THE HAVOCCRAFT

As he slithered along the main corridor of the Havoccraft, Zatan returned salutes from his space troopers while they marched along carrying the imperial flag of Zygote. Zatan looked at the image of his home world and could not help feel pride in the mighty planet that sat like an egg in space always hatching plans of galactic conquest. The latest plan was the creation of the Havoccraft. Zatan could feel his ship turn suddenly while navigating its way through an asteroid field. He could imagine the Havoccraft sucking in rubble and debris as if it were some ravenous beast enjoying needed prey. The bulkheads and deck plates actually rumbled as the space dreadnaught gorged itself and Zatan felt like a sinister mother giving her baby a bottle. But though the ship was his, Zatan was not in command.

As the high commander of Zlythetaur forces, Zatan had overseen construction of the Havoccraft but for some unimaginable reason the Imperial Council had awarded leadership of the mammoth warship to another; they chose the outworlder called Darklone. Perhaps they couldn't resist the idea of Earth being destroyed by one of its own kind or perhaps the council, knowing his great desire to lead the Havoccraft in the conquest of Earth, chose another just to screw Zatan over; that was the nature of Zlythetaurs. In any event, Zatan always followed orders.

Zatan approached the commander's command chamber. Standing in the corridor next to the guards were sub-commanders who offered the Zlythetaur salute.

"Hail hate!"

"Hail hate," Zatan replied while forming his claws into a fist. They entered the command room where Darklone was perched high above in a chair staring at the black walls that surrounded him. Slowly, he swiveled about, looked down and immediately issued orders to his subordinates.

Zatan never cared for the look of humans. They had none of the sinister features that made the Zlythetaurs so attractive, but Darklone was different. Though he did not have serpentine eyes and a forked tongue or a row of small horns that formed a ridge over his bulbous head he did have wonderful crags that twisted his face, red-rimmed eyes and a diabolical mustache and beard.

"Zatan did you hear me?" Darklone pointed from his chair.

"Yes, Darklone, we will deploy our fighters into the asteroid field," Zatan said. "But the asteroids could cause major damage to our fighters."

"That does not concern me." Darklone raised his hand. "I know what Seasqrd is thinking. I have power as he does." He tapped the side of his head. "Now as we speak, he'll be sending whatever forces he has to intercept us. Here is where we will wait, refuel and trap them."

"We are somewhat confused by your recent strategies," Zatan said.

"Why am I not surprised," Darklone said. "You wonder why we stopped to attack the outpost."

"By now Cosmos-Corps must be on the alert." Zatan awaited a reply most anxiously.

Darklone raised his hand, twisting it until his palm pointed upwards and said, "It was worth it if it allows me to hurt him, my dear Zatan."

"Sir?" Zatan replied.

"By attacking Deep Space 1999, I have stirred a feeling of dread in Cosmos-Corps and that hurts Seasqrd and I want to keep hurting the great Gene Lucas Seasqrd... I like how it feels."

"But certainly your clone will have deduced your strategy and is preparing a counter attack," Zatan said.

"I am more than capable of deducing the deductions of my brother. Let him bring a fleet of cosmicrafts... so much the better." Darklone's eyes seemed to burn with animosity. "We will wait here and lure Seasqrd into a trap. Once Cosmos-Corps is crippled we can descend upon the Earth with nothing in our way and conquer it in one swift stroke!"

Again Zatan found himself admiring the human. Though he was not of Zygote, Darklone was evil enough to be a Zlythetaur, but his thinking seemed unclear. "But?" he asked, politely.

"Or better still we will take Seasqrd captive and force him to watch as the Havoccraft descends upon Earth. He sees himself as the protector of Earth; I can think of nothing that would hurt him more or maybe better still...." Darklone raised his fist.

"Should we deploy our fighters?" Zatan asked.

"Yes," Darklone said, stroking his beard.

"As you command," Zatan said. The other Zlythetaur commanders bowed and backed out of the room. Darklone spun about in his throne-like chair and faced the empty wall once again.

"By the way, my leader," Zatan said. He paused by the open doorway; he looked about the stark empty command chamber. "What do you do up there when we are not here?"

Darklone, with his back still facing them, replied, "It does get a bit boring."

*   *   *

Down in Zenith's hangar, Peter Pulsaar nervously paced up and down, pretending to inspect the falcon fighters that were under his command. Secretly, he was dwelling on his feelings of dread and inadequacy.

"Lt. Pulsaar," a voice said. Peter turned around and saw Dya was pointing towards the Aeon Owl. She asked, "May I inquire as to the combat readiness of this thing?"

"She's not a thing and as for her readiness see for yourself." Peter crooked a finger towards Dya and they climbed inside the Aeon Owl and he began showing her all the facets of his ship.

"This main fuselage is what's left of an old Saturn XX rocket. The wings and main engine are off an old Mercury miner probe except the top wings and maneuvering thrusters. They came off a Jovian flyer."

Dya shook her head knowingly. Peter climbed up into the Owl's upper saucer section and pointed about to the random computer components with fiber lines interconnecting them. "This section is used as a piloting, communication and navigation control room. It's actually from an old Alpha Centauri Romeo," he said as he smiled.

Dya remained unimpressed as Peter continued she remained silent, but kept blinking rapidly as if the sight of each intraositator and ionic capacitor was being programmed into her brain. When they stepped back onto the hangar deck though, she was bewildered by the sight of what Peter called his "special modifications." He was happy he had finally stumped her. She looked under the large metal box before her and saw it had been welded to the hull. From it sprang what she called a spider's web of wires and coils that poked their way in through the fuselage. Dya finally looked up at Peter and said, "I fail to comprehend."

"That's a ram-rocket, Ray and I took it off an old space shuttle that used to carry commuters from Earth to the Moon," Peter said. "So what do you think of her?"

"It looks like junk," Dya said.

"That's the best part of her."

"I'll assign a maintenance detachment."

"I don't want other people touching my ship." Peter stood protectively with his hands and arms spread across the Owl's fuselage.

"You are a most fascinating case. You feel you are too inadequate to solve your own problems but your distrust for the super-technology of our age will not allow you to use machines to solve problems for you yet you love your space ship."

"She's not a product of super-technology; I built her. All I need is her and all she needs is me and we don't need anything from you and your crew."

"At least the hangar crew could scrape the rust off, not to mention these numerous wires, opticables and fiber lines should be unknotted and properly sealed within the fuselage," Dya said.

"Don't you dare I know she's not perfect and that's the way I like her," Peter smiled.

They climbed back aboard the Aeon Owl. Dya scanned about in disgust, looking down at the rubbish surrounding the pilot's seat and said, "I'll have someone clean out this cockpit."

"I like my cockpit the way it is, thanks." Peter shrugged his shoulders and his shook his head. "I'm sorry. I didn't mean that the way it sounded."

Peter looked about, making sure they were all alone in the Aeon Owl. He whispered to Dya, "I could use a quick one before our mission."

"What did you say?" Dya stepped back, her antennae shaking.

"Your mind-mesh, it really boosted my confidence," Peter said.

Just as Dya was about to answer, Peter heard someone climbing into the lower fuselage. "Pulsaar, are you ready to address your fighter crews?" asked Captain Atamz.

"Huh?" Pete asked as he leaned over the hatchway from the saucer section.

"It's customary for the squadron leader to give a speech to his pilots before they sortie," Atamz said.

Peter nodded reluctantly and gestured reassuringly towards the deck below; as he climbed down he said, "I'll try."

143

He stepped onto the hangar deck. Standing before him were seven young pilots. He felt like his stomach had just fallen into a wormhole.

"What do you think of your squadron?" Ray Atamz asked.

"They look good," Peter said quietly.

"You'll find they perform like a well-oiled machine," Atamz said. "They've been debriefed on the mission. They're just awaiting final instructions from you."

Atamz saluted Peter, indicating now was the time to speak to the crew. He stared at them and mumbled a little before Dya shoved him forward.

"Hi," Peter raised his arm and waved. The pilots looked at each other in unease. "Uh... don't worry men. Just follow me into battle. I know this mission is dangerous." Peter paused; he tried thinking of something else to say. "But risk is what being a Cosmos-Corpsman is about. It's our duty to boldly go where no one else is dumb enough to go."

Peter closed his eyes, not wanting to look at the expressions on Ray and Dya's faces. He said, "I mean everyone else is smart enough not to go where we must go... well... you know what I mean."

"Very good, Lt. Pulsaar; pilots dismissed!" Atamz said. The pilots walked away trying not to laugh. Captain Atamz saluted both Peter and Dya and said, "Now I must go; anything else you need from me?"

Peter asked, "Ray, what if the Havoccraft finds the Zenith before we find the Havoccraft?"

Ray gave Peter and Dya a proud and knowing smile and said, "The Z aren't the only ones coming up with new technology."

As the captain exited Peter felt a twinge of panic. Some of the worst disasters at Cosmos-Corps Academy occurred when Ray Atamz had some new tech to play with.

Peter looked at Dya and said, "I know you know I'm worried. Don't you ever get worried?"

"Never, I always focus on a positive outcome," she replied.

Peter admired her self-assurance and the way she filled out her gold flight suit, but it was difficult for him to think positive while his genetically enhanced ears could hear his pilots at the end of the hangar chuckling as they mocked him out.

"Come on Dya," Peter said, clasping his hands together in front of his nose. "I need it bad."

"No," Dya said.

"One more time," Peter said. "I'm begging."

"No, you will have to take this matter into your own hands," Dya said.

The chuckling of the pilots quickly changed into hilarious laughter until Commander Nammock turned on them and said, "Get to your posts!"

The pilots scurried off except one who shot a disdainful look at Dya.

"I heard what you were thinking. Consider yourself on report!"

Peter waited until the pilots dispersed and Dya cooled off before saying, "Dya, I can't do this on my own."

"You will never know unless you try," Dya said. Then she pointed at the Aeon Owl and said, "Now squadron leader get into that piece of garbage you love so much and lead us into battle."

* * *

"Come in Aeon Owl!" Atamz's voice came over the mic. "Status report!"

Peter screamed into the mic, "We've encountered a bat squadron, we're barely dodging runaway asteroids and we're low on fuel! How's that status, Captain?"

"Excellent, where the bats are, the Havoccraft can't be far. Let us know when you have exact coordinates," Atamz replied.

"Thanks for the concern, Ray," Peter slammed the mic off.

"Stay positive," Dya said.

"I'm positive were going to be destroyed," Peter Pulsaar said as the Aeon Owl dodged another asteroid and stayed ahead of the Zlythetaur bat fighters that pursued them. "We have to turn back!"

"Try to remain positive."

"I have to get the squadron back to the Zenith."

A laser blast just missed the Owl and Peter did some evasive maneuvers. On the computer screen he could see three bats closing in. When he looked up he saw another asteroid straight ahead. Peter pulled back on the control stick and wiped the sweat off his brow.

"Peter, if we go back to the Zenith we're just leading the Z to her coordinates. We have to elude these bats and find the Havoccraft," Dya said.

"I can't do all that."

"Yes, you can."

"No I—"

Suddenly, Peter felt something metallic on his head but before he could ask what it was he was deep in the Youkan mind-mesh and an instant later he said, "I got the power!"

Peter got a firm grip on his control stick. The Aeon Owl suddenly spun around asteroids, dodging the laser attacks of the pursuing bat fighters. Looping upwards, the Owl circled into a wide arc while inside Peter yelled, "Hold on to your antennae, Dya."

Pushing down on the control stick, Peter Pulsaar took the Aeon Owl into a dive. He did not need to wait for the targeting computer to line up his opponents; he fired at will and destroyed all three bats. Wasting no time, Peter grabbed onto another lever and twisted a few dials. The Owl responded by flying about in a fluid motion and soared over the pack of bats chasing down his squadron.

"Drop proton bombs!"

Dya took Peter's cue and pulled down on the proton launcher.

"Proton bombs away!" Peter heard Dya say as he watched a flurry of glowing, gold, energy spheres explode over the bat fighters. His squadron of falcon fighters dispersed, then quickly regrouped and swarmed over the crippled bats.

"Activate long range sensarrays," Peter said.

His co-pilot smiled and replied, "One step ahead of you."

"It's time to find the Havoccraft."

Through the canopy of the Aeon Owl, Peter could see a satellite-dish spin about then suddenly lock in one direction.

"Havoccraft located!" Dya said.

"Send those coordinates to the Zenith."

"No, need to." Dya tapped his shoulder, reached in front of his face and pointed. "I think they have them already."

"Oh no, what is he doing?" Peter looked around and spotted the Zenith emerging from a cloud of asteroid dust.

Pulsaar slammed his hand across the mic control and yelled, "Ray, what are you doing? The Havoccraft is just beyond those huge asteroids. They will pick you up."

"No, they won't," Atamz's voice said over the mic. "Watch this while you can."

Peter watched the Zenith glide around, and then he could not believe his eyes. The Zenith's hull faded in color, turning from gray to white. She began shimmering from bow to stern, and then the Zenith disappeared. She could no longer be seen; it was incredible.

"She became invisible!" Peter said. He looked at Dya and asked, "A lurking device?"

"Affirmative," Dya said.

"I know of the theory, but I didn't think there was one in operation."

"You were wrong," Dya said, bluntly. "May I submit the most positive thing to do would be to get over your awe and order the squadron back to the Zenith for refueling?"

"One problem with that, Commander," Peter said as he pressed another button. "The squadron may return to the Zenith, but the Aeon Owl cannot."

Suddenly, the ship shook. Dya adjusted the ship's attitude and said, "Bats on an intercept course."

"I see them," Peter said, "so is the Havoccraft!"

"We can't head back to the Zenith," Dya said. "That will divulge their position to the Z."

"Affirmative; we'll have to lure the enemy deeper into the asteroid field so as to buy time for our squadron!" Peter twisted the control stick and grabbed some levers.

"I know what you are thinking, Peter, and—"

"Hey, I got the power," Peter said as he turned to his pretty co-pilot and gave her a cocky smile. "And so does my ship!"

Reaching forward, Peter pressed a large red button in the middle of the dashboard. The controls to the ram-rocket lit up.

"I hope you like a man who can handle lots of thrust." Peter turned the ignition of the ram-rocket and the Aeon Owl raced away like a bolt of lightning.

*   *   *

Across the blackness of space, within the malevolent Havoccraft, Darklone stalked the deck of the Havoccraft's battle bridge. As Darklone paced back and forth, the Zlythetaurs cringed in fear. This pleased him; suddenly, he pointed through the portal and said, "Track the odd looking fighter racing away."

"Why are you so interested in that tiny, dilapidated spacecraft," Zatan said in puzzlement.

"I have a hunch it will lead us to Seasqrd." Darklone said. "Intuition may seem like a strange human foible to you

Zlythetaurs, but it is a power of command and no one should underestimate my power."

Zatan tilted his bulbous head and asked, "Why not wait for a clear transmission from our bat fighters, all we have on their recon is static and —"

The High Commander was a fine minion and sinister lackey but he occasionally needed to be shown who was in charge. Darklone gripped Zatan's throat and said, "Why not obey my orders?"

Zatan slithered back after Darklone generously released him. The rest of the crew busied themselves at their posts avoiding eye contact with Darklone. Zatan slowly gulped and whispered "Hail hate."

Immediately, the frightened Zlythetaurs began pushing buttons and Darklone could feel the Havoccraft slowly moved forward, plodding along the dark fabric of space blasting asteroids out of its way in pursuit of its new quarry.

*   *   *

Aboard the bridge of the Zenith, Captain Raymond Atamz was in his element, barking orders at his bridge crew while they prepared the myriad of weapons, devices and gizmos of his cosmicraft.

"Lurking device in perfect operational order," Lt. Meedioride said.

"Good thing I ordered you to conduct a diagnostic," the captain said.

"Captain, all departments and computer stations report battle ready," Lt. Andrea Romeda reported from her networking command console.

"I told you those drills were necessary," Captain Atamz said as he pointed down at Lt. Romeda. He noticed that Romeda's face was not quite as annoyed as Meedioride's, but of course, she had served longer aboard the Zenith and knew the captain's routine.

"Charge laser-blazers and put all auxiliary power to our deflection plates," Atamz said as he walked across the triangular room. He pointed at Ensign Vector. "Prepare proton bombs for maximum spread."

Ray Atamz watched with glee as his crew followed his orders. He sat down in his reclino-chair and said, "Lt. Romeda, raise the cartographic-cart!"

Out of the floor rose a rectangular metal cart with four micro-projectors protruding from its corners. The projectors aimed beams at the glass plate in the cart's center and, suddenly, geometric images representing nearby spacecraft and wandering asteroids took shape. Admiral Seasqrd got up out of his chair and stood next to Ray; the captain felt a little nervous with the admiral looking over his shoulder.

"Our falcon fighters are coming in for a landing." He pointed at the cartographic-cart.

"The Zenith will be ready for battle as soon as our fighters refuel, sir." Atamz said. "By the way, would you want my chair? It is bigger."

"Not the entire squadron has landed, and a commander isn't measured by the size of his chair," Seasqrd said.

"Sir?" Atamz asked.

"You're pushing this crew too hard, let them do their jobs," Seasqrd whispered.

"But I have to push hard; they're just not as good as the machines," Atamz whispered back.

Vector and Meedioride slowly turned in their chairs; they stared at their captain, then at each other then they looked at Lt. Romeda. When Ray turned to see Romeda's face she had a scowl across it. He then turned back to the admiral and spoke from the side of his mouth. "They're not a great crew, but they do have great hearing."

Ray was about to order his crew around some more when the admiral tapped his arm. Seasqrd pointed directly at one of the geometric shapes. Atamz recognized the little blue triangle as the Aeon Owl. It was moving away from the mean looking red ovals that represent Zlythetaur bats. Seasqrd moved his finger and poked at the top of the holograph where a very large, green rectangle was coming down.

"The Aeon Owl is acting as a diversion. Peter's decoying the enemy so the squadron can reach the Zenith without giving away our position," Seasqrd said.

"With the ram-rocket engaged those little, red ovals will never catch the Aeon Owl," Atamz said.

Seasqrd looked at the cartographic cart intently. "What about the big, green rectangle?"

"He can outmaneuver them all the way he's flying."

"That's still quite a few red ovals for our little, blue triangle to handle. What happens when the ram-rocket exhausts its very limited fuel supply?" Seasqrd asked.

"That's a good question," someone said.

Ray Atamz spun around in his chair. He was outraged to see his chief medical officer on the bridge at a time like this. "Your place is in hosp-hold," he said.

"Ray, do something, Peter needs your help. I feel it," Jane MaCardiak said. Ray knew there was no arguing with the good doctor. She was always overprotective of that kid.

"Captain to Zenith computer," Ray Atamz said, looking up at the ceiling mic. A transistorized voice spoke back in laconic tones.

"*Computer is computing.*"

"Correlate solution to current problem. How the heck do we rescue our friends?" Ray Atamz asked.

Jane MaCardiak leaned up next to Lt. Andrea Romeda and whispered, "You see he thinks more of the opinion of his ship then he ever did mine."

"I hate it when people whisper behind someone's back." Ray shifted back, sinking into his chair while facing the scowls of his entire bridge crew. "Come on computer; I'm waiting."

* * *

Out in space, a few quick lazer-blazer salvos followed by a proton bomb barrage proved quite effective in luring the bats away, but suddenly the Aeon Owl sputtered to a halt.

"Oh no," Peter said. "We've lost ram-rocket power."

"Don't lose confidence," Dya said. "You're in the zone."

Inspired by Dya's words of praise, Peter Pulsaar thought of a scheme to get them out of this jam. Fuel was low and the shields were going, but Peter had a hunch about being in the zone.

"Set a course for coordinates one thirty by three forty-five!" he said.

"That will take us directly into the Unknown Zone." Her antennae popped up.

"Let's say I have a positive feeling about it," Peter said.

The Aeon Owl dove and spun with the bats closing in for the kill. Ahead of them lay the twirling, ominous gas clouds of the Unknown Zone. The Owl pierced through the mauve mists in an explosion of static; the bats followed right behind breaking through the venomous vapors just as Peter anticipated. Peter spun the Aeon Owl around then fired his weapons. As they emerged from the Unknown Zone, Peter looked at his smiling co-pilot with pride.

"You got them. You got them! You have got the power!" Dya said.

"Let's hope so, beautiful," Peter said. "Now I have to land on an invisible cosmicraft."

*　　*　　*

Back aboard the bridge of the Zenith, Ray Atamz prepared for battle; the air was electrified by combat even though no weapons had been fired and it wasn't the Z he was worried about.

"Damn it, Ray!"

"That is enough, Doctor!" Captain Atamz turned away from Jane MaCardiak.

"Would you and your precious Zenith do something!" she said.

Ray faced the cartographic cart. "It's been my experience that thinking too much can be bad. My belief has been when in doubt fire. There's no problem a few laser blasts can't handle. The Aeon Owl bought the Zenith time, now the Zenith is going to return the favor!"

"Stop the speech making! You have to rescue Peter!" the doctor screeched.

Admiral Seasqrd raised a hand as if trying to slow Jane down. He said, "I think I see what Ray has in mind and I have a hunch it'll work."

"Activate the see-plate," Atamz said. Lt. Andrea Romeda touched a button by her console. The steel plating on the far wall of the bridge slowly slid open, revealing the see-plate. The plastic screen lit up and went from blue to black and then the crew was able to see the Havoccraft in front of them.

"Reduce to lowest magnification," Atamz said, staring at the massive war craft that filled the see-plate.

"It is on lowest magnification," Lt. Romeda said.

"Wow!" Atamz said.

"Steady, Captain Atamz, steady," Admiral Seasqrd said as he took a place by Ray's side. "You're a cosmicraft commander. Let them know who is in charge."

"Fire lazer blazers! Launch proton barrage!" Captain Atamz ordered.

Moments later the see-plate exploded with bursts of energy and explosions of laser light. The admiral put his hand up to shield his eyes and said, "That's great, Ray, but I meant you should show your crew."

The captain, the doctor and the admiral watched as the onslaught Ray commanded fell upon the Havoccraft. Slowly the horrible warship spun about and headed away from the Aeon Owl.

"Ray you did it!" Dr. MaCardiak clapped her hands together. "Peter is safe."

"Great work, Captain." The admiral patted Ray's shoulder. On the see-plate the Havoccraft grew larger and larger. The gaping maw of the monstrous head at its prow opened, firing a force beam. Electrorays fired from its eyes, while upon the Havoccraft's amidships, powerful ionizers fired devastating bolts.

"Only now they're after us!" Atamz said. He paused, trying to conceive of the perfect counter attack. "Helm take evasive action!" he yelled.

The bridge tilted as the Zenith outmaneuvered the Havoccraft. Disruptorays fired from the Havoccraft's wings and bombarded the general vicinity of the Zenith, but the cosmicraft floated away to safety.

"This is great!" Atamz said to the admiral. "The Z have no idea where we are. I'm going to launch another attack."

"But just as they can't find us," Seasqrd said.

"Neither can the Aeon Owl." Captain Atamz put his fingers to his mouth and gasped.

*   *   *

Out in space, Peter Pulsaar and Dya Nammock sucked in what was left of the air within their vessel.

"We're out of fuel," Dya murmured. "I'm switching life-support over to battery power. That will buy us time."

"You can think all the positive thoughts you want, but I have no clue where to find the Zenith. I've wasted our fuel flying in circles. I'm a rotten pilot. I've lost the power," Peter said.

"You've lost nothing. Remain posit...." Dya Nammock fell silent as she went unconscious.

Peter drew in one final deep breath and said, "I've lost something: our lives."

CHAPTER 11
THOSE SCI-FI GUYS ESCAPE INTO THE UNKNOWN ZONE

Back aboard the Zenith bridge, Captain Atamz was still locked in two battles. He continued ordering attacks against the Havoccraft then evasive maneuvers then listened to the rantings of Jane MaCardiak.

"Damn it, why doesn't Peter land?" she said.

"He can't while we're lurking," Atamz said. He turned to his crew and bellowed, "Fire full lazer-blazers!"

"Can't you help him land?"

"He knows as well as I do that a homing beacon, distress signal or any communication between the Zenith and the Aeon Owl will divulge our coordinates." Ray backed away from a control panel that burst into sparks. "Damage control procedures for all decks... especially the bridge!"

"Can't you shut your dumb lurking device off long enough for him to land?"

"And let the Havoccraft lock their arsenal onto our exact position," Atamz said. "They're hitting us this hard and they don't know where we are."

"Typical man." MaCardiak folded her arms. "You have an answer for everything. You weren't this smart when you were begging me for help on your quantum chemistry exam and what about when you frat brothers tricked you with that shape shifter from Seti Gomorrah?"

"That really is enough, Doctor!"

Admiral Seasqrd leaned over one of the many scopes and said, "Readings show only a minute left of air aboard the Aeon Owl."

The admiral and his yeoman stared at Captain Atamz. Jane MaCardiak stared at him. Lt. Romeda, Lt. Commander

Meedioride, Ensign Vector and the rest of the bridge crew stared at him.

"It's your decision, Ray," Seasqrd said.

Ray had trouble thinking of what to do. He looked upward for guidance.

"Captain to Zenith computer."

"Oh Ray, please," Dr. MaCardiak said.

"Engage tractor beam!" Atamz said.

*   *   *

The Aeon Owl screeched to a halt and bashed against the bulkhead. Through blurred vision Peter Pulsaar could see the hangar crew, led by Admiral Seasqrd, race towards the wounded space vessel. It seemed like they and everything else was going in slow motion until Seasqrd opened the canopy. Dya and Peter began sucking in gasps of air. Jane MaCardiak administered some medical treatment with her injecterdermic.

"Peter, Peter!" she said.

"He was quite remarkable." Dya took in one last breath. "He went beyond even the hopes of my positive thinking. Fuel gone, engines down, life support failing and he was still able to pilot us in."

"He has the power," Seasqrd said as he patted Peter Pulsaar's face.

"I was just lucky. Any pilot could've done it." Peter closed his eyes and felt Admiral Seasqrd lift him from the cockpit. When he opened his eyes he watched Dya being helped by Jane's medical staff.

Suddenly the deck rocked and the crew was thrown off their feet. Peter and Dya fell to the floor. Again the ship rocked, the lights flashed and the crew flew across the hangar, bouncing from bulkhead to bulkhead.

"Is everyone alright?" Admiral Seasqrd asked.

"I'm fine," Peter said. But Jane ran to him anyway.

"You sure you're alright?" she asked while her hands were all over his face and body.

"Really I'm fine. What about Dya?" Peter said.

Jane had a blank expression on her face. "Who?" She looked at Dya. "Oh her, I'm sure she'll be fine. She just needs to think positive."

Dya rose to her feet, brushing off her tight flight suit. "Thank you doctor; I remain unharmed."

"What hit us?" Peter asked.

"It's the Havoccraft!" Seasqrd said.

Dya's antennae ears sprang up as she said, "They must have locked on to us by tracing the tractor beam to its source."

"It's all my fault. We're going to be destroyed because of me." Peter got to his feet and gently pushed Jane away.

"No one is going to be destroyed, but I'm sure Ray will need me," Admiral Seasqrd said.

"I'll join you," Dya said, following the admiral.

"Wait!" Peter said. "I want to talk to you."

Dya stopped in confusion; she looked at Peter waiting for him to explain further but Peter didn't know how to explain what he wanted from her.

"No. Hosp-hold is the place for you. Come with me," MaCardiak said grabbing Peter's arm.

"Jane, really, I am fine. I want to be with Dya," Peter said, politely.

The doctor stood back, acting affronted. The admiral turned and said, "His genetically enhanced metabolism will have him back to normal in no time, Jane. Now, I'm sure there are plenty of secureaDy guards on their way down to hosp-hold. You know how they never last."

The admiral then dashed through the open hangar doors while the ship rocked again. Dr. MaCardiak looked at Peter and said, "Fine, you don't need my help."

She pointed at the rear of the hangar and her medical staff immediately followed. Peter felt bad but anxiously waited for Jane to retreat out the opposite end of the hangar. The doctor stopped to glower one last time before the doors swooshed closed across her more than slightly miffed face.

"Emotional thing, isn't she?" Dya said.

Peter didn't have time to explain how things were and always had been between him and Jane MaCardiak; he looked around, making sure no one was looking, then he put his hands around Dya's shoulders and waist. Dya pulled back ready to deliver the Youkan punch.

"What are you doing?" she asked.

Peter whispered, "I need you —"

"How dare you?" Dya exclaimed. "We're both officers."

"No, you didn't let me finish," Peter said, "I need you to give me that mind-mesh again."

*   *   *

Up on the Zenith bridge Ray Atamz waved his hand through puffs of smoke as flashing lights beeped louder and louder. He stopped biting his nails long enough to order the Zenith about and then ordered a spread of proton bombs. Lt. Meedioride followed the captain's orders and brought the Zenith around at full speed. Out maneuvering the Havoccraft's counter attack the Zenith swiftly descended below her massive foe.

"Captain, the enemy is descending upon us," the yeoman said in between chokes.

"It's as I feared, they've locked onto our energy signature from our old position. They're using it to guide their assaults," Atamz said.

"Our deflection plates are at twenty percent power!" Ensign Vector yelled.

"Why aren't we firing back?" Atamz asked.

"The energy conviculators are off line," Meedioride said. "We can't get power to the weapons."

"Captain!" the yeoman stumbled across the bridge. "I did an extra-credit project on energy conviculators back at the academy."

"Go for it, yeoman!" Atamz said.

The yeoman saluted and ran to the jetevator. As the door slid open, Admiral Seasqrd stepped forward. They bumped into one another. She put her arms around him to keep from falling. Ray was about to ask the admiral if Peter and Dya were alright, but he did not wish to interrupt Seasqrd and his yeoman as they embraced.

"Where the devil are you off to?" Seasqrd asked as he held her in his arms.

"Just wish me luck, Gene Lucas." She kissed his cheek and darted into the jetevator. The doors swooshed closed just as Admiral Seasqrd said, "Good luck... yeoman... I keep forgetting her real name."

Captain Atamz stood clinging to his reclino-chair waiting for the admiral to turn around.

"Has the Owl landed?" he asked.

*   *   *

Peter Pulsaar was following Dya Nammock down a narrow passageway, pleading for her help; they then bounced about the corridor as the ship shook.

"Dya, wait!" Peter put his hands up bracing for another bounce against the wall.

"I need to be on the bridge!" Dya steadied herself trying to keep her balance.

"I need you!" Peter said.

She ignored him, continuing on her course for the nearest jetevator. Peter headed her off and pounded his fist against the bulkhead, leaving a dent in the metal plating. He looked at Dya and said, "You see it's only when I get mad that I'm able to fully utilize my power. That is until you came along and helped me with your mind-mesh."

"You cannot become dependent on me," Dya said. "You need to be able to utilize your abilities on your own."

"So what do you suggest?" Peter asked. "I get someone to irritate the hell out of me every time I have a task to do."

159

Dya stood in front of a control panel in the wall. She flipped a switch and a hatch in the ceiling opened, allowing the escaladder to lower.

Then she said, "My duty is on the bridge. You must find your duty and do something with it."

A pair of boots appeared on the top rung of the escalader and hastily climbed down. It was Admiral Seasqrd's yeoman; she suddenly dropped down and landed on Peter. Dya climbed up onto the ladder as the yeoman and Peter got up. The hatch closed.

"Sorry Lieutenant. It's my duty to fix the energy conviculators to our weapons!" The yeoman raced down the hall.

Peter watched her disappear down the corridor and for some reason he followed.

*   *   *

Admiral Seasqrd stepped out of the way of one scurrying crewman only to bump into another. He took a place next to Captain Atamz, but the captain was looking around at the jetevator doors.

"Good to have you back on the bridge, Commander," Atamz said as Dya Nammock stepped out of the jetevator then he looked at the ceiling. "Computer compute computations on Captain's scope."

"What is your plan, Captain?" asked Seasqrd while Ray's face turned blue from the glow of the scope he stared at.

He did not answer; he looked up at Dya and said, "Bring plasma capacitors up to full capacity and reroute the radioactive waste vents into our propulsors."

"But, Captain," Dya said, "won't that leave an energy wake a half a parsec wide behind us."

"Exactly," Atamz replied. He turned to Michael Meedioride and said, "Use a hyperbolic resonance wave to create a harmonic static field through our deflection plates."

160

"Captain Atamz," Admiral Seasqrd said, "I... uh... what are you... never mind."

The admiral became silent as he watched the helmsman busy himself pressing buttons while Dya Nammock ran from computer console to matrix monitor, making sure the rest of the bridge crew were on task. Admiral Seasqrd just watched and scratched the power port on his head. He said to himself, "Speaking of a parsec, Sam would love this."

"Capacitors capacitating and radiation rerouted, Captain," Dya said.

"Good," Atamz said. "Now, use our probe plate to flood the area with neutrinos."

As Dya walked by, the admiral swung his arm about hers, pulling her to the side. "I hope you understand what he's talking about because I sure don't," Seasqrd whispered.

"Watch the cartographic-cart, sir," Dya said, "If my hunch is correct, the captain is about to forge our signature."

* * *

Though she knew it was a human superstition based on frailty, Dya crossed her fingers as she, Captain Atamz and Admiral Seasqrd glued their eyes to the cartographic-cart, watching the image of the mighty Havoccraft drift over the little Zenith Three. The Zenith's deck plates rumbled and her bulkheads shivered as the Havoccraft floated right above them.

The crew waited in suspense while Captain Atamz peered upwards, listening to the roar of the Havoccraft's engines and said, "Now raise the Zenith 10,000 space-fathoms."

"Aye, Captain," Dya said.

Slowly, the little, blue trapezoid that represented the Zenith Three on the cartographic-cart elevated itself until it was right behind the Havoccraft.

"They can't find us." Ray Atamz pointed at the see-plate. "Our signature is covered by their energy wake."

"Excellent, Ray!" Seasqrd said.

The bridge crew rejoiced.

"And once we have our weapons back on line, we shall hit them with everything we've got right at their stern!" Ray threw his fist in the air.

The bridge crew cheered all except Dya.

Commander Dya Nammock stood by the cartographic-cart and said, "Captain, sir."

"The technology of the Z is no match for ours!" Atamz said,

The bridge crew applauded.

"Captain Atamz, you're attention is required," Dya said.

"As her name implies, the Zenith has risen to a new height!" Atamz said.

Dya stamped her boot on the deck plate and said, "Captain, please!"

"Oh what is it Dya?" Captain Atamz said.

"The Havoccraft is reversing course!"

"It's doing what?" Atamz asked. He looked at the holograph, watching the great big, green rectangle float backwards into the oncoming trapezoid.

"Take evasive action!" Atamz commanded.

"Too late," Dya said as she fell into the cartographic-cart; Admiral Seasqrd pulled her back into his arms. She watched other crew members fly against the floor while Captain Atamz staggered back into his chair. As the lights flashed and sparks flew from the command console the beeping sounds of the bridge stopped beeping and the lights went out. One moment later amber emergency lights were on and the ship lurched forward.

"*Warning! Collision!*" stated the voice of the Zenith computer.

"We know!" Dya wrenched herself from the Admiral's brawny arms. She punched a button on the computer console and said, "Captain, they have us in a tractor beam."

The captain looked around but said nothing.

"Orders?" Dya asked.

162

"Uh, I think...." Atamz said.

"Sir?"

"I'll be in my ready-room. Admiral, you have the conn!" Captain Atamz said then darted for the narrow doorway at the back of the bridge. The door swooshed open and Captain Atamz stepped in. The doors swooshed closed behind him.

Then the jetevator doors swooshed open; Doctor MaCardiak stepped out. Dya wondered why the ship's chief medical officer wanted to be on the bridge all the time.

"Should you not be in hosp-hold, Doctor?" Dya asked.

"Does anyone up here need medical attention?" the doctor replied. "Where's Peter is he alright?"

Dya was about to order her off the bridge when she remembered she wasn't the ranking officer in charge. Just then she felt Admiral Seasqrd's hand on her shoulder. He asked, "What's Captain Atamz doing in the captain's ready-room?"

"Difficult to say, sir," Dya said. "It's not a ready-room. It's a bathroom."

"What?" Seasqrd asked.

"Captain Atamz just likes to call it the ready-room. He thinks it sounds more military," Dya shrugged her shoulders.

The deck shook beneath their feet again. Both Dya and the admiral stumbled back against a short-circuited console. Ensign Vector looked up at them and said, "The conviculators are back on line!"

"We have power to the weapons," Dya said.

"No we don't. Keep those weapons off line," Admiral Seasqrd said to the stunned bridge crew.

Dya felt her antennae sloping back around her head as she said, "Say again, Admiral?"

* * *

Admiral Seasqrd sat in the captain's reclino-chair and said, "Open a communication with the Z. Their commander will want to talk with me regarding our surrender."

The entire bridge crew spun around. Lt. Romeda, while blinking rapidly, asked, "You want to talk surrender with Darklone?"

"You heard me." Seasqrd turned to Lt. Romeda. "Do it."

As the lieutenant opened hailing frequencies the admiral turned towards the chief medical officer and said, "And Dr. MaCardiak you have a patient awaiting you."

The doctor turned her head towards where the admiral was pointing and said, "You want me to hide in the bathroom with Ray?"

"Doctor!"

"Alright, I'll try and help," MaCardiak said.

A hatch opened within the ceiling and a large teletube lowered down. The inside of the wide, cylindrical, glass tube became shiny with static. Lt. Romeda said, "We've opened a ship to ship communiqué with the Havoccraft."

Admiral Seasqrd looked at the teletube, the static slowly cleared, and staring back at him was the face of Darklone. At first, Seasqrd felt like he was looking in a mirror, but the mirror image was twisted and warped and had sinister crags in its face and a malevolent mustache and beard dangled like wire cords around the mouth and chin.

"Seasqrd, my old comrade, it seems I have you at last," Darklone said as the lights about his power port began to flash.

"Darklone, you have the Zenith, but you don't have me."

"I have defeated you," Darklone said, as he twisted his triangular beard.

"No old friend. Your Havoccraft with its superior might has defeated this cosmicraft, but you still have not proven that your power is greater than mine. If you want to prove who has the mightier power than you have to beat me," Seasqrd said

"What is it you propose, Admiral?"

"I'll have a portahole brought to the Zenith bridge," Seasqrd said. "You have one brought to your bridge. I will teleport to you and you let the Zenith go free, then we will have it out—one to one."

Though the bridge crew stood exchanging incredulous looks of dismay the admiral knew he had hit his mark. Darklone's face was pensive as it stood framed within the teletube, nodding. He finally said, "Yes, in the end I will be the one."

"Then you agree to my terms."

"I agree if," Darklone said then he paused. "And only if you bring the schematics for your ship's lurking device with you."

Seasqrd put his head down and laughed. "You drive a hard bargain, but I agree."

"I will give you seventy microns." Darklone's face disappeared from the teletube.

"Admiral you can't do it!" Dya said.

Admiral Seasqrd rubbed his chin. He said, "Just think positive, Commander."

*   *   *

Dr. Jane MaCardiak had finally gotten used to the smell, but she was finding that getting into the captain's head was not as easy as just stepping into the bathroom. Jane sat on the toilet with Ray lying on the tile floor next to her. She could tell Ray was a manic mess. His eyes were flitting about at light speed as his trembling lips had become chapped.

"My ship, my ship," he said.

"Why are you being so hard on yourself?"

"My ship," he said again. "But it's not my fault. It's not my fault."

Ray lifted his head, placing his hands to his chest. Jane did not know what to think.

"Seasqrd distracted me." Ray closed his eyes. "If he hadn't then I would have seen the danger to my ship; they're all blaming me I know it, but it wasn't my fault!"

Jane placed her finger beneath Ray's chin, lifting his face; he opened his tearful eyes. She said, "No one blames you."

"Yes they do because they hate me and… because… I am to blame."

"You're being too hard on yourself. You're a good captain. Now get out there and take command."

"You don't understand the pressure of sitting in that chair."

"Do you prefer the one I'm on?" She pointed at the toilet.

"You don't understand! It was my fault!" Ray pounded his fist on the tile. "Why didn't I see that the enemy was reversing? I let my guard down for one moment and I… I…."

"You made a mistake."

"How could I malfunction like that?" Ray buried his head against Jane's thigh. "I'm a cosmicraft captain. This isn't supposed to happen to me. I am supposed to be like one with my ship."

"There, there, there." Jane patted the back of her captain's head. "You haven't changed a bit. You know everything about machines but nothing about people and that includes yourself."

Ray pulled away in scorn. "What do you mean?" he asked.

"You've gotten so obsessed with technology that you think you can just do a self-diagnostic to keep yourself from making mistakes. Well, take it from someone who has studied the human machine. We are a bit more complex than these gadgets you adore so much."

"Jane, I don't want a lecture." He lifted his head and leaned away.

"What the heck do you want?"

"Oh, Jane, you're the one who hasn't changed. As soon as I lower my shields you let me have it amidships." Ray slumped back against the wall.

Jane realized she had always been too tough on Ray. She had been so since their days at the academy, but she only did it because she knew that if he would just stop the swaggering and posturing he could be more than a truly great captain; he could be a great person. Then she came to a startling realization — she and Ray were much more alike than she would ever admit. The exception at the moment was that she was not the one laying next to a toilet whimpering.

"Ray listen, I'm your doctor and your ex-girlfriend. Leave this bathroom and get back on the bridge before you really do become pathetic," Jane whispered.

She kissed him on the cheek; he rose and walked to the door. The bathroom door swooshed open and Captain Ray Atamz stepped out of the bathroom, pulled the toilet paper off the bottom of his boot, wiped the lipstick off his face and marched over behind his chair where Admiral Seasqrd sat before a blank teletube.

"Just don't stand there; someone give me a status report," Atamz said.

Admiral Seasqrd spun about in the reclino-chair and winked at Dr. MaCardiak as the bathroom door swooshed closed behind her. She knew what Seasqrd was thinking; it was good to see Raymond J. Atamz, pompous, arrogant and back to his old self.

Just then, face appeared within a teletube that hung in front of the admiral; Jane stepped back against the bulkhead, letting out a gasp. The face was like that of Admiral Seasqrd's but it was malevolent; it was evil; it was the face of Darklone.

"What the photon is going on aboard my ship?" Atamz pointed at the teletube and gestured towards Dya, who was placing a portahole in front of Admiral Seasqrd.

"Good to have you back, Captain Atamz, now get out of my way," the admiral said and Ray immediately stepped back.

"Your time is up, Gene Lucas," Darklone said.

Ray and Jane exchanged looks of total confusion.

"So it is, lower your shields and here I come," Seasqrd replied.

Ray stepped forward, taking the admiral's arm and pulling back. Seasqrd pulled free and Ray landed on the floor. Seasqrd looked down and said, "Sorry but a hero must do what he must do."

"Admiral..." Ray said, "Gene Lucas, you're not going to...." Captain Atamz got up and was about to try stopping the admiral again but Dya stood in his way, blocking him.

Darklone snickered. "Look how worried Cosmos-Corps is about the great Gene Lucas Seasqrd."

Seasqrd sneered but said nothing until he asked, "Has the Havoccraft lowered its shields yet?"

"The Havoccraft has lowered its shields," said Meedioride.

Jane stood waiting; she knew something was about to happen; there was something up the admiral's sleeve besides his muscular arm. All of a sudden Admiral Seasqrd stepped back from the portahole and commanded, "Bring weapons on line and fire!"

Meedioride and Vector merrily and swiftly followed his orders. Jane wasn't sure but she guessed by all the lights and sounds of the bridge getting so bright and loud at once that the Zenith's weapons were about to launch a devastating attack. Darklone must have surmised the same thing because of his reaction to Seasqrd's action.

"NO!" Darklone screamed so loud that the teletube containing his image rattled.

"I got the power," Seasqrd said and ordered communications closed as the Zenith's arsenal blasted away at the Havoccraft's stern. Jane had to shield her eyes from the bursts of exploding lights that filled the see-plate.

"We're free of the tractor beam," Dya shouted, while scanning a screen.

"Computer, provide computations on quickest escape route," Atamz said, looking up at the ceiling mic, but Admiral Seasqrd countermanded him.

"Helm, course twelve thirty by ten fifteen," he said.

"But, Admiral, you're taking us into the Unknown Zone," Atamz said.

"You know another way out of this?" the admiral replied.

Jane watched Ray shrug his shoulders; they then stared at the cartographic-cart. Jane watched a little trapezoid lumber ahead into the wispy clouds of what she assumed was the Unknown Zone. The fiendish murkiness seemed to reach out and envelop the trapezoid. Up across the see-plate the screen was filled with a fog of celestial dust and vapors. Then a noise Jane knew would be terrible to the captain's ears filled the bridge. It was not a red alert; it wasn't a hull breech; it was worse.

"Hooray for Admiral Seasqrd! He saved us from the Havoccraft!" shouted the helmsman.

"Hooray!" shouted the bridge crew.

Ray Atamz turned around and looked at Jane again, who simply shrugged her shoulders.

"If anyone needs me, I'll be in my ready-room," Atamz said,

Suddenly, the jetevator doors swooshed open.

Jane grasped her chest in shock. Standing in the open jetevator doors was Peter Pulsaar. He held the yeoman's body in his arms.

* * *

"How could you reptiles let them escape?" Darklone bellowed. Zlythetaurs cowered before the rampaging Darklone as he stomped across the battle-bridge. "Such ineptitude cannot go unpunished!" he said.

He kicked the gunnery officer under the tail, sending him flying over the weapons console. He took the boatswain by the tail and flung him into the naviterminals; then Zatan intruded by saying, "No need for this excessive physical violence. May I suggest the tortucalator?"

With the ship's pilot squirming in his grip, Darklone said, "The tortucalator; what's that?"

"We Zlythetaurs are very sophisticated in the ways we dispense cruelty." Zatan withdrew a flat, round object with tiny spikes around its diameter and a single button in its center.

"No... no, it wasn't my fault," said the ship's pilot as Darklone took the tortucalator from Zatan.

"Take your discipline with pride, please," Zatan requested as he showed Darklone where to place the device. Darklone placed the tortucalator on the Zlythetaur's bulbous head finding it fit perfectly within his ridge of horns. He pressed the button.

All the Zlythetaur could do was reply in garbled chokes while the tortucalator lit up. Darklone smiled with delight and pressed the button again driving the ship's pilot to his knees.

"This is an amazing bit of technology and so easy to operate," Darklone said.

He pressed the button again and the Zlythetaur's head seemed like it was about to burst.

"Indeed it is and since there are only intense thought waves of pain, with no anatomical damage, you may apply it indefinitely," Zatan said.

"Really," Darklone said. The pilot finally began to rise when Darklone hit the button on the tortucalator again. The Zlythetaur's snake eyes welled with tears just before he dropped to the floor in agony. Darklone smiled again and said, "You see this is the problem with Cosmos-Corps. They would never conceive of such a device."

"We have found the tortucalator to be an excellent means of enforcing obedience," Zatan said.

"I certainly agree," Darklone said.

"The tortucalator averts insurrection and insubordination; it maintains discipline and prevents incompetence," Zatan said.

"Yes," Darklone said as he removed the tortucalator from the grateful but drooling pilot and stalked towards Zatan, who became confused. Then he became frightened.

"I am the High Commander," he said.

"Yes and as High Commander, are you not responsible for the training and performance of the crew?" Darklone said.

Zatan stood back and said, "But I—"

"Incompetence cannot be tolerated." Darklone raised his arm. "Take your discipline with pride, please."

Zatan looked around, finding no sympathy amongst the crew of the battle-bridge especially the ship's pilot. He leaned forward, allowing Darklone to employ the tortucalator and said "Hail, hate."

Darklone pressed the button.

Only a few moments passed before the Zlythetaur High Commander fell to the deck plates, but soon after Darklone removed the tortucalator, his reptilian eyes began to flicker and soon he rose. Darklone nodded approvingly at the small device in his hand.

"Have this ship repaired," Darklone said. "We must move on with great haste."

"The Havoccraft will be prepared to continue our mission of Earth's conquest."

Darklone stared at his second-in-command and said, "No you fool! We are charting a course into the Unknown Zone. I have not finished hurting Seasqrd."

"But our mission is to—"

When Darklone raised the tortucalator to his Zatan's face, the wretched reptilian bit his forked tongue, coiled his tail under his back and ordered the crew to set a course for the Unknown Zone. "I told you before I like to hurt Seasqrd. He hurt me with that trick that allowed him to escape so now I must hurt him back and keep on hurting him. I like hurting things," Darklone said.

He saw the look of confusion on Zatan's lizard-like face and realized it was shared by the entire crew as he looked about the battle-bridge. Darklone moved his head back and his chin up, letting out a heavy sigh. He said slowly and pedantically, "We will find the Zenith and capture her lurking device. That will make the Havoccraft completely invincible. And I will at last have revenge on Seasqrd. Good enough?"

CHAPTER 12
THOSE SCI-FI GUYS GET LOST IN SPACE

Down in hosp-hold, Dr. MaCardiak pulled a sheet over the yeoman's head while Admiral Seasqrd and Peter Pulsaar stood, trying to hold back their tears. Jane had known the torment of losing a patient; she had lost count of how many secureday guards she had pulled a sheet over but this time felt especially painful. There was a swoosh sound and Dya walked in. She stood motionless by the table next to Jane and said, "I grieve with thee, Admiral."

"She was a fine yeoman and a fine shipmate." Seasqrd dried his eyes.

"An excellent epitaph," Dya said remaining emotionless. She turned to Peter and asked, "You are unharmed?"

"My genetically heightened stamina allowed me to withstand the radiation burst," Peter said. He moved his hand over the yeoman's lifeless body and said, "She stayed in the conviculator room though I ordered her out. She was determined to get them back on line."

"I'm sorry, but we must not give up hope," MaCardiak said.

Dr. MaCardiak walked over to a table where the brain she had just removed floated in a jar of blue liquid. "Though her body was poisoned by radiation, her mind still lives in this hibernation fluid. There may come a time when our medical science could place her brain in some host body, but for now there's nothing else I can do. There was no other way."

"Of course, if Peter had brought her right to hosp-hold rather than bringing her to the bridge first, it might have given you some valuable time to operate on her—"

Jane MaCardiak yelled, "It would have made no difference! You inhuman—"

"Stop it both of you!" Peter said. "I know it was my fault. I know I'm not perfect and damn it who would want to be?"

Peter Pulsaar ran out of hosp-hold knocking an ensign out of the way as he fought from bursting into tears. The doors swooshed closed. Admiral Seasqrd said, "Well, I'm on my way to the bridge while you two fight it out."

The doors swooshed closed again.

"Doctor, I merely wanted to point out Lt. Pulsaar's error in judgment in hopes he'd be inspired not to repeat such an action."

"You could've employed a little more tact, Dya."

"Why do you humans put such value on subtlety and tact? Subtlety and tact do not solve problems, as well as constructive criticism. Why do humans fail to see the importance of developing a proactive path in life?" Dya asked.

"Why do you fail to see that your destructive criticism does more harm than good? Could it be because you enjoy pointing out imperfections in others so you can show off how perfect you think you are?" Dr. MaCardiak stood with her arms folded. "You totally destroyed Peter and all because you couldn't keep your big Youkanian mouth shut."

"Nonsense, my purpose was to... that is I merely... my intent was to solve... I just wanted to equate...."

Dya paused; she acted like she was about to finally finish her statement when, with pouting lips, red eyes and hard stomp against the floor she rushed through the swooshing doors of hosp-hold.

Jane muttered, "Good and stay away from him."

*   *   *

Up on the bridge, Admiral Seasqrd was still dwelling on his yeoman; he had just stepped out of the jetevator when Ray Atamz immediately took him aside.

"Admiral, it is just as I feared; our probe plate and navigatrometer are useless inside the Unknown Zone and we also cannot activate our chronosphere. Without our technology I don't what to do. I hate to admit it, but we're lost in space,"

Atamz said quietly, trying not let the crew over hear him this time.

Seasqrd knew that Captain Atamz needed a boost of confidence; he needed to be reassured of his many talents. In a very philosophic tone the admiral answered, "Many ships have been lost within the Unknown Zone, Ray, but not the Zenith. Remember what makes the Unknown Zone truly fearsome is that it's not just a segment of space filled with nebulous clouds of ionized gases and static emissions; it's a dimension that stretches from the pit of our despair to the pinnacle of our fear but we are only bound by the limits of our imagination. You must not give into the fear but use your imagination; be creative and a way out will appear."

Captain Atamz began nodding his head in acknowledgement. "I see what you mean, sir."

Seasqrd placed his hands on Ray's shoulders. "I'm glad you do."

Ray rubbed his chin and said, "Well, without our machines we will have to rely on my piloting skills."

"What?" Admiral Seasqrd said.

Ray Atamz smiled and placed his hand about Seasqrd's waist; he patted his back and said, "You remember, Admiral, what a navigator I always was."

Though he tried to hold it back, tears filled Seasqrd's eyes and, suddenly, he began to sob. Ray Atamz placed his arms about the admiral and said, "There, there, sir, I know how you must feel over what happened to your yeoman."

*　　*　　*

The Zenith drifted aimlessly through the Unknown Zone. Without navigational control it was up to Captain Atamz's piloting skills to steer the ship and as Admiral Seasqrd had anticipated within only mere macrons the Zenith became hopelessly lost. Finally, the wandering cosmicraft floated near a planet with a hospitable atmosphere.

Admiral Seasqrd stood before the see-plate with his arms folded behind his back while listening to Ray Atamz shouting orders.

"Helm come about. Okay, come about some more. Whatever it takes to get us into a landing pattern for that planet," Captain Atamz said. Admiral Seasqrd turned about to face Ray as the captain approached from behind. "Once we touchdown, sir, we can effect repairs?"

Seasqrd nodded. He looked at the strange new world before him and placed his fingers about the pendant that dangled from his neck; he found himself thinking of the Animazon Queen and ole Sam Parseck.

"Attention Earth ship!" a voice came over the ship's communication system. Seasqrd and the entire bridge crew looked at the audio-alerter in the ceiling in bewilderment.

"Someone or something has opened a communiqué with the Zenith, sir," Lt. Romeda said as she swiveled around in her chair.

"Where's it coming from?" asked Captain Atamz.

"I know that voice," Seasqrd said and again found himself drifting into the past.

"It's some sort of hyperadio transmission being beamed from that planet," Romeda said to the captain.

"Hyperadio is only a theory," said the captain.

"I make theories into realities," said the voice.

"Now I know who it is!" said Seasqrd.

The admiral walked quickly over to Lt. Romeda's station. She began touching buttons, attempting to get a fix on the source of the transmission and clear it of static. As the blinking vertical lines across her computer board switched to horizontal, the transmission became more audible.

"Earth ship," the voice repeated. The white crystal centered in the audio-alerter flashed red faster and faster as the voice became more insistent. "Please veer off. Do not approach this world. Go away!" it shouted.

Seasqrd stood over the communications console and replied to the voice of warning in a gleeful tone. "Rozwelles!" he said, "It's me Gene Lucas. I thought I should never hear from you again!"

"Gene Lucas Seasqrd!" Rozwelles said in a tone that showed cheer through all the static. "Though I'd love to catch up on the latest ways Earth has misused my genius, I must insist you do not land your ship on my planet."

Captain Atamz, Commander Nammock and Peter had joined Seasqrd by the communications console. Seasqrd looked at them in befuddlement. Ray replied with a grunt and Peter squinted hard like he was having trouble seeing the communications board. Realizing he was going to get nothing from the captain or pilot, Seasqrd looked to Commander Nammock. She mouthed her words and in his mind Seasqrd agreed; Rozwelles was hiding something.

Seasqrd scratched his head looked down at the console and said, "Negative, Dr. Rozwelles. Our ship is in desperate need of repair. We must land."

"Once again you refuse to heed my advice," Rozwelles shouted back. "This is the copyclator all over again."

"Uhh...the copyclator was your idea, remember?" Seasqrd said.

"There you go again blaming me. It wasn't my fault you couldn't control your clone. My original idea was to — "

"Now is not the time for that, Doctor! Will you let the Zenith land or not?" Seasqrd said.

There was no answer just static. Just as Seasqrd was about to speak again, a reply came. "Very well, I'll let you land on my planet, but I will not and cannot be held responsible for the safety of your crew. I will send a homing beacon. Over and out," Rozwelles said.

"Did he say his planet?" Peter asked.

The jetevator doors swooshed open. Jane MaCardiak stepped onto the bridge and said, "Rozwelles' words were heard by the entire ship."

"She really doesn't like staying down in hosp-hold does her?" Dya said.

Seasqrd, ignoring Commander Nammock's comment, approached Peter and stated, "To answer your question, Peter, it wouldn't surprise me if Rozwelles regarded this foreboding planet as more a home than Earth. Rozwelles was a genius, but he had grown bitter. His inventions seemed to do more damage than good... or so he thought. He grew resentful towards all humanity and so he fled into deep space with a rag-tag fleet of research vessels; a convoy of super-scientists who dreamt of finding a new world, where they could start over."

"A world they could make their own," Dya said.

"What a shame the world never recognized his genius," Captain Atamz said.

"Genius? He experimented with improving evolution by re-programming life-forms at the genetic level; theorized about creating living machines and envisioned a future where humanity is reduced to spare parts," Jane MaCardiak said.

"Pity his dreams never became reality," Atamz replied.

While Jane sank her face into her hands and shook her head, Admiral Seasqrd placed his hand on Ray's shoulder and said, "Those whom the gods wish to destroy, they first make mad." Then he rubbed the pendent that hung beneath the collar of his uniform once again. He then said, "And didn't Dr. Rozwelles sound pretty mad at me?"

*   *   *

Captain Atamz wasn't quite sure what Admiral Seasqrd had meant but it was obvious the admiral sensed something dangerous about Dr. Rozwelles and his planet. But one thing the captain knew for sure was his ship needed repairs. Following the homing beacon, the Zenith plodded forward on an uneasy heading for the foreboding planet of Dr. Rozwelles.

Captain Atamz ordered the ship's anchordroids to be launched. The anchordroids rocketed down into the planet's orbit, spearing into the sandy soil of an open plain. Each of the six anchordroids fed a landing pattern to the Zenith. Though she was badly injured the cosmicraft, Zenith, touched down gently on the planet's surface and up on her bridge her captain sighed in relief. Then Captain Atamz said, "Landing party, join me!"

As the gangplank slowly lowered, Ray Atamz led Dya Nammock and Peter Pulsaar down; he immediately took notice to the whirling cloud of dust off on the horizon and pointed it out to the commander and lieutenant.

"What is that?" Ray Atamz asked.

"I don't know," Peter said.

Ray did little to cover up his annoyance at Lt. Pulsaar and said, "Well, get your conclusionator and make a conclusion."

"Yes Captain," Peter said.

Ray Jay Atamz did not care for Peter's tone but was not going to address his insubordination with someone else coming down the gangplank behind them.

Dr. MaCardiak and the admiral had made their way down and spotted the dust cloud which by now had grown to the size of a small tornado, spinning its way up over the azure mountains of the alien landscape and into its purple clouds.

Ray and Dya drew out their plasma-pistols, preparing for the worst while the cloud stormed its way to a halt only a few meters off the bow of the Zenith. When the dust cleared, there appeared a strange looking automobile of sorts. The vehicle was a long platform with eight wheels and two rockets at the back, but what Ray Atamz found even more fascinating then the rocket car was what was driving it.

The robot driving the vehicle stepped out from under the transparent dome that shielded the rocket car. He stood on two columns of spheres connected by hydraulic joints that acted as legs. His torso spun about on a thick plate that sat atop his legs joining them like a pelvis. Sprouting from the sides of his torso were two accordion-like tubes, which extended out to become arms. At the end of each arm was a three pronged claw. One arm reached outwards as if to offer a welcoming gesture while the other touched the top of the robot's circular head, which framed a plastic human face.

"Greetings," a voice said from a speaker in the middle of the robot's torso, but the mouth on its plastic face remained silent, although it produced a very warm smile. "I have been sent by Dr. Rozwelles to escort you to his dwelling. Would you step in please?" the robot asked.

While lights brightened and dimmed within the glass sphere that rose from the robot's head, his arm pointed towards the rocket car.

"This is amazing," Ray Atamz said with delight.

"Certainly polite but it's freaky the way his face looks," Peter said.

"Apologies for my mouth lacking vocal power," the speaker within the robot's chest spoke again. "My creator had hoped that a human face, even if it be mute, would add warmth to my cold mien."

The robot's plastic face grinned and winked.

"I would not think it possible," Dya said, "but I am actually sensing some sort of emotional state from him."

"As if he were more than a machine; he is a mechanical man," Seasqrd said.

"Incredible." Atamz stared at the robot, eyeing the inner workings of the giant bubble that sat on top of his plastic face. "The most advanced robotic engineering I've ever seen. It actually acts autonomously of human control; it's nearly sentient. You are quite an automaton"

"Why thank you," the robot said. A look of pride crossed the plastic face while gyros and antennae spun about within the bubble above his head as if he were thinking of what to say next. "You may call me Otto."

"Otto, is that what Dr. Rozwelles calls you? Otto the automaton," Seasqrd said.

"Yes, he is awaiting you," Otto said.

"Let's get in." Seasqrd headed for the rocket car. "We have much to discuss with Rozwelles."

Ray Atamz nodded towards the admiral then turned to Dya and raised his middle finger. Dya raised her fist. Atamz said, "Let's check eyerings."

"Aye, Captain."

From the flat surface of the ring on Ray's finger rose a conic blue beam of light and at the top of the light was a picture of Dya's face.

"Eyering functioning normally," Dya said while speaking into her ring and pointing it at her face.

"Aye, Commander," Atamz said. He turned his ring towards his face. "I'll ring the bridge. Bridge, this is your captain. Launch the fixallites!"

From the top of the hull, protruded a long pipe. Out of it shot five fixallites. The fixallites floated down from the sky and hovered over the scarred Zenith. From beneath their spherical heads emerged three mechanical arms that drew repair implements from the tool belts that wrapped around their cylindrical bodies.

"Dya, you have the conn. You and Peter see to the fixallites as they make repairs on the ship. Jane, why don't you come with us?" Atamz said.

"But I...." She paused, looked at Peter longingly, then said, "Yes, sir."

Otto's plastic face was crinkling its nose as if the fixallites gave off a bad aroma. Ray assumed he must have viewed them as rather primitive. Otto turned his lumbering metal body about, opened the door for the doctor and said, "After you, my dear."

Captain Atamz watched the fixallites as they flew about the Zenith and was satisfied his cosmicraft was in good hands then he followed Admiral Seasqrd and Dr. MaCardiak taking a seat under the transparent dome of the rocket car. Otto climbed back into the driver's compartment.

"Remember, any problems, I'm only a ring away." The captain saluted.

Suddenly, the rocket car blasted away leaving Peter and Dya coughing on the dust as they tried saluting back.

"Don't let anything happen to my ship," Ray Atamz shouted to them from the back of the racing rocket car.

* * *

The home of Dr. Orson Rozwelles was a chain of four domes of opaque glass interconnected by plastic tubes and surrounded by blue leafed trees, red shrubbery and golden lawns. The rocket car had just screeched to a stop before the largest dome. Admiral Seasqrd stepped out of the rocket car and looked over the grounds with his genetically enhanced vision. Bordering the complex was a series of posts, which Seasqrd surmised engaged a force field and an advanced scanning and communication system. Seasqrd had to squint but beyond the posts looked like a cemetery.

"I must park the rocket car in the garage." Otto slowly climbed out of the car and extended a claw to Jane, helping her out of her seat. "It requires a flushing of its nuclear radiator and I require a diode-diagnostic. Dr. Rozwelles said he would meet you here."

Gene Lucas Seasqrd stood patiently before the main entrance of the largest dome as Ray Atamz watched the car soar away. Jane MaCardiak held her stomach and said, "That was some drive over here.

"You must forgive Otto; he only drives me and usually it's too far," said a shadowy figure standing on the porch. "You must also forgive this old recluse for his ill-mannered comments and lack of hospitality. Hope my I did not sound too hyper on my hyperadio transmitter."

182

Admiral Seasqrd was about to reply when Captain Atamz stepped in front of him and said, "That hyperadio transmission was really something."

"It's also something you really should've listened to."

Seasqrd stepped back in front of Captain Atamz; the figure stepped down to greet Admiral Seasqrd. He was still tall, thin and sophisticated looking, wearing black from head to toe. His eyes were as dark as always but his beard and hair had become salted with gray as were his menacing eyebrows.

"Greetings, Orson." Seasqrd shook his old friend's hand. "You're literally the last person I'd expect to find on some planet in the middle of the Unknown Zone."

Dr. Rozwelles remained cold and detached. Seasqrd made the introductions of Captain Atamz and Dr. MaCardiak.

"Dr. Rozwelles, I must say it's a great honor to meet you. You're kind of a hero to me. Your breakthrough on dark-matter propulsion and your design of cold friction engines are acts of true genius. I've studied all your work. Even if I couldn't understand it, I still studied it," Atamz said.

Dr. Rozwelles acknowledged the compliments with a brief smile before saying, "Thank you my boy but there's no reason to state the obvious."

Rozwelles held his arm out before the doorway. Seasqrd followed the gesture entering the domicile. Right behind him, Dr. MaCardiak cautiously walked up the stairs while offering a mock smile to Rozwelles. Seasqrd reached for the captain's arm as Dr. Rozwelles slid the door shut and whispered to Ray, "Keep flattering him, Ray."

Jane MaCardiak's forehead creased as she stared at Seasqrd in disbelief; she raised an eyebrow. Seasqrd gave her a reassuring wink, but the doctor's brow remained knitted and her lips became pursed.

He whispered to her, "I have a plan."

CHAPTER 13
THOSE SCI-FI GUYS AND THE POWER OF MOMM

Despite her misgivings about Seasqrd's plan and her concerns about Rozwelles, Jane MaCardiak thoroughly enjoyed her meal; she offered Dr. Rozwelles compliments about the delicious lunch and to Jane's and everyone's surprise the food had been prepared by Otto the automaton.

"Yes, Otto makes an excellent servant however the filet mignon could have been slightly more well-done but not too bad." Rozwelles wiped his bearded mouth clean of crumbs.

Leaning over to take away the dirty plates, Otto turned his plastic face, which was puzzled, towards Rozwelles. Jane found it odd but she felt bad for the robot. She watched the glass dome upon his head spin around while he tried fathoming his master's criticisms. After a few things clicked and lit within his glass dome head he went about clearing the table. Jane was kind of hoping he would have dumped the dirty dishes on Rozwelles' lap.

"Fortunately, you did not program feelings into him otherwise they'd be hurt," MaCardiak said. "What would you do if your machine turned on you?"

"Impossible," Rozwelles stated. "Allow me to showcase some further works of my genius. Otto! Activate the Recycla Tube."

At his master's command the automaton pressed a button and a large, glass cylinder rose from the floor. At one end the tube was wide then it tapered down to the end.

"Watch and be prepared to be amazed," Rozwelles said.

Otto began tossing leftovers from lunch into the wide end of the tube including the plates and utensils; each time Otto tossed in a dish there was an enormous spark. Jane did not want to admit it but she was amazed.

"The plates are disintegrating!" she said.

"Not to worry; the reintegrater in the kitchen creates whatever we need." Rozwelles pointed. "Now look at the other end of the Recycla Tube."

Jane and the others looked at the smaller end of the where small crystal squares were sliding out.

"Each of those boxes is a concentrated mixture of silicon, metals, nitrogen, and potassium and so on. They're placed in the ground where they'll enrich the soil for years to come."

"What an excellent means of replenishing the Earth," Atamz said. "Although we're not on Earth... but it is earth... well still dirt... soil."

"Thank you captain," Rozwelles said. "Would you be interested in assisting with another demonstration?"

"Certainly."

"Excellent." Rozwelles came close to smiling. "Otto, take Captain Atamz and toss him into the Recycla Tube."

"What?" Atamz said.

"What?" MaCardiak said.

Jane got out of her seat but Seasqrd urged her to sit down. It seemed Ray Atamz was still willing to go along with the demonstration but it was obvious to anyone looking into his eyes that fear had replaced eagerness. Suddenly Otto's claws had Ray by the seat of his pants and the collar of his uniform; Jane gasped as he carried Ray to the mouth of the Recycla Tube but as his metallic pelvis spun Otto's head began to flash. The glass dome seemed ready to burst as Otto's speaker screeched, "Error... error!"

"You see he cannot do it," Rozwelles said. "And do you know why?"

"I think I can answer that," Atamz said as he was swung backwards and forwards. "You must have programmed him with a permanent, repeating safety algorithm."

"Quite correct."

"His base programming is to obey you but it cannot override his programming forbidding him to harm a human."

"Error... error...." Otto said as he held Captain Atamz by his collar and by the seat of his pants and kept trying to toss him into the Recycla Tube.

"He's locked in a sub-electronic exigency." Ray Atamz pointed his thumb back at Otto, smiled and then tapped the side of his brow while pointing at Rozwelles with glee.

"Precisely young man!" Dr. Rozwelles said. "Otto put him down."

As the robot's head stopped flashing and Ray got onto his feet, Otto turned to Dr. Rozwelles and asked, "Did I do it?"

"No," Rozwelles said shaking his head.

"How disappointing," Otto said while his face formed a frown.

"Why does he seem saddened?" Jane MaCardiak asked.

"He wishes to make an error," Rozwelles replied.

"It is the one thing I am incapable of." Otto's speaker lit up from his torso.

"Spare us your computerized complaints you cybernetic simpleton," Dr. Rozwelles said.

Otto lowered his head. After scolding his mechanized man-servant Rozwelles looked at Ray and said, "With a giggagoogle of information stored within the database of his memory he tends to ramble. I only wish I had built a brevity chip into his synaptic relays."

"I'm not sure I understand what you mean, Dr. Rozwelles." Otto's speaker lit up while his plastic face looked as if someone had just kicked him in the diodes or something. "Is it not more productive to know all the facts on an issue before making a decision? As La Rochefoucauld once said —"

"Shut up," Dr. Rozwelles said, holding up his hand.

"Said... said... said...." Otto's speaker darkened, as the robot became silent; his plastic face still looked wounded while he deactivated the Recycla Tube and stomped into the kitchen.

"Forgive my abruptness, I did find it pragmatic to program an immediate silence default code in his matrix otherwise if you ask him what time it is, he'll provide the history of the temporal continuum," Rozwelles said.

Dr. MaCardiak leaned over towards Captain Atamz and asked, "Do you think he could program Dya with one of those shut-up codes?"

Atamz waved his hand at Jane while he listened to Dr. Rozwelles.

"I don't know what I'd do without Otto. He's cook, maid, gardener and bartender and he's invaluable to my research. He can answer any question and fix any machine. He is quite perfect. Aren't you, Otto?"

"Please, sir, do not rub it in," Otto said. His plastic face frowned while setting the coffee urn down.

"What's wrong with being perfect?" Atamz asked.

"Pay no attention to this lead-lined lamenter," Rozwelles said. "He doesn't like being designed perfectly."

"It's not easy being perfect," Otto said.

Atamz nodded as if in sympathetic agreement. Jane MaCardiak jabbed her elbow in the captain's side.

"If only I could perform just one error," Otto said. "Just once."

"Strange, a mechanical man who longs to make mistakes. And real men who long to be flawless," Dr. MaCardiak said.

"Jane, please, Dr. Rozwelles is leading the discussion," Atamz whispered.

"I'd like to discuss some answers," Seasqrd said.

"Answers to what, old friend?" Dr. Rozwelles asked.

"You fled Earth. Why?"

"You know better than anyone." Dr. Rozwelles pointed at the port in Seasqrd's head. "All my inventions backfired; you and Darklone are the perfect example."

At the mention of Darklone's name Admiral Seasqrd's forehead lit up.

"Earth has never been a paradise, but we need people with your genius," Seasqrd slammed his hand on the table, "and now more than ever!"

"No, you don't." Dr. Rozwelles shook his head, though MaCardiak was not sure whether he was shaking his head in disgust over the admiral's harsh tone or the damage Seasqrd had just done to the dining room table. "I discussed it with my fellow super-geniuses and we decided it was better for the brightest minds to take their highest hopes into deepest space."

Dr. MaCardiak leaned forward in curiosity. She asked, "So where are the other scientists?"

Rozwelles scratched the bridge of his nose and said, "We decided that humanity had grown too dependent on the inventions we gave them. We wanted a world with no technology. So on this planet there would be no machines."

"That's wonderful," Dr. MaCardiak said.

"That's awful," Captain Atamz said.

Ray and Jane stared at one another then looked back at Dr. Rozwelles.

"When we first started, we thought like Dr. MaCardiak," Rozwelles said. "But then very quickly, after experimenting with lavatories based in the woods and morning ablutions involving the river water in winter, we began to think like the captain. So we tried going in a new direction."

"You still haven't answered Dr. MaCardiak's question," Seasqrd said.

Rozwelles slowly rose from the table and stood by the glass wall. He pondered while looking out in the distance. The admiral rose and joined him.

"Once on this pristine world there was an unnatural evil," Rozwelles said. "One by one each of my colleagues was consumed by it. Their graves lay out beyond that hill."

Ray and Jane walked by the glass wall and pensively gazed out at the hilltop along with Rozwelles and the admiral.

Atamz clasped his hand over Rozwelles' shoulder and said, "You buried them with your own hands."

"I should say not," Rozwelles said. "I had Otto do it."

"Oh, yeah," Atamz said. "Of course."

"What kind of evil?" Seasqrd asked.

"Some... thing... a monstrosity of some kind," Rozwelles spoke like he was trying to describe a nightmare. He fixed his gaze on the distant gravesites and said, "It suddenly appeared, then disappeared and somehow there was always a feeling of its omnipresence. It is still out there. It's just lurking. It's just waiting. It's ready to strike again."

"Father."

At the sound of the unexpected voice from the staircase Jane jumped in the air and landed in Ray's arms; Seasqrd put his back to the wall and Rozwelles stood with his hand over his chest. Everyone stood motionless until Rozwelles spoke.

"My child," he said. "Did I not tell you to stay upstairs until lunch had ended?"

"But lunch has ended," she said.

Jane's jaw dropped as she looked up at the staircase. Ray's eyes were bulging and the hair on top of his head stood on end and if Seasqrd had any hair there it would have stood on end as well Jane thought.

"This is my daughter, Barbralta," Rozwelles said.

The young woman descending the stairs was as jolting as a full injecterdermic of B-1012. Her glimmering silver dress clung tightly to her curvaceous figure; the lower portion of her skirt of transparent plastic revealed long legs wrapped in light grey stockings that bore silver sequins and red slippers on her tiny feet. Her blonde hair was woven in a tall spiral that let cascades of curls fall from the end over her bare shoulders.

"Hello," Dr. MaCardiak said.

"Hello, hello." Seasqrd smiled. "Strange I don't remember you having a —"

"And hello." Ray Atamz knocked over a chair as he rapidly ran to the bottom of the staircase to take Barbralta's hand. "I'm Captain Ray Jay Atamz."

"It's a pleasure," she said, "I'm sorry, Father, but you couldn't expect me to stay upstairs and miss the only chance I may ever have to meet a man."

"Beg your pardon," the captain said.

Barbralta just smiled and squeezed Ray's hands between her own while looking him up and down.

Jane clenched her teeth.

"You heard correctly." Rozwelles turned suspicious eyes on the near-panting cosmicraft captain. "My daughter has never met a human male other than myself."

"I see. I'm sure she'll never know what she has missed." Dr. MaCardiak looked at her nails, wondering if any of the men had heard her.

Dr. Rozwelles continued introductions as Otto poured coffee. Dr. MaCardiak offered a hand to Barbralta but was ignored. Barbralta stood before Admiral Seasqrd.

"Admiral you have quite a physique for someone your age." She traced her finger over his chest. "What is that?"

"Oh, just something your dad gave me," Admiral Seasqrd said grinning as he pointed at his forehead.

Barbralta sauntered over towards Ray and said, "Captain Atamz, are all Earthmen like you?"

"No, I'm especially handsome," Atamz said.

While Barbralta patted the captain's chest and shoulders, Rozwelles reached for his coffee and said, "Please forgive her. Years of isolation on this planet have left her with a certain social clumsiness towards the amenities."

"She seems pretty smooth to me," MaCardiak said. "By the way, I'm Doctor Jane MaCardiak."

"Oh hello, Doctor," Barbralta said. "I'm sorry, I didn't see you."

"I'm a woman," MaCardiak said. She looked Barbralta up and down, only not quite as avariciously as Ray had and whispered, "One who likes wearing clothing."

"Beg your pardon," Barbralta said.

Ray Atamz took the puzzled Barbralta by the hand. "Your dad and the admiral will want to talk. Why don't you give me a tour of your domicile?"

Otto rotated his head and said, "Sir, I am more than capable of providing — "

"No! No!" Atamz reached up and put his hand on Otto's speaker. "I have the conn."

Jane MaCardiak made a fist and watched the space-princess lead Captain Atamz back up the stairs. Then Jane remembered the admiral's so-called plan and his comment to the captain about flattering Rozwelles; she said, "Strange you don't want to sit and enjoy some tech-talk with Dr. Rozwelles, Captain Atamz."

While Ray and Barbralta paused on the stairwell, Jane turned to the admiral and nodded. "While we were landing, all Ray did was talk of your great genius, Dr. Rozwelles."

"Do you really think my daddy is a great genius?" Barbralta asked.

Ray Atamz looked down at his boots and replied in a coy yet sickening voice, "Well, I have read all about him."

"He certainly has," Seasqrd said, nodding back to Dr. MaCardiak then he waved for Captain Atamz to join them at the table. "Why not ask Dr. Rozwelles about everything you'd like to see."

"That's a splendid idea." Barbralta put her hands over the captain's shoulders and snuggled her nose up under his neck.

Atamz pulled in a deep breath and said, "Yes, please, Dr. Rozwelles, I was hoping to see some more of your creations." Upon seeing the look of shock on Rozwelles' face, Ray added hastily, "I meant in addition to your robot; do you have other inventions?"

Dr. Rozwelles put down his cup and said, "Indeed, it has been awhile since I've had guests. For quite some time I have longed to share the brilliance of my work with beings worthy of comprehending the intellect behind them, but I guess you people will have to do."

They walked with Rozwelles across the room. He pressed a button on the wall and an enormous portal opened within it, revealing the entrance to a narrow passageway that led down into the planet.

"Follow me," Rozwelles said.

*   *   *

Dr. MaCardiak thought Ray Atamz was shimmering brighter than a magnatar as Dr. Rozwelles conducted a tour of his vast underground laboratories. There were machines, computers and all sorts of gizmos buzzing, bleeping and beeping everywhere; it was everything Ray loved. He was so enthralled by the technology he had actually stopped gaping at Barbralta.

Inside a catacomb, they followed Rozwelles to what appeared to be the final stage of his tour. With great pride he led them to a door. There they stood as Rozwelles waved his arms about crossing his hands through some force beams. The door slid upwards, revealing the opening to an immense cave that to Jane's shock was one giant machine. Above them these electrode things hung, shooting bolts of electricity from one end of the cave to the other. Fat cabinets, bulging with cables and wires, stood row on row next to each other. Bubbling beakers and test tubes filled with a rainbow of chemicals were scattered over the numerous lab tables.

In the center of the cave, rising from a glowing, circular floor plate, was something like a computer tower and on top of it was what appeared to be an enormous balloon of aluminum foil, but it seemed to be alive as if the aluminum was made of living tissue. The shiny balloon of skin expanded and shrunk like it was breathing and out of the pulsing foil were tendrils that connected it to power lines that hung from the ceiling like thick webbing.

"The cables pulse almost like arterial veins. Is this the heart of your laboratory?" Dr. MaCardiak said, pointing at the machine, disgustingly.

"Seems more like the brain," Seasqrd said, rubbing his chin warily.

"This is great!" Atamz said. He nudged Jane's arm and said into her ear, "Even you must be impressed."

Jane was not feeling impressed; she felt frightened.

Rozwelles pointed across the walls of computer cabinets, which were covered by rows of dials. He said. "The gauges are calibrated by ten. So it's ten and another ten and another ten and another ten and another –"

"We get the point. There a lot of dials," Seasqrd said. "Go on."

"The power of ten raised to an astronomical figure," Rozwelles said.

"What's the power supply?" Atamz asked. Rozwelles pointed to the large round plate beneath the computer tower that supported the brain.

"Seven meters beneath us rests a ten negaton furnace," he said.

"Ten negatons?" Ray Atamz placed his fingertips to his bottom lip as he peered down at the shining plate. Then he asked, "Only seven meters deep?"

"An ingenious job of micro-engineering if I do say so myself." Rozwelles stuck out his chest and shoved his hand back through his hair.

Jane was not sure why ten negatons was so phenomenal but judging by Ray's awe and Rozwelles' boastfulness it seemed to represent quite a breakthrough.

"I'll say," Atamz said. "So little mass but yet so much power."

"And all fed into my MOMM," Rozwelles said.

"Your what?" MaCardiak asked.

Rozwelles pointed to the throbbing ball of foil and said, "My Mind Over Matter Machine. Not too long ago, I created a synapses cell chip and began reproducing it; think of them as microchips that emit brain waves. The result is a mechanism that works similar to your Imagarenas except no need for a framework. It sends out psychic waves of corporeal energy which can be materialized into whatever form the users wish."

"That's incredible," Atamz said. "Such a device would mean civilization without dependency on ambulatory operations."

"What does that mean?" Jane MaCardiak asked.

"We wouldn't have to get up to do anything!" Atamz said.

Rozwelles nodded with great pride as the captain looked at him with admiration and added, "Just think all of humanity could spend their entire lives sitting on their asses doing nothing forever!"

"Sounds terrific, an entire race of immobile slobs," MaCardiak said.

"So this is what you meant when you said you went in a new direction," Seasqrd said. "So is it machine or a being?"

"Both but then again neither; to me, she is my MOMM and what would a guy do without his MOMM?" Rozwelles said with a smile before leaning over to hug and kiss the foil ball.

Dr. MaCardiak nudged the admiral and said, "This guy is worse than Ray; he talks about that machine like it's alive."

"I think that's how he thinks of it," the admiral said with his hand over his mouth.

"Sometimes it's difficult. I get busy with my work and forget to visit her. But my MOMM always wanted me to be a doctor!" Rozwelles suddenly broke into laughter, slapping his thigh. Ray Atamz laughed along with him.

"Do you bring it flowers on Mother's Day?" Dr. MaCardiak asked.

"Jane!" Atamz said. He placed his index finger to his lips.

"I may be able to tolerate insults about me, but not about my MOMM," Rozwelles said, waving his finger at Jane.

Admiral Seasqrd raised his hands, gesturing towards the giant ball of foil and said, "How could anyone say anything about your MOMM? Please continue."

"Allow me to demonstrate a modicum of my MOMM's power," Rozwelles said.

He then directed them all towards a small table and a crystal headset with shiny spikes poking out of it. Within the table was a glass dome. Rozwelles sat before the dome and lifted the transparent head set.

"This is the uraniumcranium. It acts as the activator to my MOMM and as a repository for all my vast knowledge." Rozwelles eased the headset down over his skull until it rested on his shoulders. As he did this, a purple cloud arose within the glass dome. The cloud twirled, changing colors from purple to red to blue. Finally, the cloud cleared and standing underneath the dome was a living person.

"Why that's Barbralta!" Captain Atamz wiped a bit of drool from his mouth. Barbralta smiled and clapped her hands together. Jane cleared her throat.

"You think her own father would've imagined her in something less revealing," she said.

"It's not imaginary, Doctor." Rozwelles opened his eyes and spoke from within the uraniumcranium, watching the little Barbralta wave to him and blow a kiss. "The image is real. My daughter is alive in my mind and so therefore she lives here."

"Amazing, the power of creation," Seasqrd said.

"Can I try?" Atamz asked. "Please, please, huh, please."

MaCardiak and Seasqrd indicated to Rozwelles that the captain would not stop unless he was given a chance. Rozwelles gave a brief nod and pulled himself away. He removed the uraniumcranium and instantly the miniature Barbralta vanished. Meanwhile, the genuine Barbralta eased Captain Atamz into Dr. Rozwelles' vacant chair and massaged his shoulders ardently, but briefly, just before her father pushed her away. Placing the headset snuggly on the captain, Dr. Rozwelles said, "Now concentrate. Think of someone you think of often; use your strongest thoughts on the person you feel the strongest about; make it someone you truly love."

Ray closed his eyes and suddenly another cloud appeared. Out of it walked a little living image of Raymond Jay Atamz and Jane groaned. Ray opened his eyes and waved at the miniature version of himself.

"You see you can do it," Rozwelles said. "Obviously, you have made a strong impression on yourself and what kind of an impression has my MOMM made on you, Gene Lucas?"

Admiral Seasqrd took Rozwelles aside and said, "You must come back to the Earth with us. An invention like this could be the difference in our latest struggle against Darklone and the Z."

"I've been waiting for you to make that fool statement," Rozwelles said. "Was it not made clear that Earth is not ready for my ideas? How many times have I seen my inventions turned to tools of destruction?"

"Then why did you show it to us?" Seasqrd asked. "Ego?"

"You, sir, are way out of line; you genetically enhanced jack-n-ape." Dr. Rozwelles shoved his finger at the admiral's nose.

"Forgive me for being brutally candid, Orson, but if you can't see how much you're needed then maybe you're not as great a genius as you think you are." The admiral pointed back.

"Spare me your venomous verbal abuse, Admiral."

"But, Father, wouldn't it be wonderful to visit Earth?" Barbralta said as she stood behind Rozwelles, resting her head on his shoulder.

While Barbralta was resting her head on her father Jane noticed it gave Ray a chance to rest his eyes on her curvaceous shape. Jane was about to interrupt his lingering stare on Barbralta's long legs when another cloud appeared within the glass dome beside her. Out of it stepped a living image of Barbralta. Soon the miniature version of Ray and Barbralta were in each other's arms.

Jane tapped Ray's shoulder and shook his arm, but he refused to take his eyes off Rozwelles' daughter. She made sure Dr. Rozwelles was not looking as she gently tapped the glass dome, waving her finger and trying to stop the miniaturized love scene. Little Ray Atamz and little Barbralta continued their amorous interlude beneath the glass dome while Jane tried to capture the admiral's attention, but Seasqrd was standing toe to toe with Dr. Rozwelles.

"So you intend to keep this to yourself?" he asked.

"No, someday if I judge humanity worthy then my invention will be disclosed to Earth." Rozwelles was about to turn and Jane moved quickly, blocking his view of the table. Ray was still enjoying himself under the uraniumcranium as the argument between Seasqrd and Rozwelles heated.

"So, I see," Seasqrd said. "The Earth must wait patiently for the judgment day of the great Orson Rozwelles."

"Indeed," Rozwelles said.

Jane kept one eye on Rozwelles and the other on the little Atamz who was now undressing the little Barbralta. She tugged at Ray's epaulettes, but the captain sat quietly eyeing Barbralta while she nestled against her father's arm.

"Father, while you stand judging all of humanity why not let me go and visit the Earth?" Barbralta stroked Rozwelles' beard. "I've grown to like these Earthlings. I wish to know more about them."

Rozwelles turned to face his daughter's plea, and then he turned back to face Seasqrd. Jane was still trying to break Ray's concentration and block Rozwelles' view of the glass dome and the passionate scene within.

"Now you have my own daughter speaking against me." Rozwelles closed his eyes and wrinkled his eyebrows. "You go too far; I will not let my genius be...."

Jane finally batted the uraniumcranium and broke Ray's concentration which could not have happened too soon for the little Ray Atamz and the little Barbralta were steaming up the glass dome. Rozwelles turned about and witnessed the wispy images of his daughter and Ray just before they vanished. Admiral Seasqrd rested his elbow in the palm of his left hand while placing the bridge of his nose into the palm of his right; he closed his eyes and frowned.

"Oh, Ray," he said.

Jane pulled the uraniumcranium off Ray's head, but both realized it was too late. Ray Atamz wilted under Dr. Rozwelles' glowering glare. The captain smiled in mock-innocence to which Rozwelles responded, "Like I was about to say, I will not let my genius be perverted!"

Dr. Rozwelles took his smiling daughter by the hand and stormed out of the underground lab, ranting.

CHAPTER 14
THOSE SCI-FI GUYS AND THE KANINEITES

The fixallites soared from the stem of the Zenith back to her stern, repairing everything from her dark-matter gills to her retro-rockets. Meanwhile, Dya Nammock had grabbed some smartools and attempted to replace the damaged hyperotors on the propulsors, but the propulsor plate proved difficult to remove due to some stripped siliscrews.

"*Don't give up on me,*" said the magnadrill. "*I can do it.*"

"Sorry, right tool for the right job," Dya said as she put the magnadrill down.

"*No, I think you just need to adjust my torque,*" said the magnadrill.

"*Sorry, drill,*" said the protoping hammer as Dya picked it up. "*Your idea has too many holes in it.*"

"*Oh screw you!*" said the magnadrill.

Dya paid no attention to the bickering of the smartools. Her mind was preoccupied. Worry was a human weakness, at least that is what she kept telling herself, but when she swung the protoping hammer and merely dented the propulsor plate she grew frustrated.

"I am a Youkanian!" she said. "I will not give into pessimism. I shall only think positive."

She swung the hammer again and knocked the siliscrew loose.

"*We nailed that one,*" said the protoping hammer just before Dya tossed it back in the tool bag.

As the fixallites continued their work, Dya stood looking at the two moons that surfaced on the horizon. Night was about to fall, then she saw a spinning cloud of dust and knew it had to be the captain and his company returning from Dr. Rozwelles' estate. The rocket car screeched to a halt and the mechanical man extended a claw-hand to the doctor. He escorted Jane out. Captain Atamz immediately looked over the ship.

"It was a pleasure making your acquaintance." The automaton bowed respectfully.

Moments later the tornado trail of the rocket car twirled off into the distance. Captain Atamz stood looking down at the smartools then up at Dya. He asked, "What are you doing to my ship?"

"Assisting in repairs, sir."

"You know I prefer to let machines fix machines." The captain waved his fingers at Dya.

"Yes, sir, but in this case I thought I could hasten repairs which would lead to a more positive outcome," Dya said; she was not going to mention her need to keep busy.

Admiral Seasqrd said, "I hope repairs will be done soon; we've just been ordered off the planet."

"The fixallites are right on schedule," Dya said. "I was merely lending a hand."

"But the rest of the crew is not tampering with the Zenith are they?" Captain Atamz asked.

"No, Captain," Dya said, reassuringly.

"Good," Atamz said in relief. "You know how I hate that human touch on my machinery."

"You mean you don't let your crew work on your ship," Seasqrd said.

"Eewh," Atamz said.

"Where is Peter?" the doctor asked.

"It could be conducive to the crew's morale if they were allowed to do some repairs," Dya said, quickly.

"I asked where Peter is?" the doctor said looking eye to eye with Dya and briefly attempting to smile.

"I remain optimistic about the Zenith's repair schedule," Dya said. She then looked down at the ground and mumbled, "But we have a... a problem."

"Where is Peter?" the doctor demanded.

Dya realized it was time to speak the truth.

"Lt. Pulsaar led a one-man reconnaissance when his conclusionator sensed some unusual humanoid life-forms out there." Dya looked towards the hills. "He has not returned nor can we contact his eyering."

"What were you thinking, you wire-headed weirdo?" Dr. MaCardiak asked.

"Please, Doctor, your outbursts are not conducive to creating a positive outlook," Dya said. "I'm sure Lt. Pulsaar is fine."

"Why did you let him go alone?" MaCardiak asked.

"I insisted he take some secureday guards, but he insisted he did not want to be responsible if any harm came their way, which it always does."

"That is a good point," Atamz said. "How long since you've heard from him?"

"Captain, if I may quote regulations," Dya said. "Standard operating procedure is to wait a minimum of twenty macrons before sending search parties."

"We'll send out search parties now, Commander." Ray Atamz turned and looked at the admiral. "I shall lead one. You and the doctor will lead the other."

"Captain," Dya said. "It would be inappropriate for an officer of the admiral's rank to lead search parties. May I suggest that I lead one?"

"No, you've done quite enough, Commander Nammock," Atamz said.

"If we use the probe plate we should be able to lock onto him," Seasqrd said, as he began walking up the gangplank back into the Zenith followed by Dr. MaCardiak and the captain. Dya stood down below rather confused, and asked, "What should I do?"

Dr. MaCardiak hollered. "Just think positive and everything will be fine!"

As the doctor and captain stormed off Admiral Seasqrd turned back from the hatchway that led into the Zenith. He hollered to Captain Atamz telling him to assemble the search parties and he would join him momentarily. He strode back along the gangplank retracing his footsteps until he stopped and leaned against the probe plate. Dya suddenly realized he was waiting for her to speak.

"Admiral, have I done something wrong?" Dya said. "At the Cosmos-Corps Academy we were instructed to follow procedures. Is not going by the book the best way to achieve the most positive results?"

"Yes," Admiral Seasqrd said. He placed his arm about Dya's shoulder, carefully avoiding her antennae ears and said, "And no. This is not the academy, Dya, and we humans have a need for doing things our own way. Let me give you some advice."

Suddenly, the maximum alert signals went off; Ray Atamz came running down the gangplank yelling, "Prepare defenses! Where are the secuready guards?"

"Captain Atamz," Seasqrd said. "What is happening?"

"The probe plate located something approaching the Zenith," he said.

"Ray, calm down!" Admiral Seasqrd placed his hands up before the captain's face. "No need to panic over some little thing."

Atamz said, "This thing is not little. It's some thing big!"

Dya knew it wasn't very Youkanian but she crossed her fingers anyway.

*   *   *

When his eyes opened, Peter Pulsaar thought he had not truly awoken and was in some sort of nightmare. He was tied to a stake that stood in some kind of a cave with high vaulted ceilings; he tried pulling himself free but his genetically enhanced strength failed him. He was too weak and groggy; he couldn't even remember how he had even gotten here. All he could recall was moving through the woods following the signals of his conclusionator when he found a village. But all he could remember after that was hearing some growls and barks.

Peter shook his head, trying to wake himself up. He looked at the walls of the cave; they were smooth and clean as if someone had carved and polished them. Hanging from the ceiling were a series of burning urns that acted like torches and below the furthest one, at the far end of the cave, was a high bench. Seated behind the bench were three creatures, who sat like judges at a trial.

They were strange looking creatures. They were more than hairy; they were furry. They also had strange noses protruding from their faces that joined their mouths in tapered snouts. One of the creatures then began scratching his misshapen ear with his paw. Peter shook his head again believing he was only semi-conscious; then he reached the realization that he was awake and that these creatures were a strange mix of canine life and humans. As his head cleared further, Peter looked about and found the judges were not alone. Several more dog people walked in, their paws softly padding against the sandy soil of the cave. Their robes reminded Peter of the days of medieval Europe. They took seats on some stone benches that lined the cave's walls; they sat and stared at Peter.

"What is this... a madhouse?" Peter said.

"The interloper will remain silent," barked the judge.

"You can talk!" Peter said.

"Please be quiet," a dog woman said, waving her paw.

"But you can speak," Peter said.

"Of course," she said.

The judge took a gavel in one of his paws and slammed it against the top of the wooden bench.

"The court of the Kanineites will come to order!" he announced.

"Kanineites," Peter whispered to the dog woman next to her. "Is that what you call yourselves?"

She didn't answer but merely placed her paw over Peter's mouth. The judge looked at Peter with angry eyes, awaiting his total silence which Peter gave him.

"Is the defense and prosecution ready?"

"I, Brutus Boxer stand ready to attack this criminal!" said the Kanineite to Peter's left. He was a short pugnacious cur, with broad shoulders and a pushed-in muzzle.

The slender female Kanineite on Peter's other side stood forward. She had long strands of chocolate colored fur that hung from her head like fine hair. Her snout was pointed and she did not speak in growls like the others but in a slight whimpering voice. Standing before Peter she addressed the judges, "I, Spanielius, stand ready to speak defense for this poor creature," she said.

"Then I, Caesar Shepherd, stand to hear this court. Prosecution, you will begin."

"What is our law?" Brutus Boxer asked. "It is what our Lawgiver commands!"

Peter noticed that when the word lawgiver was used the Kanineites all bowed in reverence. Then Brutus Boxer continued, "This interloper was collared on our territory after leading an invasion. He is obviously not one of us, and if he is not one of us then he is one of them, for all those who are not us must be them, and they must be condemned to the Dog House of Pain."

He bowed his head before the judges then turned at Peter and lifted his lip to show his teeth. Peter grew nervous. The other Kanineites in the audience of this strange tribunal applauded and grunted approval; they seemed anxious to condemn him to this Dog House of Pain. Peter knew what it was like to be in the dog house metaphorically courtesy of Ray Jay Atamz but something told Peter that this Dog House of Pain was no metaphor and it would be slightly uncomfortable. Peter was about to voice his argument when the Kanineite female charged with his defense spoke.

"Honorable Kanineites, we beg for mercy," Spanielius said. "We do not know that the interloper came as an invader and for that matter how do we know he's not one of us."

The judges began deliberating amongst themselves. As Peter's nervousness worsened he decided he had better start talking for himself, before these dogs buried him like a bone. He said, "I am Peter Pulsaar. I am a Cosmos-Corpsman serving aboard the ECC Zenith."

"You should stay quiet," Spanielius said. But Peter could tell, already, he should have kept his big mouth shut. The judges whispered to the prosecution in rapid conversation. Caesar Shepherd stood and said, "Bring forth our Sacred Scrolls. If he's one of us then he shall be able to recite our laws."

"But I ... uh," Peter said.

"Please be quiet," Spanielius said.

"Bailiff Bernard!" Brutus Boxer said. "Bring our Sacred Scrolls!"

Plodding across the cave floor was an overweight Kanineite with a huge muzzle for a mouth and from the mouth came plenty of drool. In his paw he carried rolled up parchment. The Kanineites all bowed before the scrolls of papyrus the bailiff held. Suddenly, Brutus Boxer turned on Peter Pulsaar, pointed at the scrolls and asked, "Tell the court what the fifth law of the Lawgiver is?"

"I'm sorry," Peter said, "I don't know your religion."

The judges shook their heads disdainfully as Spanielius sulked. Brutus Boxer stood next to the scrolls and stated proudly, "The fifth law says to always walk on two legs; that is the fifth law. Now tell us what the eighth law of the Lawgiver is?"

"This is unfair. I can only guess," Peter said.

"The eighth law states never to lift your leg; that is the eighth law! Now tell us the tenth law of our Lawgiver."

"Thou shalt never hump thy neighbor's bitch."

The audience burst out in growls and yelps.

"He speaks sacrilege!" Brutus Boxer said.

"Such contempt cannot be tolerated," Caesar Shepherd said. He pointed at the one called Bailiff Bernard and bellowed, "Give him a rap-rap on the head!"

Bernard, the large slobbering bailiff, rolled the sacred parchments into a taunt roll and swatted Peter Pulsaar across the nose.

"Ow!" Peter said. "I'm sorry, but your Lawgiver's laws sound pretty silly."

Spanielius placed her paws over her snout and closed her eyes.

"You must learn obedience," Caesar Shepherd said. "Another rap-rap on the head."

Bailiff Bernard did not hesitate to punish Peter again with the rolled up scrolls.

"You're making me mad," Peter said.

"Now he threatens us," Brutus Boxer said. "Tell me, interloper, what will happen if we anger you? Will you attack us with your weapons of destruction?"

Peter raised his eyebrows in shock, watching Brutus Boxer play with his conclusionator, eyering and plasma-pistol.

"Be careful with that!" Peter said.

"Do not give us orders! You are not the Lawgiver!" Caesar Shepherd said.

Brutus Boxer waved his paw and said, "Time for another rap-rap on the head!"

Again Peter was subjected to a rap on the head by the bailiff and again he grew angry. Peter choked down before speaking, trying to control his temper, "Stop doing that rap-rap on the head, Bernard, you're gonna make me mad."

The judges gestured towards the bailiff indicating they wished another rap on the head, but Spanielius stood before Peter blocking the bailiff.

"Thanks," Peter whispered in Spanielius' floppy ear.

"You're making this very hard for yourself," she whispered back.

"He is not one of us!" Brutus Boxer said. "He must go into the Dog House of Pain!"

The prosecution flapped his paw to the guards. One of them stepped forward carrying a brass collar; Brutus took hold of it and cast it before Peter's gaze.

"You are not putting that thing on me," Peter said. "You're not tossing me into the Dog House of Pain."

Seeing the fear on Peter's face, Brutus Boxer cheerily chanted, "He must go into the Dog House of Pain."

Soon the cave echoed his words as everyone repeated his chant. Peter tried to control his temper.

"You must not," Spanielius said. "It's incanine."

"He must be destroyed for the good of us!" Judge Shepherd said.

The other judges nodded in agreement. Brutus Boxer stood proudly and Spanielius seemed desperate. She whimpered and wagged her tail. Then she held up her paw as if she just had an idea; she shouted, "What of the Prophecy?"

The judges stood back while their jaws dropped. Brutus Boxer went before the judges and said, "This is heresy!"

"It is not! We all know of the Prophecy of the New Lawgiver. Someone made in the image of the Lawgiver. Well here he is!" Spanielius pointed at Peter.

The judges began discussing matters amongst themselves. Though they still seemed unsympathetic, they showed signs that they were concerned about something. Peter tugged at the ropes that bound him, hoping he could just break free and make a run for it. Suddenly he heard the sound of the gavel again.

Caesar Shepherd stood. He said. "It is decided that we cannot risk the wrath of our Lawgiver. Captain Doberman and his guards will bring the prisoner before the great monolith. The Lawgiver will tell us what to do as he always does."

The guards of black and tan dragged Peter from inside the cave out to the center of a tribal compound. Peter looked at the semi-circle of doghouses standing on columns of timber. They stretched around a wide fire-pit. In front of the fire-pit stood a tall monolithic crystal, half buried in the sand.

The Kanineites stood before the monolith in silence. They raised their paws and lowered them. They raised and lowered their paws again. Caesar Shepherd spoke.

"Oh great and glorious Lawgiver, tell us through your oracle what to do," he said.

Surrounded by guards, Peter was made to kneel on the ground. The crystal slab became illuminated like a mirror in the sun with a shiny image within. He watched in amazement as the image evolved into the likeness of a man. Peter found the face of the man very familiar. He knew he had seen the face before.

"Dr. Rozwelles!"

Peter shut his mouth after he was kicked by one of the guards. As Peter held back a groan he watched the giant image of Rozwelles come to life before the reverent Kanineites. Then a voice emanated from the monolith.

"What is the law of the Lawgiver?" the crystal monolith asked. "Speak!"

The Kanineites began to bark, howl and yelp. The monolith spoke again.

"Behold the Lawgiver!" it said. "Look at me. Look at me."

The Kanineites began to stare unwaveringly at the monolith.

"Good look," the monolith said. "Now sit. Sit! Good sit."

Peter watched in bewilderment as these thinking beings did everything this machine told them to do.

"Now roll over and play dead."

"Stop it!" Peter yelled as he looked at all the Kanineites on their backs putting their legs and arms in the air. Caesar

Shepherd rose. Brutus Boxer came to his feet and pointed at Peter. Spanielius waved her paws, begging Peter to be silent.

"I will not be quiet!" Peter yelled at the Kanineite council. "You let a recorded voice rule your lives? You dumb dogs!"

"Rap-rap on the head!" Bernard the Bailiff said as he lowered his club of sacred scrolls on Peter's head. As he listened to Captain Doberman and his guards snicker and Brutus Boxer call again for the Dog House of Pain, Peter Pulsaar became very, very mad.

*   *   *

Captain Ray Jay Atamz surveyed his defenses. Anchordroids stood about the cosmicraft, Zenith, forming a perimeter. About the ship's base stood a troop of secuready guards, armed with plasma-pistols. The ship's probe-plate glistened as it sent out waves of sensarrays. Captain Atamz liked what he saw but not what he heard.

The Zenith's maximum alert signal again pierced the silence of the night. Ray spoke into his eyering and said, "Atamz to bridge! Dya what is going on?"

"Sir, our probe plate has detected a gigantic 'thing' making its way through the canyon," Dya said as the virtual image of her head took shape over Ray's hand.

"Further analysis required." Ray scratched his head and bent his neck.

"Scientifically what is out there cannot be."

"Specify," Ray Atamz said moving his ring closer to his face. "Cannot be as in cannot be out there or cannot be in existence."

"Both!" Dya replied. "It is an entity composed of pure energy yet it registers as an organic life form."

"That's impossible!" Atamz said. He looked at Admiral Seasqrd in puzzlement then turned back to his ring and said, "Complete a diagnostic on the probe plate. I'll be up to the bridge in a moment. Maybe it has a few bugs in it."

"Ray, I suggest you have the anchordroids raise a repellozone around the ship. Don't ask why. Something just tells me to do so," Seasqrd said.

"Very well, Admiral." Atamz smiled. "Raise the repellozone!"

Atamz turned off his ring. "But I'm telling you a monstrosity like that cannot exist. It must be a glitch in the—"

"What did you call it?" Seasqrd said.

"A monstrosity." Captain Atamz clasped his hand over his mouth. "Oh no!"

Suddenly, there was the sound of plasma-pistols blazing away. Streams of energy shot at the repellozone as something tried to break through it. Captain Atamz ran to the scene of battle.

"I'm the captain don't worry I'm here." He took a position behind some crewmen. "Tell your captain what is going on?"

The secureedy guard lowered his plasma-pistol and pointed at the ground outside the perimeter. Massive claw-prints were being formed in the dirt as if some unseen creature was striding about the edge of the repellozone searching for its vulnerable point.

"The gamma-damn thing is invisible!" Atamz announced.

"Ray!" said Jane MaCardiak.

Captain Ray Atamz jumped up and quickly grabbed the plasma-pistol he just dropped. "Don't do that to me in front of my crew!" he said.

Dr. MaCardiak smiled apologetically.

"What are you doing here?" Atamz asked. "Get back aboard the ship!"

"Something tells me, with all these secureedy men on patrol you will need my medical assistance very soon," she said.

"Look!" Seasqrd pointed to the claw-prints. "It's instinctively heading for the weakest point in our defenses. Men rush over there and set up a cross-fire."

Atamz held up his hand and said, "With all due respect, sir, I'm captain of the Zenith." He faced his secuready guards and ordered, "Well men, what are all of you waiting for? Go set up a cross-fire!"

After staring at each other in disbelief, the Zenith secuready guards lined up by the anchordroids waiting for the creature to attack and they did not have to wait long. An explosion of blue energy waves surged across the repellozone as the monstrosity assaulted it. The creature seemed to be ramming itself against the force field while it withstood plasma fire. The wreath of flames that surrounded the monstrosity's head raged into an inferno as it pressed against the repellozone. Ray stepped back in fright but felt Admiral Seasqrd's hand at his back forcing him forward. Sparks rained down on Ray and the Zenith crew while the face of the creature materialized.

"It looks like the devil, himself!" Atamz said.

"No, someone else!" Admiral Seasqrd said.

Atamz and Seasqrd drew their plasma-pistols and joined the fray. Relentless in its assault, the monstrosity butted, rammed and jammed its huge head through the repellozone until finally it broke through becoming invisible once again. Ray kept one eye on Jane and another on the claw prints in the soil.

"Jane, please get back inside the ship!" he yelled.

Suddenly, two secuready men burst into flames while another secuready guard seemed to be caught in the grip of the monstrosity's claw; he was lifted into the air and tossed into the Zenith's hull. The monster's claw prints came forward like it was ready to stomp on Atamz and Seasqrd, when suddenly there was an explosion of red and orange smoke. For a slight moment Ray Atamz thought he could see the monstrosity's face as he peeked around Admiral Seasqrd's shoulder.

"It's gone!" the admiral turned around towards Ray who was still hiding behind him. "It simply dematerialized."

Just then, and to his surprise, Ray found himself in Jane's embrace. "It was like some sort of a nightmare!" she said.

*   *   *

Asleep at his table, Dr. Rozwelles suddenly opened his eyes as his daughter knocked on the glass of the uraniumcranium He lifted his head to see Barbralta standing before him weeping. He pulled the transparent headset off as quickly as he could and took his daughter in his arms barely noticing that the many gauges and dials of his MOMM were slowly dimming.

Stroking Barbralta's long blonde hair he held her tight and asked, "What's wrong?"

"I had a bad dream."

"Oh, my dear." He braced her face between his hands. "Dreams cannot hurt us."

CHAPTER 15
THOSE SCI-FI GUYS AND THE SECRET OF ROZWELLES

Dya Nammock found Captain Atamz kneeling over the body of one of the secureadt men lost in battle. Dr. MaCardiak had just pulled a blanket over the secureadt guard's face and said, "I'm sorry, Ray. He's dead."

Captain Atamz placed his fist over his lips so that his knuckles were beneath his nose. He bit against his thumb.

"Don't be too saddened, Captain," Dya said. "We have lost many secureadt guards. We always do."

"You don't understand, Dya." Atamz lowered his fist from his mouth and looked up at the purple sky. "I knew this man's family. His father was my first commanding officer when I graduated. His mother had helped me get into the academy. What will they think?"

"Probably that you're the man who got their boy killed," Dya said.

The captain tucked his face against his shoulder, turned and strolled off with a quivering lip.

Dya felt puzzled.

"I thought he was asking for an honest opinion," Dya said turning to the doctor. "But if I were to invoke some positive thinking —"

"Spare me your plentitude of platitudes on the powers of positive thinking." Dr. MaCardiak ordered her medics to raise the body onto a hovering gurney and float it up the gangplank.

Hurt by MaCardiak's angry alliteration Dya sank her head down and said, "I only wish to help people. Is that such a harmful thing?"

"No, no, not at all," a tranquil voice said.

Dya spun about, not realizing anyone was behind her. Admiral Seasqrd smiled while placing his arm around her. Dya said, "It's like I said Admiral; you humans confuse me?"

"How do we do that?" he asked.

"Why do so many take offenses to my statements? I certainly do not mean to be offensive; it is the way I am. Is not better though to show others the error of their ways? Not pointing out mistakes only allows someone to repeat the mistake." Dya folded her arms about her waist.

"You see, we humans like to improve ourselves, but not at the expense of hurt feelings." Seasqrd said as he stood before her. "There actually is a fine art to offering sage advice and helpful counsel without damaging a person's confidence. Didn't they teach you that back on the planet, Youkan?"

Dya shook her head then pensively propped her chin against her fingers and gulped. "That thought had not occurred to me." She whipped her head about and asked, "So you mean when Ensign DiNova complained that no one wanted to dance with him at the Solar Solstice Dance I should not have indicated that his yellow teeth and lack of hygiene could be a contributing factor."

"Well...."

"And when Lt. Kosine was distraught about not being promoted for the third time my point that someone of such limited mental ability should be satisfied that she even reached the rank of lieutenant was less than consoling."

The admiral nodded his head reluctantly.

Dya leaned against his shoulder and said, "I have always picked up on the negative signals of my shipmates, but I never knew it was because I am mean."

"No, you're not mean." Seasqrd patted her arm. A beeping sound began emanating from the admiral's eyering. Seasqrd lifted his hand and said, "Seasqrd, here."

The face of Lt. Meedioride appeared and said, "Admiral, the shuttle car has been fueled up."

"Meet you around the bow," he said, lowering his hand and switching the eyering off. "You really are a splendid officer, Dya, and a fine Cosmos-Corpsman, that is from a certain point of view."

"Wait, where are you going?" Dya grabbed onto the admiral's arm.

"I have to go." Seasqrd gently pulled her hand away. "There's some unfinished business to attend with Dr. Orson Rozwelles."

"But I wanted to finish our talk?" Dya watched the admiral disappear around the Zenith's hull. She had never felt a feeling of failure; feelings of failure were forbidden where she came from. But Dya felt like she had achieved nothing positive for her shipmates. There had been only one who claimed that she had done him a world of good and then she let him wander off into danger. She looked out on the hills and decided there was some unfinished business she had to attend to.

"Anchordroids open the repellozone!" she said. "If anyone is to ask, I'm conducting a solo search for Lt. Pulsaar."

After making sure her plasma-pistol was fully charged, Dya ventured beyond the repellozone. Though she kept trying to remain positive, she was consumed with dread that she would be too late to save Peter Pulsaar.

* * *

"Spanielius," Peter said, "slow down!"

Peter watched Spanielius scamper through the brush and around shrubs. She became a blur in the early light of the sun. Even with his genetically enhanced stamina, Peter was just about able to keep up.

"They have fallen far behind," Peter said.

"You don't understand." Spanielius panted. "You destroyed the monolith of the Lawgiver. They will hunt us down."

The danger he had placed the Kanineite female in struck his heart like a neutron bullet. "Why don't *you* go back?" he asked.

Spanielius did not answer. She was panting too hard. Finally, after her tongue was done flying in the wind like a flag, she said, "I stole these for you."

Peter looked down into Spanielius' paws. He took his plasma-pistol and eyering. "Thank you," he said.

Spanielius smiled. Her big, brown eyes finally stopped looking sad. Peter pushed back her furry hair and draped it back around her neck. She licked him passionately and said, "I like you. I always have. Even if you're the ugliest thing I've ever seen."

Peter caressed her ears and nodded his head in thanks. He raised his middle finger to himself and was about to contact the Zenith when he realized that somehow Ray would blame him for this and that would start another fight between him and Jane. He thought about contacting Dya, but knew he would have to listen to a speech, so he contacted the one man in Cosmos-Corps he had always looked up to.

"Pulsaar to Admiral Seasqrd," he said. "Come in Seasqrd."

Peter shook his hand, "What's wrong with this thing?"

Just then a computerized voice spoke from his eyering.

"You have reached the ringmail of —"

Spanielius lurched back in fright at the sight of Seasqrd's head. Peter took her paw, calming her down as he listened to Seasqrd's image.

"Gene Lucas Seasqrd," it said.

"Is not available," the computer voice interjected. *"If you wish to leave a message please do so at the sound of the tone."*

At the beep, Peter began speaking rapidly. "Admiral, I was captured by a race of dog-people called the Kanineites. They took me before a statue of Dr. Rozwelles. They seem to worship him like he was their god or something," he said. He wanted to say more but was cut off by a second beeping tone.

"I sure hope he gets the message soon," he whispered.

Just then, Spanielius began acting quite nervous. A whiff of air reached Peter's nostrils and he knew why she acted as she did.

"What's that?" he asked.

"I smell it too," Spanielius said. Her ears perked up.

"Yes, and I just heard something," Peter said.

"You have senses like a Kanineite," Spanielius said.

Peter looked at his furry friend and winked, realizing she had just given him a great compliment. Then he thought he saw something move. He crept down next to Spanielius, looking for another sign of movement.

"You go around this way," Peter whispered. "I'll go the other way. Whatever it is we will catch it between us."

Peter prowled through the underbrush, sneaking forward but keeping an eye back on Spanielius. He hid behind a tree then heard a yelp. He dove from behind the tree and caught Spanielius as she went flying through the air. She landed in his arms, unconscious.

"I recognize the Youkan punch anywhere," he said. "She wasn't going to harm you, Commander."

Dya Nammock stepped out from behind the tall shrubs with a plasma-pistol in hand. "I was afraid it would lift its leg on me," she said.

"She wouldn't do that, she's my friend," Peter said.

Peter knelt down with Spanielius in his arms and patted her head while she still lay unconscious, then gave her a belly-rub. Dya leaned over and asked, "Do you require privacy?"

"If I didn't know better I'd say you're jealous. What are you doing here?" Peter then thought of the answer before Dya could reply and that seemed to bother Dya. She didn't like her thoughts being read. He looked her into her eyes and said, "You are trying to save my life."

"It seemed like the only positive thing to do," she replied as she pushed her hair back behind her antennae ears. Dya knelt down beside Peter. She put her arm around him and kissed his forehead. "I find seeing you alive to be a very positive experience."

Just as Peter leaned forward towards Dya's moist lips, Spanielius awoke and snapped. Dya fell backwards, pointing her plasma-pistol at the fierce Kanineite. Peter pulled Spanielius back and held her while talking in soothing tones.

"Down girl," he said. "She's okay."

But Spanielius kept snarling and growling then whimpering. Her tail went limp. Peter couldn't understand what was bothering her. Dya turned around as a shadow crossed over them; she pointed upwards and said, "It's not me that's bothering her. It's up there."

Peter Pulsaar glanced upwards at the darkening sky and saw the Havoccraft looming above.

* * *

Admiral Seasqrd did not even wait for the turbines to cool on his shuttle car before hopping out and storming up to the home of Dr. Rozwelles. He had just checked his ringmail and the frantic, virtual face of Peter Pulsaar had left him quite concerned; he had to hope that Pulsaar would be fine on his own until he got to the bottom of what was up in Orson Rozwelles' head.

Forgetting his superior strength, the admiral pounded on the door so hard he left a few dents, but he did not care. He had little time.

Casting a shadow across the domes of the domicile was the Havoccraft. Seasqrd briefly turned to look up at the malevolent warship when the door finally rolled up and standing in the doorway was Otto the automaton.

"I'm here to see Dr. Rozwelles," Seasqrd said.

"Sorry, but Dr. Rozwelles requested that he not be disturbed," Otto replied politely as flashing lights gleamed in the glass sphere above his plastic, human face, which bore a look of remorse.

"It is urgent Otto; we shall need Orson's Mind Machine to thwart our enemies." He pointed upwards to the Havoccraft. "He must see me; he must listen to me."

"Sorry, sir, but as I stated before — "

Seasqrd sucked in a deep breath and said, *"SHUT UP and SHUT DOWN."*

"I stated… I stated… I stated…."

Otto's human face went blank and the lights in his bubblehead head dimmed. He slowly slouched over.

Seasqrd wasted no time opening the secret portal that led into Rozwelles' underground laboratory. He raced down to the cave. After executing a perfect power kick, Seasqrd stepped through the shattered doorframe and found Orson Rozwelles standing with his uraniumcranium on.

"Come in Kanineites," he said.

"Rozwelles!" Seasqrd said. "I ought to break your neck."

"What's going on?" Rozwelles pulled the glass helmet off his head. "Stand away, sir."

"I see what is going on," Seasqrd said, rushing forward. "How could you?"

"How could I do what?" Rozwelles backed away in fright to the other side of his chemistry table. "I said keep your distance, sir."

"Orson, the one thing a person with your IQ cannot do is play dumb." Seasqrd stood at the opposite side of the table. "You're acting like the god of this world and you want us off at any cost you self-righteous super-genius!"

"Spare me your brutish barbs," Rozwelles said while maintaining his distance from the admiral.

"Then tell me the truth about this planet." Seasqrd tossed the table out of the way. As the potions and chemicals splattered across the floor, Rozwelles backed up against the wall. Seasqrd took him by his collar, hoisting him up on his toes.

"What do you think is going on?" Dr. Rozwelles asked.

"I think you've been creating your own life-forms here. Your own personal pets that you can evolve at your pleasure and with your mind over matter machine you can act as their omnipotent deity."

"Bah," Rozwelles said just before he was thrown across the room.

Rozwelles rose off the computer terminal that lay next to him and said, "You don't understand. I may be their creator, but I'm not playing God. Oh, sure they've built some statues in my likeness and I gave them a few commandments, but I prohibited them from holding a holiday feast in my honor."

"Oh, that makes things all together different."

Dr. Rozwelles shook his head. "You don't understand the symbiotic relationship between the Kanineites and me. They need a culture. I gave them one. They are my people and I will help them grow into something greater than humans ever dreamed of becoming. At least they appreciate my genius. You humans are all alike; you and my dearly departed comrades."

"Yes, let us talk about the deaths of your fellow scientists that you brought to this world," Seasqrd said.

"I'd rather not." Rozwelles circled around, keeping his distance from Seasqrd.

"You will!" Seasqrd said; he circled around, following Rozwelles' path. "They did not approve of your experiments with the Kanineites did they? So when they voiced disapproval what became of them?"

"I don't see where you're going with this?" Rozwelles moved around the MOMM.

"How can a mental-colossus be so dumb?" Seasqrd asked. "Your mind over matter machine did what you could not bring yourself to do. It murdered those who opposed you."

"Rotten hypothesis!"

"Your anger drove the machine to conjure up a monstrosity that would destroy anyone who threatened your chance to play God." Seasqrd cornered Rozwelles off.

"Your theory is all conjecture." Rozwelles backed into his uraniumcranium.

"Then how do you explain the monstrosity that attacked the Zenith last night?" Seasqrd asked.

"Indeed," Rozwelles said. "You explain how I could have sent a monster to attack your cosmicraft last night when I was asleep… oh, shit."

Rozwelles crouched as if someone had just kicked him in the stomach. For a brief moment, Admiral Seasqrd actually felt sorrow for him then he walked towards him and said, "Orson you must listen to me."

"No, no, I won't listen anymore," Rozwelles said, stepping away. "I'm going to tell my MOMM!"

As soon as Rozwelles placed the uraniumcranium upon his head the gauges on the wall sprang to life. Seasqrd was about to pull the crystal headset off of Rozwelles skull when two power cables lowered down from the ceiling and wrapped themselves about Seasqrd's arms and torso. Acting like they were alive, the power cables tightened their grip, constricting about Seasqrd's body, then an electro-optic line descended, acting like a snake ready to attack, it seemed poised to thrust its high-energy tip into Seasqrd's chest.

"You're finished, Gene Lucas," Rozwelles said as he slinked back across the lab floor.

Admiral Seasqrd struggled against the attack of the MOMM but he wasn't scared and Rozwelles knew it, and the doctor was obviously perplexed by it. Seasqrd smiled at the super genius and said, "You forget I have the power!"

CHAPTER 16
THOSE SCI-FI GUYS VERSUS THE SAUCERPIONS

Peter Pulsaar ran about in a panic searching for a safe place for him and the females to hide. Up above, he saw Zlythetaur Saucerpions fly by; he had seen these CGIsms before. They were a menacing mix of arachnid life and disc-shaped flying crafts. The flying cybernetic organisms swung their fiendish tail-guns about, taking aim at the Kanineite compound and firing deadly incinerays. At the bow of each Saucerpion grew an organic cephalothorax that housed an array of mechanical eyes, which seemed to target Kanineite warriors, and as the Saucerpions swooped down the Kanineites were seized in clutches of the Saucerpions' pedipalps.

Below, Peter watched the Zlythetaur Colossoroids come smashing through the forest, attacking the village of the Kanineites. As their enormous boots pounded across the terrain, the Kanineites panicked. Peter felt broken hearted seeing Kanineite mothers flee with their puppies in their mouths. He watched the terrible Colossoroids scan the scurrying Kanineites and Peter dreaded what was next. The mechanical giants shifted their metal heads around and their iron jaws opened, revealing speakers that pierced the air with thunderous siren whistles. They lifted their massive robotic arms and their photon-phalanges fired laser beams, blasting Kanineite doghouses and reducing the village to rubble.

Amidst the flame and ashes, Peter Pulsaar, Dya Nam-mock and Spanielius ran with Kanineite warriors who fled in terror as they held their ears. They scurried into the woods and hedge country except those who were caught in the pinchers of diving Saucerpions.

"My people are brave, but the Lawgiver did all the thinking for us. We are leaderless," Spanielius said.

Peter saw the way Spanielius was looking at him and quickly replied the only way he could, "You're better off letting someone else do the thinking for you; it's less headaches."

"Peter!" Dya said. Stray laser bolts from the Colossoroids struck. As the terrible titans stomped by Peter, Dya and Spanielius dove for cover.

"You destroyed the oracle of the Lawgiver," Spanielius said, placing her paws on Peter's arm. "You must now take command. You are our Chosen One. I feel it."

"You don't understand," Peter said. "Look out there! Your weapons and defenses are useless against their kind of power."

"The power!" Dya pointed at Peter. "You have the power."

The Zlythetaur Colossoroids plodded across the land pointing their fingers, pulverizing a path through the towering trees and stepping on what was left of the Kanineite village. Peter and Dya withdrew behind a large stone as the ground quaked beneath them.

"I cannot help them," Peter said.

"Peter, you're a Cosmos-Corpsman. You're a G-Man! Just act on your natural instincts!" Dya said.

"Good advice," Peter said but as he turned to run he felt Dya grab his collar while Spanielius bit onto his leg.

"Where are you going? I didn't mean those instincts!" Dya shouted as she and Spanielius pulled Peter back and they all fell to the ground.

Peter rolled over and said, "I can't do anything!"

"Yes, you can!" Dya shouted over the blasting of the rocket rifles that were being fired by the Z shock troops that followed the Colossoroids.

"What about Cosmos-Corps' primary rule of minding your own business?" Peter asked.

"That mind-your-own-business directive is only for healthy, growing cultures. This society knows nothing of war, violence or hate. It's up to you to show them what human civilization is all about."

"Say that again."

Dya placed her hands on either side of Peter's face and said, "You must stand and help them fight the Z!"

Dya's positive words echoed in Peter's mind and a surge of confidence overcame him as she completed her mind-mesh. Then there was another explosion followed by a series of rocket bombardment but now Peter was unafraid. The Saucerpions flew back over igniting the treetops while the Z shock troopers descended over the hill. Peter told Dya and Spanielius to take cover behind the stone.

There was tremor; Peter lifted his head over the stone to look around. His eyes assessed the latest Z assault; he found a column of seven Atomatanks crossing the horizon. Their spiked wheels were spinning at high speed carrying armor-plated frames with heavy sonicannons mounted on top. One of the Atomatanks rolled towards them, crushing underbrush and shrubbery. Its sonicannon let out a blast turning the stone Peter, Dya and Spanielius hid behind to pebbles.

Peter flew back from the sonic attack landing flat on his back; he slowly got up choking on dust and peered back to see Dya kneeling over the fallen Spanielius. Peter raced to Dya's side and looked down at Spanielius in her arms. The poor girl remained motionless. Dya broke out her emergency medi-kit from her belt.

"Is she going to live?" Peter asked.

"We shall see," Dya said. "I for one am remaining positive."

Peter watched the Saucerpions fly off in the distance as the Colossoroids marched along clearing a path for the Atomatanks. He turned to see the Z shock troopers slither along in a slow yet relentless approach, searching for stray casualties and fleeing victims. He looked at Spanielius and he felt more than confident; he felt mad.

"These darn Z must be stopped."

Dya removed a pack of pills from her kit. "What did you say?"

"Nothing," Peter knelt next to Spanielius, "I don't know if she should be moved but we'll have to take that chance," he said. Peter picked up Spanielius' limp body and cradled her in his arms. He sought out an area of safety beyond a ridge. There he placed her down and Dya knelt by her side.

"We should be safe here for the moment," she said.

"She doesn't look good," he said.

"Must I tell you again?" Dya began administering medical treatments. "Be positive!"

"I'd rather get mad!" Peter dropped back behind what was left of some smoldering tree trunks, avoiding the search of the Z troopers.

Suddenly, a Kanineite Peter recognized came scurrying up out of the hollow. As the one called Caesar Shepherd darted by, Peter Pulsaar grabbed a hold of him and yanked him back.

"We must stand and fight the Z!" he said.

The Kanineite judge pulled away and ran. Peter chased after him but bounced into Brutus Boxer. He screamed, "We must fight back!"

Brutus Boxer ran off, disappearing into a crowd of fleeing Kanineites. Finally, Peter cupped his hands over his mouth and yelled, "STOP!"

The Kanineites stood dumbfounded. Peter could not believe the confidence and power in his voice. He did not know what he had done yet he was pleased the Kanineites had obeyed his words though the pursuing Z were advancing around the hollow and were taking aim with their rocketrifles. Peter commanded the Kanineites to charge into an adjacent grove, hoping the Z troops would follow.

They reached an opening in the grove of trees where Peter commanded the Kanineites down on the ground. Brutus

Boxer seemed confused. He looked at Caesar Shepherd and said, "Why do we suddenly listen to the interloper?"

"He sounds like he knows what he's doing," Caesar said.

"I do," Peter said. "Please trust me and *play dead!*"

The trees shook and swayed and finally cracked in half as a column of Z soldiers marched through the forest, blasting everything in sight with their rocketrifles.

"Stop!" Peter yelled. "This is your only chance to surrender."

The Z stood in confusion. Peter continued with his illogic. "You are surrounded! Drop your weapons!" he said.

The Z were stunned with miscomprehension. Clad in their armored uniforms of gold and black, they moved in closer to Peter, pointing their rocketrifles at him and ignoring the motionless Kanineite bodies that littered the grassy field.

Finally they took aim. Peter looked at the Kanineites strewn across the ground amid the Z troopers.

"Now bite like dogs!" Peter commanded.

At Peter's command the Kanineites rose from the ground and pounced on the Z, punching them with their paws and whipping them about by the their tails. They bit and chased after them and one by one the Z were trounced.

When the last of the enemy had been vanquished, the Kanineites held rocketrifles up over their heads and cheered for Peter Pulsaar. Peter could feel a rush through his genetically enhanced heart like a neutrino going through matter. He had never known such a thrill until one of the Kanineites sprang on Peter, knocking him over and licking his face.

"Spanielius!" Peter said. "You're alive!"

"And you are our Chosen One." She ran her snout through his hair, sniffing him. Dya reached down and yanked Peter to his feet.

"You have defeated the Z troopers, but where are the Colossoroids?" Dya asked.

"No doubt on their way to crush the Zenith," Peter said. He called for Caesar Shepherd and Brutus Boxer and explained that Dya would instruct them on how to use their new weapons.

"I must go and thwart the Colossoroids," Peter said, but before he could dash off the Kanineites took a hold of his shirt and nipped at his pants, begging him to remain with them.

"*No!*" Peter said. "*Stay!*"

"Where did that voice come from?" Dya asked.

"I don't know but they sure listen to it," Peter said and winked.

"Why not wait for us?" Dya said. "You cannot combat the Colossoroids alone."

Peter poked his thumb into his torso and said, "Hey, I've got the power."

*   *   *

Captain Ray Atamz watched the skies with dread. Zly-thetaur Saucerpions descended from the clouds and converged on the Zenith. The flying ships hovered about, with their tails whipping about aiming their incinerays at the Zenith.

"Get back into the ship!" Ray Atamz ordered and the secure-ready guards followed their fleeing captain up the gangplank. "Activate deflection plates!"

Up on the bridge, Captain Atamz leaned over to read hull temperatures that were rising to danger levels. Jane MaCardiak stepped out of the jetevator and grabbed the captain by his collar.

"Ray, they're turning the Zenith into a toaster. Do something before we pop!" she said.

Atamz looked upward and said, "Zenith computer correlate a battle plan that will thwart the Saucerpions."

Dr. MaCardiak slapped the captain's shoulder. He pulled away from her and said, "It will only be a few moments before—"

"*Correlation complete.*" The speaker in the bridge ceiling lit on and then off. "*Strategy has been programmed.*"

"Excellent," Atamz said. He said to Jane raising his index finger and said, "You see the Zenith is quite capable of defending herself."

"You're quite a man," Jane patted Ray's shoulder.

Slowly, the snowy screen of the see-plate displayed an image of the battle outside. While Dr. MaCardiak and his bridge crew became glued to the scene, Captain Atamz ran over to a computer console and began tapping buttons as fast as he could. He turned and pointed so that MaCardiak and the rest of the crew would notice the targeting system that had been displayed across the see-plate.

"What's with the cross-hairs bobbing over your see-plate?" MaCardiak asked.

"This ship has quite a few tricks and so does her captain!" Atamz said.

He sat in his reclino-chair and snapped his fingers. Lt. Romeda immediately approached with a box with a long lever protruding from it. MaCardiak seemed to be dismayed when Ray placed it between his legs.

"If you're going to spend more time on my bridge then in your hosp-hold at least be of some technical support." He tossed a long cord to the doctor. "Help me plug in my joystick."

"I beg your pardon," MaCardiak said.

"Ensign Vector reroute the meson machinegun's tactical matrix through the see-plate and have it connected directly to my remote control," Atamz said.

"Yes," said the ensign. "The meson machinegun will take them down."

"Exactly," Atamz said. "Jane, stand back, while I play with my joystick."

"Typical man," Dr. MaCardiak said.

Ignoring Jane's comment, Ray quickly and proficiently locked the crosshairs onto one of the Saucerpions and fired. The Saucerpion exploded.

"Direct hit!" Atamz said.

231

"Now get that one," MaCardiak said. "You need a tighter grip on your joystick."

Atamz fired on another Saucerpion and moments later its burning wreckage fell to the ground.

"Captain, you're doing it," Lt. Meedioride said.

"Of course," Atamz said, maneuvering his joystick with glee.

"One left," MaCardiak said.

A tremor shook the deck plates of the Zenith. Another tremor quickly followed, shivering the bulkheads.

"Ray, what was that shockwave?" MaCardiak asked.

"Nothing to worry about, Doctor. It was just the last Saucerpion crashing to the ground." Atamz sighed. "Status report."

"Hull temperature returning to normal," Romeda said, "however, our deflections plates are damaged."

"Put the fixallites onto the task." Ray shook in his chair as another tremor rocked the Zenith. "What is that?"

"That's what I asked," said the doctor.

There was another tremor and Captain Atamz realized there was another opponent on its way.

"Captain," said Lt. Meedioride, studying his helmscope. "There are three Z Colossoroids approaching our repellozone."

"Lt. Romeda switch helmscope to main view," Captain Atamz said with a snap of his fingers.

The see-plate became a wall of static then went to black but then came back on and revealed three elephantine robots stomping forward.

"Oh no, Colossoroids" Ensign Vector said. "And they're the new Double X –Execution models."

Ray and the whole crew watched with trepidation as the Colossoroids slowed to a halt momentarily while each chest of each Colossoroid unfolded. Within the cavity of each robot's chest was an array of warheads.

"What are they doing?" asked Dr. MaCardiak.

"They're preparing to launch their pecpedoes at us," said Lt. Meedioride. "Our defenses will never be able to withstand the blast."

The Zenith rocked and pitched again as the Colossoroids drew nearer. Atamz fell forward out of his reclino-chair. He quickly got back to his feet, but held a lever in one hand and a cracked control box in the other. Dr. MaCardiak and the bridge crew looked towards Captain Atamz. He knew they were awaiting some brilliant strategy to come out of his mouth.

"Well Ray?" Jane MaCardiak asked.

Ray Atamz looked around then stared at Jane and whispered, "My joystick is broken."

CHAPTER 17
THOSE SCI-FI GUYS VERSUS THE COLOSSOROIDS

Peter Pulsaar leapt down the hillside, swung down on a vine and hit the ground running. One of the Colossoroids was just ahead and while its massive feet smashed into the surface, beating a path towards the Zenith, Peter leapt over the footprints, one by one until he jumped up and wrapped his arm about a bolt that emerged from the Colossoroid's heel. Jumping onto the top of the metal monster's pod-like hoof, Peter began climbing up its leg until he reached the Colossoroid's power source, right between its legs. He aimed his weapon and fired directly at the small hatch, blowing it open. He set his plasma-pistol to overload and tossed it into the power core chamber.

Peter jumped to the ground and rolled to safety just before the explosion. He looked up and saw the jaw of the Colossoroid dangling wide open. Its mechanical hands draped about the smoldering power core station between its legs. Its once threatening siren call turned to a high-pitched wail. The metallic titan stumbled forward as if it were in severe pain and tumbled to the ground as its pecpedoes launched.

The small missiles rocketed outward and careened into the legs of the other Colossoroids, blasting their footing out from under them. The Colossoroids collapsed backwards as their pecpedoes fired skyward.

Peter raced away to safety using every bit of speed his genetically enhanced leg muscles could muster. He darted behind a ridge of rocks. From there Peter took in the victorious sight of the pecpedoes descending back down onto the Colossoroids leaving them in molten wreckage. He couldn't help jumping up and clapping but just as Peter was done smacking his hands together his super-sensitive hearing picked up on the rumble of Zlythetaur armored cavalry rolling in. He rose up from behind the rocks, watching Atomatanks drive down the hill behind him. The lead tank, which was bigger and a different color than the others, suddenly swerved and moments later Peter found himself standing before a heavy duty Z Atomatank with its sonicannon pointed right at him.

As the Atomatank ground to a halt before him the others sped down towards the Zenith. Peter wanted to race to the rescue but, a great feeling had consumed him and for once it was not fear it was curiosity; he had to know who had come to face him. The Atomatank's lid slowly flipped open. From within rose an ominous figure. He was dressed in black, but across his wide shoulders were two red, crescent shaped arm bands while a black cape rustled across his back in the wind. His billowy gray hair seemed to flow off his balding head like an icy waterfall, revealing a flashing power portal; it was just like the admiral's. In fact, the man was the spitting image of Admiral Seasqrd and suddenly Peter knew who he was facing.

"So you are Darklone," Peter said.

The man in black spoke. "Darklone to Zatan; launch second wave."

"Then you are Darklone!" Peter said.

"No, you fool!"

"You are not Darklone?" Peter said. "Who are you then?"

"You are delaying our mission," Darklone said.

"Me? I'm delaying our mission," Peter said. "We're not even on the same side."

"I'm not talking to you yet!" Darklone turned to the side and pressed his fingertip against the fang shaped communications device plugged in his ear. "Zatan!"

Peter shook his head in acknowledgement, trying to conceal his embarrassment about not recognizing the sabretooth. "Go ahead; finish your call," he said.

Darklone shook his fist in the air and said, "Just obey my commands and send them or else it's the tortucalator for you again."

The lights across his forehead seemed ready to singe his eyebrows. Darklone said, "I feel your power, my young friend, but you are no G-Man."

Peter paused then Darklone nodded and said, "Yes, I'm talking to you now."

"Well, wrong again Darklone!" Peter said defiantly as he stepped around keeping his distance from his foe. "I am a G-Man as my father was before me."

"I don't know who you are, but Gene Lucas was wise to keep you hidden from me." Darklone leapt down from the Atomatank and squared off against Peter, who assumed a nervous yet staunch fighting posture.

"Were you talking to me?" asked a voice.

"No, Zatan. Damn this thing!" Darklone tossed his sabretooth to the ground and squashed it beneath his boot.

Peter drew on some of the anger he had left and said "How do you know he wasn't protecting you from me."

He then charged at Darklone who sidestepped the maneuver, allowing Peter to land in a growth of shrubs. Darklone stood waiting patiently for Peter to climb out. He said, "You are the one who is wrong about several things."

Peter brushed a few thorns from his Cosmos-Corps uniform then stood agape while Darklone lifted a massive rock up over his head, preparing to hurl it at Peter.

"G-Men do not inherit the power," Darklone cried out. "They must be programmed with it. Why do you think we have these stupid computer ports imbedded in our heads?"

"What?" Peter asked, leaving his mouth open while the rock flew towards him. He ducked down only a nanosecond before the rock careened over his skull.

"Gene Lucas never shared that fact with you," Darklone said. "What else didn't he share with you?"

"I will not listen to you!" Peter flung himself at Darklone. They hurtled backwards into a tree. As Peter tried to get his hands about adversary's throat, Darklone shoved his foot under

Peter's stomach and sent him flying backwards with one kick. Peter collided with another tree and sank to the ground. He shook his head, reached up and tore a thick limb from the trunk. He swung the club at Darklone, but his foe was too agile, ducking each swing.

"I'm beginning to see what happened," Darklone said. "Seasqrd did not care for the way I used my power. So he went back to Rozwelles' original plan."

"You talk too much!" Peter attempted to plant the tree limb's knotted end right between Darklone's red-rimmed eyes, but Darklone caught the strike in the palm of one hand and cleaved the limb in two with the edge of his other hand. Peter dropped back, staring at the shard end of his wooden weapon.

"You are nothing more than an experiment gone wrong," Darklone said.

"What do you mean?" Peter asked. In the distance he could see the Atomatanks ramming themselves against the Zenith's repellozone. Their sonicannons sent shockwaves through the force-field and the anchordroids were straining under the relentless pounding. Peter wanted to do something, but Darklone's words had cut deep into his mind and heart.

"G-Men aren't born but they can be cloned. Get it?" Darklone smiled. "When his first clone turned to evil Seasqrd tried again and made an even bigger mistake."

Peter watched Darklone raise his finger at him. He shook his head, saying "No! The admiral would've told me!"

"Not if he were ashamed!" Darklone withdrew a weapon; it was some sort of a whip but it seemed mechanized.

"Yes, he must have been quite ashamed of you." Darklone cracked his whip at Peter.

"Ashamed?" Peter said.

"Well, I turned out bad, but you must be a real screw up for him to have denied who you are all these years." Darklone whipped his lash at Peter's legs. Peter felt the metallic cord weave about his knees. Darklone flipped him around and up in the air.

"I don't feel so good," Peter said while dangling upside down.

"That is how you should feel," Darklone said. He plopped Peter down into a mound of dirt. "You've probably caused Cosmos-Corps a great deal of disgrace."

"Stop it," Peter murmured.

"*Your mission to save Earth has failed and so has your effort to save your ship,*" Darklone said.

Peter felt the words of Darklone's booming voice sink deep within his head.

"*Failure!*"

"You're mean," Peter said. He lay face down in the dirt.

"*Pathetic, incompetent, loser.*"

"I lost the power," Peter said as he crawled away on his belly. The memories of all those he disappointed at Cosmos-Corps Academy raced through his mind. Darklone cracked his whip at Peter's face. Peter squirmed away in fright; he knew he didn't stand a chance.

"But you need not live this way anymore," Darklone said as he stood victorious. "Join me and I shall show you the real way to use power."

"No," Peter said.

"If you won't give me your power," Darklone stalked forward; the tip of his whip was snaking its way towards Peter's head, "then I will take it!"

"It's all yours," Peter said with a wave of his hand.

Darklone's sinister face was gleeful until he realized there was no power port on Peter's forehead. He said, "Oh darn, I forgot you don't have one."

The whip's tip poked at Peter's forehead a few more times until Darklone said, "Then you will just have to die."

Peter was terrified; Darklone's whip wrapped itself about Peter's neck and began choking him. He tugged in vain at the tightening noose but the cold cord remained unyielding. Peter realized it would all be over soon, but before he Darklone finished him off he needed to know something; he choked out a few last words. "I must know one last thing."

"You must know what?" Darklone asked. "What? What?"

Peter couldn't talk the whip was suffocating him. Darklone repeated teasingly, "What? What? What?"

Then his voice became serious, "What are they doing?"

Darklone was distracted by some howling and barking and explosions. He was so distracted the cord about Peter's neck lost its tension. Peter pulled it loose and looked at what Darklone was staring at. As he gasped for air, he beheld his Kanineites on the attack. Darklone screamed, "Tell those damn dirty dogs to take their stinking paws off my Atomatanks!"

The Kanineites fired their rocketrifles point blank into the sterns of the Atomatanks. Peter watched Brutus Boxer lead the way as a group of Kanineites grabbed hold of one of the burning tanks and flipped it over. The rest of the pack followed, turning the Atomatanks over and firing rockets into their soft underbellies.

Caesar Shepherd then stood on top of one of the vanquished Atomatanks, pointed in the distance and cried out, "Just one left!"

Immediately, Darklone fled towards his Atomatank trying to reach it before the yapping Kanineites destroyed it. Peter rose up and shouted, "Wait you, I want to know more about you, me, Seasqrd and the G-Men!"

Darklone raced ahead as Peter crawled along then slowly rose to his feet. He pursued Darklone as quickly as he could. "Wait, I still want to know more."

He stumbled to the ground but jumped back up, but he was too weak to keep his balance, but he had to know what Darklone knew. He wanted answers about his past; he needed to know about Seasqrd and himself. He tripped over a stone as Darklone reached his Atomatank.

Darklone pressed a button on a remote control he had withdrawn from his sash. As he reached his Atomatank, the back hatch flipped open, revealing a portahole. Darklone tossed the teleportation device to the ground, looked at Peter and said, "Why not ask the perfect Seasqrd for your answers?"

"What," Peter said. Then a plasma-pistol fired and hit the tank. Dya came running ready to fire another shot with Spanielius scampering behind her. Darklone looked at them then turned towards the pack of Kanineites, charging upon him with rocketrifles in paw. He raised his hands.

"Your invasion has been thwarted." Dya took aim. "Step away from the portahole!"

"You may have stopped my Saucerpions, Colossoroids and Atomatanks, but my invasion is not over yet; you'll never stop them!" He glanced at the hillside.

Peter watched Dya reluctantly turn around to see what Darklone had glanced at. She turned back to make sure he had not moved, and then slowly turned around again, lowering her plasma-pistol to her side.

"Dya, he's getting away!" Peter yelled, but it was too late.

Darklone had dove into the portahole and dematerialized into the space-time continuum. Peter leaned over the portahole and said, "I need to know more."

"Get away from that portahole," Dya said, grabbing Peter by the collar.

"He is gone," Peter said. "You drove him away."

"That is a negative thing?"

"Well, yes, when I wanted answers from him." Peter pointed down at the portahole. Spanielius kept shoving her snout into his face and sniffing him; he gently shoved her back and said, "I'm okay."

"I wouldn't concern myself with Darklone." Dya pointed at the horizon. "I'd be more concerned about them!"

Suddenly, the cheering Kanineites dropped their rocke-trifles. Spanielius' ears drooped and she hid behind Peter who just shook his head in disgust. Up on the hillside, scanning the area with their antennae, compound eyes and clypeuses were three gigantic, robotic insects.

Peter and Dya both sighed and said, "Mechan-Ants."

The Mechan-Ants gave off a shrilling sound from their living heads as their metallic limbs stabbed into the ground, carrying them closer to the Zenith. Peter, Dya and the Kanineites were forced to flee the path of the Mechan-Ants and hid behind a dense patch of brush and rocks.

Rock and soil seemed to dematerialize before the mechanical mandibles of the Mechan-Ants as they burrowed deep underground. Peter watched the soil that lay before the Zenith's hull. Within the repellozone the ground erupted; the Mechan-Ants emerged from their tunnel and began attacking the Zenith, ripping apart her hull and shredding her bulkheads.

"They're going to slice our cosmicraft to bits unless you do something," Dya said.

Peter watched the Mechan-Ants devour the Zenith's hull plates then sank his head between his hands.

"I've lost the power. Darklone knocked it out of me," he said. "I'm weak. I'm hopeless. I'm useless."

"Maybe this will work," Dya said.

Peter felt Dya's fingertips about his head. He shrugged. Her nails pressed into his skin.

"Amazing, even the mind-mesh cannot rouse your confidence," she said. "You need to get angry."

"Not gonna work," Peter said. He wrapped his arms about his stomach.

"Think of what they're doing to our ship," Dya said, while pointing at the Zenith.

"No good," Peter replied, wrapping his arms tighter about his stomach. His chin dipped down over his chest.

"Think of what they'll do to Dr. MaCardiak and Captain Atamz and all your shipmates." Dya raised her hands in the air; the Kanineites mimicked her gestures with their paws.

Peter looked at the dog people and knew they were anxious for him to lead them into another battle but all he could say was: "Still nothing."

Peter felt Dya's nails digging into his arm as she said, "Think of me."

Peter crinkled his nose and squinted; he said, "Sorry."

Dya put her hands on her hips and scowled. She asked, "What would Admiral Seasqrd do?"

"Seasqrd!" Peter jumped up and flexed his muscles. "He makes me angry!"

Dya stood back in shock, but the Kanineites howled in joy as Peter climbed onto Darklone's Atomatank and ripped the cannon out of the turret. He waved his arm at his canine compatriots; Brutus Boxer, Caesar Shepherd and a cohort of other Kanineite warriors followed Peter into one of the Mechan-Ant tunnels. Peter popped his head out the other side, grabbed his sonicannon and said, "Attack!"

Peter and his pack of allies pounced on their cybernetic foes. As he rammed the vibrating tip of the sonicannon into the first Mechan-Ant's abdomen, it trembled then began to shake apart. The Kanineites finished off the gigantic insect, pouncing on its head and thorax and pulling it to pieces.

Peter attacked the second and third Mechan-Ant beating on them with the sonicannon. The shock waves of the weapon blew the insects' circuits and cracked the joints of their jointed legs. The Kanineites soon stood among a pile of broken bolts, torn girders and fractured petioles. The anchordroids finally raised the repellozone while the gangplank of the Zenith lowered. Soon Peter Pulsaar found himself embraced by Jane MaCardiak.

"Peter! Peter!" she hugged him ardently. "I'm so glad you alright."

"Never mind that," Peter said. "Where is our fearless leader?"

"Ray is back on the bridge," Dr. MaCardiak said. "He's trying to fix his joystick."

"What did you say?" Dya said.

"No, I meant Gene Lucas Seasqrd," Peter said. "Where is that bald-headed bast—"

"Peter! That is no way for you to talk about the admiral." MaCardiak stood back.

"You mean my father?" Peter said. "My clone father I never knew."

"You know," MaCardiak said with her eyes opening wide.

"So you knew too," Peter said. "But you never told me."

"I would like to interject something," Dya said.

Peter ignored Dya.

"Peter, there are things you don't understand," Dr. Ma-Cardiak said.

"I really must intercede into this conversation," Dya said.

"I'm still waiting for your explanation," Peter said to Jane. The Kanineites began whimpering and begging for his attention.

"Go lie down. What's wrong with them?" he asked Dya.

"Perhaps I could elucidate the situation," Dya said.

"Dya, please, we don't have time to listen to the positive aspects of the situation," MaCardiak said then she looked down at the dark shadow crossing the ground. "Oh my, how strange."

Peter looked about as the Zenith became shrouded in darkness.

"I don't see anything positive in this." Dya pointed skyward. The Havoccraft had taken a position directly over the Zenith. Suddenly, the voice of Darklone could be heard.

"The young one has defeated my Z army and so I have decided it is futile to try and capture your ship and its lurking device."

Dya stepped next to Peter and held his hand. MaCardiak stood in front of him like she was shielding him from the Havoccraft. There was something furry nudging Peter's hand and he knew it was Spanielius.

"Is he going to surrender?" Peter asked.

"I severely doubt that," Dya said.

"Tell the young one he has left me with no alternative but to destroy you all," said the voice of Darklone. "Just as I destroyed Alpha Arthritis II, Deep Space 1999 and will soon the Earth. Tell Seasqrd I have finally hurt him enough."

Peter felt like his heart had just crossed the event horizon of a black hole. He yelled, "DARKLONE!"

"No, do not blame yourself," Dya said.

"She is right, Peter. Darklone would have destroyed us anyhow," Dr. MaCardiak said.

"Maybe... maybe not. Seems I just keep doing the wrong thing," Peter said. He kicked the ground. "Why did he have to say that? Now, I am going to die just as I always lived — worried."

"There's nothing to worry about." Ray Atamz was storming down the gangplank. "My joystick is working again."

"Good for you," MaCardiak said. "Think you can do something about that."

"Mother photon," Atamz gasped as he looked at the Havoccraft then he took Jane in his arms.

From beneath the Havoccraft two rods lowered and suddenly a violent wave of energy shot from the tip of one rod to the other; the blue beam of energy began pulsating. The rods spun beneath the Havoccraft's keel and the pulsing wave of energy turned red.

"It's their climate killer," Dya said as she clung to Peter.

"Where is the great Admiral Seasqrd now?" Peter asked.

CHAPTER 18
THOSE SCI-FI GUYS AND THE WRATH OF MOMM

Admiral Seasqrd agonized under the grip of the power cables while they shot high voltage waves into his body. His skin shuddered to the point that he thought it was going to crawl off his body until he finally broke free. The MOMM sent the cables after him once again, but Seasqrd grabbed the cable.

"*Power chop!*" he said as he severed the cable in two with one swipe of his hand. The second cable seemed stunned providing Seasqrd enough time to wrap it up, tying it in a knot.

"It's not over yet," Rozwelles said, touching his fingertips to the top of the uraniumcranium and shutting his eyes. Seasqrd looked about the lab trying to anticipate the next attack by MOMM.

Two large electric cabinets rose from the floor and flew at him. Seasqrd ducked and rolled across the floor just before the two cabinets collided together above him. Metal parts splattered over the floor as Seasqrd jumped to his feet. The MOMM sent the cabinets flying at him once again. Seasqrd waited for the first cabinet to soar down and lifted his leg.

"*Power kick!*"

When his foot impacted against the cabinet it bounced back against the wall of gauges and exploded, but he turned too late to kick the second cabinet and it hammered Seasqrd across the room.

"*Power lift!*" Seasqrd said as he gripped the sides of the cabinet, pressed it over his head and sent it careening into the glass dome, where Rozwelles created his living virtual images. Rozwelles ducked away from the blast that resulted from the cabinet's impact and looked at MOMM; more gauges on the walls began to light up.

Seasqrd scanned about and instinctively knew where the next attack would come from. A glass cabinet stood at the opposite side of the cave; the label across its door read: DANGER HAZARDOUS CHEMICALS.

Its door suddenly shattered revealing an array of rather lethal looking glassware standing upon the shelves. Seasqrd ran along the wall, making a path for the doorway as a barrage of bottles, beakers and flasks followed him. The glass containers darted across the room and burst against the wall over Seasqrd's head, raining bubbling chemical compounds down upon the floor. Seasqrd turned and raced up into the entranceway. He turned and took cover outside with his back to the wall and watched a final salvo of phials and test tubes soar from the mouth of the cave and impact against the stone wall opposite Seasqrd; the rock wall became a cascade of smoking flames and sizzling liquid.

Seasqrd slowly turned his head to look around the entranceway; he immediately ducked back as a large graduated cylinder flew over his head then a woman's scream echoed off the smoldering wall. Sprawled across the floor beneath him was the gorgeous yet limp body of Barbralta.

"Orson!" Seasqrd shouted into the cave. "Your daughter has been hurt."

"What have I done?" Rozwelles stepped forward and took the uraniumcranium off, "oh, the pain of it all."

"See what playing God has done," Seasqrd said as he knelt over Barbralta. He took her hand and began patting it. Rozwelles knelt by his daughter.

"Barbralta speak to me," he said. "Say you're alright. Tell me you don't blame me."

Seasqrd knelt next to the kneeling super-genius who dared think of himself as a deity and felt sad for the brilliant fool. Barbralta reached for her father. Rozwelles took her hand.

"Daddy," Barbralta said as she slowly rose to her feet. "Look what you've done to my best dress."

"Oh, how sharper than a serpent's tooth is it to have a thankless child," Rozwelles groaned and dropped her hands.

"You're lucky to be alive." Seasqrd steadied Barbralta. "Are you sure you were not harmed?"

"You know you're never to enter the MOMM cave without permission," Dr. Rozwelles said. "Why are you here?"

"It's PMS," Barbralta said, brushing off her charred dress.

"What did she just say?" Seasqrd said. He looked at Rozwelles in disbelief.

"Seasqrd, if you don't mind," Rozwelles said. He turned to his daughter and asked, "Has the Planetary Monitoring System has gone off?"

"Yes, but Otto has shut down and I couldn't get you on the intercomicator so I came down to show you," Barbralta said.

Seasqrd and Rozwelles followed Barbralta into the cave. She flipped a few switches and one of the monitors lit. Across the screen was the picture of the Havoccraft rising over the ECC Zenith. Seasqrd was taken aback; he squared his shoulders and stuck out his chest. He had almost forgotten who the real enemy was.

"You need not worry." Rozwelles held his daughter's hand. "They pose no threat to us. They're just here to destroy Seasqrd and his crew."

"Oh," Barbralta said. Then she looked at her father, then at Admiral Seasqrd.

"I feel sorry for your people," Rozwelles said, turning to Seasqrd.

"Feel sorry for your own people if we may call them that." Seasqrd pointed back at the monitor. Rozwelles stared in befuddlement at the Kanineites surrounding the Zenith.

"My babies! What are they doing there?" Rozwelles' face turned white. "Gene Lucas, you must do something!"

"Even my power is not great enough to fight off the Havoccraft, but you do have the power," Seasqrd replied.

Rozwelles' lips quivered. "What do you mean?" he asked.

Seasqrd spun Rozwelles around to face the MOMM and said, "You must try to use your Mind Over Matter Machine."

"But even my brain is not strong enough." Dr. Rozwelles placed a trembling hand to his chin.

"Father you can do it, you always told me the power of the human mind is the most powerful force in the universe," Barbralta said.

Seasqrd clasped his hands firmly about Rozwelles' shoulders. "You're not going to tell me that Dr. Orson Rozwelles doesn't have the brains for this."

Rozwelles nodded his head in agreement and he darted to fetch the uraniumcranium.

"Never fear, Rozwelles is here," he said. "I'll stop them if it's the last thing I do."

Barbralta latched onto Seasqrd's arm and whispered quickly, "I wish he hadn't of said that."

*   *   *

The only thing louder than the wail of the Zenith's maximum alert signal was the crying of the Kanineites and Peter Pulsaar was sure the only thing louder than them was the shrieking of Captain Atamz.

"As Captain I have one thing to say! Do not think of this as utter doom, defeat and death," he said. "Simply think of it as one of those no-win scenarios they simulated for us back at Cosmos-Corps Academy. Only this won't be a simulation because we're really going to be destroyed!"

Atamz put his hands over his face, attempting to conceal his tears. Dya patted him on the shoulder and said, "Sir, we have a saying about death on my planet… you only have to face it once."

Atamz dropped to his knees, his hands still over his face while he shook his head.

"Have I said something wrong again?" Dya asked.

The Havoccraft appeared ready to unleash its primary aggression weapon when, suddenly, a whirling vortex appeared over the Zenith. At first Peter thought it was another weapon in the Z arsenal but then he realized it was something else. The wisps of plasma and bolts of electricity coalesced into the form of a frightening skull.

"What's that?" Peter asked.

"It's the monstrosity," Ray Atamz gasped while his hands pulled back revealing his colorless face.

Peter did not know what Ray meant but he could see the monstrosity was an entity of enormous power.

"Is it something Dr. Rozwelles dreamt up?" he asked.

"Could be," Dya answered while holding Peter by the arm. They both looked skyward anticipating the battle to come. "It attacked our ship last night."

"So which side is it on?" Peter asked, holding her hand tight.

"Not sure," Dya said as she moved closer to Peter. They held one another while watching the battle above.

The fiery head of the monstrosity looked up at the Havoccraft, letting out a roar of anger. Its tentacle-like hair whipped about. It flew upward like an animal lunging towards an enemy. The monstrosity attacked the Havoccraft, its tentacles burning their way into the malevolent dreadnought's armored hull.

Just then the Havoccraft's primary aggression weapon fired, driving the monstrosity back with a devastating force beam. At first the monstrosity seemed to be wounded by the beam of pulsing blue energy then it opened its gaping mouth and began feasting on the beam. The Havoccraft's force beam relentlessly drove its way down the monstrosity's throat but rather than shrink from the attack the monstrosity grew.

Peter turned to Dya and said, "It's taking in everything they dish out."

They watched the monstrosity grow larger with each pulse and shock wave that entered its mouth until it became a behemoth larger than the Havoccraft. The monstrosity raised itself upward, let out a final roar then swallowed the Havoccraft. Peter could not believe his genetically enhanced eyes. There was an almost gleeful look on the monstrosity's hideous face just before it exploded. The sky seemed to burn as the Havoccraft left a trail of smoke through the clouds while crashing into the hills beyond. The land shook, dropping the Zenith crew and the Kanineites to the ground.

Peter got up first; helped Dya to her feet and said, "That's the end of Darklone and the Z."

They both looked at the plumes of smoke rising over the hills and they hugged. The Kanineites yipped and squealed in joy. Peter was so joyous he felt enough courage to kiss Dya but just then they picked up Peter Pulsaar and carried him about.

"Our new leader has done it!" Spanielius shouted. "The new Lawgiver has saved us all. He is truly the Chosen One."

"Peter, who are these dog-people?" Jane MaCardiak yelled.

"And why do they call you their Lawgiver?" Captain Atamz asked. "And what do they mean you saved us all?"

"If I may, Captain, these are the Kanineites. They believe Peter to be their prophesized chosen one," Dya said.

The Kanineites placed Peter down in front of Ray, Jane and Dya.

"They are my friends," Peter said. "At last I have people who accept me as I am."

"But you are their Chosen One?" Atamz scoffed.

"Ask them," Peter said. He turned to Spanielius and said, "*Speak!*"

Ray jumped back from Peter and asked, "Hey, where'd that come from?"

Jane clasped her hands together and said, "Our little Geneti-Man's voice is changing."

252

Peter let out a sigh of disgust and pointed at Spanielius; Ray and Jane slowly turned their attention towards the Kanine-ite female.

"It is the truth. He is our Chosen One." Spanielius said, gesturing to Peter with open paws. "We were told that a leader would come who would have powers similar to ours."

"You see," Peter said. "It had to be me."

"He would stand when our old Lawgiver had fallen," she said.

"You see, that's me," Peter said.

"And that he would save us from certain doom," Spanielius said.

"You see, that's me," Peter said.

"And of course he would be pure," Spanielius said, "a virgin."

"You see, it had to be...." Peter froze. He closed his eyes.

"So that was the innermost secret I could not tap into!" he heard Dya announce.

Peter did not even bother to look at Dya let alone answer her inquiry. He plodded up the gangplank hanging his head. The Kanineites, holding their tails low, began to follow.

"You're not bringing them aboard my ship," Atamz said.

Peter pointed at Spanielius and the other Kanineites.

"*Stay!*" he said in his power voice.

The Kanineites were confused, but they obediently stood on the ground at the edge of the gangplank. Peter stopped half way up, looked at Captain Atamz and said, "By the way our mission is over so I no longer consider myself a Cosmos-Corpsman. I'm going aboard to grab some things from my cabin, then I will return to my people and you guys can go back to the Earth without me."

He pulled his C-C insignia off his shoulders and chest and dropped them to the ground.

"You don't mean that," Dr. MaCardiak said. The Kanine-ites turned and snarled at Jane who backed up by Ray. Atamz was about to say something when the Kanineites began growling at him as well.

"I hope I never see another human again," Peter said. He strode up the gangplank into the Zenith where he punched a hole in the bulkhead.

"Hey, watch what you do to my ship, pal."

Peter heard Ray's shout from the bottom of the gangplank then he and Jane began following Peter up into the Zenith, arguing all the way.

"Stop thinking of yourself and your precious ship and think of him."

"You always did enough of that for the two of us."

"Peter, wait for us!"

Peter stood at the top of a stairwell. He was enraged; he spun around and shouted, "*STOP IT!*"

Peter clasped his hands over his mouth but it was too late. His power voice had just bowled the captain and the doctor down the gangplank. He looked down at the two senior officers as they lay sprawled across a mound of dirt.

"Oh my, I just struck two superior officers. Of course I really didn't strike them but I did cause their fall. Well, who cares; I'm not in Cosmos-Corps anymore," Peter said.

"Peter, wait for me," Dya said as she walked to the bottom of the gangplank, stepping over the captain and chief medical officer. Peter looked down at the commander's beautiful face and the long slender antennae springing up over her luxurious hair.

"Sorry, Dya, but you're the last one I want to see," Peter said, then he ran down the corridor to the nearest jetevator.

* * *

The shuttle car roared to a stop beneath the Zenith. Admiral Seasqrd stepped out. He turned to help Barbralta out as Otto climbed from the open hatch on the side. He cautiously approached the Kanineites and slowly extended his hand while making kissing sounds with his lips. The Kanineites sniffed at Seasqrd, turned their noses up and walked away.

"What is going on there, Admiral, sir?" Barbralta pointed to the bottom of the gangplank.

"There is an odd sight." Seasqrd looked at his two most senior officers wrestling on the ground.

"Get your hands off me, sir!" the doctor said.

"You're on top of me!"

"Shut up!" MaCardiak said jumping to her feet.

"Ray!" said the admiral.

Captain Atamz suddenly saw his superior officer; he jumped to attention and tried to offer congratulations on the destruction of the Havoccraft and flirt with Barbralta at the same time; Admiral Seasqrd had no patience for either and he said, "No time for that now, Ray; where is Peter? Is he safe?"

"Your junior G-Man is fine, but he has resigned from Cosmos-Corps again and he claims he's going to stay on this planet with these mutant canines."

"He can't do that!" Admiral Seasqrd said. Spanielius approached Atamz and Seasqrd smelled their groins then backed away in disgust. The rest of the Kanineites showed their teeth; Atamz backed up and stood behind the admiral. The Kanineites' growl turned to a low roar. Seasqrd faced the snarling Kanineites and said, "None of us can stay here. This planet is about to explode in twenty-four macrons."

The Kanineites tilted their heads in confusion as Ray, Dya and Jane began bombarding Seasqrd with questions, but it was Barbralta who offered explanations.

"My father is dead," she said.

"How sad, how unfortunate, how about you lean on my shoulder?" Captain Atamz asked and placed his arms about her narrow waist.

"Always there for a woman in need aren't you, Captain Atamz," Jane MaCardiak said.

"Let her continue," Admiral Seasqrd said. He was really losing patience with his officers. And he was concerned about Peter.

"It was my father who saved your cosmicraft. By use of his Mind Over Matter Machine, he was able to conjure up that hideous monstrosity, but it took all the power of his incredible mind to vanquish your enemies. The strain was obviously too much; just as obvious was his fear that his MOMM would fall into the wrong hands. While he lay dying on the floor of his lab, he ordered Admiral Seasqrd to throw a series of levers and then requested that he take the Kanineites, Otto and me back to Earth and also this." Barbralta pointed to the uraniumcranium. The glass headset lay upon a red velvet blanket in the back of the shuttle. "It holds all his vast knowledge; then with his last words he explained that the MOMM's negaton furnace had been set to self-destruct.

"And with all the super-genius of his incredible brain had he forgotten that the Zenith is still under repair?" Dr. MaCardiak asked.

"It seems Earth's greatest scientist overlooked that one little problem," Seasqrd said.

"Sir, we have another problem. Peter knows you are his father through cloning," MaCardiak said.

"What?" Seasqrd said. "How?"

Dr. MaCardiak waved her hands in befuddlement as tears filled her eyes. "I couldn't say."

Dya stepped forward and said, "Pardon me for the interruption but Peter was fine until his confrontation with Darklone. As a matter of fact upon Darklone's escape Peter stated a need for more answers. I submit Darklone used your identity as his long lost father to eradicate any confidence Peter may have had or ever will."

"That is all well and analytical, Dya but does it really matter?" the doctor asked.

"It matters to me," Admiral Seasqrd said as his guts churned. He pounded his fist into his open palm so hard the thud made the Kanineites jump. He thought about his evil clone; he looked off in the hills where the Havoccraft had crashed and said, "At least we need not worry about anyone else suffering under Darklone's menace; status report."

He said directly to Ray, "Status report."

"Huh?" Atamz said as he consoled and caressed Barbralta.

Seasqrd was really losing patience. "Captain, I would like a report on the status of Zenith repairs."

Ray Atamz took a break from massaging Barbralta's shoulders and was about to say something when the ground trembled. A rush of wind swept through the air; a malevolent specter hovered over the hillside. The Havoccraft slowly rose into the sky. Suddenly, Otto the automaton began flailing his mechanical arms.

"Warning!" he yelled. "Danger! Incoming projectile!"

Bursting from the clouds was a missile headed right for the Zenith. Ray clung to Barbralta as the Kanineites spread in panic. Seasqrd stood firm and said, "It is only a txt messile."

"Are you sure?" MaCardiak asked.

"It must be Darklone." Seasqrd stepped aside. The small missile landed right in front of him. From the upper end of the txt messile emerged a notification emblazoned across the illuminated screen:

SRT say IB & AAS! GT & noble EF4T but futile. ATM I am OMW to refuel the Havoccraft. UMR U will be destroyed. IMAO there is NWO — TMWFI.

Darklone (GMBO W A VEG)

"My txt speak is a little rusty," Seasqrd said to Captain Atamz.

"Sorry to say I'm back and alive and smiling." Atamz pointed at the text screen. "Great try and noble effort but futile. At the moment, I am on my way to refuel the Havoccraft. Upon my return, you will be destroyed. In my arrogant opinion there is no way out. Take my word for it. Darklone."

Atamz drew in a deep breath before finishing. He looked at the admiral, who remained patiently, awaiting a translation of the final txt within the parenthesis.

"Giggling my butt off with a very evil grin," Atamz said.

Admiral Seasqrd slammed his fist into his palm again; his lip began to quiver, then he let out a violent yell.

"DARKLONE!" Seasqrd said with his fist now in the air and watched the Havoccraft ascend into the upper atmosphere.

"Admiral, I'd like to suggest something positive," Dya said as she took the admiral's fist and lowered his arm. "I suggest we get the hell out of here as fast as we can."

"No, Dya." Seasqrd shook his head. "It's always the same. They attack and we run. Well, it's time to draw a line in the sand."

Seasqrd slid the toe of his boot across the ground. "And that line must be drawn here. Oh, yuck!"

He began scraping dog crap off his boot, while one of the Kanineites held his head down in shame. Dr. MaCardiak approached the admiral and said, "Don't tell me you have another hunch."

"More than a hunch, I have a plan," Admiral Seasqrd said. Satisfied that his boot was clean he turned to Ray once again. "Captain Atamz."

The captain reluctantly pulled his arm from around from Barbralta's hip and asked, "What is it Admiral?"

"Ray, you and Dya and the crew get the Zenith repaired." He pointed at Ray. "We need every hand; no not mechanical ones real ones!"

"Aye, Admiral." The captain saluted with a sad face.

"Oh, Captain, I've always been very good with my hands. May I be of assistance?" Barbralta asked.

"Certainly." Atamz now smiled with glee. "I'd be glad to work on you. I mean work with you."

"Very well," Admiral Seasqrd said. "Otto and I will utilize our extraordinary strength to bring back the negaton furnace."

"Do what?" Atamz asked. "What exactly is your plan, sir?"

"It's something Sam Parseck told me. He had thought of a way to destroy the Havoccraft." Seasqrd tapped his head as he thought back to Darklone's attack on Alpha Arthritis II.

"I'm sorry, Ray I wasn't listening," Seasqrd said to the perplexed captain.

"How?" Atamz repeated.

"Negatons," the admiral walked up and gently patted Ray's face, "negatons."

Ray Atamz nodded as if he was beginning to understand while Jane said, "Huh?"

We must use the greatest weapon available to us and the only weapon that will stop Darklone once and for all and save this world from destruction and of course save our own."

"And Peter?" MaCardiak said.

"First, I will talk to Peter," Seasqrd said raising his hand and pointing his finger upward.

"No, I will go and talk to him," Jane MaCardiak said.

"But, Doctor, I need you to take the uraniumcranium to your hosp-hold where it will be safe."

"I need to talk to Peter!"

Ray Atamz obviously didn't want to listen to Jane talk about Peter and took Barbralta around the bow of the Zenith. Dya began walking up the gangplank and said, "I'll gather the crew." She got about half way up the gangplank when she turned pointed at Jane and added, "Oh and take it from someone with psychic powers, she's made up her mind."

"Very well." Seasqrd cautiously nodded to Dr. MaCardiak. As she stepped up the gangplank he said, "Don't take too long Jane. We shall need Peter very soon."

"Yes we will!" Captain Atamz shouted. Seasqrd was pleased to hear that Ray was finally starting to appreciate Peter's value; then he watched Ray lift his foot up and say, "His Kanineites are leaving loads all over the ship's perimeter."

*　　*　　*

Peter Pulsaar became tired of the bleeping and finally allowed his cabin door to swoosh open. Dr. MaCardiak entered the cabin and finding him sitting on the edge of his bed, sat down next to him.

"What troubles you?" she asked. "You can tell me?"

"I was lied to my whole life by the man I looked up to the most and the woman I care for the most thinks I'm pathetic."

"How could I ever think you're pathetic?" she held his hand.

"That's not what I... never mind." Peter did not have the heart to clarify.

"What do you mean you were lied to?"

"Seasqrd lied to me. He never gave me a choice in my destiny. I was a preordained copy, and the man I was copied from never even had the guts to disclose this to me." He held Jane's hand tight.

"He had reasons." Jane moved closer and put her arms about Peter. Usually Peter felt uncomfortable regarding such displays from Jane, but now he nestled his head on her shoulder.

"We've been away from each other for far too long." Jane kissed his brow.

"You know what it is like to be a freak your whole life, and then to find out you weren't even created normally; that you were some kind of weird experiment. Then you discover that the one you were created from was too ashamed of you to let you know the truth."

"No. You don't know how wrong you are." Jane pulled him in close, jamming his face into her bosom.

260

"Oh, Jane," Peter spoke from deep within Jane's cleavage, "I'm tired of resisting your feelings."

He pushed her back down across the bed and began kissing her neck and shoulders.

"To hell with Atamz and to hell with Gene Lucas Seasqrd," Peter said in a voice hoarse with passion. "It's about time I thought about me. It's about time we thought about us."

"But you don't know the whole truth," Jane MaCardiak said in a voice shrilled with shock.

"I know enough." Peter nibbled at her ear.

"Peter… you don't understand how things are between you and me." Jane spoke rapidly.

Peter replied in an equally rapid voice, "Oh, but I know how I'd like them to be."

As Peter nestled his face beneath her ear he heard her say, "Darklone only told you who your father was but not your mother."

Peter slowly pulled his lips off Jane's neck and looked down into her eyes. He whispered, "No, you're not about to tell me… please don't."

She said, "Yes, I am your mother."

Peter began trembling and said, "No, no… it's not possible!"

"Peter, you know what I say is true." Jane's eyes stared into his without blinking.

"No!" Peter got up off of her and began wiping his hands up and down his chest and legs. "Yuk!"

"Thanks for the compliment," she said, sitting up.

Peter looked at the wall; he couldn't stand looking at Jane. He said, "No offense but this is… eewh."

Jane began to explain. "Years ago, it was decided to once again try cloning our greatest hero, Gene Lucas Seasqrd, only this time it would be done differently."

Peter continued staring at the wall. He heard Jane say, "Look at me, will you?"

Peter refused; he knew he was being stubborn and rude, which was not his way, but he couldn't help it. This was all too weird for him; then Jane said, "Alright just listen. Unlike Darklone who was a product of the copyclator you were impregnated in me."

Peter slowly turned to face Jane as she sat on the bed and continued saying, "You were not made in a test tube as part of a lab experiment gone wrong. Do you understand?"

"But wait, you're only a little older than me!" Peter raised his index finger at Jane.

"Biologically, yes," Dr. MaCardiak said as she put her hand up. "Chronologically, no; besides all of Gene Lucas Seasqrd's pre-programmed genetic abilities you were given a good dose of growthmones."

"Growthmones?"

"Yes." Jane nodded her head. "So in a few months you went from a toddler to puberty. By the chronological age of two you were ready for Cosmos-Corps Academy."

"No wonder I'm so messed up," Peter said, shaking his head.

"It was hoped that unlike Darklone, who got all his power at once, you would be able to slowly cultivate your power under our guidance at C-C Academy, but things went wrong."

"You better believe they went wrong," Peter said. Slowly, he began to understand. He sat on a chair opposite her and asked, "Then why was I never told?"

"You had to be kept a secret. Remember Darklone was bent on destroying all the Geneti-Men. You don't know how painful it was never being able to tell you," Jane stopped for a moment as tears filled her eyes, "about us."

She began to cry. Suddenly, Peter found himself leaning forward and yelling, "Oh Mommy!"

Peter hugged her hard, sobbing on her shoulder.

"My baby," Jane MaCardiak said. "I've waited so long for this. Now at this time I can only say one thing."

Trying to keep his puffy eyes from crying, Peter looked at Jane face to face intently waiting for Jane's words of wisdom. Jane said nothing; she just slapped him across the jaw.

"What did you do that for, Mommy?"

She slapped him again.

"Ow!"

"I'm tired of your whimpering. I have all these great powers but I don't know how to use them. Boo-hoo, I can't be a G-Man. What happens if I fail?" She stood up. "No son of mine is going to sit here feeling sorry for himself while his shipmates need him."

"What do they need me for?" Peter asked. "Darklone and the Z are finished."

"No!" she said. "The Havoccraft has risen.

"How?" Peter asked.

"You would know this if you had stayed on duty instead of quitting Cosmos-Corps and running to your cabin to sulk. By the way this planet you wish to runaway to is going to blow up."

"What?" Peter asked.

"Never mind all your silly scientific questions; you can have that girlfriend of yours from Youkan answer them later. Now the Zenith needs all the help she can get and heaven knows your captain needs all the help he can get. In other words, get off your ass and get back on duty. Lt. Pulsaar."

"But, Mommy." Peter sank his head down in disgust.

"Peter!"

"Alright already." He moved swiftly to the door. "Stop nagging me."

Just as the doors swooshed open, the Zenith's computer voice called into Peter's cabin over the audio-alerter. Dr. Ma-Cardiak tilted her head back looking at the ceiling as the voice announced that she was need in hosp-hold immediately.

CHAPTER 19
THOSE SCI-FI GUYS AND THE LAST FLIGHT OF THE AEON OWL

At first, Dr. Jane MaCardiak thought the medical emergency was Ray Atamz's anxiety attack. It was not until he began explaining the accident that she realized it was Barbralta's life that was in peril.

"We were about to recharge the plasmicators," Atamz said. He paused.

"And what happened?" Dr. MaCardiak asked.

"She was under me... I mean... she was beneath the control panel. I was checking her legs... her work," Atamz said as he backed into the table. He steadied the jar of hibernation fluid that held the yeoman's brain. "Well, maybe I wasn't concentrating. There was an explosion when the relay overloaded."

Moments later, Dr. MaCardiak finally got Ray Atamz out of hosp-hold. She told him she could not help Barbralta while he remained in the way. Barbralta's limp yet curvaceous body was placed under the bio-checker. MaCardiak glanced at the yeoman's brain.

"Too many have been lost on this mission. I'm not going to lose another." MaCardiak put out a hand. "Sterilazers!"

The orderlies followed the doctor's orders. Dr. MaCardiak checked the anatoscope and said, "How strange."

She took a stethoscanner from the medicoptor that flew overhead. She ran a scan then dropped the implement to the floor. She couldn't believe it and more importantly she knew she'd never get Ray to believe it. She stepped back in shock.

"I always knew Ray loved machines," she said, "but this is too much."

*　　*　　*

Peter stepped out of the jetevator, feeling like his head had just been through a nuclear accelerator. Coming around the corner and standing right behind him was Admiral Seasqrd. They both immediately looked down at their boots while waiting for the other to say something first.

Seasqrd finally broke and asked."Did you talk to Dr. MaCardiak?"

Peter replied, "You mean my mother?"

"I see you have." Admiral Seasqrd motioned for Peter to follow as he strode down the compartment way. "How do you feel about the situation?"

"Well, let's see, so far I have a group of dog-people worshipping me because I'm a virgin. They announce this in front of the only woman who has ever made me feel like someone important and just recently I tried making a sexual advance on my mother. But other than all that, the situation is fine," Peter said.

"Good," Seasqrd said. "Peter, there is so much to talk about. I know you have a thousand questions, but let me just say what I need to say uninterrupted."

The admiral drew in a deep breath before continuing, "You know though my career in Cosmos-Corps has been fabulous there have been some errors. I can honestly say not telling you the truth was the biggest mistake I ever made."

"What did you just say?" Peter was shocked.

"I said it was my biggest mistake. Please let me get this off my chest—"

"You're saying you made a mistake." Peter pointed at Seasqrd.

"Yes," Seasqrd said. "Now I often think back to what Sam Parseck once said to me."

"And if you're saying it was the biggest, then you must have made others so that you can compare." Peter pointed at the admiral again.

"Yes, why are you so happy about this?" Seasqrd said. "Stop pointing at me please."

"So you're not perfect," Peter said. "And if you're not, then it doesn't mean I have to be."

"Are you going to let me finish?" Seasqrd asked.

"Admiral, you've just lifted a dwarf star off my heart." Peter took the admiral's hand, shaking it hard. "You really do have the power!"

"Yes. So do you, my son." Seasqrd said. "We both do!"

Peter then gripped the admiral's forearm and he did the same to him. Peter asked, "What do you need from me?"

Seasqrd said, "First let go of me then you and I have to find Ray Atamz."

"I have a hunch he's down in the hosp-hold." Peter smiled.

Peter and the admiral took an escaladder down to hosp-hold. It was easy to find Captain Atamz. He was locked in verbal combat with Jane MaCardiak once again. The admiral gestured at his bickering senior officers as if to say what else is new. Peter smiled, though he did not like the tone of voice old Ray Jay was using with his mother.

"Captain, Doctor, what is this?" Seasqrd asked.

"She seems to have forgotten who the captain is aboard this cosmicraft," Atamz said.

"Ray, I am in command of hosp-hold and I say who visits a patient and when," MaCardiak said.

"But I miss her!"

The doctor turned to the admiral. "You outrank us all. Can you explain to the captain that I understand what is wrong with Barbralta better than he does?"

Peter saw Jane wink. Admiral Seasqrd cocked his head back. "Jane, I think I understand exactly what you mean."

Jane cocked her head back then nodded knowingly. They both turned to Ray.

"I'm sorry," he said, "ever since I laid eyes on Barbralta, it's like a star went nova in my stomach, like a cosmic-string pierced my heart and my head dropped into a black hole."

Jane MaCardiak lowered her head then raised it back up; she looked at Ray and said, "Before you get to the big bang I have to tell you something."

"Ray!" Admiral Seasqrd interrupted. "I'm sure the doctor will let you know all that she knows when the time is right. Until then I need your help; we all need your help. Let us go over my plan."

Peter watched the admiral gently place his hand under the captain's arm and coax him along. Atamz reluctantly followed Seasqrd and Peter down the corridor, occasionally looking back at hosp-hold with a look of dashed hope in his woeful eyes.

"Gentlemen, in order for my plan to work we are all going to have to make sacrifices," Admiral Seasqrd said.

Peter stopped.

"What kind of sacrifices," he asked.

The admiral went over his plan and then he went over it again and then one more time before Peter and Ray finally agreed. Then without saying a word to each other both Peter and Ray knew where they had to go. The admiral excused them with great understanding and sympathy while he and the robot went to the Rozwelles domicile.

Microns turned into a macron as Peter and Ray stood side by side in the Zenith hangar looking at the Aeon Owl. Each knew what the other was thinking. There was no need to speak, but Ray had to say something anyway.

"I know how you feel, but the admiral is right." Captain Atamz patted Peter's shoulder. "Life in the Cosmos-Corps is not easy. It calls for sacrifice."

"That's true, but this one is gonna hurt," Peter said.

"Yes, but we are beings of duty. The Cosmos-Corps has taught us to deal with adversity with confidence, courage and self-reliance."

Then Atamz through himself against the Owl's hull, hugging it and kissing it. "No, No, I helped make you I cannot destroy you!"

Peter yanked back on Captain Atamz's collar almost tearing the captain's uniform, so he placed his hands about the captain's waist trying to get a good grip without being too physical with a superior officer.

Then someone said, "Perhaps I may be of assistance."

Peter whipped his head about dreading to see who stood behind him.

"Nothing positive can come from this," said Dya Nammock as she leaned towards her weeping commanding officer. She then assisted Peter in hauling the captain off the Owl's hull, which was wet with drool.

"Sorry, I just hate it when bad things happen to good machines," Ray Atamz said.

Dya Nammock looked at Peter and asked, "How are you dealing with this?"

Peter averted her eyes, but Dya moved around trying to reestablish direct visual contact. Peter backed away. "I'm sorry Dya, I'd rather be alone," he said.

The immense sliding doors of the hangar parted, but before Peter could rush through he found Otto the automaton blocking his path. The robot was carrying the end of an immense cylinder. The admiral was carrying the other end. Peter realized that this was the negaton furnace everyone had spoken of.

"Admiral, if you don't mind I'd like to see the Kanineites." Peter watched them head for the Aeon Owl. "I'd rather not watch this."

Admiral Seasqrd quietly gave permission and Peter Pulsaar was gone; he never bothered to look at Dya though he could feel her looking at him.

Peter wandered down the Zenith's compartment ways and corridors until he reached the gangway leading to the gangplank. He sucked in some fresh air and tried once again in vain not to think about Commander Nammock.

Outside, Peter Pulsaar watched his new friends, the Kanineites, acting as if they had not a care in the world. They had just finished a meal courtesy of the Zenith galleyroids and now they played tug-o-war with one another and ran about chasing each other's tails and, after making many circles and digging away at the ground, they finally rested in the grass.

"It's a dog's life," Peter said to himself.

"What?" Spanielius said. She crouched down next to him and sniffed at his hair, like she was curious as to his mental well being.

"Just an expression back where I come from," Peter said. "Have you always been so care free?"

"The Lawgiver always provided us with everything we needed," Spanielius said. "Everything but freedom."

"Well for better or for worse, your Lawgiver is no more," Peter said, rubbing his jaw.

"It matters not, we have you. You will take care of us and teach us how to grow," Spanielius said.

"Spanielius, I have to tell you something" Peter said. He swallowed hard. "I might not be around much longer."

"But you are the Chosen One. You must stay with us!"

"Yes, but you know that thing," Peter pointed towards the sky, "the ship in the air that attacked us."

"The monster ship in the sky," Spanielius looked up and drew closer to Peter, "I know it causes you and the others, who look like you, great trouble."

"That's putting it mildly," Peter said. "They want me to join in a battle against the monster in the sky. I know you won't understand, but I am going to fly up and try and destroy it."

"Of course," Spanielius said. Peter could feel her tail brushing against his back as she wagged it in excitement. "As Chosen One you must use your powers to destroy the great monster."

"Something like that but I may not come back. Can you understand that?" Peter said.

Spanielius' tail drooped and she lowered her snout. Peter knew she understood. In between whimpering she spoke. "Why go then?"

"Because you and my shipmates are many and I am just one," Peter said.

"Yes, you are the One. You are the Chosen One," Spanielius said.

"I know, but that's not what I meant," Peter said. "I mean you are many, so your needs are many. My needs are less because I am just one."

"You are not just one." She shook her head. "You are our Chosen One."

"I know," Peter said. "I know I am the Chosen One, but I am still only one. Do you get it?"

Spanielius shook her head; her furry ears flopped about. Peter took in a deep breath and made another attempt.

"Let's try this," he said. "Many people have many needs and that outweighs the needs of one. Wait I shouldn't have —"

"Not if he's the Chosen One," Spanielius said.

"Spanielius, please try to understand." He lifted her floppy ear in his hand, caressing it. "If I do not go on this mission we will lose and our enemies will have won."

"No," she said. "You are the One."

"Oh, forget it!" Peter got up and stormed up the gangplank. "I'm going on this mission! Good-bye!"

*   *   *

The captain looked about the Zenith hangar and was convinced everything would be ready for battle; unfortunately he couldn't say the same about himself. Dr. Jane MaCardiak hollered and Captain Ray Jay Atamz cringed.

"Don't give me any of that garbage about the needs of many." Jane's hair looked like it was on fire and her eyes burned as she brought them to bear on Captain Atamz. Ray wasn't sure if he could withstand her full attack.

"Now, Jane try to understand," he pleaded.

"The whole ship is talking about what you have planned, but I said it can't be true. So I came down here to see for myself."

Ray could feel his defenses buckling under Jane's intense fire. Dya approached and said, "Doctor, you must see the positive aspects of our plan."

"Get this outer-space jack-rabbit away from me," MaCardiak said.

Ray Atamz immediately stood in a position to block his executive officer from delivering her Youkan punch. While Dr. MaCardiak stood back scowling.

"Would someone just tell me why? Why?" the doctor's words echoed off the walls of the Zenith hangar. Ray had noticed that Admiral Seasqrd had seemed to remain purposely distracted by the modifications to the Aeon Owl, but with Jane's words reverberating off the bulkheads he finally stepped away from the Aeon Owl and watched Otto push the negaton furnace forward. He put his hand up then turned it slightly, guiding the robot. Otto's laser torch then began welding the negaton furnace of the MOMM to the fuselage.

"We are pursuing the only option we have, Jane, at least from my point of view," Seasqrd said.

"Your point of view?" MaCardiak slapped her hand across her head.

Otto finished with the laser torch and approached the admiral seeking to know if his work met Seasqrd's approval. Seasqrd nodded but Ray wanted to point out a few flaws in the robot's work. He turned to the automaton and saw that Otto's antennae and probes were spinning about in his bubblehead as if he were scanning Dr. MaCardiak.

"Doctor, perhaps I could elucidate on our plan," Otto said.

"It's suicide!" MaCardiak said.

Otto plodded forward with a consoling look on his virtual face and said, "The feeding aperture goes directly into the Havoccraft's positon core. When the negaton furnace is fed into the aperture and meets the positon core they will cancel each other out totally."

"Sam Parseck once tried explaining the positon-negaton reaction to me; that's what gave me the idea," Seasqrd said.

Feeling left out Captain Atamz said, "Listen to the robot, Jane."

"But why the Aeon Owl?" MaCardiak asked.

"The ram-rocket will give us the thrust necessary." Seasqrd looked over the Owl's fuselage.

"Why not program the ship?" MaCardiak asked.

"No auto-pilot program could maintain such a treacherous course." Seasqrd shook his head.

"Why him?"

"Who's our best pilot?" Seasqrd asked.

"Listen to the admiral, Jane," Atamz said. "What am I saying?"

"You men certainly have an answer for everything," MaCardiak said. She folded her arms over her stomach. "From my point of view."

Seasqrd turned towards the doctor and glowered.

Though he was now feeling fortunate to be left out of the dialogue, Ray Atamz felt compelled to make a point. "It's a two man job though." Atamz said. "While Peter is piloting someone has to navigate."

"Yes, it would require someone with almost machine-like precision," Seasqrd said while nodding his head.

Captain Atamz took a step forward and brushed off his uniform, awaiting the admiral's next words.

"There's only one I can think of," Seasqrd said.

Atamz put his shoulders back. The admiral looked directly at him; Ray smiled. Then Seasqrd looked at Otto with concern and said, "Ray, do you think the robot will fit in the cockpit properly."

"What?" Atamz said. "Not me!"

"Sorry, Captain Atamz, you try to perform like a machine, but he is one," Seasqrd said.

"I'm cursed with perfection," Otto said.

"Oh," Atamz said as he waved his hand at the automaton, "shut up."

"No, no" Dya said as she ran to the robot trying to reactivate him.

"There is one last concern I have." Dr. MaCardiak raised her hand, pointing her finger. "If Darklone senses the way you think, Admiral, won't he suspect something."

"Not if he's expecting something else," Seasqrd said. "Which reminds me, Doctor, how are your skills at plastic surgery?"

Jane looked back at Ray. Ray turned and looked at Admiral Seasqrd pensively and raised an eyebrow. He wondered what was going on behind that power port.

CHAPTER 20
THOSE SCI-FI GUYS JOURNEY TO THE CENTER OF THE HAVOCCRAFT

The Aeon Owl blasted its way into the clouds. Inside the cockpit, Peter Pulsaar wiped the side of his face. His cheek was smeared with lipstick; Jane MaCardiak had smothered him with kisses while he stood in the hangar. He had not bothered saying good-bye to Dya. He knew she would have only said something about the positive outcome of the mission when underneath it all she would be laughing at him.

He tried not to think about Dya Nammock but it was difficult. Not only had she reached into his heart, but she had also touched his mind... literally. And Peter found it very difficult to get her out of either place.

"Think of something else," Peter said.

"Sir?" Otto asked.

"Nothing."

"My audio sensor received a signal from your mouth," Otto said.

"I was just thinking out loud," Peter said. "I was thinking about the Kanineites."

"Yes, it was Dr. Rozwelles who had implanted the idea of a Chosen One in the brains of the Kanineites," Otto said. "His belief was that it would make it easier for him to come to the Kanineites in his human form and lead them to greatness. But you know I think you fulfill the prophecy much better for it is obvious to my scanners that you truly care about the Kanineites; just as they truly care about you."

"Gosh darn it, you're right, Otto. They do care about their Chosen One, but not because they expect me to be perfect; it's because they just care a lot about me," Peter said. "It's time to accept my fate and make this mission work. I must return to them. I can't let them down! My problem has always been being afraid of not living up to expectations; I'm sick of fear holding me back! That's the solution to my problem. Hey, I finally solved a problem on my own. We're going to do it!"

Peter tightened his grip on the control stick and flipped the switch for the ram-rocket. The Aeon Owl soared upward breaking through the planet's atmosphere and into space.

"To be brutally candid, it would not be totally unsatisfactory for us to be destroyed," Otto said.

"Say again," Peter said, with his head and chest pressed back by g-force.

"It would at least be a sign that I am not perfect," Otto said. "I have noticed that humans have an aversion to things that are too perfect. I wish I was capable of making an error."

"I understand completely, but do me a favor. Wait until after this mission to make your first mistake," Peter said.

"I understand completely as well, sir." Otto gave Peter what seemed to be a claw up.

Peter smiled. He thought about Otto's quest for imperfection. Peter knew firsthand what a burden perfection could be and what a relief it was to have that burden lifted. Now that he knew he did not have to be perfect he was actually looking forward to fulfilling his life. He had to return for Spanielius and the Kanineites.

*   *   *

Gene Lucas Seasqrd was pleased to see the look of shock on Ray Jay Atamz's face as the doors to hosp-hold swooshed closed behind him.

"I'll be the son of a gamma gun" Ray Atamz exclaimed. He almost dropped the portahole down on the floor. "If I hadn't been warned I would have what's left of our secureadymen on you in a minimicron."

Admiral Seasqrd played with the long beard that Dr. MaCardiak had attached to his face as he looked in a mirror. He looked so much like Darklone he felt a little sick to his genetically enhanced intestines. "Let us hope this disguise will fool the Z long enough to allow me to get to the Havoccraft's engineering and divert Darklone's attention away from Peter and the Aeon Owl," he said.

"It will work, Admiral," Atamz said. "You look enough like Darklone to fool any Zlythetaur. Jane did a great job."

"As captain you might want to render that compliment to your chief medical officer," Seasqrd said as he wriggled his eyebrows.

Captain Atamz stood silent then said, "I'll give the signal to Dya."

Atamz switched on the teletube. As the large, square monitor lit the wall, he signaled the bridge.

"Dya!" he said and waited for her to appear on the screen. "Begin transmitting the go-code to the Aeon Owl. Then run a final diagnostic before switching controls on the Metaphysical Teleportation Apparatus to auto. I want nothing left to human error."

While Ray barked his orders, Admiral Seasqrd stood before the portahole the captain had placed on the floor. He took in a deep breath.

"Sir!" Atamz said. "I have to warn you that even with my great technological skills, I'm not sure whether or not this will work. With no portahole on the receiving end, you could get stuck within the space-time continuum."

"That's neither here nor there." Seasqrd prepared to jump.

"Admiral, I just want to say one thing before you go," Atamz said.

"What's that, Captain?" Seasqrd asked.

"I never told you this but, though I have an ego the size of Betelgeuse, I've always felt inadequate next to you."

"That's kind of you to share that with me." Seasqrd prepared to jump through the portahole.

"I'm not done," Atamz said as he blocked him. "Maybe being a pompous, swaggering martinet was my way of covering up for my insecurity."

"You shouldn't feel that way." Seasqrd looked down at the portahole.

"What is your secret?" Atamz asked.

"Now, may not be the best time for this." Seasqrd was about to finally jump into the portahole when he took note of the captain's frown; Admiral Seasqrd stood back and said, "Okay, you'll never be a great cosmicraft commander without a great crew and they'll never think of themselves as great crew unless you make them feel that way."

"Well, I don't know if you ever noticed, but I've always been more comfortable around machines than people."

"I once knew someone very much like you," Seasqrd said. "But he changed; if Sam could so can you."

"It's not that I don't like people, but I think I can't trust anything I can't take apart and put back together. But when you picked that robot over me I realized how threatening technology can be," Atamz said.

Admiral Seasqrd stood patiently waiting to see if Captain Atamz was done.

"It's not that I like machines more than people," he continued. Seasqrd pulled up a chair and sat by the portahole. "It's just that I feel I can trust machines more than those incompetent boobs I have for a crew."

"If you think of them that way, you'll never be able to trust them and they'll end up resenting you and you'll find yourself isolated and alone and by the way, I think you should've switched off the teletube before you started this whole conversation." Seasqrd pointed across the room at the monitor that hung across the wall.

Captain Atamz turned and found himself, staring at the insulted faces of his bridge crew. Seasqrd said, "See a commander can't always trust technology, but he must always be able to trust his crew. Run that through your diagnostics."

Then Seasqrd jumped into the portahole, disappearing into oblivion.

* * *

Aboard the ECC Zenith's bridge, Dya Nammock scanned the diagnostics of the Meta-physical Teleportation Apparatus. "MTA responding within normal parameters," she said. "Locking on auto."

"You are a computer in a dress."

Dya looked up to find that she was staring eye to eye with Jane MaCardiak. "Doctor, shouldn't you be in hosp-hold?"

"I've done what I needed to do with the admiral," MaCardiak said. "Now I'm here to ask you what you're intentions are toward Peter Pulsaar."

"I don't have time to engage in your human jealousies." Dya turned away from the doctor. "I have more positive things to do."

"He's out there risking his life and you go about your duties on the bridge as if you don't care."

"I do care!" Dya said.

She watched disdainfully as the other officers began to put their consoles on hold, turning their attention towards the mounting conflict between their executive officer and chief medical officer.

"I know what you're thinking." She tapped her antennae.

The crew lowered their heads and went back to work.

The doctor continued, "Then why didn't you even say good-bye to him?"

"He's been avoiding me!" Dya said.

"That's because he cares about you and I want to know how you feel about him!" Dr. MaCardiak said.

"And how do you know he cares about me?" Dya asked.

Jane tilted her and said, "A mother knows."

"A what?" Dya said as she turned and looked at the incredulous faces of the bridge crew. "You're his… eewh… you humans are disgusting."

Dr. MaCardiak was about to answer when she too noticed the stares of the bridge crew. Quietly, Lt. Romeda spun around in her chair, Ensign Vector focused on his weapons console and Lt. Meedioride pressed a few buttons on the helm control.

"Never mind!" MaCardiak swept her hand across the air. "I don't want my son involved with a woman who has no heart. He could be on his way to his death and that seems to mean nothing to you."

Dr. MaCardiak pointed towards the cartographic-cart.

"My worries aren't going to insure his safe return." Dya pulled in a deep breath while watching the Aeon Owl drift closer to the Havoccraft. MaCardiak approached Dya raising her hand to her face. She touched a tear that rolled down Dya's cheek.

"I might not be from the planet Youkan, but I think know how you feel, Dya. You do love him," Dr. MaCardiak said. "Don't you?"

"This is not positive. Crying is a sign of worry. Worry is caused by negative thoughts." Dya wiped her face. "I've been exposed to humans too long."

"You certainly have, Dya." Jane MaCardiak smiled. "You most certainly have."

* * *

After getting the signal from Dya, Peter Pulsaar busied himself turning knobs, pressing buttons and flipping switches.

"Chronometer set." He pointed to the clock in the middle of control panel. "That's how much time we have before this negaton furnace blows. I'm rerouting emergency power into our shields."

"I am adjusting heading for the maw of the Havoccraft." Otto's claw hands set the navigatrometer.

The Aeon Owl raced through space; Peter decided to let Otto do the piloting as he sat staring at the distant specks that seemed to hang from the dark blanket of space, but as they grew closer the small specks became large asteroids except one long, narrow speck which was the Havoccraft.

Peter Pulsaar sat in awe of the monstrous, malevolent warship as it pulverized asteroids and pulled the debris into its evil orifice. Peter's eyes fixed themselves on the Havoccraft's chomping jaws as they crunched giant rubble.

"I've got the timing down," Peter said, pushing the throttle forward. "Here we go right down their throats!"

The Aeon Owl soared towards the biting teeth of the Havoccraft, but just as they were about to race into the deadly dreadnought's mouth.

"Hey, what are they doing out here?" Peter swung the control stick around while two bat fighters swooped down in an intercept course. Suddenly, the ship quaked and the panel burst into flames. Bouncing off the Havoccraft's teeth, the Owl spun about while the two bats pursued.

"Reroute what's left of the battery into our weapons," Peter said while he hung from his seat.

"Disengaging weapons!" Otto said, his bubblehead bouncing off ceiling of the canopy. Peter looked at Otto's virtual face. His eyes were crossed and his plastic lips acted as if he was trying to blow bubbles. The bats attacked again. A power surge ran through the console up Otto's claw and into his head.

"No!" Peter said. "Don't disengage the weapons! Power them up!"

"I'll lower our shields," Otto said.

"No!" Peter said. He swatted at the robot's claw hands. "Run some self-diagnostics. You're making too many errors."

"Errors!" Otto's speaker flashed rapidly. "I made an error! I am in error!"

His virtual face smiled.

Peter ducked down as flying glass burst from Otto's exploding bubblehead. Another blast hit the Owl. Peter grabbed the control stick and circled the Aeon Owl around one of the Havoccraft's titanic teeth. He raised the Zenith.

"Come in Zenith. Ray! Otto got short-circuited!" Peter spun the steering column and the Aeon Owl looped around. Otto's lifeless frame dropped onto the floor of the cockpit. The Owl soared as its ram-rocket roared. Peter aimed his ship right between two of the attacking bats just as they were about to close in.

"Come in Pulsaar!" Ray's voice erupted from the ship's mic.

"Ray! I'm here!" Peter said. "Otto is not. He was severely damaged. I have no navigator!"

"Prepare a portahole!" Ray Atamz said. "Send the robot back. With my engineering skills, I'm sure I can fix him!"

"Yeah, sure you will," Peter said.

*   *   *

Dr. Jane MaCardiak watched Ray Atamz impatiently as the captain patiently watched Lt. Meedioride and Ensign Vector grab onto Otto the automaton's mechanical arms and heave with all their might.

"Don't just stand there, Ray," Dr. MaCardiak said. "Help your crew!"

"Oh, yes, certainly," Captain Atamz said.

Atamz grabbed Otto's claw and helped Meedioride and Vector hoist the robotic corpse out of the portahole Dya had placed on the floor, but just when they had lifted him about half way through, Atamz let go.

"Oh, no!" Atamz looked at Otto's cracked bubblehead and checked the dials and screens on his chest. "Well, he's not perfect anymore."

"Ray help them out, damn it!" MaCardiak said, watching Meedioride and Vector struggle with the robot who was about to slip back into the portahole.

"Sorry!" Atamz took a hold of the antennae on the side of Otto's bubblehead and pulled. Together they managed to get Otto across the floor. "Thanks, shipmates!" Atamz said, saluting Meedioride and Vector.

They looked at the captain then at each other.

"Not bad for a pair of incompetent boobs, right sir." Meedioride saluted the captain back.

Atamz lowered his head pretending to examine Otto, but Jane MaCardiak knew he was really trying to avoid eye contact with his crew. He kept his head down in shame and said, "Otto's not perfect anymore and I never have been, but I have to try and help Peter."

"You what?" MaCardiak said. She stood in front of the portahole. Captain Atamz moved around her attempting to leap into the portahole as he said, "I know you don't think I can do it, but I believe we have to ask what Admiral Seasqrd would do in such a predicament."

"Don't say you have to do it for your ship," Dr. MaCardiak said, swinging herself around, blocking the captain from the portahole.

"No!" Atamz said. "I think he'd say something like doing it for the best crew in Cosmos-Corps!"

"What did you say?" Jane MaCardiak asked.

"Sir?" Dya said her antennae going up.

"What did he call us?" asked Lt. Romeda.

Jane was just as bewildered as the rest of the crew; she stood with her mouth agape and her jaw askew. She had never heard Ray Jay Atamz speak so highly of humans. As she shook her head Jane suddenly found the captain between her legs.

"Wait stop!" she said but it was too late. Jane looked down at the whirlpool of energy that swirled within the open portahole.

"I didn't even have a chance to say goodbye to him," she murmured.

"When he returns you should make it a point to talk with him," Dya said, standing at the doctor's side. "I do not wish to sound critical, I'm just giving you the advice I intend to follow."

Jane turned, looking at Dya with a smile. She said, "Why Dya, you finally said the right thing."

* * *

Back aboard the Aeon Owl, Peter looked down at the portahole with dismay.

"What the heck are you doing?" he said.

Ray Atamz slowly popped his head up out of the portahole. He pulled himself up and climbed into the cockpit.

"Look at the chronometer. That negaton furnace is ready to blow," Atamz said as if Peter could not figure this out.

"I need to escape those bats first!" Peter pointed at the scope. Atamz glanced down at the scope.

"What do you have in mind?" Atamz asked.

"Let's hope I have a great sense of timing," Peter said, leaning on the control stick. The Aeon Owl sped forward while the bats raced after them; Peter watched the scope. The Aeon Owl soared through the closing gap of the two teeth of the Havoccraft's jaws, barely escaping their crunch. The pursuing bat exploded under the impact of the massive incisors.

"One down," Peter said. "One to go!"

Peter Pulsaar checked the energy gauge and saw they were running low on fuel then he checked the chronometer and saw they were running low on time.

"Hammer rays dead ahead!" Atamz pointed forward. "They're used to smash big chunks of space rubble into little ones."

"Never mind the schematic explanation!' Peter exclaimed. "Help me maneuver around them or we'll become space rubble."

The Aeon Owl thrust forward, carrying the negaton furnace; before them lay an array of force field discs interconnected by threads of energy. The Aeon Owl dove under one disc just before it impacted against another disc. Behind the Owl, firing blazer attacks was the last bat fighter. Peter turned the control stick around as the Aeon Owl looped about and flew around one of the energy rays just before going into a dive. The bat followed. Peter turned to Ray Atamz and said, "Hold on!"

The Aeon Owl skimmed across one of the force field discs just as the disc above was about to crash down. The Owl raced upwards away from the shards that burst from the exploding bat fighter.

"Great piloting!" Atamz said, clinging to his chair.

"Thanks," Peter said. "Now comes your end."

Filling the cockpit with waves of light was a cascading wall of energy resembling a waterfall of golden lightning bolts. Peter smacked Ray's shoulder. "The attachyon field. What do we do?"

"I'm setting a harmonic field around the ship that matches the frequency of the attachyon field," Atamz said.

"Sounds good to me," Peter said. The Aeon Owl shook while passing through the attachyon field. It rocked backwards and pitched forward. Peter gripped the control stick, using all his super-human strength to try to keep a steady course.

"It's choppy," he said, "but better than being chopped up."

Atamz gripped his seat belt, saying, "I know what this ship can do; remember I helped build her."

Peter said, "Maybe she'll hold together anyway."

*   *   *

Aboard the Havoccraft, Admiral Seasqrd finally dried his clothes. Disgruntled that the teleporter ray had shot him through a Zlythetaur toilet, but thankful that they had a very powerful solar dryer in the bathroom, Seasqrd slowly walked down an empty corridor. He suddenly stopped when he felt a weapon at his back.

"Stop, human!" said the voice of the Z guard. Seasqrd slowly turned hoping Jane's plastic surgery would work.

"Darklone, a thousand apologies." The Z guard lowered his rocket rifle.

As the Z guard bowed, Seasqrd delivered a blow to the back of his head then sprinted down the corridor. He passed a guard, who saluted and opened the hatch to a Z turbovator. Seasqrd wondered if MaCardiak's plastic surgery was that good or if these guards were that dumb or had Darklone sensed his power and ordered the guards to allow him to make his way to the engineering room.

"No," Seasqrd muttered to himself. "They're pretty stupid."

Seasqrd stepped out of the turbovator and onto a scaffold that overlooked the engineering section of the Havoccraft and was welcomed by Z hails from the Zlythetaurs.

The massive room was a long rectangular compartment, lined with steel plates across the floor and walls. Rising from the center were two pyramidal batteries and on top of them were two golden orbs. Connecting the two orbs were a series of glass tubes that sent pulses back and forth. Across from Seasqrd was another scaffold, which the admiral was examining as a means of escape when one of the Zlythetaurs began shouting from below.

"Darklone, your presence is an unexpected honor," he said. "We are almost completely refueled. Shall we begin charging the gravity magnetron?"

"No," Seasqrd said.

"Did you say no?"

"We are abandoning the attack on the cosmicraft, Zenith."

The Zlythetaurs tilted their massive heads in disbelief. Then a voice Seasqrd knew all too well spoke from the darkness.

"Countermand that!" the voice ordered.

He looked across the engineering room at the scaffold on the opposite wall where the real Darklone emerged from the shadows.

"How did you know to find me here?" Seasqrd shouted across the engineering section. "Did you telepathically sense my presence, were you able to psychically anticipate my strategy?"

"No," Darklone said. "I was in the bathroom stall next to you."

Darklone waved to the squad of Z troopers standing beside him. He pointed at Seasqrd. The Zlythetaurs pointed their rocket rifles at the admiral, but Seasqrd remained calm, and then he got angry.

"You fools!" he said. "Can't you see he is the imposter?"

"Nice try, Gene Lucas," Darklone said. The Z turned around, aiming their weapons at him. "A very good try, indeed."

The power port upon Darklone's head lit up. "You dolts!" he screamed. "I'm the one who ordered you down here, so follow my orders."

The Z troopers turned and faced Admiral Seasqrd with their rocket rifles.

"That's just what I would have said, Gene Lucas." Seasqrd stroked his fake beard. The Z turned on Darklone again.

"Incompetent bunglers!" Darklone rolled his eyes back and pointed at Seasqrd. "I brought you down here to capture him, so capture him!"

The Z turned on Seasqrd. The admiral tried thinking of something Darklone would say. He through his head back and shouted, "You'll all be executed for this."

The Z turned on Darklone who said, "I am DAR-KLONE!"

The Z turned around totally confused. Darklone stroked his beard; he withdrew his intelli-whip from his belt and said, "It seems the only way to prove which one is the real Darklone is to settle this Geneti-Man to Geneti-Man."

Gene Lucas Seasqrd raised his fists, took a fighting stance and said, "Just as it as we should've done years ago."

*   *   *

Deep within the innards of the Havoccraft, Peter Pulsaar flew the Aeon Owl into the deepest bowels of the warship, ready to flush away the Zlythetaur's power source.

"Ray!" Peter said. "You got us through the attachyon field."

"No! I should have anticipated this!" Atamz exclaimed.

"What is wrong?"

"Interference from the magnetic accumulator has put our engine fluxuator out of flux yet the chronometer is still ticking away."

"We have to be at full thrust to get the Owl through the containment field," Peter said. "Can't you bypass the fluxuator?"

"I wish… that is I'd feel better if I could talk to the Zenith computer," Atamz said looking up at the ceiling.

"Maybe it's time to rely on yourself instead of your machines, old friend."

"Haven't you noticed?" Atamz said. "That usually doesn't work too well."

"You can't give into fear, Ray. I've made that mistake too many times myself. Peter said. "Solve your own problems, Captain."

"Maybe, if I could get into the main board beneath this panel."

Atamz shielded his eyes from the sparks that flew across the cockpit after Peter rammed his fist into the control panel. A moment later the captain was up to his wrists in fiber lines and optic relays.

"I did it," Atamz said. "Let's get out of here!"

Peter flipped on the pilot lock while he stared into the burning mass that lay ahead.

The Aeon Owl floated ever closer to the fiery furnace. The inner temperature of the cockpit was rising rapidly while the Owl flew closer to the burning vortex of the positon containment field.

"Atamz to Zenith." Ray held up his eyering. "We're going down the portahole."

* * *

Up on the Zenith's bridge, Dya and Jane MaCardiak stared at the portahole that had been left on the floor. Suddenly, a puff of smoke blew out of it. The doctor gasped, placing her hands to her face. Dya darted over to the MTA. "Prepare another hole!"

* * *

Within the Aeon Owl, Captain Atamz and Peter had just been belched out of their portahole. Atamz screamed into his eyering, "Dya! What happened to the portahole?"

"Energy levels are too low. The hole is closed!" Dya's voice shouted back as her face took form over the captain's ring. "We have another in place. Try again, gentlemen!"

Peter and Ray Atamz dove into the portahole but were blasted back into the cockpit. Peter looked up at the chronometer. "Not much time left!"

Captain Atamz, held his eyering so he was face to face with his executive officer and yelled, "You really have to open this hole!"

* * *

On the Zenith's bridge Captain Atamz's head had just finished shouting at Dya. She shouted back, "I'm now cross-circuiting."

She felt her antennae ears wiggle as she ran her fingers over the buttons of the MTA; Dya pulled back on the three-pronged lever that energized the MTA. There was only a small explosion and a puff of smoke.

"I suggest you teleport us aboard," said Captain Atamz as his head shot up over her eyering.

"We're attempting that very task, sir," Dya said. "We'll have re-cross-circuit from the navigatrometer."

"No!" the captain's little face became angry. "You blow the navigational banks."

But it's the only way to achieve the positive outcome of saving your lives, sir."

"I order you—"

Suddenly the captain's tiny head disappeared then reappeared then was gone again; when it finally appeared again it was fuzzy and the only audio was choking sounds. Dya said, Sorry, Captain Atamz, you're over and out."

*   *   *

Within the cockpit of the Aeon Owl, Peter Pulsaar pulled away from the helm as the equipment began to burn and fume. The Owl's outer hull sparkled with energy as it crept ever closer to the positon field. Peter slapped the shoulder of his petrified co-pilot. Captain Atamz suddenly raised his eyering to his mouth while staring into the fiery mass of the Havoccraft's positon core, which now filled the entire canopy like a flaming sun.

"Zenith, teleport us aboard," he whimpered.

"There is only enough power to teleport one of you," Dya's head said.

Peter's eyes locked onto the captain's, their lips quivering.

"I guess as captain I must go down with the ship," Atamz stated bravely. "You jump into the portahole."

Peter was impressed with the captain's fortitude except that after this courageous statement, Ray folded his arms around his knees, which were pressed against his chest and began sucking his thumb. Peter looked down at Captain Atamz and smiled.

"Sorry, but this is my ship," Peter said.

He cradled the cringing captain in his arms. Before Ray could object or even open his eyes Peter dunked him into the portahole.

Peter stood staring at the portahole awaiting his chance while the Aeon Owl floated into the positon field and was wrapped into swirls of energy and flame. He checked the time; the negaton furnace was about to explode.

* * *

Down in the Havoccraft's engineering, Gene Lucas Seasqrd faced off against his archenemy, Darklone.

"Well, my brother, I finally have you right where I want you." Darklone put his fist at his hips.

"Yes, old friend." Seasqrd put his fists at his hips. "It seemed like the only way of stopping you from killing everyone else!"

"I'm going to miss you Seasqrd," Darklone said. "We were so very much alike."

Seasqrd could feel his power port tremble upon his head. "Darklone," he said. "We are nothing alike. You did something I would never do... could never do. It wasn't good enough that you destroy our ship and blast away at helpless puppy-people; you had to drain away what little confidence that boy had and turn him against me. Why do you do these things?"

"Sorry, Gene Lucas, I like to hurt things." Darklone said. "Pity I cannot keep hurting you and your young one after you have been destroyed."

Seasqrd lunged forward and attacked, stepping forward and jamming the butt of his palm at Darklone's face. The Zlythetaurs, still in confusion, circled around the combatants. Darklone blocked Seasqrd's next blow and shoved Seasqrd backwards while sweeping his whip at Seasqrd's belly. Seasqrd withdrew hastily to avoid the attack.

Again the intelli-whip slashed through the air. Terminals and monitors blew as magnetic pulses swept the room. Seasqrd and Darklone pulled back from their duel and circled about one another. Darklone aimed his lash at Seasqrd's sternum and suddenly it began to spin about like a drill. Darklone charged. Seasqrd stepped back and hurled himself straight up in the air. Realizing he was hanging from plasma conduits, he got an idea.

Beneath him, Darklone was swinging his intelli-whip about waiting for his prey to drop. Quickly, Seasqrd pried the braces that held the piping to the ceiling off their bolts, ripped his fingers across the lines and bent the severed plasma conduit down. Energized gas sprayed out and descended on Darklone as Seasqrd swung himself to the other side of the room.

"No!" the gas lit up as it contacted Darklone's intelli-whip and the evil clone was trapped in an ionized gas bubble that formed a force field about him. Yet Darklone would not yield to defeat.

"Zatan, old pal," Darklone said. "Get me out of here!"

Seasqrd looked at the Zlythetaur, who had just stepped forward; he was dressed in high ranking robes and as he inched his way towards the gas bubble he gave Darklone a look of disdain then he turned his reptilian glare towards Seasqrd.

"Kill them both," he commanded. "It's the only way to ensure the imposter fails to survive."

Seasqrd watched Darklone's portal light with a brilliant incandescence as a look of shock masked his face.

"Zatan, you forked-tongued fool!" he cried from within the ion bubble. "You can't see it's me? I'm still your commander. I'm your superior... I just got accidentally stuck in this energy bubble. Now do your duty!"

The Zlythetaur called Zatan turned; he held a small circular device up for Darklone's view and said, "I do have one last duty to perform."

Seasqrd was not sure what was about to happen but he could see the dread on Darklone's face and that surprised him.

"Not the tortucalator!" Darklone gasped. "You cannot."

"I must. Incompetence cannot be tolerated," Zatan said with a sneer. "Take your punishment with pride."

Seasqrd stood back as Zatan stuck the device to the field of ion gas that trapped Darklone and pressed a button at its center. Within the bubble, Darklone was fried by static shockwaves that electrocuted his body until finally the bubble burst, driving the Z back. Darklone's smoldering body dropped to the floor. Seasqrd grabbed a rocket rifle from one of the Z, pointed it at the commander, called Zatan, and said, "Order them to drop their weapons and withdraw!"

As the Z cautiously obeyed Zatan, Seasqrd knelt at Darklone's side; his burnt body was gasping for breath. To his surprise Seasqrd felt pity.

"I know what you're thinking, old friend. You are about to remind me of the consequences of a life dedicated to evil," Darklone said.

"And I know what you're thinking, I'm too much of a good guy and even though I have won this battle the Havoccraft is about to attack all those I hold dear and I am powerless to stop it," Seasqrd said.

"We know each other pretty good," they said simultaneously.

Suddenly, an alarm wailed across engineering. A warning voice spoke, *"The positon field has been breached. Positon/negaton explosion imminent!"*

"Our thoughts have always betrayed ourselves to each other," Seasqrd said, while holding tight to the Animazonian pendent that was chained about his neck. "You know what I'm thinking now?"

Darklone looked at Seasqrd with fright. "Yes, Gene Lucas, I do."

Again Seasqrd and Darklone spoke together.

"We're screwed!"

CHAPTER 21
THOSE SCI-FI GUYS AND THEIR VOYAGE HOME

"No! No!" Ray Atamz said. He remained crouched in a fetal position when someone pulled his fingers from across his eyes. Ray realized where he was, got up and resumed his normal, pompous posture.

"Good to be aboard the Zenith again," he said. "Well done, Dya."

Commander Nammock ignored her captain; she went back to the MTA, reset it and pulled down on the lever but the portahole remained still. Ray's eyes teared.

"Where is Peter?" MaCardiak asked.

Ray could not answer. He pretended to be concerned with the work of Lt. Romeda and Lt. Meedioride, who busied themselves reconnecting cables that stretched across the bridge floor. Romeda received a nod from Meedioride and she pressed a switch on the cartographic-cart.

"Where is Peter?" MaCardiak asked.

"I thought he'd be right behind me," Atamz said as he looked at the empty portahole and wiped his eyes.

"Captain, we have a managed to get a visual from the probe plate to the see-plate." Lt. Romeda pointed at the wall where there was an image of the Havoccraft. Atamz shifted his attention from his sobbing medical officer to the see-plate. The Havoccraft began to yawl as if the dreadnought were in death throws. Its terrible maw heaved a stream of flames then the wicked warship exploded. Captain Ray Atamz led the bridge crew in cheering for the defeat of their enemy, and then Jane MaCardiak tapped him on his shoulder. He slowly turned around and looked into her puffy yet still beautiful eyes.

"I'm sure Peter was not aboard," he said.

"Then where is my boy?" Jane MaCardiak asked as she looked down into the empty portahole. Captain Ray Atamz wanted to speak, but his words became choked. He finally conjured enough strength to say something as he walked Jane away from the portahole.

"He sacrificed himself for the good of the Zenith." He held Jane in his arms. The doctor rested her wet cheek against his shoulder. "Your son... my friend... was the bravest Cosmos-Corpsman I knew."

Captain Atamz and Dr. MaCardiak held each other, weeping. Then he heard Jane say, "Dya, join us in a good cry,"

Jane held out her hand to the pretty, yet stoic Youkanian. Ray Atamz turned to face his executive officer who remained motionless.

"He's not really dead you know," Dya said.

"I know the people of your planet try to find something positive in everything but we need to grieve," Atamz said while holding his hand next to Jane's. "Join us; it's only human."

"But I cannot believe he is dead," Dya stood like she was in shock.

"Are you sure you are alright, Commander Nammock?" Atamz asked.

"I am positive." She pointed behind the captain at the portahole.

Both Ray Atamz and Jane MaCardiak spun around to see Peter being pulled out of the portahole by Ensign Vector. Dr. MaCardiak lunged forward with her arms extended, but Captain Atamz pulled her back, allowing Dya and Peter to have a moment together.

After a quick embrace with Dya, Peter turned to Atamz and said, "We did it, Captain."

"Yes, we did." Atamz clasped his hand about Peter's.

The crew cheered.

"You have the power," said the captain then he drew back to let Jane MaCardiak wrap her arms about her baby boy.

"Oh, Peter, I'm so proud of you."

"Oh, Mom, cut it out."

"Seasqrd was right about you," Atamz said.

"Speaking of that, where is the admiral?" Peter asked.

Suddenly, all went silent. Ray gestured for Jane to explain to her son. The doctor placed her hands about Peter's shoulders and said, "Admiral Gene Lucas Seasqrd was aboard the Havoc-craft."

Peter glanced quickly from Jane to Ray in confusion. Captain Atamz explained, "We sent him through a portahole to stage an incursion; his plan was to divert the enemy's attention while you led your mission aboard the Aeon Owl."

Peter dropped his chin in comprehension as he whispered, "My father sacrificed himself for me... and for all of us."

Then Ray and the rest of the Zenith crew lowered their heads in reverence to their fallen leader. Ray watched Peter wipe a tear from his eye; Dya held him. Ray took Jane's hand and leaned his face against her red hair.

"He's not really dead you know." Ray heard Dya say.

"Yes," Peter said, holding Dya tighter. "We will always have fond memories of my father."

"And his exploits will live on in Cosmos-Corps history," Captain Atamz said.

"No, I think she's doing it again," Dr. MaCardiak said, while tilting her face towards Dya.

Dya stepped back pointing while everyone twisted their heads around, looking at the lifeless body of Otto the automaton being energized with life once more.

"He's alive again!" MaCardiak pointed to the robot, standing before them.

"Yes, I am!"

Ray and the Zenith crew stood in disbelief, staring at Otto's virtual face. It had changed. It had morphed into the exact likeness of Admiral Seasqrd and when the speaker spoke it was in the voice of the admiral. "Incredible," Captain Atamz said.

"I am Gene Lucas Seasqrd," he said. Then the robot smiled.

Jane MaCardiak kept closing and opening her eyes. "I don't believe it."

"The MOMM's explosion changed the power of my mind into an ethereal essence." The speaker lit brightly. "For a time I was one with the cosmos. That is how I saved Peter from certain doom."

"How could the MOMM do that?" Atamz asked as he rapidly blinked.

"Never underestimate a MOMM," MaCardiak said.

"And never underestimate a woman's tulipathy."

"Come again, Admiral?" Atamz asked. Ray couldn't believe what he had just said but it seemed apparent that Gene Lucas Seasqrd had taken over Otto's mechanical body.

"Nothing Sam... I mean Ray," Seasqrd shook his new plastic face. "I have come back to dwell within the short-circuited body of Otto so as to speak to you mortals."

"It seems you have," Atamz said. "And what is it you want to tell us?"

"Peter," Seasqrd whispered while his robotic face swiveled about. "I know what your destiny is. You must stay on this planet and lead the Kanineites. Show them how to grow. Train them well. They have the ability to be great with your help; never let them forget that there is a great power that dwells in believing in one's self."

Peter bowed his head and smiled. Dya held his hand. Peter said, "I can't wait to tell them."

Peter wanted to dash off to the jetevator but Dya wouldn't let go of his hand. She reached with her other hand and took Peter's arm. She said, "But there's much we need to talk about. If you know what I mean?"

Peter stood confused then he said with a sudden look of comprehension, "Oh, yes, sure. Perhaps we could discuss it in your counseling chamber?"

Dya stood face to face with him and said, "I'm positive we can."

"Hmphh," Jane MaCardiak said. But Ray placed his arm about her and shook her shoulder. He knew it would be tough for her, but she finally seemed ready to let go of her baby boy.

Peter and Dya were about to step into the open jetevator when the commander turned and said, "Oh, but Captain Atamz there's something we must discuss as well."

"We do?" Captain Atamz said. His eyes opened wide.

"Whatever you need to discuss with your captain can wait," Admiral Seasqrd said. "What you need to discuss with Lieutenant Pulsaar has waited long enough."

"Oh, of course," Dya said as the jetevator door swooshed closed on her and Peter.

Captain Atamz stepped before Admiral Seasqrd and asked, "And now that you have delivered your message must you disappear into oblivion, leaving us mortals behind?"

The admiral raised his mechanical hand and said, "No, I have also foreseen that you people need as much help as you can get, especially you, Ray."

Ray placed his hand over his chest in bewilderment. He felt Jane's hands over his shoulders giving him a quick yet consoling massage.

Seasqrd continued, "Fear not Ray. Behind every great man there is a woman." He gestured with his claw towards Jane.

"Yes!" Captain Atamz clasped his hands together. "Doctor, take me to hosp-hold so I can be with Barbralta."

"Oh Ray, we must talk," Dr. MaCardiak said.

* * *

Jane MaCardiak watched the captain pace across hosp-hold with his chin down over his chest. He then leaned over one of the gravigurneys. Burying his face into the pillow, Ray Atamz muttered, "She a machine. How could I've been so dumb? I can't believe I let my heart get me in so deep."

Atamz began pacing about the room again; Seasqrd followed him, stomping his robotic feet in the captain's trail. Atamz flopped on the gurney once again.

"I know how you feel, Ray, I remember how I felt when I lost my yeoman," the admiral said from the speaker in his chest.

"Strangely they have the same problem in reverse," Dr. MaCardiak said. "Barbralta has a body, but the neuronic matrix of her mind has been fused. The yeoman has a mind but no body."

Suddenly Captain Atamz lifted his head and stared into the plastic face of Admiral Seasqrd, who asked, "Are you thinking what I'm thinking?

"What are you two thinking?" MaCardiak asked while turning her head back and forth.

"It could be a way to save two lives." Ray Atamz slammed his fist against the gurney. It then dawned on Dr. Jane MaCardiak what was being thought of; she shook her head. She backed away, but the admiral's claws took her by the arms.

"No!" she exclaimed. "It's beyond my knowledge. I can't take a living brain and shove it into an android body. I don't have the skill. I could kill what's left of both of them!"

"I'm starting to see where Pulsaar gets his lack of confidence from." Atamz stood behind Dr. MaCardiak. She felt his hands against her back.

"Maybe we can do something about that." Seasqrd said while turning his mechanical head towards the uraniumcranium.

"An incredibly good idea, sir," Captain Atamz said. "Take her."

Jane got shoved towards the admiral and his claws took her hands. The captain had the crystal helmet of Dr. Rozwelles in his hands and gently placed it over the doctor's head.

"Don't you dare, Raymond Jay Atamz. Seasqrd take your claws off of me!" MaCardiak said. "You keep that thing off of me!"

300

"Just let the genius of Rozwelles flow through you," Seasqrd said, soothingly.

Jane MaCardiak shook her head violently as Ray Atamz lowered the uraniumcranium down. Slowly she calmed. She closed her eyes then it was as if a great and glorious epiphany had descended upon her medical mind. She opened her eyes. She looked at Captain Atamz and Admiral Seasqrd and whispered, "Why it's so simple even a man could do it."

*   *   *

Peter stood patiently in Commander Nammock's counseling chamber waiting for Dya's return. He heard the door swoosh open.

"I'm so proud of you." Dya walked over and hugged Peter. "It seems like we had quite the positive outcome."

Peter sat down on. "The first time I came into this office of yours I was so worried you would read my thoughts. Now I wish you would. I'm too embarrassed to discuss certain things with you," he said.

Dya sat down on the opposite end of her couch. She slowly crept towards Peter. She placed her hand on his. "Instead of making our minds mesh maybe we should work on our hearts."

Peter wanted to say something profound, but he found it difficult to speak with Dya's lips pressed tightly against his. She finally pulled away. She looked at him anxiously anticipating a reply.

"Wow!" Peter said. "Suddenly, losing the Aeon Owl doesn't mean as much as it used to."

"That's the best thing you could've said." She hugged Peter. "And I knew you were going to say that before you said it."

Peter smiled broadly. "You're reading my mind that means we're really connecting."

She began kissing his neck, cheek and ear. She whispered, "Forgive the bluntness of this statement, but I love you."

"I think something very positive can come from this." Peter kissed her. He opened his eyes and was happy to see Dya's antennae rising. But then she shook her head, making her antennae wobble. She got to her feet and said, "This isn't the proper place."

"What do you mean?" Peter asked as she took his hands and got him to his feet. "We need something more romantic. We're going to the Imagarena."

*   *   *

Down in hosp-hold, Ray Atamz felt like his heart was ready to blast off into the upper exosphere. Jane MaCardiak had pulled off a medical miracle, placing the brain of the yeoman into Barbralta's android body. Atamz stepped into the hosp-hold waiting room as the doors to the operating room swooshed closed behind him.

"It was amazing. You should've seen Jane go and now I'll have Barbralta back," Atamz said.

"And I'll have my yeoman back," Seasqrd said.

After an awkward moment of silence, Atamz said, "I didn't think of this."

"Yes," Seasqrd's speaker lit as he said, "We have a problem."

"Who will she choose?" Atamz asked.

The admiral's face seemed puzzled; it was still quite strange looking at Admiral Seasqrd's face in its robotic form. Suddenly he was done ruminating and said, "We must leave it up to her; it's the only way. Forcing a choice upon her or coercing her into a decision or fighting it out could cause irreparable damage."

"Well, we wouldn't want that. And I would never want us opposing each other. I just hope she makes a choice that will make us all happy," Atamz said as he slapped Seasqrd's mechanical shoulder.

"I agree completely," Seasqrd said.

"Then why do you have what are supposed to be your fingers crossed?" Atamz asked.

"What?" Seasqrd's plastic face was gripped in shock and his audio speaker began flashing brighter. "No, it's not what you think. I'm still getting used to these robotic hands."

"Oh sure, I'm supposed to believe that," Atamz said.

Just then, the admiral's mechanical torso twisted about and the relays in what was left of his dome head flickered.

The doors swooshed and Barbralta stood with her arms up as she gazed across the room.

She said. "There you are, the love of my life!"

Then she ran up and jumped into the mechanical arms of Admiral Seasqrd and Ray's heart crashed back into the troposphere. He felt Jane's hand on his arm; she pulled him aside, but he kept watching Barbralta smother kisses on the Admiral's plastic face. Finally, Dr. MaCardiak yanked his arm and said, "Ray, don't be too hurt. It's Barbralta's body but the yeoman's brain. She was obviously going to go for the admiral even if he's trapped inside a mechanical body. When you think about it, it all makes sense. They're both machines."

"Yes, but that's what I loved about her. She was the most beautiful machine I'd ever met," Atamz said, turning away from the love scene.

"Ray, if you think about it you got your wish," Seasqrd said in between kisses from Barbralta. "This is a choice that'll make everyone happy."

"What does he mean?" Atamz said to the doctor.

"Ray," she replied as she put her hands on either side of his face. "He means this!"

She pressed her lips against his, kissing him hard and passionately. For a brief moment Ray tried to pull back then he quickly surrendered to the doctor's ardor and embraced her.

"Where did that come from?" the captain asked.

"From the bottom of my heart," Dr. MaCardiak said. "You reached it when you jumped into the portahole. You were ready to give up your life for our lives. What a human sacrifice? Well, you know what I mean."

Ray Atamz could not help notice the admiral and Barbralta. They were making even more sparks then he and the doctor, although they had a natural advantage when it came to making sparks he thought.

"I think we should leave them alone," Atamz said. "I know my passion for machines has made you mad now and then, but I have this little program I created for the Imagarena."

"Is it anything like the one we played back at the academy?" Jane MaCardiak asked.

"Better!"

The doors swooshed closed behind them.

* * *

Peter could not believe what he was seeing as he and Dya stood holding hands at edge of the corridor. Captain Ray Atamz had just peeked around the far end of the corridor then signaled to Jane MaCardiak to follow; they crept along never noticing Dya and himself at the opposite end of the corridor. Just as they stepped before the Imagarena doors Dya shouted, "Captain Atamz, what are you doing?"

Both the captain and the doctor stepped back from the Imagarena door pretending as if they were just strolling casually down the corridor. Ray then replied, "The doctor and I were... well... um."

Then Jane said, "You see he and I... that is...."

"Wait, what are you two doing here?" Ray Atamz asked.

Dya and Peter looked at one another; it became awkward and uncomfortable faster than the speed of light. Peter was not about to try to explain to his mother why they were going to the Imagarena so he looked at Dya and said, "You tell them."

With her antennae straight up, Dya said, "Oh we... I... I came to find Captain Atamz. I have something to explain."

Ray Atamz seemed quite anxious to change the subject and said, "Uh... yes... now what was it that was so important?"

"The navigatrometer was destroyed when I routed the MTA through it," she said. "It was as you predicted, sir, but it was the only way I could think of to save you two."

"Blast," said the captain.

"The navago—what ever she called it, is that important?" Dr. MaCardiak asked.

"Sure is; I mean it was. Without it we'd have no way of piloting ourselves through deep space and out of the Unknown Zone and even if we could then we'd have no way of chartering a time-bend course back to Earth." The captain became disgusted but to Peter's surprise instead of being critical Ray Atamz became consoling as he said, "It was the only way Dya; you had no choice. But I'm afraid it means we're marooned on this planet."

"We can all stay here with the Kanineites," Peter said and clasped his hand together then realized he was the only one smiling. "The admiral... my father did say it was my destiny."

Ray Atamz raised an eyebrow and tilted his head. "You may want to stay here on a planet gone to the dogs but I don't."

"Well I'm just looking at the positive side of the situation." Peter looked at Dya; she held his hand and smiled.

"He's starting to sound like her." Dr. MaCardiak bent her head down while pinching the bridge of her nose.

Dya looked back and forth from Peter to Jane and asked, "Now what's that supposed to mean?"

Peter feared yet another confrontation between his girlfriend and mother when a voice sounding like it came from a speaker echoed from the adjacent corridor. It said, "You people at it again?"

*　　*　　*

Gene Lucas Seasqrd stomped down the passage way; it was difficult but he was growing comfortable with his new robotic body and he knew the yeoman at his side had no complaints about her new body. As they turned the corner, Seasqrd was curious to see what his officers were arguing about again;

305

he looked at their shocked faces and asked, "What are you all doing here? I thought you'd be—"

Before he could finish, all four began in unison saying a lot of 'wells' and 'we-ums' and 'I-uhs" as they tried very hard not to look at the Imagarena doors. Peter was surprisingly the first to speak loud and clear. He said, "Good to see you're alright again Barbralta."

"No, I'm the yeoman," she said. Both Peter and Dya stood wide-eyed. "Don't I look great?" she asked.

Peter nodded and gulped as Dya asked, "But how is such a thing possible?"

"I did it?" MaCardiak said with her thumb at her chest. "It was a simple brain transplant."

Peter and Dya were even more wide-eyed then they were before. Then Jane added, "Well I had the help of her father's genius."

Everyone looked towards Barbralta who said, "My father runs a fueling station on Demos."

Jane's face became confused and the admiral said, "Baffling isn't it?"

"It really is the yeoman in there." Peter stood in front of her looking into her eyes as if they were windows to peer through. "I'm glad it's you in there."

She took a step back and smiled. "It's good to see you again, Peter."

"I blamed myself for what happened to you," Peter said with a frown.

"Oh that's silly; conviculators can be touchy things but if it hadn't been for your super-human abilities, Peter, I would've been fried in there."

As Peter found himself in an affectionate embrace he said, "You mean I felt guilty and I worried all for nothing."

Admiral Seasqrd reached out with a mechanical claw and shook Peter's hand. "I'm afraid so, son."

"Don't feel bad, Peter," Jane MaCardiak said quickly. "You've come a long way on this voyage."

"But I'm afraid he's not going any further; none of us are, sir," Captain Atamz said.

Seasqrd rotated his torso around and focused on the captain. He asked, "What do you mean?"

Ray and Dya exchanged looks of remorse and then he said, "Unfortunately, I've been told our navigatrometer has been destroyed. We can't even get off this planet much less get back to Earth."

"Have you people learned nothing?" Seasqrd asked. "Something will come up."

"Or maybe down," Peter said pointing behind the admiral.

Admiral Seasqrd rotated his torso back around the opposite way and saw an escalader had dropped and down came the bridge crew. Ensign Vector and Lieutenant Meedioride carried a portahole and placed it before the admiral. Lt. Andrea Romeda saluted and said, "Pardon the interruption, sir, but we received a communiqué from a ship orbiting this planet."

"A ship is orbiting this planet out in the middle of the Unknown Zone!" Seasqrd said so loud he thought he might break the speaker he spoke out of. "What did they say?"

"They requested we place a portahole in front of you," Lt. Romeda said.

"What's the name of the ship?" Peter asked.

"It's called the Saturn Seventy," Romeda answered.

"What did you say it's called?" Seasqrd asked and when the lieutenant repeated her answer Seasqrd said, "What does that remind me of? Wait! It couldn't be!"

Seasqrd looked down at the portahole with gleeful anticipation. The silver center began to glow and then whirl as if the space-time continuum was about to erupt then out of the vortex of energy came two bare arms. They reached about as the back of someone's head appeared; the man struggled for a moment while his arms pressed against the portahole's rim and his dark skinned torso raised itself upward.

The man climbing out of the portahole had a svelte frame, curly black hair and he wore what appeared to be a grass skirt. As the man's bare feet hit the deck floor he spoke to Meedioride and Vector.

"Where is the great Gene Lucas Seasqrd?"

Seasqrd said, "I don't believe it!"

The man spun around and Seasqrd yelled through his audio-speaker, "Sam! It is you! I wouldn't have recognized you! You've gone organic."

Sam's ebony eyes almost crossed in shock as he replied, "You wouldn't have recognized me; what about you? You've become mechanical."

Seasqrd extended his accordion like arms up and out and said, "Yes, I must admit I've been through a few changes on this voyage."

"I'll say," Sam said as he leaned over and looked over Seasqrd from bubble head to metal toe. He scratched his curly hair and asked, "Gene Lucas, is it really you in there?"

"Yes, my old friend," Seasqrd said. "But look at you, what happened?"

Sam Parseck flexed the little muscle he had and said, "I have become one with nature. The Animazon women really revitalized me and gave me an appreciation for the beauty of all things natural. If you know what I mean, old buddy?"

"Sam, you never cease to amaze me," Seasqrd said. "Now how'd you find us in this Unknown Zone? Were you able to follow our radiation wake? Could you trace our distress call or did you recognize our energy signature?"

"No, I used tulipathy!" Sam placed a hand about the pendent he wore.

"Huh?" Seasqrd said. He couldn't believe it but Sam Parseck was wearing a tulipathy pendent like the one the Animazon Queen had given him so long ago.

"Really, Gene Lucas, you think too much about technology." Sam patted the pendent as it rested against his chest. "I sensed my best friend was in trouble and its natural force led me to you. But unlike you guys I was smart enough to release several solar buoys so we'll be able to follow a reverse course right out of this Unknown Zone."

"Sam, you've done it again!" Seasqrd said as he slapped his claw hand against the extended palm Sam had just offered. "Ooh sorry."

Sam pulled his hand back and said, "You still don't know your own strength."

"But I now appreciate what you always talked about," Seasqrd extended his accordion like arms upward, "regarding machines and their might!" He turned to his crew and said, "And thanks to Sam's new ship and his solar buoys we'll find a way home!"

As the crew smiled Sam Parseck interjected, "But were it not for my human intuition that guided me here the Saturn Seventy wouldn't have found you in the first place. Remember folks the human soul is the greatest machine."

"Sam I was just showing some support for your technology," Seasqrd said.

"But as you always used to say the human heart, brain and brawn; no wait how'd it go?" Sam Parseck placed his hand over his lips and cheek in confusion.

Seasqrd was about to speak when the yeoman stepped forward putting Barbralta's alluring android figure in between the squabble and said, "It was heart, bone, sinew and soul and do you two have to do this now?"

Seasqrd realized she was right and as much as he relished arguing with his old shipmate once again he knew there were other things more pressing. Sam must have been thinking along the same lines because they said simultaneously, "Good to see you again."

Seasqrd plodded backwards and asked, "Sam, do you remember Captain Ray Jay Atamz?"

"Of course." Sam shook Ray's hand.

"It's a pleasure to see you again, sir," Captain Atamz replied. "I'd like you to look at our navigatrometer; it's been damaged real bad."

A look of fear engulfed Dr. MaCardiak's face and she bolted forward, seized the captain's arm and said, "But first we have to look at that glitch in the Imagarena programs, right, Ray."

And with that the doctor pulled Ray away from the stunned Sam Parseck and behind the swooshing doors of the Imagarena. Dya and Peter seemed to want to just stare at the closed doors in despair. Seasqrd said, "And you remember my son, Peter Pulsaar?"

"Yes, I do!" Sam clasped Peter's hand. "He's the boy who is supposed to be just like you. Ow!" Sam pulled his hand from Peter and shook it in the air. "Well, he certainly has your strength." Sam turned his eyes towards Seasqrd then tilted his head at Peter. He continued, "So he knows who he is?"

"Indeed he does and he's ready to be the first in a new generation of Geneti-Men."

"Yes, sir," Peter said while saluting, "but right now we have to get back to the counseling chambers so I can boldly go where I've never been before."

Peter took Dya's hand; the counselor's antennae ears were popping up as she said, "You read my mind."

Then they raced down the corridor disappearing around the next companion way. Sam looked at Seasqrd in disbelief. Seasqrd said, "I'd like to explain but the yeoman and I have ship affairs to attend to."

"Seems like everyone has," Sam Parseck said. "So in the meantime I'll borrow your crew." Sam hooked a finger at Romeda, Vector and Meedioride and asked, "Would you mind following me to the Saturn Seventy. We need to upload a resonance relay system between our two ships by downloading a singularity signaling application and by the way I never travel without a spare navigatrometer."

"Excellent Sam!" Seasqrd said as he watched all four dissolve down into the portahole one after the other. Seasqrd lifted the yeoman's new, appealing automated body into his mighty mechanical arms and headed down the corridor but then his super-acute, robotic audio sensors picked up on a strange sound. At first he couldn't discern what it actually was. As he revolved his torso about the sound came in clearer. It was Ray Atamz.

"Jane! Stop this crazy machine! Jane, help; help me!"

Seasqrd turned back around with his yeoman in his arms and continued down the corridor. He said, "Why does all this sound so familiar."

About the Author: During the summers and winters, when R. Jay Carissimo is not teaching or gardening, he's writing. His fantasy novel, *Thieves of the Vormonde*, came out in 2015 and his children's book, *Two Familiar*, came out in 2016. *Those Sci-Fi Guys* is his humorous tribute to all the great science fiction he grew up on. He hopes it's as much fun to read as it was to write!

About the Artist: Marcus Malara is a New Jersey based artist, songwriter and playwright. He has been a freelance artist since the age of fifteen. When he's not working on some creative project, he works to develop his business, Diatessaron Group — a company that focuses on arts as wellness.

CPSIA information can be obtained
at www.ICGtesting.com
Printed in the USA
FFOW03n0040280617
37224FF